WOLF, NO WOLF

✦ AND ✦

NOTCHES

*For Ken; Innocent
Best*

[signature]

WOLF, NO WOLF

AND

NOTCHES

TWO MONTANA MYSTERIES
FEATURING GABRIEL DU PRÉ

Peter Bowen

St. Martin's Minotaur ≈ New York

www.minotaurbooks.com

ISBN 0-312-28963-4

First St. Martin's Minotaur Edition: April 2002

10 9 8 7 6 5 4 3 2 1

Wolf, No Wolf

For Alston

✤ CHAPTER 1 ✤

Du Pré fiddled in the Toussaint Bar. The place was packed. Some of Madelaine's relatives had come down from Canada to visit. It was fall and the bird hunters had come, to shoot partridges and grouse on the High Plains.

The bird hunters were pretty OK. The big game hunters were pigs, mostly. The bird hunters were outdoors people; they loved it and knew it, or wanted to. The big game hunters wanted to shoot something big, often someone's cows.

Bart had bought a couple thousand dollars' worth of liquor and several kegs of beer and there was a lot of food people had brought. Everything was free.

Kids ran in and out. The older ones could have beers. Bart was tending bar. Old Booger Tom sat on one of the high stools, cane leaned up against the front of the bar.

"You do that pretty good for someone the booze damn near killed," said Booger Tom. "I know folks won't be in the same room with the stuff."

"Find Jesus," said Bart. "It's not too late to change your life."

He went down to the far end of the bar and took orders. Susan Klein, who owned the saloon, was washing glasses at a great pace.

One of Madelaine's relatives was playing the accordion, another an electric guitar. They were very good.

Du Pré finished. He was wet with sweat. The place was hot and damp and smoky, so smoky it was hard to see across the room. The room wasn't all that big, either.

Madelaine got up from her seat, her pretty face flushed from drinking the sweet pink wine she loved. She threw her arms around Du Pré and she kissed him for a long time.

1

"Du Pré," she said, "you make me ver' happy, you play those good songs."

Du Pré took a glass of whiskey passed hand over hand from the bar.

"Pretty good," said Du Pré, looking at the whiskey.

"What is pretty good?" said Madelaine.

"Only two people they drink a little from it, on the long journey from the bar to me."

"They love you, Du Pré," said Madelaine. She laughed. She was wearing a red, gold, green, and blue vest she had beaded herself. It had taken four years to do; the beads were tiny and she had four children.

Someday this fine woman marry me, thought Du Pré, soon as that damn Catholic church, it tell her OK, your missing husband is dead now so you can quit sinning, fornicating with Du Pré.

"Du Pré!" It was the big clumsy priest, Father Van Den Heuvel. Du Pré liked him. When Madelaine badgered Du Pré into going to confession Du Pré would confess to living in sin with Madelaine Placquemines. The priest would say, Good, I am happy for you, five Hail Marys, say them, the words are pretty.

"Such fine music!"

Father Van Den Heuvel could hear and he had a beautiful singing voice, but he was so uncoordinated he often knocked himself out slamming his head in car doors.

"Play 'The Big Rapids,' " said Father Van Den Heuvel.

"OK," said Du Pré. "I will get you some food, here."

"I can . . ."

"No," said Du Pré. "You spill a plate, fine, you knock the whole damn table over, people go hungry. I go get it."

Du Pré snaked his way through the crowd, got to the food table, piled a big plate full of meat and potato salad and fry bread and cole slaw. He carried it back.

"You sit down," said Du Pré, "then I give it to you."

The priest sat at Madelaine's table. She stood by the chair so he wouldn't go over getting into it.

Du Pré stood, sipping his whiskey.

The out-of-state bird hunters were easy to spot—very expensive hunting clothes, usually British; they smelled of dogs and gunpowder and sage. Some of the ranchers leased their land for hunting. The bird hunters who lived in Montana weren't bitter yet, but they would be when the hunting lands were all closed to them and given over to flatlanders, who could afford large fees.

"Some good party, eh?" said Du Pré to Madelaine.

She nodded. More people were coming in. Two couples from the west side of the Wolf Mountains. Stemples and Rosses. Du Pré had inspected their cattle many times, checking the brands, never any problem. Du Pré waved to them. The two couples snaked their way through the crowd and up to him.

"Du Pré!" said Bill Stemple. He held out his hand. Du Pré shook it and nodded and smiled at the others.

"We got a problem," said Stemple.

"Ah?" said Du Pré.

"Couple days ago a couple came to the house and asked if they could hunt. They seemed OK. Californians, but what the hell. We said sure. Didn't get the license numbers, of course. And then I was out driving to check my water tanks and I found some cut fences. Cattle out all over the place."

"Jesus," said Du Pré.

"Well, you don't like to think bad of folks 'less you know it," said Bill Stemple, "and it got worse. A lot of cows had been shot, with a twenty-two. I got a vet out there and it looks like I'll lose about twenty. Some were already down and dead. I have stock up in the mountains still, too, sent a couple hands, bring them down early, I'll hay 'em out."

"Got us, too," said Sally Ross. "Same story, we lost seventeen for sure and might lose that many more."

Twenty thousand dollars maybe, thought Du Pré, each. Depends. When they count it up, all, I bet twenty thousand.

"OK," said Du Pré, "I will get my coat and we will go."

"Oh, tomorrow," said Sally Ross. "They're gone, whoever they were—they didn't come to our place."

"What they look like?" said Du Pré.

"Twenties, city people, new hunting clothes. Had a springer in the back, so I thought they were all right. Those are good dogs."

"You talk to Benny?"

"Why we came," said Sally Ross. "His office said he was here." Benny Klein, the Sheriff, and his wife Susan owned the bar. Not much happened in the county that they didn't know about, and damn soon at that.

"I have not seen him," said Du Pré. "You maybe ask Susan."

The guitar player was tuning. Du Pré went back up to the little stage in the corner and he twisted the pegs on his fiddle till the tones held right.

Some shit, he thought, we got people steal cattle. Had a crazy person once poisoning people's dogs. Cattle are very valuable. Cut the fences, run them into a truck. Plenty of small places butcher them out and make real good profit. Ninety-nine percent.

Well, Du Pré thought, plenty big fight over the West, now. These new people, they sure don't care for anything that was here, or anyone. Place like this too good to last. Well, it is worse out in the west part of the state. Not so many people here, good.

Something is changing.

Du Pré fiddled for another hour, long songs, backup, no breaks. His fingers began to hurt and then they went numb and then his hand began to cramp. He hadn't been looking out at the crowd.

The people were all silent and staring at him. Then they began to clap and hoot and whistle. It went on for several minutes.

Me, Du Pré thought, I always play fiddle better, I am angry or want to fuck or I am happy drunk, lose myself in this music. This time I am mad.

Why these people come here? Do I go to their house, mess it up? Why?

Benny Klein came in, stood, spotted Du Pré. He waved to him, come over. Du Pré put his fiddle in the case and he took it to Madelaine and then he wound through the crowd to Benny. Benny put a hand on Du Pré's shoulder and pulled him outside.

"They told you?" said Benny.

"Yah," said Du Pré. "Pretty strange, lot of money. You know what it is about?"

"Oh," said Benny, "it gets worse. There was more over north and east. But they did find, the next county over, some of that get-the-cattle-off-the-public-lands crap."

"Yah," said Du Pré, "I thought so."

Du Pré had read an article which said all the ranchers and their cattle and their families and towns should be removed from eastern Montana and the western Dakotas. Then those tens of thousands of square miles could be a big park for buffalo and wolves, so that tourists could play in it. So some of those people who wanted that could not wait; they killed the ranchers' cattle, to try to drive the ranchers away. Hah.

"Du Pré," said Benny, "I got a real bad feeling. These idiots are here, and they know they're right. They don't care about the people here. They just want what they want. They don't seem to much care how they get it."

Du Pré nodded.

"They don't know where they are," said Benny. "They drive through this country, and they think there ain't anyone in it. If their car breaks down, though, someone's there in what, fifteen minutes?"

Du Pré nodded.

"What bothers me is that no one saw them," said Benny.

Du Pré looked at Benny for a long moment.

Benny rolled a smoke. He looked very troubled.

"I make you this bet," said Du Pré. "I say there are maybe two of them."

Benny nodded.

"I say that you get some missing-persons reports, pretty soon."
Benny nodded.

"They are dead," said Du Pré. "We just have not found them."

Benny looked up.

"I won't bet you," he said. "'Cause I know you're right."

✦ CHAPTER 2 ✦

Du Pré waited for Taylor Martin to come in his helicopter at
ten A.M.

"The air's better then," Martin had said. "It kinda jumps
around first few hours of light."

Du Pré rolled a cigarette and lit it and he unbuttoned his
leather jacket.

Them Martins, they got a ranch so damn big takes three helicopters to round up the cattle, Du Pré thought. That is a lot more
ranch and cattle than I could stand.

He heard the thwock of the rotor blades. Taylor Martin and his
machine rose up out of a canyon five miles away and shot along
ten feet above the ground. The man flew like a cowboy rides, fast,
loose, and perfectly. He set the little machine down and Du Pré
ran for it through a stinging storm of dust and chaff. Du Pré
ducked in and fumbled with the seat belt. Martin was pulling up
before Du Pré had swung his legs completely in.

Martin set the helicopter northwest in a climb. The two men
stared out at the land below, riven with coulees, the rock outcrops
dark with junipers. Looking for something that shouldn't be
where it was.

"The scablands?" yelled Martin.

"Start there," Du Pré yelled back.

Martin quartered back and forth. Du Pré looked off toward the
ridges that led to the foothills of the Wolf Mountains, glancing at
the clusters of ranch buildings, looking for a truck or car, the flash
of sun on glass. Where a truck or car shouldn't have a reason to be.

The helicopter vibrated. Du Pré hated it.

This damn thing fly apart all at once, three bolts and some tin-foil. There I'll be. Hail Mary. Splat.

A coyote scooted across a meadow, ducked into the shadows of a rocky slit in the earth. Du Pré glanced down at the two automatic shotguns mounted on the struts. Martin strafed coyotes with them.

"Down there!" yelled Taylor Martin. The helicopter's noise nearly drowned his voice. Du Pré leaned out and looked. A tan four-wheel-drive Land Rover was crumpled down in the bottom of a narrow slit in the earth lined with rock. Magpies and ravens covered the bushes around the wreck, were hopping in and out of the broken windows.

Out on the scablands, Du Pré thought, shoot them, toss them in the back, drive the car over the slide there. Didn't even bother to burn it. Attract attention, anyway.

The helicopter sheared away and headed back. Martin was talking into the microphone. Du Pré could see Benny Klein's car roaring up the dirt road several miles away. He leaned over to the pilot's ear and shouted for him to land Du Pré in front of Benny.

He is a nice man, don't like dead bodies, eyes pecked out already by them damn magpies. Can't even shoot them anymore, they are protected.

Taylor Martin set the helicopter down on the road and Du Pré hopped out and the chopper took off. Du Pré rolled a smoke and he lit it and waited. Benny's car roared up, no lights flashing. Not much traffic here, for sure.

Du Pré moved to the side of the road. Benny slowed and stopped and Du Pré got in.

"I don't need this," said Benny. "You were right."

"We get there," said Du Pré, "I go look, tell you when to call the coroner."

"Governor's already asked for the FBI," said Benny. "I hope none of them get killed. This is real bad, Gabriel, real bad. I knew it would happen, too. I'm going to resign."

Du Pré nodded.

Benny, he never was made for that job, he thought, this will end with arresting our friends and neighbors.

But I will probably do it. Death, it is a pretty harsh sentence for being young fools.

"Up there," said Du Pré. He pointed to a rutted track.

Benny's cruiser bumped along the pounded earth. He had to move slowly and steer around rocks sticking up high enough to catch the transmission or the oil pan. The track ended abruptly. They got out and looked into the slit in the earth. The tan four-wheeler was down seventy-five feet or so.

Du Pré pitched a rock down. Some of the birds flapped for a moment and then they settled again.

A trail wound back and forth down to the wreck. Du Pré started toward it. His moccasins slid some. He skated on the yellow earth. Benny came after him.

"You stay the hell up there, Benny," said Du Pré. "You puke on me twice, you know, you don't do that again."

Du Pré went on. He slid the last ten feet straight down, fetching up on the side of the Land Rover. All the glass bashed out of it. He looked in the back window. No blood. A dead hand hanging over the back seat.

Du Pré moved so he could see from the side. Man. Woman. Birds and animals had been at their faces. Skunk smell around. Blood on their clothes. Hair matted with blood.

He looked at the front seat.

Du Pré stood up.

"Benny!"

"Yah!"

"Two. You can call now."

Benny's face disappeared from view.

Du Pré went round to the other side. A couple shotguns in their cases spilled out of the open driver's door, a cooler leaking stinking water.

OK, Du Pré thought, where is this springer spaniel? We got a dog around here, maybe the coyotes haven't eaten him yet. Maybe the dog is dead where these people they were killed.

Du Pré scrambled back up. He pulled himself over the lip of the slit, grabbing on to a sagebrush. Benny was sitting in his cruiser. Du Pré went to the driver's side and he leaned against the hood and smoked.

"Couple medical examiners flying in," said Benny. "We're gonna have a lot of help on this one. Jesus." He got out of the cruiser.

Du Pré offered him his tobacco and papers. Benny took them, though he'd quit smoking a long time ago.

"Benny, my friend," said Du Pré, "you quit now. You resign today."

Benny looked up.

"What will happen, you stay, they will think you are part of some group did this, they accuse you. They will try to scare you anyway, but don't stay, this one will maybe kill you. Please."

Benny nodded. "Susan said the same thing. But who will be Sheriff? They'll do the same thing to them, you know. I can't just leave my people to hang. I swore an oath."

"You didn't swear no oath to fight with them FBI," said Du Pré. "They don't care they get the right person, you know, just *some* person. I hear that they are better now. I hope they are, you know, but this will kill you. Then I got no place to take Madelaine, drink pink wine, play my fiddle."

Benny thought.

"I feel like a coward," he said.

"Hah," said Du Pré, "you no coward. Arresting kids, burgling, some fool swiping a car, drunk kill his wife, that is one thing. This is not that."

"I know," said Benny, "but who will do it? My deputies? I won't just dump this on one of them. I wanted this job, really."

"Not them," said Du Pré. "You are right."

"You?"

"No," said Du Pré. "We are going to have them FBIs here. Got to be someone they can't shove around, you know?"

Benny drew on his cigarette.

"We're little people here, Du Pré," he said. "No one has any money, or power. We're small ranchers, tradesmen; couple lawyers, don't have a doctor closer than Miles City. We're going to have a fucking army of FBI agents and newspeople and gapers and gawkers and folks wanting to write the whole story for the true-crime publishers. A zoo. And the meat's going to be some of our friends and neighbors. *We know these people, Du Pré, we know them.*"

Du Pré nodded.

"You come up with a name," said Benny, "and a good one, and I'll quit. If they agree to take it."

Du Pré nodded.

A siren, far off in the distance.

The helicopter was coming back, low.

"They are here already," said Du Pré.

"Who?"

"Them FBIs," said Du Pré. "That is not a crop duster." The chopper Du Pré had come in was owned by Taylor Martin, and pretty small.

This thing was much bigger, had jet engines on it.

Here come the fucking cavalry, Du Pré thought, as charming as usual. I think maybe they find their goddamned Little Big-horn, too.

They waited.

"I know the guy who will do this," said Du Pré.

"What?"

"Not kill those people, who will be the Sheriff."

"I think I do, too," said Benny.

"Bart," they both said.

"Perfect," Benny said. "He's richer'n God and he's been dried out a good long time and he don't take shit, we know that. But would he do it?"

"I ask him, he do it," said Du Pré.

My good friend. Years ago, he just a rich drunk but he is good now and people like and respect him. Very powerful man, the lawyer he got to come here, Charles Foote, got teeth way back to his asshole. Yes, that Bart, we need him now.

His lady, that pretty Michele, the cop, she dump him. She like that Washington, D.C. She crazy. He better do this, take his mind off that. She hate Montana, he was here long enough no place else good enough for him. She figure that out, too.

Life can be very sad.

The chopper began to circle the wreck, blowing dust all over Du Pré and Benny. They ducked into the cruiser.

"Pricks," said Benny.

"Well," said Du Pré, "you can count on them, for sure."

The big chopper set down and four men in dark suits jumped out into the cactus. They ducked under the blades and dashed toward Benny and Du Pré.

"I got a great idea," said Du Pré.

"What."

"Lock these doors," said Du Pré.

Benny shrugged and pressed the electric lock.

"Wait till they get here," said Du Pré.

"OK," said Benny.

"Then we give them the finger," said Du Pré.

Benny nodded.

"And then we drive home," he said.

They did and they did.

❖ CHAPTER 3 ❖

Benny swirled the whiskey in his glass and stared at the ice cubes in it.

"You got to do this, Bart," said Du Pré. "We help you, you know, but these people here, they need you now."

"Jesus," said Bart. "This is like handing me a stick of dynamite and tellin' me to suck on the end ain't lit."

He is talking Montanan pretty good there, Du Pré thought.

"We need you," said Benny.

"I don't understand," said Bart. "You resign and how do I get to be Sheriff?"

"County Commissioners appoint you," said Benny. "They can call an election, of course, or they can wait for a petition. But we need you right now."

Bart looked at Du Pré for a long moment. Du Pré looked at him.

"OK," he said. "I think I understand. I'm an outsider."

"Some people think you are an outsider if your great-grand-father wasn't born here," said Du Pré. "But not many. You are liked much. You dry out, you help, you work. How many people in trouble you help out? Many. You don't even tell me all. I hear it pretty quick, though, it is a small place."

"And what do I do when I find the people who killed these two idiots?" said Bart. "I arrest them and see them to trial. I will not do anything else. Those fools should have been spanked and sent home to Mother. Not murdered."

"No," said Du Pré, "they should not have been murdered. But you know these people, what happens, you press them too far, Bart."

Bart nodded. Old Booger Tom had probably shot the previous Sheriff. The Sheriff was shooting at Booger Tom. There was no evidence surviving and Booger Tom just looked amused when asked about it. Booger Tom made lovely horsehair hackamores and ropes and quirts; he'd learned to do that in Deer Lodge Prison. For killing two men.

I wonder what *that* was all about, Du Pré thought. All Booger Tom ever said about it was that they needed killing. They probably did.

"I'll stay on as a deputy," said Benny, "but there isn't anyone in the county who can do it but you."

Bart nodded.

"Thank you," he said.

"Thanks?" said Benny. "Jesus! This is going to be purely awful. I wouldn't blame you you pissed on my shoes."

Bart nodded.

"I'm going to call Guerdon Smith right now," said Benny. He went into the kitchen.

"It may get some worse, you know," said Du Pré. "I mean, they come here, cut the fences, shoot cows. Then there is that silly wolf thing, put them back in the Wolf Mountains. I think I will go to the hearing in Cooper, there, it is day after tomorrow. These people here have been here long time, you know, they don't like being told move on, we don't like you, got better idea for the place."

"I forgot about the wolf business," said Bart. "Are they here now, too?"

Du Pré shook his head. "Oh, I do not know. Sometime soon they will come, talk, go up in the Wolfs. I hope that they come down. You know my grandpapa, he kill the last wolves here in Montana, 1923, with that Don Stevens."

"A government hunter?" said Bart.

"Sometime, he was editor of that Great Falls paper, too," said Du Pré.

Benny came back, beaming. "I called Smith because he's the smartest, and he said . . ."

They waited.

Benny grinned. "He said he'd call the others and the whole business should be done today. Matter of fact, he said he'd come by the saloon and swear you in."

Bart nodded. "I hope I'm big enough to do this," he said. "I knew this would happen one day but I never thought I'd be the Sheriff who had to do it. Frankly, I am scared."

"Good," said Du Pré. "You weren't, you be pretty dumb."

"I suppose I'll need uniforms."

"We order ours from Chicago," said Benny. "Take a few days to get here. Nobody here's your size. You're a big man."

"Foote is going to *hate* this," said Bart. "I'll go and call him. You go on down to the bar, get some lunch. I'll be along in a moment."

Du Pré and Benny drove down Bart's drive and out onto the road.

"I never thought he'd do it," said Benny.

"Bart, he is bigger than you think," said Du Pré. "Trouble is, with lots of money, it is easier to throw it at life than take life's troubles. So you mostly never live, I think."

"He's got guts, for sure," said Benny.

There were a few people in the Toussaint Bar, having red beers and nibbling at the baskets of chips and pretzels Susan kept out for her customers.

Benny went round the bar, and then back into the kitchen. When he and Susan finally came out her eyes were wet.

She reached across the bar top and took Du Pré's hand.

"Thank you," she said. "I was half out of my mind. I knew this was going to happen, too."

Du Pré grinned. "That Bart, he need to do this."

The door opened and Bart and Booger Tom came in. Bart looked a bit stunned. Booger Tom looked grim.

"I'se working for a lawman?" he said. "All my life I been a good dishonest cuss, honorable, never stole no horse nor cattle. Well, maybe some from them Eastern-owned ranches, I forget. I only robbed banks a couple times. Well, maybe four. I never killed anyone didn't really, really need it. And I wake up this morning, belch, fart, have my coffee, and ride into town with the god-damned *Sheriff*? I need a drink, bad."

"You never rode in with a Sheriff before?" said Du Pré. "You tell me that, look in my eye while you do."

"Plenty of times," said Booger Tom, "but it was some different . . ."

"You shoulda heard him scream," said Bart. "You'd think I scared him or something."

"Shit," said Booger Tom.

"Just don't do anything I'd have to arrest you for," said Bart. "You know how much I'd love it."

It is changing, Du Pré thought, something, like maybe my people when the buffalo were gone or they fled down here from the English. Left that Red River country, Canada, 1886.

The telephone rang. Susan went to answer it and she brought it to Bart.

Bart put it to his ear. He listened.

"I know, I know, Charles," he said. "I have to do this, though. I can't in conscience demand that you come. But I would deeply appreciate it. I'll buy you a thick down bag and plenty of caviar."

Lawyer Foote was abrupt.

Bart handed the phone back to Susan Klein.

"Well?" said Du Pré.

"He said he ought to have me committed," said Bart. "But he did quite understand and he would be here late this evening, and would like to be met at the Billings airport. He hates flying in little planes, especially at night."

"Madelaine and me, we go get him," said Du Pré, "if you want."

Bart nodded, then he shook his head no.

"Benny," he said, "I'm the Sheriff now, soon's Guerdon gets here with his Bible. So I would . . . what would you think of perhaps taking Susan to Billings? You could have—"

"We're outa here," said Susan. "Who'll tend bar?"

The door opened. Three men in dark suits came in. They peered a moment into the dark, saw Benny Klein, and came over to him.

"Special Agent Hansen," said one of them, a tall, dark-haired man, his mouth sneering, "and this is Special Agent Miller and that is Special Agent Houghton."

Benny nodded.

"Unusual," said Hansen, "to find a Sheriff in a bar when a case of this gravity has occurred."

"I'm not the Sheriff," said Benny.

"We were told he would be here," said Hansen.

"He's here," said Benny. "Bart? These . . . uh . . . folks seem to want to talk to you."

"Bart Fascelli," said Bart. He didn't get off his stool and he did not extend his hand.

"We need several things," said Agent Hansen. "Office space, telephones. Fax machines."

Bart nodded. "Then I suggest you go rent them," he said. He stood up. "This is my county. These are my people. You stupid cocksuckers fuck up once and I'll throw your asses over the line myself."

"Just a goddamned minute," yelled Hansen. "The Governor requested our assistance—"

"I don't work for the fucking Governor," said Bart. "So get him to rent some offices for you."

Guerdon Smith came through the door with a couple of the County Commissioners.

He walked up to Bart.

"You swear?" he said.

"Yup," said Bart.

Bart picked up the badge Benny had left on the bar top. He pinned it on. He stood in his old boots and torn jeans and stained leather jacket.

"Ever see *High Noon?*" he said. He grinned at Special Agent Hansen.

❖ CHAPTER 4 ❖

Du Pré stood at the back of the hearing room in Cooper. There were a bunch of very angry ranchers there, and some well-dressed young people in yuppie outdoor clothes, ugly colors and stupid buffalo designs on them.

"We will now listen to public testimony in the matter of re-introducing the gray wolf to the Wolf Mountains."

"We'll just kill the bastards!" shouted a weathered rancher.

The first speaker moved to the podium. A young woman in hiking boots and multipocketed clothes.

"We need to restore the predators. . . ." she began. She stopped. There was a hail of cowshit landing on her and the Fish and Wildlife agents sitting at the long table on the dais.

She ducked and turned her back.

Something started hissing in the back of the room. Du Pré looked down at a stink bomb working up to good thick smoke. He ran for the door and made it through before the rest of the crowd caught on. They soon followed, choking in the fierce stench.

Du Pré laughed. He was wearing his Métis clothes, the high moccasins and Red River sash and hat, the doeskin pants and the loose shirt and leather jacket, buffalo with the fleece in. He rolled a smoke and lit it and watched the crowd sneeze and choke and bitch.

The high school auditorium would need to air a long time.

The Fish and Wildlife agents had been the last out. They coughed and cursed.

"Why don't you sons of bitches go bust poachers?" a ranch-woman yelled. "We aren't raisin' cattle to feed goddamn wolves, so these California bastards like Montana better. We like it just fine and we been here a hundred years."

Du Pré laughed. Jesus, he thought, they think they just march in here, tell us, hey, you get wolves back, we say fine? These wolves, they will not live very long, you bet.

The young woman who had tried to speak came up to Du Pré, wiping her eyes. She coughed a little.

"Excuse me," she said, "who are you?"

"Gabriel Du Pré," said Du Pré. "You did not get much chance in there."

She shook her head. "These stockmen, they just won't let us bring anything back. I've had cowshit thrown at me before."

Du Pré waited.

"Are you Indian, I mean Native American?" she said.

17

"Part Indian," said Du Pré. "Métis, French Cree Chippewa."

"Oh," she said. "What do you think?"

"Eh?" said Du Pré.

"About bringing the wolves back. It's a major medicine animal."

Du Pré laughed. "All animals are medicine animals," he said, "all of them four-footed, six-footed, eight. All."

"We came up yesterday and had a sweat with a Native American shaman," she said.

Du Pré grinned at her. "Maybe Benjamin Medicine Eagle?"

"Yes," she said. "Do you know him?"

"Oh, yes," said Du Pré, "I know him very well." Jesus. That little shit.

"It was very moving," she said. "We prayed for the return of the wolf."

Du Pré laughed.

"Why are you laughing?"

"His name is Bucky Dassault," said Du Pré. "He is a child molester, did time, Deer Lodge, he con his way to alcohol counselor, get fired from that, then he set himself up, shaman. He is a bad guy. How much he rip you off for?"

"Uh," she said, "oh, God."

"He didn't come here?" said Du Pré.

"Yes," she said, "he did, but then he said he had an appointment he had forgotten."

"No," said Du Pré, "I think that maybe he saw me."

"Oh," she said. Her eyes were red from the smoke.

"There are not so very many shamans," said Du Pré. "Medicine People are very rare."

"He sent us an ad," she said.

Du Pré nodded. An ad. Coupons, maybe.

"What do you think about the wolves?" she said.

"Well," said Du Pré, "it is a bad thing, bring them back, you have heard about the murders up near the Wolf Mountains, there."

"Those stockmen . . ." she said.

"You know, it is a very bad idea, cut fences, shoot someone's stock."

"They were friends of mine," she said.

"I am sorry," said Du Pré.

"I came here for them," she said. "We won't give up. But you didn't really say what you think."

"Um," said Du Pré. "My grandpapa, he hunt down the last two wolves in Montana, in the lower states here, with that Don Stevens. Old Snowdrift and Lady Snowdrift. Year before they kill them they find their pups, ship all but two of them to the Smithsonian. Don, he take one female pup and he train her, she was in some silent movies with a dog named Strongheart. My grandpapa, he raise a male but it get mean. He kill it. I still have the hide."

She was looking at him in horror.

"So if you stupid people do this I don't think that your wolves live very long. Very bad idea push these people around some. They don't take it."

The young woman reached in her pocket and she pulled out a tape recorder.

"I'm going to give this to the FBI," she said, "you bastard."

Du Pré laughed at her. He walked to his Rover and got in and drove off toward home.

Very strange, these people, he thought. The road home was a straight line north. They just come here, say everything has changed, because we told you so. I don't like this at all.

I got to keep any more of these fools from being killed. That will not be easy. So stupid. They really want to clear everybody out from the Big Dry? Just tell them, go? Dig up the graves, your people, take them with you? We want a park here? Pretty crazy.

We got them FBIs, we got these people we never seen before. We got lot of change coming, maybe I have to go to Canada. That western Montana is very sad place. Strange people move in there, all alike mostly.

A coyote ran across far ahead of Du Pré's Rover.

Medicine animal there, for sure, Du Pré thought, he is some joker. Sometimes he catch himself up, get caught in his own jokes, yelp.

I go see Benetsee, Du Pré thought, old coyote joker there, see what he says. Be three in the morning I get there.

He reached under the seat and took up a pint of whiskey and sipped while the Rover shot down the two-lane highway. He had bought a pack of tailor-made cigarettes at the gas station. He smoked and drank and drove.

He shot past a Highway Patrol car lurking in the shadows where a county road came into the highway.

Du Pré sighed and flipped the switch and turned on his flashing lights and siren.

The Highway Patrol car slowed and turned off its light bar.

I liked Montana better before all those social workers, they take over the legislature.

Piss on 'em.

Du Pré's bladder sent its message. He slowed down and pulled off onto the verge and pissed in the road and got in and went on. Snow started to fall, fat flakes, so it wouldn't last long.

He pulled up to Benetsee's shack several hours later. He fished out a jug of bad wine from the back of the Rover and went up to the shack and banged on the door. Benetsee's old dogs woofed.

"Hey, old fart!" yelled Du Pré. "I got to talk to you!"

Du Pré waited.

Someone grabbed his shoulder. Du Pré whirled round.

"Hah!" said Benetsee. "You bring me some good wine there? Some tobacco? We drink, have a smoke, you come on in." He opened the door. A stench of old dogs and old man and dirty clothes and woodsmoke and stale wine hit Du Pré in the face. He rolled a cigarette and lit it and another for Benetsee. The old man poured himself some wine in a big dirty jar and he drank it in one long swallow.

"Pret' good wine," said Benetsee.

"You know all this bad news," said Du Pré.

"People got to be knowing how to fight, they make war," said Benetsee. "Pretty sad, kids, you know, they are dead now and lot of sadness. Parents lose kids, you know, they never get over it."

Du Pré nodded. "You got anything to tell me?" he said.

Benetsee drank a long drink. He puffed on his cigarette.

"These dead people, they played," he said. "All that they do, you know."

Du Pré nodded.

"They think, bring back the buffalo, forget the people. Bring back wolf, eat the buffalo, forget the people. Make it a place fools can play. Wear feathers. Maybe try to dance. Rub them crystals."

Du Pré had a slug of whiskey.

"Long time, you know," said Benetsee, "people been here. Before the whites, we hunt meat peoples, to honor them. We kill fur peoples to honor them, keep us warm. All the peoples make themselves for us, you know, and so we all live. Between the earth and sky. Keep each other strong."

Du Pré nodded.

"These new people they just play," said Benetsee.

"Yes," said Du Pré.

"So the earth hate them," said Benetsee. "I have never felt that. Earth hating anything."

Du Pré nodded.

"I got to go sleep," he said.

He went out and drove to Madelaine's.

✦ CHAPTER 5 ✦

Du Pré," said Madelaine, "I am worried now about you, do this, do that."

"Ah," said Du Pré.

"You got a real bad temper, these people they piss you off plenty. You don't kill none of them, eh?"

"OK."

Madelaine rested her head on the pillow again. They were lying in bed. Wind and sleet beat on the windows. The glass was steamed from their breath.

"You come on to Mass with me, yes?"

"No," said Du Pré. "I got to go see this FBI, Hansen, he want to talk to me about something. I tell him I be there at ten."

"I pray for your soul," said Madelaine. "I pray for this Hansen's ass."

Du Pré laughed.

"Pray, yours," he said, kissing her.

After, they sat in the kitchen. The television racketed mindlessly in the living room. Her teenage children watched it out of habit.

"You drop me church, pick me up?" said Madelaine.

"You be there pretty early," said Du Pré.

"Confession," said Madelaine.

All she got to confess she sin with me, these six years, the church don't like it. Oh well, that Father Van Den Heuvel, he give her a few prayers for the pretty words.

Du Pré dropped her off at the little cedar-sided church. He went on down the street and turned around and drove to the trailer park where the FBI had set up shop. They had to there

22

because no one would rent to them, Bart wouldn't allow them in his building, and the owner of the trailer park was Susan Klein, who gave them a lot far away from anyone else and refused to rent it to them for more than one day at a time. She came for the rent every morning and always smiled and said how quickly they would be gone if they pissed her off.

The FBI had to truck a double-wide all the way from Miles City to work in. It was covered with satellite dishes and antennas.

Du Pré parked and he sauntered up to the trailer and went in.

Hansen looked up from his desk, slightly larger than those of his minions, scowling.

"You're late," he said.

"Kiss my ass," said Du Pré pleasantly. "Now what you want?"

Hansen glared at him.

"OK," said Du Pré, "you got fifteen seconds, say good morning, so I know I am not talking to an asshole. Then maybe I stay, we talk, you know."

"Good morning," gritted Hansen. "Have a chair. I'll get coffee."

"Not for me," said Du Pré. "I don't drink, place like this." He rolled a cigarette and dug a lighter out of his jeans.

"No smoking," said Hansen.

"OK," said Du Pré, "I go now."

"Shit," said Hansen. "Go ahead and smoke."

Du Pré nodded and lit up. Three other agents stopped what they were doing and came over, dragging chairs. They arranged themselves in front of Du Pré. Du Pré looked at them and he smiled sunnily.

"Who's doing this?" said Hansen. "Who killed those two people?"

"Ah," said Du Pré, "well, I don't know, I am sure that I know them, I know everybody, you know, but I do not know who."

"This is a small place," said Hansen. "You must have heard something."

"Dumb questions," said Du Pré. "This all that you got?"

Hansen snapped the pencil he was scribbling with.

23

"I go now," said Du Pré, getting up. He walked to the door and out and got in his Rover and backed up and turned round and went out to the street and off toward the Toussaint Bar.

Susan Klein was scrubbing the bar top with cleanser. The bleach smell cut through the old tobacco stink a little. She looked up when Du Pré walked in and she nodded.

"Stinking weather," she said.

Du Pré dug a beer out of the cooler and he put a dollar on the bar top. He popped the can open and he drank.

"Went to talk to them FBIs," he said. "Pretty dumb, them."

"They live in a different world, Du Pré," she said. "This one is real. Earth. Sky. People who know where they are. And it's part of them. They have a lot of fancy toys. Nobody will even speak to them. You know what will happen. We'll settle this ourselves."

Du Pré nodded. "A bad one, this," he said.

The TV crews had come, asked questions, got no answers, and left. Agent Hansen didn't have any, and Bart just said he'd talk with them when he had something to say. When they learned that Bart was Bart Fascelli, a multimillionaire, working as a Sheriff in deepest Montana, they came pounding up his driveway, only to pound right back down it when Booger Tom shot a few times in the ground at their feet and then said that the next slugs would hit the TV cameras.

"I wouldn't waste a bullet on you," he said.

Tens of millions had watched him say that on international television.

There were newspaper reporters coming and going, and getting nothing. One of the victims was the daughter of a Congressman.

"That Bart he burn them back pretty good," said Du Pré, "like they are weeds, you know."

"Good," said Susan Klein. "God, did we need him. Poor Benny would have gone crazy."

Lawyer Foote had arrived. Bart had promptly deputized him and put him to work as spokesman. Newspeople working on him had the feeling that they were trying to crack a walnut with a banana.

The Governor had sent several state agents, who stayed about four hours. Bart called the Governor and they left.

Du Pré sipped his beer and watched the TV. News show.

No new leads on the Montana Murders, the news anchor said. She went on to other things.

"Maybe they figure we just shoot outsiders, they'll stay away," said Susan Klein.

Du Pré shrugged. That would be just fine.

Bart and Deputy Lawyer Foote came in, brushing snow and water from their uniform jackets. Foote's uniform fitted loosely; he had borrowed one from Benny Klein.

They came to Du Pré and Susan. She looked up.

"Coffee," said Bart.

"Brandy," said Foote.

"Drinking on the job," said Bart. "I reprimand you."

"Do that," said Foote.

Foote swirled the brandy in his snifter and smelled. He nodded. It was the only bottle of that brandy in Toussaint and the only snifter, for that matter.

"Them FBIs they haul me in there, ask a couple dumb questions," said Du Pré. "They ask me who is doing this. I tell them I am sure I know them but I do not know who."

"Wasn't the Stemples and it wasn't the Rosses," said Bart. "They were in Miles City when they were killed. Hell, it was two days later they found their cattle and the fences."

"They find anything in that car?" said Du Pré.

"No," said Bart. "Maybe the feds will find something, all the toys they got. But nothing I know of. Both of them shot in the head, a high-powered rifle, went right through. So no slugs, since they weren't killed there. No holes in the Land Rover."

"Where's the dog?" said Du Pré. "They had this springer spaniel?"

"Yes," said Bart, "I thought of that. But there's a lot of springer spaniels here, they live here, and more brought in."

"There was maybe a rabies tag in that Land Rover?" said Du Pré.

Bart shook his head.

"The vets?" said Du Pré. The two veterinarians in the county largely tended big animals.

"Neither one has seen the dog," said Bart.

"Well," said Du Pré, "that dog probably dead, too. Or maybe he run off and someone find him, cold and scared and hungry, and take him home. Dogs like that, expensive."

Bart nodded. He sipped coffee. They stared at the mirror a moment.

"If we can find the dog," said Bart, "what would it tell us?"

"Dogs," said Lawyer Foote, "do not usually talk."

"All we got right now," said Bart, "unless someone walks right in and says I did it, I'll tell you how, let me sign the confession."

"Someone probably will," said Lawyer Foote, "if not several. This is a pretty spectacular case. Attracts the unhinged, like politics."

"That uniform, it is not like you," said Du Pré to Lawyer Foote.

"No shit. I ordered some."

"Fancy tailor, Chicago?"

"Fancy tailor, London," said Lawyer Foote. "Got their start making uniforms for the likes of Lord Nelson."

Du Pré shrugged.

"I got to go," he said, "just out to my car, a minute."

Get away a minute, Du Pré thought, think about that dog.

Du Pré stepped out into the storm. He heard children laughing and then three ran past. They had a dog with them, happily jumping up on them, splashing them with mud and water.

A springer spaniel.

Packy Jones's kids. The farrier.

Du Pré got into his car and started it. Jones's house was only a hundred yards away, but the weather was nasty. He drove slowly toward it.

❖ CHAPTER 6 ❖

S he was just running along the road out west, there," said Packy. "Muddy and cold. I stop and open the door and she jumped in like I was her owner."

"Where you find her?" said Du Pré.

"Way the hell up on that back road cuts off to the Forest Service land," said Packy, "behind Tor Oleson's."

Thirty miles away.

Coyotes could chase her that far, a few hours. Didn't kill her, she must be coming into heat.

Those Oleson brothers didn't shoot them, they can't *see* that well. And they would not have heard anything. Du Pré had heard them try to play that fiddle. Hardänger stuff. Awful.

"She didn't have no collar on," said Packy, "and I thought some out-of-state hunter lost her. If anybody'd set up a howl for the dog I'd have give her back, but nobody did."

The kids came in with the wet, happy dog.

The spaniel came to Du Pré, shy and suspicious. She sniffed Du Pré's pant legs. He reached down and patted her head. She rolled on her back.

She had a tattoo on her belly, clear blue on the pink skin. A phone number. Du Pré scribbled it down.

Packy's TV blared in the corner. The murdered woman was to be buried this Sunday afternoon.

"The Montana Murders," the anchor droned. "Police suspect a serial killer."

For two people, same car, some serial killer. Huh? Du Pré

27

thought. Catch these people, kill them, ditch them. Them FBIs don't got shit. Serial killer, hah.

"OK," said Du Pré, "Packy, you keep that dog, I don't tell anyone, them FBIs try to give a lie detector test to her, I think. Make her nervous, she would not pass. Lock the poor dog in a room, beat her with hoses or something. Yah, you keep her here. Don't tell nobody."

"I already told Susan Klein and Bart," said Packy, "in case someone was looking for the dog. I've had two run over, you know, it's like losing a child."

"Oh," said Du Pré. Why they not tell me about the goddamn dog?

Play a joke on Du Pré.

"Thanks," said Du Pré. "I see you. Nice dog."

Du Pré drove back to the bar. Bart was there, just sitting.

"Nice dog Packy's got there," said Bart, grinning. "And yes, it's the dog. The phone number is a tracing service. Tattoo your dog, someone finds it, they call this number. Belonged to the girl's boyfriend. I was afraid you'd tell the FBI about the dog," he went on. "Packy's kids love the dog and vice versa and the dog's happy and the dog can't read mug shots. So. They had anything, they wouldn't tell us. Screw 'em."

"You ready to play this afternoon?" said Susan.

Du Pré had forgotten. Another community supper and music.

My music. I have fun today, go chase down my neighbors later.

"I got to go and get Madelaine," said Du Pré. "We come back, she is making that lamb, rice, bay leaves."

"I love that woman," said Bart.

Du Pré picked up Madelaine at church and he dropped her at home and he drove off toward the benchlands. He saw the leaning trees around Benetsee's shack and a whiff of smoke coming up from the chimney. He drove up the rutted driveway and parked.

He knocked on Benetsee's door. The old dogs woofed, but the old man didn't come. He went around back to see if the old man was in his sweat lodge.

The fire pit was still glowing hot and the door flap was down in front of the sweat lodge.

Du Pré could hear the old man singing. He waited. The snow and rain were falling off. Some sunlight was punching down to the ground from the west.

Du Pré heard another car out front.

He walked round the house. One of the FBI cars.

Du Pré slipped back behind the sweat lodge. He squatted down behind a bush and waited.

"Some witch doctor," said Hansen, laughing loudly. He pounded on the front door.

"FBI!" he yelled. The old dogs woofed.

Du Pré whistled.

"There's someone around back," said one of the agents.

The three men came around the side of the shack. They looked at the sweat lodge. Not at the ground. Du Pré was fifteen feet away and his tracks led clearly to his hiding place.

The sweat lodge door flaps opened and Benetsee slid out. He stood up and looked at the three men in their city suits and city coats.

"I don't talk, Mormons," he said. "Go away."

"FBI," said Hansen. "You can either talk to us or we'll arrest you and take you in."

"Arrest?" said Benetsee. "For taking a sweat? Funny law, that."

"All right, you old asshole." One of the other agents lunged for the old man. His slick leather shoe soles wouldn't grip. He had to stop and get his balance back.

Benetsee grinned.

"You never find out," he said. "You can't see. Go home."

"That does it," said Hansen. "You know something. We're taking you in."

But he couldn't walk well.

Benetsee shrugged and he walked away a few steps.

An agent started to unbutton his coat.

Du Pré leaped for Hansen. He jammed his nine-millimeter in the agent's neck.

"You motherfucker," said Du Pré, "you got no right, do this to this old man. You bastards. You get your gun out slow, the others also. You drop them down. You got five seconds. Funny move, your brains are in Idaho."

"Do it," said Hansen to the other agents.

Plop. Plop. Plop.

"You get out of here now," said Du Pré. "I bring you your damn guns. You are so stupid. You do this, people, they will kill you here. Why you do this to an old man?"

Du Pré let go of Hansen.

"You bastards," he said. "You ever bother this old man you be very sorry."

"You will regret this, Du Pré," said Hansen.

"What you do?" said Du Pré. "You frame me, like you do? You guys, dumb and mean."

Du Pré walked them to their car. They got in and drove off. The FBI car's rear end swayed round; the driver didn't know how to drive in ice and snow.

There will be trouble, this, thought Du Pré. I do what? Let them shove old Benetsee around? He done nothing.

Du Pré reached in his Rover and turned on his radio.

"This is Du Pré," he said. "I need to speak to that Bart."

"You mean the Sheriff?" said the dispatcher.

God, I hate this women, Du Pré thought.

"Yah," said Du Pré.

She patched him through.

"Three them FBIs they were here at Benetsee's," said Du Pré. "They push him around some, say they arrest him."

"Bastards," said Bart.

"So I shove a gun in that Hansen's ear," said Du Pré, "and I run them off."

"Gabriel," said Bart, "*please* don't do that sort of thing. *Please.*"

"Fuck them," said Du Pré. "That Benetsee, he don't do nothing."

Du Pré walked back up toward the sweat lodge. The flaps were shut again and wisps of steam were rising from the cracks in the lodge.

Du Pré shrugged and he drove down toward town.

Where the road suddenly dipped and turned he saw car tracks going off and over the side, down toward the creek bottom. Du Pré shot down the hill and pulled over and got out and walked to the edge.

The agent's car was upside down in the little creek. Hansen was crawling out of it.

Du Pré called the dispatcher and then he got out and he slid down the side of the hill.

Another agent had struggled out. The third one was hanging upside down in the car, unconscious. Du Pré got the seat belt unbuckled and he dragged the man out and up away from the car. The motor was still running and the gasoline fumes were heavy.

Hansen and the other agent crawled away on their hands and knees.

The car began to burn.

Sirens in the distance.

Hansen looked at Du Pré, hating him.

"Answer me a question," said Du Pré. "I am guessing."

Hansen stared at him.

"You are driving, and a coyote runs across the road."

Hansen nodded.

"It was funny," he said. "The coyote crossed and then it . . ."

Du Pré waited.

"It felt like something just shoved us over the side."

The ambulance stopped on the road above.

❧ CHAPTER 7 ❧

"A coyote, eh?" said Deputy Lawyer Foote. "Life is a strange business."

Du Pré nodded. They were sitting in the saloon, eating cheeseburgers and drinking beer. The fire roared in the glass-fronted woodstove.

They were the only two people left in the bar. Susan Klein had left, saying they should pull the door shut after them. The potluck had been a success. They always were, and Du Pré had fiddled like he always did.

"Wonderful music," said Foote. "Is it Celtic? It sounds like some I have heard, Irish and Scottish."

"It is that," said Du Pré. "We got some Indian, some French, some Scot. We some stew, us."

"Did you tell me what the Métis are?" said Foote.

"We the voyageurs. Some French they come, Scot, Irish, all them Catholic, with the Black Robes, them Jesuits. Very tough priests, them Jesuits. And they marry Indians and here we are. Some of us, we live on the reservations, some of us don't, most of us are gone, part of what America mostly is, you know. Indians call us white, whites call us Indians. So we are the peacemakers, catch all the shit from everybody."

Foote laughed.

"You weren't too peaceful with Hansen," he said. "God, that could have been trouble for you."

"Why they do that to an old man?" said Du Pré.

"No one here will talk to them," said Foote. "They are very used to solving things. With a murder, you know, if you don't solve it quickly the chances of solving it ever are small. And they

32

are under great pressure to solve these cases. So three of them are in the hospital and now we get three more. Or more. I expect they will lean on you."

Du Pré nodded. Stick a gun in an FBI neck, they take it personally.

"I hope they don't any of them get killed," said Du Pré.

"Oh, God," said Foote, "that would mean we would have hundreds of them here. I have been able to forestall their . . . overcrowding . . . so far. The political reality is that fatuous rich kids perceived as defenders of the environment are thought much more valuable than the backwards sixth-generation ranchers, who I seem to remember stand or fall on how well they take care of the grass. The people who have lived here for a century or more are most independent. They don't *resent* outsiders interfering with them. They refuse to tolerate it *at all*. It worries me. A great deal."

"Worry me, too," said Du Pré. "The first time, you know, some FBI pulls a gun on a rancher, that rancher's wife, she will just blow that FBI guy away like a gopher. Them FBIs, they don't know how to act, they need to go away, let me and Bart and Benny and the others figure this out. They make things, you know, much worse."

"There is a lot of loose talk about a conspiracy," said Foote.

"You think these ranchers get together, say, these fools come here, we wait for them, shoot them, maybe next Wednesday at ten at night? Paugh. No."

"Please explain," said Foote.

"OK," said Du Pré. "These fools come here, but it is not their land, you know. They drive around it, they think, well, this is very empty land, nobody on it. But I make you a bet. You, Lawyer Foote, you go on out when the season for deer it is over. You shoot one deer from the road. You see how long it is before the game warden is with you. No, I know what happen. These people are young, city people, can't see much here. They are here, cut these fences, shoot cows, they want a nice place to play in. They are scared, too. So they are on a dirt road, don't see nobody around, they drive slowly back and forth, for Chrissakes. They maybe smoke a joint, drink a little, helps some. They are out there after dark, driving around, headlights, slow. How far can you see headlights, this country? Oh, fifty miles. So someone has seen them, they have come, they are wondering, what in the hell are these people doing out here, anyway? Then those dumb kids, they get out of their expensive four-wheel-drive, they go cut fences, shoot some cattle. Whoever is watching them says, Jesus Christ, enough is enough. So whoever is watching these fools, they grab a gun and they shoot them, they are so mad. They just kill them."

Foote nodded. "I see," he said. "I suppose out here, empty as it looks, someone is always watching."

"Always," said Du Pré. "Now, this person who shot those two stupid kids, they are pret' mad at the bunny-huggers already. Environmentalists, they just march in here, say, you are bad people, this is our land now, get off it. Jesus Christ, what they expect? Free beer? Shit."

"They don't drink," said Foote. "They expect free designer mineral water and fat-free cheese. God, everybody who lives here has guns. I know that the owner is a local if there is a gun rack in the pickup. Full of guns. Guns which it is illegal even to own, I'd bet, too."

Du Pré thought about the machine pistol in his attic. The one Catfoot, his papa, had brought home from the war. MP-40. Schmeisser. It worked just fine. Someday Du Pré might need it.

"Tell you a story," said Du Pré. "It is the early sixties and this Federal Commissioner, Aviation, is flying across Montana in a plane, he sees another plane flying along with him, it comes up suddenly. The pilot is wearing a cowboy hat and dark glasses. Pilot grins. He fires off the machine guns, the twenty-millimeter cannon, so that the Commissioner knows they work, tracers, you know. He does a flip over the Commissioner's plane, so that he sees there are no identity numbers. It is painted like sagebrush and rock and grass. Commissioner, he goes crazy, hundreds of people looking for that plane, they never find it. It is still out there somewhere, in some rancher's barn. Rancher, he figures, he's had enough of that Washington, D.C., he strafe it."

"Hmmm," said Foote. "What kind of plane was it?"

"Old P-thirty-eight Lightning," said Du Pré. "You know, it is very fast for a propeller plane. I read about it. Somebody out there, cowboy hat, he owns it, loves it, keeps it oiled up and ready."

"Jesus," said Foote, "I think I see what you're saying."

Du Pré fetched more whiskey and the brandy bottle from the bar. He sat back down and he rolled a smoke. Foote lit one of his long black cigars and he leaned over and lit Du Pré's cigarette.

"I see now why you wanted so to have Bart take the Sheriff's job," said Foote.

Du Pré nodded.

"Times will change but these people will not," said Foote, "and they won't run or bend or give an inch."

"No," said Du Pré, "they will not. You know what is needed here, I think, is some FBI from here, knows these people. Lead these agents, make them not get themselves killed. Because they will work very hard and that is where it will end, I know, sure as hell, and when it happens and they send more and more get killed, that will be all."

"I'll see what I can do," said Foote.

Foote took his brandy and went off to a corner and made two phone calls.

Ah, thought Du Pré, I am friend to a guy, he can call Washington, D.C., at three, the morning, and someone will answer.

Foote sat down, cigar in his hand, brandy snifter in the other.

"Done," he said, "if they don't screw it up. I expect them to screw it up, but not too much."

Du Pré rolled another smoke and he lit it and he looked up at the blue tendrils rising.

"Things changing," he said, "much change. A time that is bent and maybe breaking. Old Benetsee, he listen to the earth, you know, he say it is speaking to him and never has this way before."

"He has a truly terrible moral force," said Foote. "I can't quite understand how those agents could have treated him so; my impulse is to bow. Never had that before. So a coyote ran in front of the car and then an unseen hand pushed the car over the bank. Curious."

Du Pré nodded. His power, reach a long way. Du Pré remembered the River of the Whale.

"Yah," said Du Pré, "I feel him all the way east in Canada, that mess with Lucky, few years ago." When I kill a man, have to, old Benetsee he see it coming.

"It is possible," said Foote. "And I should warn you, that the FBI may send someone from the West who left because he hated it and he will be real glad to make it worse."

"Shit," said Du Pré.

"What do you mean by changing?" said Foote.

"Last time it changed this much, it is 1886, the Métis rise up in Canada, they fight the English, poor mad Louis Riel he talking to Jesus and Jesus say, hang two English. Then Louis Riel he don't let his little general, Gabriel Dumont, defeat them English and so the Métis they lose and the priests betray poor Louis Riel and the English hang him. Some the Métis, they come down here, North Dakota, the buffalo are gone and they have nothing, they got maybe a Red River cart, hoe, ax, couple horses. Nine children, probably. They stay here, Indians hate them call them white, whites hate them call them Indian. But we live."

Foote nodded.

They smoked.

"Now these new people come, they say everybody here is bad people, you go away now, we want to play on your land. Bring back wolves. Bring back buffalo. But they don't know, these people."

Foote nodded.

"So these people here, first they don't understand, they are some confused. Then they get very angry, when they do understand."

Du Pré blew smoke at the ceiling.

"And then?" said Foote.

"Then they say, it is a good day to die."

"I have heard that line in a lot of movies," said Foote.

"Yah," said Du Pré, "well, that is silly Hollywood saying it. But I tell you something, I just think of it. It means you, too."

Foote nodded and waited.

"You live this country, a time," said Du Pré, "and you walk on it and you listen to it talk with you, you listen to the many peoples—rocks, trees, four-leggeds, six-leggeds, winged peoples—you are Indian. It will happen, you don't know it, maybe you are a rancher, *hates* Indians. But it take you."

"I see," said Foote.

"We got to stop this," said Du Pré. "But me, I do not for sure know how."

❧ CHAPTER 8 ❧

Du Pré and his daughter Jacqueline's husband, Raymond, were sitting on a fence rail smoking. They had just signed off on a double load of calves headed for feedlots and tables out east. The diesel engines of the trucks taking them were fading to nothing in the distance. It was one of the warm November days, golden light and the air so clear things seemed closer than they were.

Du Pré stared up at the Wolf Mountains.

"Well," said Du Pré, "them assholes want to put them wolf back there, I guess I go kill them like my grandfather did."

"I help," said Raymond.

"No, you don't," said Du Pré. "I tell you something, you do this kind of thing ever, you do it alone and you don't talk about it."

"You just talked about it," said Raymond.

"Yah," said Du Pré, "well, now I don't got to do it. Someone else do it, you bet."

A pheasant flushed from the thick weeds in the creek bottom over the road. Then another.

"Someone down there chasing them," said Du Pré. "Wonder who?"

"What you ever find out about that dog Packy got?" said Raymond.

"Oh, he belong to that murdered woman's boyfriend. End of that, it was just a call-in service, find a lost dog, call eight hundred."

The springer spaniel broke cover and ran down again into the weeds. Du Pré looked off east and saw Packy coming, shotgun across his chest, high. A pheasant flushed in front of him and he shot it, one smooth motion, boom, a puff of feathers.

Packy waved and then he disappeared, down behind a hill.

Du Pré heard a car coming, pretty fast. Drive like they are from here, he thought.

A tan government car topped a rise and then dipped out of sight. It came up again, still roaring, then began to slow down three hundred yards or so away. The car slowed and stopped.

A woman got out, standing up in one smooth motion. She had gray hair with white streaks in it. Dressed in jeans and boots and a worn rough leather jacket. She reached into the car and pulled out a stained hat and put it on.

She walked up to Du Pré and Raymond, chewing slowly.

She nodded. Clear blue eyes, lines around her mouth and eyes. About forty. Very lean. Horsewoman.

"Gabriel and Raymond," she said. "Told I'd find you here." Her accent was Montana, down deep. "I'm an FBI agent. In charge of this mess. Name's Corey Banning."

Gabriel and Raymond took off their hats and shook hands with her. They put their hats back on.

"I thought so," she said, grinning. "Now, I got a favor to ask of you, hope that it won't piss you off too much. I need to talk with Mr. Du Pré here, and Raymond, if you could maybe drive my car back to town we'll pick it up later."

"I got to go anyway," said Raymond. "I let Gabriel bring you my house, pick it up. Nice to meet you."

He walked over to the pool car and drove away.

"Just broke a bunch of regulations," said Corey Banning, "so fuck 'em."

Du Pré went to his Rover, got out a half-full bottle of whiskey, came back. He offered it to her.

"Obliged," she said, taking a sip.

Du Pré had a good slug.

"Whew," said Corey Banning. "Now, murder is not, as you know, a federal crime, so I am here to prove who violated their civil rights, which since they are dead I think must have happened. I ain't going away till I find out who, why, where, when, and all that good stuff. Now, unfortunately us folks at the FBI have a very poor reputation in the courtesy department and I just made it very clear to the three guys who came with me and who already hated my guts that they got to sir and ma'am and not shit in the punch bowl. Or someone'll blow their fool heads off."

"Good," said Du Pré. "Now I feel some better. I thought that maybe we have a war, you know?"

"Well, yeah," said Corey Banning, "it was headed that way. Now you and me, we know what happened. The little dummies thought no one was watching them and someone of course was and they lost their tempers some and killed them. That's against the law and further it ain't right."

"Yah," said Du Pré.

"Now I'm going to find these folks," said Corey Banning, "every goddamned one of them, and I'm going to see them tried and put in prison. You can go to the bank with it. And if you or Bart—nice guy, I like him—or Benny Klein screw up, withhold information, or break the law I'll do the same to you. Only fair to warn you. I got a job to do and further I happen to like the job."

Du Pré laughed.

"So I want to hear from you today all that you know. Everything. Now, we'll just sit here if you don't mind smoking and having a drink now and again, putting a little smile on, till all my questions are answered. I like answered questions, I hang around till I get them. Real pain in the ass. Not too bright, sometimes three, four days later, I think, now I didn't like that answer, I come back, see if it's changed any. Or maybe, I think, I asked that question wrong, there."

"OK," said Du Pré. "I am very glad you are here, you know why? Now, that Benny he quit, he don't want to arrest his good friends and neighbors and so he do that. Bart, he swallow hard and then he say, well, I will do this job best I can."

"Pretty strange," said Banning. "Guy's got more'n a hundred million dollars, dried-out drunk living in the ass end of nowhere to begin with, and suddenly he's the law. Good guy?"

"Yah," said Du Pré, "I think he be a very sad guy before this is over, but he is a good guy."

"Sad families just buried their kids, Du Pré," said Agent Banning. "Those kids were too dumb to walk and chew gum all at once, but they still didn't need killing. Even if they did we don't do things that way anymore."

Du Pré shrugged.

"Like that guy you killed in New York," said Agent Banning. "You do recall your old friend Lucky? Bad guy. You did the right thing, mind you, and I can say that because we never got any evidence and you ain't going to dance on in and confess and say please hang me. But I know that you did it and of course you know it's against the law and out of fashion. Even here."

Du Pré looked at her.

Ah yes, she is something, this one, he thought.

"Now," said Banning, "the Rosses and the Stemples they come up to you and tell you about their cut fences and dead cattle, you're playing at the bar—I love that music, I'll be there next time, you bet, you bet—they got good alibis and so it ain't them. Now, you aren't exactly a cop so I suspect you're too smart to be one which I admire but when you get back you're going to find ol' Bart there at the bar with a badge for you on account of how I asked him so nice and blinked my baby blues at him and waved my ass under his nose. Actually, I just told him it would be easier and he agreed."

"How long you talk to him he say that?" said Du Pré. "Just want to know?"

"Oh," said Agent Banning, "about two minutes, I guess, you know how I get? Scream, foam, bite things. Told him I'd cut a deal with him, he slaps a badge on you, I don't let those three pussies they stuck me with out of the trailer, they can sit in there, pull each other's dicks, answer the phone, I don't care. Useless as the tits on a slab of bacon but the main office is always trying to help. Bunch of fucking social workers, don't want the poor little things out on the street. I'll get rid of them soon enough but you know they'd just get themselves killed I let them go outdoors, and how would I feel? Actually, I wouldn't really give a shit but it's against the law which I do care about so I got to arrest more people and then they get pissy, they think I'm making work for myself so I can stay here. You know how their tiny little minds work. Hardly at all. They're so dumb all I got to do is water 'em once a week, sprinkle a little bullshit on 'em."

Du Pré howled.

"Yeah," said Agent Banning, "I do a great stand-up routine, don't I? Now I got to have your help. I just have to have it. You ever want one thing so bad you can just taste it? Run your credit card over the edge getting it? Do that? Well, I just got to have you, Deputy Du Pré, just until it's over. I just won't settle for less, you know."

"OK," said Du Pré, "but we got to let Benny off this one. He's too kind a guy for this job."

"Already done," said Banning. "I talked to his wife and we agreed on it, I don't want anybody hurt don't have to be, and he'd just fuck up and I'd have to bust him."

Du Pré nodded.

"Slug of that, please," said Special Agent Banning. "Christ, I lend government property, drink on the job, show disrespect for my superiors. Oughta report myself but I don't feel like it." She had a good pull of the whiskey.

"Now my first question," said Agent Banning, "is also my last question until I think of another, which may take a bit of time."

Du Pré waited.

"How far is it to this Medicine Person," said Agent Banning. "I have some gifts of respect in a bag over by your Rover there, and I would very much like to meet him."

Du Pré looked at her.

"We go there," he said. "He is called Benetsee."

"Ben-et-see," said Agent Banning, slowly. "Mr. Benetsee."

"No," said Du Pré, "just Benetsee."

"OK," said Banning, "I won't mister him."

❧ CHAPTER 9 ❧

But Benetsee wasn't there. The sweat lodge was cold and empty and no smoke came from the chimney. The dogs were on the front porch of the shack. There was a pile of gnawed bones and scrap meat a little ways away and they could drink from the creek, eat the scraps, and sleep in the warm place under the porch.

Agent Banning scratched their ears.

"I think he's watching us," she said, "either from that bunch of rocks over on the ridge there or the willows just across the creek. You mind we wait a bit? Actually, we wait a bit. I got to talk to him. Oh, well. Tell you what, I'll just bet you there's a chopping block back there, and I'll just go and put this wine and tobacco and meat back on it and then come back and we just sit here on the front porch, have us some more of that whiskey and I'll bum a couple smokes off you and we'll wait."

"I am supposed to meet my Madelaine, hour or so," said Du Pré. "I got to go then."

"Actually, you don't," said Banning. "I talked to her, see, she was in the bar when I talked to Susan Klein and I said, look, I got to do this with your Du Pré, sorry about that. She said fine, tear your ass off if I needed to."

Yah, thought Du Pré, that sound like my Madelaine, all right. She think this is funny.

"So we'll just wait till he comes. We'll wait all night and all day tomorrow and all week and still be here when the snows fucking melt but I just got to talk to this Benetsee and I won't have it any other way or with anyone but you."

She walked round back and put the wine and meat and tobacco and a small knife on the chopping block. She pulled a twist of sweet grass out of her jacket and lit it and set it on a stone on the ground.

"Uncle!" she yelled. "I must speak with you! You can help me! Please, Uncle!"

"Good," said Du Pré.

"I hear he's a very sacred person," said Banning, "and I will not be a smart-ass with him. My mother had kidney cancer and the Mayo Clinic told her to go home and die quietly. So I took her to a person like this Benetsee and she is seventy-six and on the third husband now, the other two died."

"Oh," said Du Pré.

"My daddy was a test pilot," she said, "you know how that goes. Lost him when I was three. Next one was a drunk and a lawyer and you know how *that* goes."

"OK," said Du Pré. He waited. "Who is the third?" he said.

"A really good guy," said Banning. "A blind blues saxophone player, wonderful man. Blind and black. They live in Paris."

Du Pré laughed.

"No shit," said Banning. "Great guy. She's wonderful. Sends me these frilly things. Tells me to get married."

"And?" said Du Pré.

"Well, I got married the one time but it didn't work out," said Banning.

"What happened?" said Du Pré.

"I shot the son of a bitch for pissing out the bedroom window.

43

It bothered me, so I became an FBI agent so I wouldn't do that again."

There is a true story in there somewhere, Du Pré thought. I chew on it long time maybe I guess it.

"Now, these people who shot the kids they get murder two," said Agent Banning, " 'cause I don't think they were thinking about it till they saw the stupid little bastards cutting the fences and shooting the cattle, and you know we got to stop this because otherwise it's going to be a sport, you know, shoot anything walks funny, eats tofu, or carries around a flag with baby seals on it. You know, I know, small-town West is going to die, our wonderful government is going to kill it off. They like doing that to small cultures, did it to the Indians and now it's us but it's how history moves, and beef is a bad word now and we live in a democracy and we got a very small voice. Oh, by the way, when they release those damn wolves up there they'll last about two hours and I know that and I don't care. I don't want to hear it, or about it. That's Fish and Wildlife crap, doofuses. They pulled me off some drug murders, Jackson Hole, to send me up here. God, that place is unbelievable. Good place for a nuclear accident, you ask me. Well, we had this when it was good."

"Yah," said Du Pré, "it was. I don't think that we lose it, though. This is just one bad moment."

"Hope so," said Banning, "but I don't think so. Well, we had it when it was good and I actually feel for the poor little bastards who came here to save everything, bring back the woolly mammoth and such. It was gone when they got here because when they came they came in a tide and they just swamped it. All the drinking water in the Rockies is poisoned now with giardia. Thank you, backpackers."

Du Pré laughed.

How many more people dead before this is over, he thought sadly. It came on him suddenly. He looked down at his feet.

Banning held the whiskey bottle in front of Du Pré.

"We got to do this," she said. "It's ugly enough now, Gabriel. Really ugly. And you know how bad it could get."

"Yah," said Du Pré, "I am not going to enjoy being a good guy this time, if I am."

"Gray hats, for sure," said Banning. "I give that old bastard about five minutes before he comes round the shack. I hope I didn't leave him too much wine."

"Not possible, leave him too much wine," said Du Pré. "You know these persons. I got more, he wants it. He is some old man. I sometimes want to break his dirty old neck, but then I think, sometimes he don't know the answers, just the riddles."

"Case you are wondering," said Banning, "I just want to ask for his help and he'll do it or not and I'll take what he gives me and it's all right, whatever."

"I knew that," said Du Pré. "I tell you I help. You are right, it was not right, kill those people. I wish it had not happened. I wish for many things in my life. I wish it happened someplace else, I wish my leg was broke. I wish much. But I help you. I will find myself in front of somebody I went to school with, hunted with, drank with, maybe someone who saved my life, this country almost take it few times. I don't like this."

"Thanks," said Banning. "I didn't know if you could fly high enough to see it. I am truly grateful."

"I have lived here always," said Du Pré. "Little time, the army, but that is all. My papa is brand inspector, and when he is killed I am. I got one daughter here with many children, the other she is finishing up her doctor's degree, at Yale. That Bart, he pay for her everything. But me, I am here, I don't know too much else. Now I got to go to my life, my friends, cut some of them out, put handcuffs on them, see them off to bad prisons, have their families hate me forever. I don't like it."

Banning nodded.

"I say I help you and I will, unless this Benetsee he tells me I can't. I am sorry, I give you my word and then I think of this. If he says no I go away."

"He won't say no," said Banning. "Whatever is bad now will only be worse if you don't help and he will know that. A bad time, it's here, and we have to deal with it. Your Madelaine told me something about you, Du Pré, she knows you well. She said you'd charge hell with one bucket of water. I ain't heard that for thirty years."

The old dogs stirred. They got up and woofed wheezily. "Benetsee!" said Du Pré. "We need you, my friend."

The old man was behind them on the porch.

"Some good wine," said Benetsee. "I like maybe a good smoke. You roll it thick, yes?"

Du Pré did. He handed it to the old man and held out his lighter to him. Benetsee drew deeply on the cigarette.

Benetsee knelt down and held the smoke in front of Banning. She took it and had a long drag.

"You got a good spirit," said Benetsee, "falcon spirit. Pretty swift, little too sure sometimes, get you in trouble, crash into things."

"Yes, Uncle," said Banning.

Benetsee moved down the steps. He squatted in front of her and he looked at her face for a long time. He finished his cigarette.

"You better be my daughter," said Benetsee. "I can help you more."

She nodded. "A great honor," she said.

"No shit," said Benetsee. "You going to need it. Now, Falcon Woman, you got more to do, you know."

Banning's head snapped up. She looked levelly at Benetsee.

"Coyotes sing early this morning," said Benetsee. "They tell me sad things."

No, Du Pré thought, please, no more.

Benetsee stood up and he tugged at Banning's sleeve till she rose and she followed him.

"People, last night they let wolves out up there. They sneak them in three days ago, pen them, last night they let them loose. Eight wolves. Four people up there with them."

"Oh, God," said Banning.

"Two wolves left now," said Benetsee. "They get lucky, run right."

"The people?" said Banning.

"Coyotes say two wolves left," said Benetsee.

Agent Banning looked up at the Wolf Mountains, bright with snow. A thin line, gray as the lead of a pencil scraped over paper, stretched east from the tops of the peaks.

"It's going to snow like hell up there," said Banning.

Shit, Du Pré thought. Shit. Goddamn it.

Six.

❖ CHAPTER 10 ❖

Who do we know that can go up there on snowshoes very quietly and kill four people and six wolves and then come back down quietly and not leave a fucking trace?" said Bart. "The bastard even dug the slugs out of their heads. Chopped them open with a hatchet and fished around in their brains till he got the slugs and then off he went singing a happy song. Probably twenty-two hollow-points. He is thorough, he goes back to his home, fires up the old cutting torch, melts down the barrel, and leaves us here with our dicks in our ears."

Du Pré tossed a dart at the dartboard. It had a photograph of the Governor on it. Very tattered.

"Ah," said Du Pré, "forty people could do all that, you know. But this one it is different. This time that person was hunting those Fish and Wildlife assholes. Maybe more, Bart, they were not even from this place."

Bart nodded. It was snowing like hell outside.

"He'll be easy," said Corey Banning. "Whoever did this did it in cold blood. Means they like it, they'll do it again. They'll fuck up."

Du Pré sighed.

"What we need to do today," he said, "we maybe go down to the bar there, drink some, I play a little fiddle, lot of people there, the weather is nice bad, just snowy, not too cold, they not got much to do, don't do much more than feed the cattle, take a couple hours, we just be there, maybe someone say something."

"I got some paperwork," said Banning. "I'll see you later. Check in on my little helpers. What a priceless little bunch of peckerheads. I wonder what their mothers did to them after they cut their balls off."

Bart laughed.

She went out, cussing.

"What a lady," said Bart.

Du Pré shrugged.

"We going to have to get lucky, this one," he said. "Nobody see anything, hear gunshots, nothing. No trucks, cars they see. They blind, deaf. That bunch of people dead in the mountains, it will not take long to find out who did it. But maybe never on the first two."

"That guy who did kill those four people," said Bart, "he might have done the others. If, like Corey says, we can get him first, he might crack. Our best bet."

One fucking crack, Corey Banning had said, one crack and we get a wedge in and then we go. Just one crack. Or heat it up and pour water on it and see what flakes off. Or go ask Benetsee what he's seen lately. But find that crack, now.

They drove to the Toussaint Bar. The place was packed and smoky. Susan was mixing drinks and Madelaine was in the back frying hamburgers.

Du Pré looked at the prime rib sign. So it was Friday night.

He waved at the accordion player from Cooper and the guitarist. They had their instruments out on the little stage. Du Pré went back out to the Rover and got his fiddle. He took it in and opened the case and left it sitting on top of an amplifier left over from the country band, to warm up so it would stay in tune.

Susan shoved a glass of soda at Bart and a double whiskey at Du Pré and she bustled off.

The air was hot, damp, and close. Du Pré took off his jacket and untied the kerchief at his throat. He tossed his hat and jacket on the stage and he sat on a stool sipping whiskey.

I know every face, this room, he thought. One of you, two of you, who did this thing.

I know my people. I make a list, I write them on it, I cross them out one by one, I do this and something it will go click and then I will know before I know. I will find this one, have to smell it.

Like a coyote. Coyote looks for things aren't right. Trap there, a circle that is something's eye, something to eat. Way I track. Look for something that is not right.

Packy lurched up to Du Pré. He was very drunk, his eyes bleary. He deserved to be, pulling shoes off horses fifteen hours a day for six weeks.

"They got the sonsofbitches this morning," said Packy.

"Huh?" said Du Pré.

"Them fucking wolves. They came down to Stemple's feedlot and he got 'em, two shots."

Good, Du Pré thought. Now if they don't do it again we maybe don't get anybody more killed.

Who is a trapper?

Fur market is down so bad no one does it.

Du Pré remembered sending his furs to Sears, Roebuck and getting things back for them, thirty years ago.

Used to do it, till the bobcats got cut back so far, used to be you got three hundred fifty for a bobcat pelt.

Bill Stemple. Packy, till he got stove up so bad. Draft horse kick him, then step on the other leg. Gets around pretty good, though. And those two brothers, the St. Francis boys. They're forty. Never married. Folks are dead.

Marcus and George St. Francis.

Not Bill Stemple, he would not do that, he shoot the wolves for sure, hell, anybody do that. Spit in their faces, those fools want them here. Packy is too sweet a guy and he can't get up there.

St. Francis boys both trap once, they are of this country, they know it, I know them, they are very quiet.

Kind of crazy, I always think, Du Pré thought. Can't think why I think that.

Du Pré saw them across the room, leaned up against the wall. They were dressed in stained brown overalls and coats, farmer caps, boots with rubber bottoms and leather tops. Big guys, strong. Played basketball, high school.

Or it is somebody over the other side of the mountains, north, they are doing it.

Du Pré made his way across the room to the St. Francis brothers. They looked at him curiously.

I don't think that I have spoken to them, twenty years, thought Du Pré. But I am remembering something.

What?

Bart and Banning had talked to them and they got nothing.

Suddenly Du Pré remembered. Both of them had had some trouble as kids. They were twins, the kind that look different from each other.

Set some cars, a house on fire, got sent to the state school, Pine Hills. Kept to themselves.

Fuck it, thought Du Pré, I am tired of playing by the rules.

He stood in front of them. They smiled at him. Shook their heads.

"Bart and Banning didn't think of something," said Du Pré, "but I did. You guys shot those people up in the mountains. Left some witnesses."

The brothers looked at him blankly.

"Best place for those wolves come down was yours," said Du Pré, "but they would not. They smell you, go to Stemple's."

"You're crazy," said George.

"I am that," said Du Pré. "I am also right, you know. I be along."

He walked away.

The St. Francis brothers left right away.

"Hey, Bart," said Du Pré, leaning over close to Bart's ear, "those St. Francis brothers, they probably killed those people up in the Wolfs."

"I talked to them, Banning talked to them," said Bart. "They both had stories and stuck to them. You know what ranching is. Pretty lonely life. Half the country couldn't come up with one witness to say they were anywhere in particular on a given day."

"Them wolves come down to Stemple's?" said Du Pré. "They should have come to St. Francis place. Closer, and they got some sheep. They smelled the men who killed the wolves up there, Bart, so they went over another entire mountain. Don't make sense. It was snowing so hard then, wolves are like everybody else, you know, they got reasons to do things."

Bart nodded.

"I don't think I can get a warrant on that," he said.

Corey Banning came in. Eyes followed her across the room. She ignored them.

Bart and Du Pré waited.

When she got to them Du Pré told her what he thought. She listened, nodding.

"They kill animals?" she said. "Set them on fire, torture them? Were they bullies, beat up smaller children, laugh while they did it?"

Du Pré rubbed his eyes. Something, long time ago, what?

A dog. It had a dog in it.

Long time ago. Come on, come on.

Snap.

Du Pré had been driving by the grade school and he had seen some kids outside gathered around a dog that had been killed by a passing car.

The children had either been crying or laughing.

All but the St. Francis brothers were crying. They smiled.

They had laughed.

Them?

Maybe.

✤ CHAPTER 11 ✤

B art kicked his official desk in his official office.
"I don't fucking *believe* it," said Bart. "The ultimate god-damned alibi, for Chrissakes, I can't stand it."

The St. Francis brothers had both been in jail when the murders occurred. For beating up a whore in Billings. They were out on bond. They had spent a lot of their lives out on bond. The whore probably wouldn't press charges.

"How many times that happen?" said Du Pré.

"They're forty-two," said Bart. "I would guess this has been one of their little hobbies for quite some time."

"But we never hear of it."

Bart shrugged.

It was snowing outside. Montana snowing. Deep and still. Deep as your ass and still snowing. Snowmobiles whined unpleasantly down the streets.

I hate them damn machines, Du Pré thought. Used to be you had to know the country and how to move through it, now any asshole can get on one of those things and chase deer to death for the fun of it. Pigs, like the rest of them, off-road vehicles, dirt bikes, little four-wheelers.

Me, I drive one when I got to, only. I hate it.

"We are not thinking about this good enough," said Du Pré. "We look for murders, we find them. What are we doing? We say, it is someone that we don't like."

"Yes," said Bart, "because the people we don't like much were killed by, in all probability, people we do like. I love this fucking job. I get five, six calls a day, long distance, people screaming at me to catch the killers. The killers of the *wolves*, mind you. I want to be the only Sheriff's office in the world with an unlisted telephone number."

Du Pré laughed.

"You know, I think I go see Benetsee," he said. "I have not seen the old fart, couple weeks, take him some food and wine, tobacco. Each winter I think, he go off, we not find him till the snow melt in the spring."

Bart flipped a dart at the board.

"He'll just disappear, Gabriel," said Bart. "The coyotes will eat him and then, someday, make little coyotes. One kind of immortality."

Corey Banning's big four-wheel-drive diesel pickup pulled up and they heard the door slam on the truck. She barged in, knocking the snow off her high packs, and tossed her cowboy hat at the hat tree. The hat landed precisely on a peg.

"You ain't missed yet," said Bart.

"I never miss," said Corey. "Too bad about the St. Francis brothers. We get to wait till they kill some poor whore, I guess."

"How's tricks?" said Bart.

Corey shrugged. "I am getting nothing," she said, "which I expected to get. Killing four Fish and Wildlife agents is a federal offense and so I am here forever. I may retire here. I may die here. But I do not go away from here without I get 'em all."

"Can't die till you get 'em," said Bart, "but I don't know, we may just never find out. You remember that guy got shot in Missouri, the thug, by the townspeople? They never found out on that one."

"They didn't send me," said Corey Banning. "You don't have to be very smart to be an FBI agent if you're a guy. President, either, for that matter. I've been north and east. Nothing there. Talked to everybody that the Sheriff's said could possibly have done it. You know what they do? They shrug. Ask them where they were that day, they shrug. Ask them is there anything they can think of to help me, they shrug. They sure ain't about to give anyone up. You'd think there'd be one greedy prick or one jealous wife or one goddamned snitch here, but they haven't bothered talking to me."

"They won't," said Bart. "They think Washington, D.C., is something that ought to be nuked and they'd just have to shoot it if it came here. And Gabriel was saying just before you flounced in that it was someone we know and like and they probably won't ever be caught. We have no evidence. Nothing. Not a slug, a fingerprint, nothing. Did your people find anything at all?"

Corey Banning shook her head.

"All the killers have to do is keep quiet," said Bart, "that's all. They don't even have to be careful. Even if there were two of them, and one confessed and turned in the other, we can't get a conviction."

"I ain't looking at it right," said Corey. "It's like tracking an animal. You don't look at the ground right, you lose 'em."

"That ground up there, under ten feet of snow," said Du Pré, "you won't find nothing. You know how to track something, you know how not to leave any. I am going to Benetsee's now, see what he say. He say that these people killed, the earth hates them, he has never known the earth hating like this before."

"I would think," said Corey, "that the earth would hate rip-off miners and such a lot more."

Du Pré shook his head.

That old man know something, or maybe doesn't yet, he is lost in his dreams, Du Pré thought.

We all are.

What is for the earth to hate, anyway? It still be here long after people have left it, all. I don't think we last much.

"Well," said Du Pré, "I go see that old fart now. I got this funny feeling that even if he know something, he won't tell us either."

Several cars went by outside, laboring through the deep snow. The plows had been through and would be again soon. The county was so sparsely populated that there were few plows. Almost everyone had a high-set four-wheel-drive truck. There was damn little north of Toussaint and Cooper but the Wolf Mountains, not much against winds that came from the North Pole.

The telephone rang. Bart had his boots up on his desk and a cup of coffee in his hand. He answered his own telephone; the dispatcher for the radio calls worked out of her house, six miles away.

Bart listened. His boots thumped down on the floor.

Du Pré waited.

"Well," said Bart, "I don't blame you, Susan, but I'd appreciate it if you didn't shoot anybody. I'll be right there."

"What?" said Corey Banning.

"Unbelievable," said Bart. "There are about a hundred flat-landers in that little park across from the bar. Several of them came into the bar and they told Susan that they were having a memorial service for the martyrs who died for the wolves. Then they say that they want to hold it inside the saloon since it's snowing outside."

Yah, thought Du Pré, I can see Susan listening to that. Hear what she say to it, too. They don't move fast enough for her, down go her hand and up come the shotgun. Oh, I hope Benny is there soon.

"I guess we had better go and see what the hell is going on," said Bart, "though I don't quite understand why they are doing this now. The murder victims have been dead for quite some time, and so have the wolves."

"I don't think these people thought much about it until someone did it for them," said Du Pré. "I think we got a bunch of extremely dumb people there, probably that asshole Bucky Dassault there, too, saying he is Benjamin Medicine Eagle, and I am worried some because maybe three hours from now this snow it stop and then it get cold and a big wind from the northwest, very cold big wind. Then maybe some more snow."

Bart looked at Du Pré.

"I think we had better get the high school set up for 'em and send for the Red Cross," he said.

"You read this weather pretty good," said Corey Banning. "According to the weather reports, that is exactly what is going to happen. And there is a hell of a snowstorm coming in fifty points north of this one. The Alberta Clipper."

Du Pré nodded. "We don't have one of them for seven years, and it was very bad."

"Christ," said Bart, "we got to get that damn highway closed down. I'll call 'em now. All three of them, I'll ask the Highway Patrol to close down."

"I better go on over there," said Du Pré, "see what is going on. That Susan, they threaten her too much she will shoot, you know."

"I'll follow," said Corey Banning.

Bart slammed the phone down.

"Goddamn it," he yelled. "Those bastards!"

"Ah?" said Du Pré.

"They've had a ton of cars headed this way and didn't do dick. They could have called me. Any car left Miles City this morning ain't gonna make it here."

"Christ," said Corey.

"I don't know," said Du Pré. "Usually them ranchers will help but this word gets round they might not."

"They'll help," said Corey Banning.

"I hope so," said Bart.

"They're our people," said Corey Banning, "of course they will. They'll save 'em and shelter 'em and feed 'em. And I bet they won't say a word to these idiots all the time they're doin' it."

Du Pré nodded, and they went out the door.

❖ CHAPTER 12 ❖

It was still pretty warm out, though the air had a crystalline bite to it. The flakes of snow were getting smaller.

Du Pré had to park a half mile from the Toussaint Bar, clear out of town. There were stalled and stuck cars all over the road, and when he slogged into town there were cars and silly little four-wheel-drive station wagons all over the place, in people's yards, on the playground next to the little elementary school.

There was a crowd across the road from the Toussaint Bar, circling a bonfire made of the picnic tables the high school kids in Cooper had made for the tourists. Someone wearing a feathered headdress was ranting from the back of a pickup truck. Du Pré couldn't hear the words. He didn't need to.

Bucky Dassault. Child molester, alcohol and drug counselor, and then he is Benjamin Medicine Eagle, rubbing crystals and talking to fools.

What they call them? New Age?

Same old crap, con artists ripping off fools. Ah, hell, Catholic Church it start off that way. They all do. Jesus probably has three walnut shells, one dried pea, then he's dead and can't be questioned.

I maybe kick the shit of Bucky out of him, I don't think Bart care.

Du Pré tried the front door of the bar. It was locked.

He pounded on it and hollered.

In a couple minutes Benny opened it.

He had an eye swelling shut. Du Pré slipped through the door and Benny threw the bolt to.

Susan stuck her head up from behind the bar. She spat out a pink stream of water.

"Jesus," said Du Pré, "what the fuck happened?"

"Little fight," said Benny, "but we got 'em out finally. I got this and Susan got hit in the mouth, somebody threw a full can of beer they brought in."

Christ.

Someone pounded on the door. Du Pré went and opened it. Corey slid in. He locked it again.

"This is a mess comin' on pretty fast," she said. "We got to get those damn fools over to the high school before the Alberta Clipper gets here. Got eighty-mile winds and a lot of snow. Who's the fucking Uncle Tonto giving the speech?"

"Nobody," said Du Pré. "Listen, I maybe need your help, Corey.

You come with me. When I tell you, look over there a minute, then when I tell you it is all right, you can look back, then you speak to these people. We can take care of them at the high school in Cooper, but not here, we don't got the room."

"You wouldn't be thinking of punching out the lights of that idiot in the feathers over there, would you?" she said.

"Oh, no," said Du Pré. "That would be assault. Against the law. I would not do that thing."

"I'll judge what I see and I don't," said Corey Banning. "Let's go do something right for once."

They went out. The snow was packed down in the street and the little park. Du Pré walked up to Bucky Dassault, who had his back to him, jerked his feet out from under him. Bucky's knees hit the tailgate of the pickup, and then his hands.

Du Pré grabbed him by the collar and twisted him round.

"Shut up, you," said Du Pré. "I kick you half dead, you hear?"

Bucky opened his mouth.

Du Pré punched him hard, dumped him on the ground, and kicked him several times.

"Will you just do it and not enjoy yourself so much?" said Corey. "We got work to do, you know."

Du Pré nodded and he cracked Bucky on the back of the skull with his nine-millimeter.

The crowd watched silently.

Corey cupped her hands around her mouth.

"I am Special Agent Corey Banning, FBI," she said, "and you are in great danger. There is a terrible storm coming and you need to go back down this highway immediately"—she pointed—"to the Cooper High School. There isn't room for all of you here, and you didn't impress the natives well. Please go now. You could die. Do not go any farther than Cooper. If you try to go back to Billings you will die. Go now to Cooper. We have not got much time. Help each other. Get the cars turned around and on the way. Start with the ones in the back."

The crowd stared at her.

Sheep, thought Du Pré. I have seen these faces going into a slaughterhouse. Same expressions.

"We came to honor the people killed for the wolves," shouted one tall, greasy-looking hippie in the back.

"I ain't going to argue with you," said Corey Banning. "You've done worn out your welcome here. Get going or freeze to death. There's not much room here. If women with young children get stranded there may be room for you. Maybe not. There's no time. Get going."

The crowd shifted and then it began to break up. The people moved back toward the scattered cars, and soon the furthest ones were grinding back down the road to Cooper.

A man and a woman waited till they could get through to Corey, still standing by the pickup. Bucky Dassault was still flat on his face in the snow. Groaning a little.

Damn, thought Du Pré, I wanted to maybe kill him, he was a public danger.

"Agent Banning," said the woman, "I'm from the Minneapolis *Star*. Bobbie Larkin. He's from Seattle. Reporters. Now, you are investigating these murders, and nothing has been found? At all? You have no leads? Nothing? Why is the FBI stymied? Do you expect a break in this case? Six people have been killed and not one statement has been made by you or the regional office. What's the story?"

Corey Banning tucked a packet of snoose in her cheek and she chewed it some. She looked levelly at them and didn't say one word.

"Why did the deputy attack that man?" Bobbie Larkin went on.

"You knew him," said Du Pré. "You would maybe run over him, your car. We got a bad storm coming in and these foolish people could die in it, you know. Bucky, here, he don't care about that."

Corey Banning stepped down off the back of the truck and she walked off toward the Toussaint Bar.

"No comment?" shouted the woman reporter at Banning's back.

"You better get to Cooper," said Du Pré. "We are not kidding, it will be thirty below, three hours, then the big storm, stay cold. It is from the Arctic, not the Pacific, this storm. You will not be able to see ten feet and if you get out of your car in it you try to walk somewhere you die maybe fifty yards."

He jerked Bucky Dassault to his feet.

"You fucking prick," said Du Pré, "anybody die because you start this chicken-shit I will personally kill you very dead, I swear to you. *Anybody*. What you doing? Make a video? Sell it, these fools? I come look at your ads, such."

"I . . ." said Bucky.

Du Pré bashed him in the mouth, slammed him face-down on the bed of the pickup, and handcuffed him. He jerked him up by his hair and shoved him off to the bar.

"That's police brutality!" yelled the guy from Seattle.

Du Pré left Bucky standing.

"Listen, you stupid motherfuckers," he said, "I think lot of people die because this asshole set up this fool memorial service. Pocket all the donations, I bet. He say we have it here. He don't *care* that they die. He would never think of it. He finally think he make some money, get to screw some pretty women. He never think of it. I will be out, three, maybe four days now. All others, too. We try to save all these dumb people you know. And if they are dead, it is because of this prick, maybe some of the people come here, you know. Now he do this and I got to clean up after him. You maybe understand. This is not a lie. It is not a game. That storm she will be here soon. Anybody on the highway, they don't know how to stay alive, they are dead. You want to bet me how many, uh? I think maybe a lot. We try, but the snowdrifts, can't see so good, maybe a car in there, maybe not. And these people here, some of them maybe die trying to save people they don't like, like they didn't like the ones that got killed. Why should they?"

The reporters looked at each other.

"So I arrest him now," said Du Pré, "and I will throw his ass in jail. And when we add up the dead, you tell me I did a wrong thing."

Du Pré shoved Bucky Dassault up to the front door of the bar and he slammed Bucky's face into it.

Benny unlocked it.

"He looks kinda worn," said Benny.

Du Pré shoved him inside. He jammed him down in a chair. He pulled out his nine-millimeter and jammed it between Bucky's eyes.

"I know people will die in this," he said. "I maybe kill you now, save the time. I know people die. Some, my friends, they die, because of this I will kill you. I make you that promise."

The telephone rang. Susan Klein answered.

She listened. She waved to Du Pré.

Du Pré walked over and grabbed the phone.

"It is me," he said.

"Booger Tom just called me," said Bart, "and he said eight people took off this morning on snowshoes, headed up into the Wolfs."

"You got sleds for them snowmobiles in your barn?" said Du Pré.

"Four," said Bart.

"OK," said Du Pré. "I call Raymond, maybe Booger Tom, one of your cowboys."

"Jesus," said Bart.

Du Pré walked back over to Bucky.

"I think maybe you killed eight people," he said softly. "You better pray I can find them."

He nodded to Benny and Susan and Corey and he went out the door.

✤ CHAPTER 13 ✤

No," said Booger Tom, "I told him *snowmobiles*. Four of 'em. They had one sled, piled up with *snowshoes*, which they is gonna need, soon's their machines sink out of sight, couple thousand feet up."

"OK," said Du Pré, "I guess we go now. Catch them pretty quick. When our machines quit, we turn around, that's it. We can't get them out then."

We got the one hope, thought Du Pré, we are better on these than they are on theirs. They are stuck and we find them right away. This snow it is graining down. They make it to the steep slopes the noise they make bring down avalanche for sure. Hear one of them we turn around, too. They can't fly a helicopter in that narrow canyon without bringing all that snow down.

It is like they run into a burning house with it ready to come down.

But I got to go look.

Oregon license plates. That is about right.

"OK," said Du Pré to Booger Tom, Raymond, and Benny Klein. "We go on up and when we can't go farther we turn around. We don't got much time, find these people, you know, minute the snow stop, sun come out and wind come up then we got to turn around and head back right then. The snow start coming down. We go pretty far, when it gets bad I go on alone, far as I can, I call you I need you. When I got to turn round that is it."

"Du Pré," said Raymond, "I don't let you do that."

"Raymond," said Du Pré, "my girls, they are grown up. You are married to one, you got her the ten kids, you. I don't think we got time to talk."

Du Pré started his snow machine and moved off. The others followed. They went through Bart's big bench pasture, cutting off a couple of miles, and came down a sidehill trail to the Forest Service trail which ran up into the Wolfs in the Cooper Creek drainage.

There were some faint signs of passage; where trees screened the trail there were almost invisible dips in the snow's surface in lines too straight to have fallen from the sky.

Du Pré ran the machine up the trail, looking ahead to where the steep slopes narrowed in. The snow was heavy on them, poised to slide. He shot out into a meadow and saw the snow machines piled at the far end. Two of them were tangled; one must have followed too closely when the front one's skis sank and caught something.

The top of the damn barbed-wire gate, Du Pré thought. Pretty deep, this snow.

Du Pré slowed and his machine began to sink. He came to a stop by the jumbled snowmobiles.

There was a more clearly drawn trail headed up the canyon. Du Pré squinted. Couple places where someone had fallen over. Them snowshoes, he thought, they don't got throttles on them, got to know what you are doing. But they must have the long ones, little ones would just sink.

Du Pré checked the snowshoes strapped to the sled he was pulling. Six feet long with high raised front tips, Alaska trappers. He waved at the three men behind him, cranked up his machine, and pulled up slowly to the gate. He got out and stood on the front skis and he reached down in the snow till he found the wire and cut it with the dikes he had in his parka.

Temperature is dropping, sun is up there, light is rising. I don't got much time. *They* don't got much time.

Little spoiled brats I am trying to save. They don't let me, fuck them. I turn round, first thing they say I don't like. No, I won't. They are just plenty dumb is all.

Du Pré pulled the wire up and pushed it over. He wound the engine up and wallowed forward till the track caught on the next wire down, giving him a springboard.

Ride in, walk out, I think, he thought.

He kept the machine flat out. The rear end wallowed through the light snow; the snowmobile jumped up and down a little. Like skating on black ice. Go over it fast, fine; slow, it break.

There was a tall grove of firs at the very mouth of the narrow canyon. Canyons on the north side of the Wolfs were U-shaped, but the glaciers hadn't come down the south side. He roared out the other side onto the braided tiny plain the creek had kept from the trees. It ran high and swift in spring for a couple weeks, then sank to a trickle for the rest of the year.

Du Pré saw movement up ahead. Someone standing in the snow, waving. He pulled up to the figure and slowed and the snowmobile sank, the front end going deepest from the weight of the engine.

Du Pré clambered back to the sled and put on the snowshoes and he pumped over to the snow-covered fool waving at him, his knees lifting high to pull up the snowshoe's toes and set them again.

He stopped next to the idiot.

"Help me, help me," she said. She had a muffler wrapped round her head. Much frost where she had breathed through it. The cold air was sliding down the canyon. Blue cold.

"You, quiet," Du Pré hissed. "I get you out but we got snow above which is wanting to slide. You got snowshoes?"

She dug out a pair from the snow. She had been standing on them.

"OK," Du Pré whispered, "now I go and get the sled, pull it over, you put on these and we go back. We got to hurry, sun come out the snow it loosen."

She nodded.

Du Pré got the sled and she clambered on it and he pulled it over to the track the snowmobile had made.

He scraped the snow off her packs and got her tied to the snowshoes.

"We got to get out of here some quick," he hissed. "No noise."

She nodded.

Du Pré stomped himself around and he started down the trail.

Usually, I let them go ahead but I got to pull this one along. We got three miles, snow it come down anytime. Another avalanche go boom, jet overhead, owl he fart. We either make it or not. Probably not. I don't give us much chance.

Du Pré's ears crackled. Something talking to him. The snow.

I will kill you now, Du Pré, they find you in the spring, your face color of red wine.

I get out of here I kill that damn Bucky Dassault. I kill him with a *shovel*. I want to hear it *ring*.

Hard going, even in the pressed track the snow machine had made.

Too heavy to turn around, and once I slow down that is it. The snow it does not come down for that, maybe not for us.

I loosened it a lot.

There was a terrible boom behind them.

The other seven be dead under that, for sure, thought Du Pré.

He looked back. She was ten feet behind him, arms swinging, keeping up.

Breath coming hard, better slow down, I can't carry her. He stopped.

"We rest a minute," he said. "Soon as you can go we go. I keep looking back for you, I will not leave you."

She was sobbing, her breath choppy.

She nodded.

"We go," said Du Pré.

Ten more minutes, halfway there, the worst place just before we get out.

Hail Mary and you burn some sweet grass, old Benetsee. Need everybody now.

His ears were crackling more. A sound I cannot hear. What?

Du Pré glanced up. There were no trees above him on either side. The snowslides scraped them off. Seedlings survived the snow till they got big enough to have stiffer trunks and then they were snapped off. Just grass up there. And rock. Seventy-degree slopes.

Got a slick base, had sleet, it froze.

It come like sand down a tilted mirror when it come. Come hard enough, the vacuum suck our lungs out our mouths, look like we puking pink foam, red lumps in it.

Du Pré saw a great horned owl float past in front of him.

Very bad sign in the daylight, that. Someone die now. Always been for me, someone die I see an owl, sunlight.

Ten more minutes. Du Pré stopped. She was thirty feet behind him, laboring, exhausted.

She struggled up to him.

Du Pré held his hand in front of her. She grabbed it.

"We got just the one mile, little less, to go," he said, "but we got to move pretty quick, more the sun up top the more the snow wants to slide down here."

She gasped and moaned.

"We go a little slower maybe," said Du Pré.

They went on.

Ears are crackling more, like I got a power cable next to them.

"Help me!" she screamed behind him.

Du Pré turned. She had fallen over, her snowshoes were up on the track, and she was down in the snow at an angle. She was flailing frantically. She screamed and screamed.

Du Pré heard the boom above, the cornices breaking off and falling hard into the stacked snow below.

A loud rush, like a train.

He stood on her snowshoes so he could find her, if he lived through the snow rushing down on them.

The wind in front of the snow wave hit him. He crouched in a ball.

The snow slammed down.

Du Pré held his hands to his face, smelled the wet leather of the mittens.

Whump.

Crushed in the dark.

❖ CHAPTER 14 ❖

Du Pré dug at his eyes. He took off his mittens and scraped the snow out of his eye pits. Drops of water ran down his cheeks. He blinked. There was a very faint light. He felt for his snowshoes. They were still there.

Only problem I got I don't know which way is up, now. If I ever know which way is up. Could be I am upside down.

Don't know how far up to the light, six inches? No, light too dim. Very dim.

No light at all.

Du Pré reached in his coat and fumbled for his cigarette lighter. Not there.

He tried his other pocket. A book of matches.

He spent a few minutes trying to light them but his breath was melting the snow and he couldn't strike them with mittens on and they got wet and stayed that way.

OK. I got spit. Du Pré pushed some spittle out on his lip. He felt for it with a finger. Sitting on his cheek. Left cheek is down some.

He wriggled and moved in that direction, tried it again. Felt for a drop. Not there.

He spat again, softly.

The spittle landed in his palm.

Thank you, whichever god, I know where down is now.

Du Pré began to claw his way up. He shoved and packed the snow, making a chamber. He pulled his snowshoes round to where he thought they would be more or less parallel to the ground.

Another goober, my palm.

Straight down.

Well, if I am not forty feet under here I may live, you know.

But the bad storm it is coming. I hope those goddamned fools go on home before they can't get there.

They won't. My friends, they die here with me.

Du Pré reached as far as he could out and down.

He yelled.

She was not there.

He took off his left snowshoe and poked down.

Nothing.

Well, that is the owl, I guess.

All of this for nothing, I guess.

Du Pré dug and dug and pulled his snowshoes up and dug some more.

He couldn't get any higher. He had reached as high as he could. He took off his parka and set it to the side, then stepped on it with his right snowshoe. He lifted the left one and poked upward. The long trapper gave him another six feet of reach.

Light.

Now all I got to do is get to it.

He dug his hand into the snow wall beside him.

A tree. Little cottonwood.

Climb up the tree to heaven.

Like when I was little kid, there, the big spruce in the back of the house, get that pitch over me, my hair, my mother she go crazy. Your clothes! Your hands!

Du Pré shifted round till he could get his snowshoes on each side of the tree.

Not a very big tree, this.

A stub.

He struggled till he could hook his left snowshoe on it and then he slowly lifted himself. Brushed the snow away from his right snowshoe.

I need these, I get out.

Hope all the snow come down. Not just one side of the canyon.

His hands slipped off the top of the tree, where the avalanche had broken off the crown.

Du Pré shoved the snow back into the hole behind him.

He could see up. The mountainside was bare.

He struggled a long time to get perched on the broken top of the tree and then he slowly rose up.

He heard a snowmobile.

He waved. The machine turned toward him. The driver saw him. Raymond.

Du Pré hauled himself up on the back seat. He undid the ties of the snowshoes and he pulled them off and tossed them in the sled Raymond was pulling.

"Where are Benny, Booger Tom?" said Du Pré.

"They are up the canyon. When the snow come on down it make it easier, they were to take one last ride up, look for you. You find anybody?"

"I find a woman," said Du Pré, "but she is pulled away, the snow."

Du Pré heard the other machines screaming back down the canyon toward them.

Booger Tom and Benny whined up. They cut their throttles back. The snow was tighter than it had been before the avalanche.

"We go home!" said Du Pré.

Them owl, they don't lie. We stay here, the Clipper hit, we stay here till spring.

No one could hear him. He pointed down the canyon and they nodded and took off. Du Pré threw himself at the sled and crawled in and Raymond pulled away, traveling a little faster than the others. The sled's bottom kept his track from digging in too deep.

They made their way through the gate and down to the trail up to the bench.

The clouds far off in the northwest were black and headed in fast. Silver-black, snow and cold.

The sun shone bright. It seemed warm.

It feel warm, thought Du Pré, even though it is twenty below.

Bart's house came in view, smoke rising straight up and quickly, because of the cold, cold, still air.

They roared into the compound, pulled the snowmobiles into the barn, and walked to the house.

Du Pré was suddenly freezing. He was wet from snow falling inside his clothes. He began to shiver.

Hypothermia.

He went into the house and got his clothes off, dropping them as he moved toward the master bedroom and the whirlpool bath. It was full and hot. He got in and switched on the jets.

He leaned back with his shoulders against one of the jets. Hot water played hard against his back. He stuck his feet against another.

Still shivering, little black spots danced in front of his eyes.

Booger Tom came in with a steaming pot of tea. He poured it into a big glass and handed the glass to Du Pré.

Hot whiskey toddy, lemon.

Du Pré sipped. Not too warm. He gulped it down and held out the glass again.

He leaned back.

"I thank you, my friend," he said.

"You're welcome. Glad you dug yourself out. See, I said, well, I won't leave till I find him, and then Benny said he wouldn't leave if I didn't. Raymond said he'd leave, he's got all them kids. Smart, and we admire him for it. And then he wouldn't, either."

Du Pré nodded. All my grandbabies there, good, he got to take care of them. We both dead, it is tough on Jacqueline.

"Benny, Raymond, they go home?" said Du Pré.

"Yup," said Booger Tom. "You drink that, 'fore it gets cold."

Du Pré did. The hot whiskey was blooming in his belly.

They tell me, medic class, don't do this. Screw them. We get a different kind of hypothermia in the mountains.

"Did you call my Madelaine?"

"Sure," said Booger Tom. "Why a beautiful woman would want anything to do with you, you worthless son of a bitch, bumfoozles me, but she does, and I did."

The front door opened.

"Du Pré!" Madelaine yelled.

"Back here!" said Booger Tom.

Her boots thumped on the puncheon floors.

She came into the steamy bathroom.

"Ah," she said, "how you feel?"

"Some better," said Du Pré. "I start that hypothermia."

Madelaine nodded. "How many go up?"

"Eight," said Booger Tom. "Dumb shits."

"Du Pré," said Madelaine, "you don't go up there, when you know the people dead."

"I found one," said Du Pré. "Bringing her back, tell her be quiet. She fall down, she scream. Avalanche."

"You get killed I hate you for it, these fools," said Madelaine.

Du Pré nodded.

I had to go. I don't argue, me, now.

But not again.

When they got no chance.

The Alberta Clipper slammed against the house suddenly. The place shook, the wind screamed overhead.

Madelaine was praying. For all the lost souls.

Du Pré didn't have to ask her.

❖ CHAPTER 15 ❖

Du Pré," said Madelaine, "we are just going to run out of food here, you know, I hope they get that damn road open."

"It is open," said Du Pré. "Bart just got the word. Plowed. No more snow. So they go now."

The pilgrims had been stuck in the Cooper High School gym all week. The local people had done what they could to feed them and make them comfortable. One end of the basketball court was a big soup kitchen, and they had rolled out the wrestling mats. The place stank.

"That damn Bucky Dassault," said Du Pré. "I find him . . ."

"It is not him," said Madelaine. "You have not been in the gym. It is four, five people live in that Jackson Hole come here, sent out all these flyers, do this. I don't know what is the big deal. Plenty wolves up in Alaska, Canada."

Du Pré shook his head.

Who these people? Some reason, them politician say yes, here we are. Got fourteen dead people. They more or less murder themselves. Like me, come home, find some tourist in my house, feet up, drinking my whiskey, saying I beat my dog, starve my horses.

Du Pré was hollow-eyed and ready to fall over. No one had slept much, searching the roadsides for buried vehicles. One six-year-old kid he decide, my appendix needs to infect, Benny has to cut it out while a doctor in Billings talks to him. Worked out pretty good.

"I will go see about my horses," said Du Pré. "Glad I sold all them cows, I would have a couple ten ton of dead ones to bury, March."

And Benetsee. He will be all right.

The telephone rang. Madelaine picked it up, motioned to Du Pré.

"That Bart," she said. She was mad at Bart for some reason.

"Yo," said Du Pré.

"They're going," said Bart, "moving out pretty fast. Course us folk who live here want 'em gone, couple of the plow drivers got pretty good at scraping just enough off the cars parked by the road to total 'em and leave 'em drivable.

"Which is not why I called," he went on. "I arrested four of these little assholes for public endangerment and threw their little butts in jail. Guy I know in Billings called, said the TV people and the journalists are ten deep waiting to leave and come here. I told him to tell them we are wholly swamped and we can't provide lodging or food for 'em. So some of them are chartering helicop-ters to fly 'em back and forth. Big story, murders, now this. They're going to be after you because of the lost dumb bastards up Cooper Creek."

"Foote is here, yes?"

"Foote is here in two hours or so, yes," said Bart.

"Well," said Du Pré, "I will just send them to him, not talk to them. Pretty pushy people, them."

"I knew that," said Bart. "What I want you to do is come here pretty quick and chew these little assholes up real good. They're sitting in the cells singing 'We Shall Overcome,' for Chrissakes. The prisoners' lockers are full of designer expedition gear."

"OK," said Du Pré. "I want to see about Benetsee, my horses."

"Booger Tom went over and your horses are fine," said Bart, "but I don't know about Benetsee."

"East, how the storm?" said Du Pré.

"Terrible," said Bart. "Worst one in history, if you think history is what people write down. Finally went out to sea after pasting the South. Funny thing is, they don't know where it came from. No warning, no blip on the spy satellites. Out of the Arctic and away we go."

"Yah," said Du Pré. "Well, I will go see about that old fart, then I come see those people. They sure are funny people down there on the flat. Think no one lives here or if we do we don't know how. How many people out there under the snow, huh, Bart? Missing persons? Calls they come in when?"

"Already coming in," said Bart. "Parents. Break your heart. My kid hasn't come back, my environmentalist kid. Earth First! Stone tools and raw hides. Course, they got no idea how tough it is to live off what you can *shoot*, let alone run down with a club."

"Well," said Du Pré, "that mob, gets to Miles City, Billings, they call home some."

"Not all of them," said Bart, softly. He hung up.

"Here," said Madelaine. She held out a big wad of blankets. "Got a hot meal in there. Jug of that wine he like is by the door."

Du Pré shrugged into his coat, pulled on his packs, went out, and started the Rover. He came back in and smoked while the car warmed up. Madelaine's kids were watching television. The oldest boy was in the army, and the next one down would go to the navy in June.

This time, it go faster and faster, Du Pré thought, I wonder how fast it go for old Benetsee? Faster till you are dead? Run so fast you are in the dark before you know it?

Madelaine bent over to kiss him.

"I get anything for you?" said Du Pré.

"Well," said Madelaine, "we need groceries but it will be some time we can go buy them."

"I got some, my place," said Du Pré.

"No, you don't," said Madelaine. "You don't got a can, creamed corn, I go out there while you poking in snowdrifts."

Du Pré nodded.

"Maybe I bring Benetsee, few days," he said.

"Benetsee is welcome all the time," said Madelaine, "you know that. I am some worried, old man like that, out there."

"I go by yesterday he got smoke coming out his chimney," said Du Pré.

Madelaine kissed him again. Du Pré went out to his Rover and got in and drove off. It was very cold and the snow gave good traction.

The road up to Benetsee's had been plowed but the wind had drifted the snow back in many places and Du Pré got up to fifty and bashed through the drifts.

Hope that there is not a car in one of these, he thought. Well, the plows made it through OK, hope someone's gas line did not freeze, car sitting here after the plows come through.

How many hundreds of people this storm kill? Still digging out, Alberta, Saskatchewan, east of here. Snow fall where it never did fall before.

Du Pré saw the trees that huddled close around Benetsee's cabin. Smoke rose straight up to the white-blue sky.

There was a place big enough to park in, chewed out of the

drifts by the plows. Du Pré crunched over to the path between the trees. He stopped, startled.

The path was clean and so was the ground around Benetsee's little shack. It looked like a tornado had set down, swirled the snow up into drifts, and moved on. A very gentle tornado.

Du Pré walked up to the porch and Benetsee opened the door and grinned at him.

"You are alive," said Du Pré.

Benetsee nodded.

"OK," said Du Pré, "I get your things Madelaine send for you."

The old man's old dogs looked out on either side of Benetsee's knees.

Du Pré sat next to the stove while the old man drank some wine and smoked. He ate hungrily all the good food that Madelaine had sent.

Like a coyote, thought Du Pré, he eat a whole lot and then he don't need to eat a long time.

"You worried me, going to look for those fools," said Benetsee. "They thought that they could do something very smart but them mountain eat them. Hee."

"Yah," said Du Pré. "Well, I had to try there, you know. It is my job, now."

Benetsee nodded.

Du Pré started to ask about the snow and the wind around his cabin but he stopped himself. The old man would just tease him with some damn riddle. Oh, I dance, he would say. Know how, dance.

"What you going to do, them reporter come here, ask you questions?" said Du Pré. "Turn into a raven, fly away?"

"Oh, they will not bother me," said Benetsee. "I disappear."

Du Pré had seen the old man disappear many times. In rooms, people in them, no quick way out, poof, he was gone.

"I got to go, talk to those assholes set this thing up," said Du Pré. "Killed a bunch of people. That fucking Bucky Dassault I think have something to do with it."

Benetsee nodded. He drank another big glass of wine.

"He is not smart enough, be bad," said Benetsee. "Pretty dangerous. Well, I go talk to those fools, the jail."

Du Pré nodded.

Benetsee belched.

"One glass wine," the old man said, "and we go."

✤ CHAPTER 16 ✤

"Ah," said Deputy Lawyer Foote, "I just finished chewing their asses off—my, how I talk in the sagebrush—and now I suspect Benetsee will do the same."

"Hee," said Benetsee.

"The old man gets done with them I'll let 'em go," said Bart. "I was appalled to find out that you cannot arrest people on suspicion of being stupid assholes. Lucky for Congress, ain't it?"

Booger Tom was sitting in Bart's chair, drinking coffee. The smell of whiskey got stronger the closer you got to Booger Tom's cup.

Du Pré and Benetsee followed Bart back to the cells. They were old and primitive and cold. The five people in the holding cell were all shivering in orange jail jumpsuits. Two men, three women.

Benetsee dragged a chair over to the cell and he sat down. He held his hand up for a smoke. Du Pré rolled him one, lit it, and stuck it in Benetsee's old brown fingers.

Benetsee smoked and he stared unblinking at the people in the cell. They began to stir and shift like a bunch of horses when the wrangler comes to cut one out.

Benetsee stared.

They could not look him in the eye.

"Why you come here?" said Benetsee, suddenly.

No answer.

"You maybe ask Bart for a red bag?" said Benetsee, turning to Du Pré. "Not a big one, maybe some flat, about this big." He gestured with his hands.

Du Pré shrugged and went on out.

Bart listened and he dug around in the locker and found the red bag, about the size of a long briefcase, very thin, made of nylon cloth. Du Pré carried it back to Benetsee.

Benetsee held it on his lap. He unzipped it. The people in the cell stirred uncomfortably. Benetsee pulled out an eagle's wing, bald eagle. He held it up, looking at the feathers.

"I keep this," said Benetsee, "it only cause you trouble. You think you can make magic? Hah. You, you maybe make coffee, boiled eggs."

Du Pré laughed.

"You come here with bad hearts," said Benetsee, "and you get a lot of people killed, one way, another. Very foolish. You don't kill them with your hands, you kill them with your foolish talk."

The people in the cell looked at each other.

"You go home maybe," said Benetsee. "You don't come back here. Not ever. This place eat you if you do."

The old man stood. He looked levelly at the people cowering in the cell. Benetsee tucked the eagle wing under his arm and he walked back out into the room.

"Fools," he said to Bart. Bart nodded.

"I go, Toussaint now." Du Pré put his coat on.

They drove out of Cooper, down the white road. There were still some cars shoved off to the side, their engines frozen. Du Pré parked in front of the Toussaint Bar and they went in.

Susan Klein was serving several couples lunch, rushing about. Du Pré and Benetsee sat and waited on stools at the bar.

"You need lunch?" said Susan, when she got back behind the bar. "I'm serving mooseburgers. All we had left. Illegal as hell, but hungry is hungry."

"Sure," said Du Pré.

Susan poured Du Pré some whiskey, pale yellow, a local product. She gave Benetsee a big glass of wine.

"You can drink all the damn wine you want," said Susan to Benetsee. "But you're going to have to eat. All free."

Benetsee grinned, his few old worn brown teeth like chips of walnut.

Bill Stemple got up from his table and came over to Du Pré. He was picking his teeth. He fished in his pocket and took out a cigarette and lit it.

"Ain't this some shit," he said. "We lost some more cows, they had their damn mouths freeze shut while me and my hands were going up and down the road to find the little fuckers. Found six. Had to keep 'em in my house and feed 'em."

"Yah," said Du Pré, "well, it was plenty quiet here, long time, now we got all this fuss. But maybe it teach somebody something, I don't know."

Stemple shrugged.

"That damn FBI woman, Banning," he said, "hell, she's all over everybody, asking the same damn questions over and over. I understand that she's got to, but, Jesus, no one's gonna walk forward and say 'I did it' and nobody else knows anything. We wasn't even *here*."

Du Pré shrugged. "Soon, we going to have another bunch of newspeople," he said. "They are coming, see the disaster. Probably say, did someone take those people, kill them, bury them under the snow?"

"I got work to do," said Stemple.

"We all got work to do," said Du Pré. "You keep your gates closed and don't shoot any of them. I do not like to arrest you."

Corey Banning slid in the door and shoved it to. She had a dark red muffler wrapped around her head. A sheepskin coat. She unwrapped the muffler. She wore a pissed-off expression.

"Christ," she said, "it ain't one thing it's another."

She stalked up to the bar and Susan poured her a double brandy.

"They're sending me some more agents," she said, "in the middle of the fucking winter. They'll freeze and get lost and die and such."

"Um," said Du Pré. "Do you care, them?"

"As much mother instinct as I got," she said, "I hate to see it. You know, frostbite. Crippled for life. They'll all be from Florida, I just know it. Christ."

She sipped her brandy.

"We got a big bunch, press coming," said Du Pré.

"Hah," she said. "That guy Foote is a plenty smart guy, there. He's got this one-page press release which says not one fucking thing in the most elegant English. Me, I just got no comment. We'll starve 'em out."

"Yah," said Du Pré. "Well, one more bad storm like this, it will not melt till June, you know. Maybe people be out there, frozen, till then."

"The bottom canyons in the Wolfs'll be eighty feet deep in snow," she said. "It may not melt down before the summer after."

Banning shrugged out of her coat. She was wearing simple ranch clothes and a stainless-steel nine-millimeter and cop holsters on her belt, handcuffs, pepper spray. She walked over to Benetsee and she put her arms around him and hugged him. She put her head down on his back.

"You know," she said softly. "You don't want to tell me and you won't and I can't make you. But you know it all, don't you. And there's not really anything that you want, so you can't be bought, and you're too old to care about anything much except praying."

Benetsee reached back and he patted her hair. He patted the stool beside him.

"You come sit here, my daughter," he said. "I will tell you what I know to tell you."

She got up on the stool and put one elbow on the bar top and she leaned her ear close to his old lips.

Benetsee whispered.

She nodded.

She listened and listened.

The other people in the bar paid and left. Du Pré went to the poker machine and lost money in it. Dumb machine, electronic.

He had a pocketful of quarters and it took him some time.

When he turned around Benetsee was gone, and Corey Banning had turned round and was looking off into the distance.

Du Pré walked over to the bar. He got another whiskey and he sat beside the FBI agent.

"Old Benetsee he just see the riddles most times," said Du Pré. "I would not get mad with him."

"Even the fucking riddles would help," said Banning.

"Sometime," said Du Pré, "you get one of them things, you know, it seems like you can untie it but you can't. You know, my father Catfoot he kill Bart's brother and we take a long time to figure it out, many years later. We never could have, but for a coyote Benetsee sent me."

Banning nodded.

"Fourteen people dead is a lot of people dead, and whoever killed 'em is very smart," said Banning, "and there's more'n one of 'em."

Du Pré nodded.

"I know," he said, "that is a bad thing, they should not have done that."

"Lot of pressure on us," said Banning. "I may get shoved out, you know."

Du Pré nodded.

"Yah," he said, "then they send someone in who make evidence up, convict anybody, guilty, not, they don't care."

"Yeah, well, shit happens," said Corey Banning.

She sipped her brandy.

"I don't give a shit about the eight suicides under the avalanche," said Corey Banning. "I got my plateful."

❧ CHAPTER 17 ❧

The TV crews came in big motor homes with satellite dishes on the roofs. The print journalists came in rented cars and they looked for motel rooms.

Finally someone rented them a run-down house on a back street in Cooper. The place leaked water through the roof every time the heat came on and melted the snow above. The attic was full of raccoons. Raccoon shit. Nests. And they liked it there.

They shoved cameras in Du Pré's face, and they asked him questions about the dead under the avalanche. Du Pré shrugged. And he walked past them.

He was getting into his Rover outside the Toussaint Bar when a fat sleazy woman offered him several packets of hundred-dollar bills for an "exclusive" story for one of the cheap magazines sold in checkout lines at grocery stores.

Du Pré shrugged and got into his Rover and he drove off with a few reporters in pursuit. He went up the back roads, pounded and now drifted, and left them stuck there.

Du Pré stopped high up on the benchlands and he looked down on the bleak white land below, marked a little, a house here, barn, one or two rocky outcrops, the rest white on white on white.

The sun in the east high up had sun dogs on each side.

Very bad sign, that, three suns ride the sky. My people, long time since, it was colder then, I was told, pile the good buffalo robes in the lodge, get in the little hot-burning alder sticks for cooking, everyone live under the robes till the cold pass, eat a lot of pemmican, meat, fat, and berries.

You got to wait for this country, sure. This country, you be like the water, it is cold, you go to sleep till the sun comes back, then you can move through it, animals, too. Live under the snow where it is warm.

Them big white owls come down, times like this, hunt animals under the snow. Owls sit, wait, got ears so good they hear mouse under the snow, owl plunge into the snowdrift and grab that mouse.

But you got to let this country tell you what to do.

You try to tell it, it will kill you plenty quick now.

Yes.

Them people who got shot, they think these ranchers are not part of this country. They say, you are to move right on. Take your dead grandparents with you, dig them up and haul them away, we want to play here.

It is more than they cut a fence, shoot a cow maybe. That is dumb kid stuff.

But these ranchers are not so dumb, though maybe they cannot say why this make them so angry they just kill them.

Always, this country, more people come and say to the people who were here, you go away and starve, this is ours now, we want it, we are right and you are wrong.

The wind was rising up and a ground blizzard started. Du Pré put the Rover in gear and drove back down while he could still see the road, sort of. He went by another route, so he wouldn't have to help stuck reporters out of drifts and so forth.

There were several cars outside the Toussaint Bar, Benny's four-wheel Sheriff's rig, the usual battered ranch pickups.

Du Pré parked and walked up to the front door. When he put his hand on the door pull he happened to look down and there was a badly broken television camera, half sunk in the snow.

It took Du Pré a couple of minutes to see in the dim bar. The light outside was bright even through the high white haze.

Remember that time I got myself snow-blind, spent three days couldn't see and a month feeling like hot sand packed around my eyeballs.

Madelaine came over to him. He recognized her footsteps. Broke an ankle as a little girl, made her left foot a little bit stitchy, pull the sole just some there.

"Hey, Du Pré," said Madelaine, "you don't remember me, eh?"

"Can't see you," said Du Pré. "You live here, maybe?"

"You die here you don't think pretty quick, now," said Madelaine. "Say something funny quick, it is how you guys survive so long. You make us laugh we don't tear your plums off, shove them down your throat, eh?"

"Interesting times," said Susan Klein, washing the bar top. "That's an old Chinese curse. May you live in interesting times. These damn journalists are all over, blocking the doorways. Or they were till Ol' Jim found them between him and his afternoon smile."

Old Jim was in his seventies, still ranching, still breaking horses clamped down in an old bear-trap saddle. He was sitting off in a corner with a big glass of whiskey. He called a glass of whiskey a smile.

"Ill-mannered bastards shoved a microphone in my face and wouldn't get out of the damn way," boomed Old Jim, "so I cracked a couple of their heads together. Christ, it used to be quiet round here."

Du Pré laughed.

One of the newspaper reporters came out of the men's room and he saw Du Pré and edged toward him.

"Not in here, you," snapped Susan. "You got a question for Gabriel, you find him someplace else. I have absolutely had it with you people bothering my customers."

The man slunk toward the door.

"They'll be gone soon," said Susan, ignoring the journalist. "No story here, I guess, until the snow melts enough to find those poor fools up Cooper's Canyon. Almost got one out, didn't you?"

The reporter had stopped.

"Shit," said Susan.

Du Pré shrugged. He tapped the bar top and Susan poured him a whiskey.

Old Jim and Susan and Du Pré and Madelaine stared at the man till he gave up and left.

"Good thing this all didn't happen in the summer," said Old Jim. "As it is the bastards get frozen pretty quick and then they go away."

They will be back, though, Du Pré thought, they will be back.

"We are at Jacqueline's and Raymond's for dinner," said Madelaine. "Couple hours. My kids are liking cook for themselves, when I am gone they can use the phone all the time."

Du Pré sat thinking, while Madelaine and Susan chatted. He drank whiskey. Old Jim joined them. Benny arrived, then Bart and Booger Tom and Packy and his wife and several other townsfolk.

Deputy Lawyer Foote came.

"The journalists are pulling out," he said. "They starve rather quickly."

Du Pré grunted.

Bart stacked wood in the big old stone fireplace at the far end of the barroom. He lit the fire and stood back and poked at it till the flames caught well.

It was growing dark, fast. The shortest days of the year were on them. Christmas. A new year after.

Du Pré got his fiddle from his Rover and he let it warm for a few minutes and then he tuned it and he played some slow tunes, laments, the songs of the voyageurs on sleepless nights when they were homesick and lonely for their families and women, all the things there were not in the endless black-green forests of the North.

Bales of furs.

Carry them for the Hudson's Bay Company. Sucking the furs out of all Canada, pulling them in with trade guns and rum, blankets and beads, axes and hatchets and knives and brass kettles. Priests pull the souls along into heaven.

If that was real.

But the Hudson's Bay Company was. HBC. Here Before Christ.

On them old-time long voyage, take a whole year, sometimes

two, while the women raise babies and make the canoes. Make them good and tight and strong so their men don't drown.

Du Pré thought of the dark he had been buried alive in, holding himself hard to the light, reaching up through the snow above him to heaven, shining through the hem of the storm come down from the North where hell really is, it is cold.

Dark forests. Ice. Sun dogs. Big land waiting and hungry.

Du Pré played his heart. Up out of the ice, the dark ice.

Eight people under the avalanche, frozen faces turning dark red, long frost crystals growing out of their eyes. Maybe even some still alive, yes, it could be. Nothing to be done.

How many voyageurs end up in the bellies of wolves and coyotes, badgers and skunks and magpies and ravens?

Play for them.

Play for everybody ever died in the cold.

I will rot in the earth but the music is forever, God breathes it in and out.

Du Pré let the last note die.

He reached out for the whiskey in front of him.

He drank. He looked over at his friends and his lover.

They were staring at him.

Corey Banning had come in while he was playing.

Tears ran down her cheeks.

"It is time we go to dinner," said Madelaine. "You come now."

Du Pré nodded, and finished his whiskey, and packed his fiddle away.

✤ CHAPTER 18 ✤

Right after New Year's an arctic air mass lumbered down the front of the Rockies. The mass was huge and very cold. It stretched from Montana to Minnesota. Some nights, the temperature fell to fifty-five degrees below zero. Water pipes burst. Smoke from chimneys rose straight up in yellow-white columns.

Du Pré walked out behind his house one glittering morning, looked up at the white sky, and shook his head. He glanced at the outbuildings and a wispy plume of steam caught his eye. It was coming from a crack in the siding of the barn.

He went back in the house and got a shotgun and shoved some rounds of buckshot into the magazine, racked one home.

Bear in my damn barn.

He went in cautiously. He gauged where the plume of breath had come from outside against the dark shadowed walls. The bear had crawled under some bales of straw and broken the ties. Fluffed the straw up for a bed and comforter.

Du Pré stood a few feet from the animal. He heard gentle snoring.

He shrugged.

Me, I wish that I could sleep till it gets warmer. When it gets warmer, out you go. Not now.

He had his Rover plugged in to an electrical outlet, so the engine was warm, but when he started the engine the belts shrieked piercingly for fifteen minutes before friction warmed them enough to grab properly. When he drove off, the flat spots where the tires had set against the ground thumped loudly.

He'd left little trickles of water running from the taps.

If them cast-iron drainpipes freeze up I'll have fun, he

thought, as he drove slowly down the snow-packed county road. Thump THUMP thwap THUMP. The paved highway was pretty clear when he got to it, but the tires were still out of round and didn't warm up enough to pop back to their intended shape until just before he turned off into Toussaint.

Benny Klein had tacked a temporary airlock out in front of the bar, a sloppy arrangement of plastic and scraps of lath, to cut down on the blasts of arctic air that burst into the saloon every time the door opened. Du Pré pushed through the hanging sheets and he rearranged them; they were tattered and breaking from the cold. He opened the door quickly and slammed it shut. A pane of glass in one of the front windows went pop!

"Little more respect for my property there, Gabriel," said Susan Klein. She came out from behind the bar with a roll of wide clear tape. Several other panes were patched.

"When we last have this?" said Du Pré. "Maybe '89? Yeah, three weeks it was fifty below every night. Old man Thompson froze to death, went out to check his stock, slipped and broke his hip."

"Yeah," said Susan. "Benny went out to check on him that afternoon, but he was dead. Benny's still sad over it, felt he should have gone that morning, but old man Thompson, he didn't like being hovered over, remember, he'd about run Benny off the day before."

"You see that Bart?"

"He called a little bit ago, looking for you. Said he'd be in for lunch. I told him we were having iceworm salad."

"Nobody doing ver' much right now," Du Pré said. He thought of the FBIs in the trailer, all the pipes frozen—spraying water had hit a fuse box and blown all the neutral wires out, and then the cold had pulled the aluminum skin away from the frame, so the next good wind would shuck the hide off the roof.

Couldn't happen to a nicer bunch of folks, Du Pré thought sourly. But I like that Corey Banning. She is pret' edgy these days, like a hawk don't got anything moving down on the land below. Nothing to do.

Susan Klein shoved a bottle of whiskey across the bar top and a short glass.

"The ice machine froze up," she said. "If you require ice, you may just hump your stumps outside there, where you will find all you need."

Du Pré laughed.

"Anything happens to satellite TV," said Susan, "the murder rate here'll look like Miami's the first night. By eleven P.M. Gives us a little idea what it was like here a hundred years ago, people going insane."

Du Pré poured himself a whiskey. He rolled a cigarette and lit it and he looked at the smoke rising to the ceiling.

Oh, yes, them winter, maybe 1910, when that Black Jack Pershing he come and round up the Métis and shove them in cattle cars, it is forty below, and he send couple of thousand of us, North Dakota, to Pembina, throw us off.

Don't take us here, we are citizens, take the poor Métis from Great Falls, Helena, Lewiston, they don't know what country they are in. How many die that time? Four hundred, I think my grandpère say, they froze in the boxcars, they starve in North Dakota, under the three suns in the sky, them sun dogs.

People. Damn. All them honyockers Jim Hill sucker into homesteads, little farms on the plains, whole families found frozen round the stoves in the spring. Starved to death. Some live, there are raving crazy people screaming in the spring mud, everybody that knew who they were has died. Coyotes, they eat the dead in the houses. Here, the Dakotas, down to Nebraska, they say there are twenty thousand poor farmers and their families die that winter.

This damn winter, when it is like this it scares my *bones*.

My blood, it remembers the taste of boiled moccasins, worse things that my people ate.

Got no songs about that. 'Less you count the burial hymns, the church. So cold, the fiddles, they broke.

The door banged open and Bart and Corey Banning came in, their faces red from the short dash from car to warmth. Bart shoved the door to and they both stamped their feet, in their heavy felt-lined packs.

The saloon was hot. Benny had put a second woodstove in,

near the door, and both of them were roaring. But if you went near the walls the cold reached out. The single paned windows had sketches of frost in their corners.

Corey and Bart shucked off their down parkas and vests. They came over to Du Pré.

"What's shakin'?" said Corey.

"Um," said Du Pré, "I got a bear in my barn, he is sleeping, I did not have the heart to run him out."

"What kind of bear?" said Bart.

"Sleepy one," said Du Pré. "He is under the straw there, but he is not big, his tracks are maybe a two-year bear's."

"I love this weather," said Corey Banning. "My superiors are sitting on their big fat warm asses in Washington, wondering why I ain't run all these foul perpetrators to earth. Two of the Butte office's turkeys went off to nail some poor schmo on a warrant, car stalled, they walked for a ways, and they are both in the hospital, not too bad, one lost four toes and the other the tips of some fingers. Oh, yeah, when they got cold, they ran like hell. *Bright guys.* Frostbit some of their lungs, got necrosis pneumonia."

"Ol' Corey here's always pleased to hear her fellow agents have about died," said Bart. "Always perks her up. Got such sympathy for 'em."

"Wussies," said Corey, "the lot of 'em."

"You going to the party?" said Bart.

Du Pré nodded.

"Party?" said Corey.

"Every January, Martins, they give a big party, cheer everybody up, they got this huge paddock they use to train horses, they build a square dance floor, barbecue couple of steers, bring in some good musicians. Everybody is invited, unless they are in jail," said Du Pré. "You should come, dance some, it will make you kinder, maybe."

Corey looked at Du Pré for a moment.

"I'll do just that," she said.

"You seen old Benetsee?" said Bart.

Du Pré shrugged. He'd been by, but the old man was gone and

so were his dogs. Or the dogs had frozen to death and the old man was out under the snow somewhere.

"He is probably Club Med, some island in the Caribbean," said Du Pré. "He don't send postcards. No, I check his house and he has not been there. You know him, he comes, goes, who knows?"

"How long you know the Martins?" said Corey.

"All my life," said Du Pré. "They have that ranch, I think it is as big as Rhode Island, I read. I go there, when they ship, never any trouble."

"Never any trouble," said Corey. "I checked with Booger Tom, he worked on their ranch a while, he likes them. Booger Tom don't like anybody much."

Du Pré shrugged. He didn't know the Martins well. No one did. They kept to themselves other than the ordinary business of being good neighbors. They sent all their children east to private schools.

"There's Taylor," said Corey. "War hero, helicopter pilot, rodeo cowboy, and he's also a veterinarian. Enough to do on the ranch, he doesn't have a practice. Then there's his kid brother, Clark, West Point and he made Nam a little later. There was a third brother."

"Hall," said Du Pré. "He died pret' young, flew a plane up a box canyon and got trapped, couldn't fly out. He was only maybe nineteen."

"I like to dance," said Corey Banning.

Du Pré nodded and sipped some more whiskey.

✤ CHAPTER 19 ✤

Bootheels thumped on the hollow wooden floor. The Western swing band had been flown up from New Mexico and they were superb. All the musicians were dressed in Flash Western, expensive custom clothing heavy with embroidery.

"Bet all their boots got chipmunks fucking butterflies on 'em," said Booger Tom.

Du Pré laughed. The three hundred or so people on the dance floor were two-stepping fast. They were merry with drink and the bright music.

"Good band," said Du Pré.

Booger Tom snorted.

Bart was standing in his uniform, fully belted, over near one of the huge double-drum woodstoves. Corey Banning stood with him, in a leather jacket long enough to cover her gun.

Clark Martin, tall and dark blond, was teaching one of his little girls to dance. The child stood on the tops of his boots and she laughed and bounced as Clark shuffled.

There were huge trestle tables against one wall of the paddock, piled with food. The far corner of the building had a new false-front saloon built in it; the raw wood oozed sap and gave off a thick scent of pine. Five barkeeps shoved drinks across the bar top.

"They put on a good party," said Du Pré. He turned around and saw Booger Tom sliding around the milling couples, on his way to the bar again.

That old goat can drink some, Du Pré thought, especially when it's free.

A few people, too old to dance or too drunk, were scattered in a mass of smaller tables to the side of the bandstand. The Martin family had their own. The elder Mrs. Martin sat at it, her son Taylor next to her. She wore a purple silk blouse and a beaded vest, and she had a choker of emeralds and diamonds at her throat. White-haired and pale-skinned, fingers glittering with rings, she sat slender and erect, smiling faintly when someone would stop and say something.

Her husband die about five years ago, Du Pré thought. She looks like the queen of a small country. Small, tasteful country, lots of traditions.

Taylor was laughing a lot. He got up and took glasses in his hands and he headed off toward the bar. His mother stared straight at the dancers on the floor. She tapped with the band's rhythms, her red nails against a white saucer.

"The Queen Bee there," said Corey Banning, at Du Pré's side. Du Pré turned. "Where's Madelaine?"

"She has a kid got an ear infection," said Du Pré.

"She thinks rich folks are silly, more like," said Corey. "So do I, but I got to snoop. I'd never seen the Queen Bee—I didn't have a good enough reason to request an audience. If I got one, I'd get nothing, maybe a nice glass of sherry, some petit-fours, an offer to help me. Jesus, the old broad's moral force about blows my dandruff off, here to there. You know her?"

Du Pré shook his head. Me, I am just the nice cattlebrand inspector comes to sign off on three million dollars' worth of cows when they ship. You want to buy a thousand head of yearlings, ask if they got 'em, they nod and pause, then ask, you want them all one color? What color?

Taylor Martin returned to the table and he set down the drinks he was carrying and he looked over at Du Pré and Corey Banning and he waved generously at them to come over.

"The prince bids us come," said Corey. "Now, don't pick your nose and you can't fart within a hundred yards of the Presence, there. Come along, Du Pré, remember to genuflect when I do."

They made their way to the table. Mrs. Martin rose to greet them. When Du Pré shook her hand, it startled him. Her horse-woman's strength gripped him hard.

"Are you finding enough to eat and drink?" said Mrs. Martin. She had soft southern notes in her voice, and deep education.

"A surfeit," said Corey Banning. "What the hell do you do with this place between shindigs? Train cavalry troops?"

"Just horses," said Mrs. Martin. "The long winters are hard to bear. At least with this place, one can work. Helps me to make it through."

"Morgan and her horses are something of a family joke," said Taylor. "If my father hadn't employed cooks, her children would have starved to death."

"I had the children," said Mrs. Martin, "and that was, I think, something of a contribution. Diapers, bottles, and the daily feedings, I said, would be up to someone else. Anyone else."

Corey laughed. Du Pré smiled.

She laughs at herself, Du Pré thought. This Mrs. Martin, there is a good deal here.

"You want to talk to me, dear," said Mrs. Martin to Corey, "so let's us just go do that. Taylor, could you have some brandy sent to the greenhouse?" She lifted a suede jacket from the bench and hung it over her shoulders. She took Corey's elbow and steered her toward a door at the far end of the paddock.

"We are well out of what's next," said Taylor Martin. "Come on, I need to dispatch the brandy, and we can have a drink."

They walked over to the bar, and Taylor spoke with one of the barkeeps. The man nodded and grabbed a bottle of brandy from below the bar and he set it on a tray and put two snifters on it and filled them halfway with boiling water.

"Corey, she is kind of frustrated," said Du Pré. "It is kind of your mother to talk with her."

"Very funny," drawled Taylor Martin, "since the two of them will be sticking skewers in each other and never a hint of pain. Banning's been following very faint tracks. They don't stop here, mind you, but she naturally wonders just what goes on in our little kingdom here."

Du Pré shrugged.

If it is you people, he thought, you will come out of here and do it again, anyway. All I can do is wait.

Taylor handed Du Pré a drink. Du Pré glanced down at the man's hand. There was livid scar tissue on the back and the fingers were twisted. One of the fingers was missing, and the two joints of the little finger were gone.

"Mortar round," said Martin, holding up his hand. "I'll not forget that day. You in Nam, Du Pré?"

Du Pré shook his head. "Germany," he said. "Drank a lot of beer."

Martin nodded.

He glanced up and his jaw tightened and Du Pré turned and looked. There was a little knot of men at one corner of the dance floor starting to fight.

Martin set his drink down and moved toward them, gliding across the floor, the floating dance of a fighter closing in. Du Pré followed him. The men were yelling by now and a couple had squared off while the others backed away.

"Not here," said Taylor Martin sharply.

Young cowboys, all set for their Saturday night sport. Du Pré didn't know who they were. Maybe hands from a neighboring ranch.

The two ignored him and one balanced back to throw a punch.

Martin stepped between them and the cowboy swung. Martin reached out idly with his damaged hand and he grabbed the cowboy's wrist and twisted and then half idly swung his right bootheel into the man's kneecap. The cowboy yelped and went down.

"None of that here," said Taylor Martin, "and not outside, either. It's too cold. Now, come on, let's all go get a drink." He reached down and grabbed the fallen cowboy's shoulder and lifted him easily to his feet. The cowboy looked dumbly at Taylor.

"Damp it down or I'll break your fucking neck," said Martin.

"OK OK sorry," said the cowboy, both hands on his knee. "We just forgot ourselves, you know how it is."

Martin led the cowboys over to the bar. He told a funny story or two, saw to their drinks, and then he clapped a hand on Du Pré's shoulder and steered him away.

"Youth is very young," said Martin. "If one starts, they all do. The happy cowboy idiocy of fistfights for the fun of it."

Du Pré nodded. He'd been in a lot of them himself.

The band took a break, the fiddle and steel guitar rippling behind the lead singer's smooth and practiced voice. Talk erupted on the dance floor and knots of people headed for the bar.

"Taylor!" a voice yelled. It was Clark Martin, grinning and striding toward them.

"Saw you break the fight up," said Clark. "One of those boys works for us, you know."

Taylor nodded. "Well," he said, "till he knocks my block off he still works for us. Can't blame a man for wanting to fight a little on a Saturday night, especially with a winter as long and mean as this."

"Where's Morgan?" said Clark.

"Took that lady FBI agent to the greenhouse," said Taylor.

"Investigate the orchids?" laughed Clark.

"Place is plumb full of exotic blooms," said Taylor, "so let's get us a drink."

Du Pré couldn't help but agree.

✤ CHAPTER 20 ✤

A March blizzard lashed hard at the land. The huge flakes shot along, pushed by winds that screamed overhead. It was fairly warm, but impossible to see fifty feet.

Corey Banning and Du Pré stood at the bar. Corey was rolling a cigarette, one practiced seamless motion. She licked the paper and flipped the smoke into her lips and lit it and tapped the lighter on the scarred wood.

"Darts," she said. "This place needs a nice dartboard."

"Wrong season," said Susan Klein. "Little later, most folks stand a tourist against the wall over there and throw knives as close as they can to them. See the stains on the floor? Makes the tourist real nervous."

The winter had been hard. Snow and cold alternating. Starving deer and elk were dying in the fields. The ranchers put out hay for them, but all the willow shoots had been browsed down and the animals couldn't digest the grass. They were starving to death with full bellies.

"You talk to that Morgan Martin," said Du Pré, "at that party. But you never tell me what she said."

"Morgan Taliaferro Martin," said Corey Banning, "to the likes of you and me. Oh, the Queen Bee and I admired the orchids and she, in her royal way, inquired gently as to just what the fuck it was I wanted. So I said that I was investigating these murders and did she have any employees she thought poorly of. She said she didn't employ people she thought poorly of. We drank very good brandy. The center of that bitch is frozen stone. No damn wonder sonny boy was such a hero. After growing up around her, not much would scare anyone ever again."

Du Pré laughed.

"You don't like her," he said.

"Actually," said Corey Banning, "I like her a lot. Strong women are my favorite. I must, however, find these swine who slaughtered six people so efficiently, and though the county is fairly well peopled, my nasty little mind has been reduced to essential thoughts. Like who is there competent enough to pull something like this off and tough enough to keep it hid. So my mind wanders back, inevitably, to the Queen Bee and her lovely sons. I had hoped for just a couple of psycho rednecks who'd get drunk and brag. I love guys like that. I hunger for 'em. But there ain't any around smart enough, unfortunately."

"Maybe they were not even from here," said Du Pré.

"Hogwash does not comfort me," said Corey Banning. "What I would really like to do is talk with Benetsee. I have flat picked the real world I am sentenced to to bits. I need that old man, get him to tell me what he sees in his world. But he's gone."

"I'm kinda worried about him," said Susan Klein.

"Oh," said Corey Banning, "he's just fine, I am sure. It's just he wants me to toss and turn at night and fret over him. He's doing this just to piss me off. I just know it."

Du Pré laughed. Whenever he had tried to pin Benetsee down, he felt like he was trying to nail water to the wall.

"Maybe he's there, home," said Du Pré. "Just decided to not leave no tracks in the snow."

Corey looked hard at Du Pré.

"I'm gonna go on out there," she said. "I'd appreciate it if you stayed here. No offense. Actually, I don't give a shit if it does offend you."

"You see him," said Du Pré, "you tell him Madelaine wants him to come and eat, do that often, he don't want to worry Madelaine."

Corey shrugged into her leather coat and pulled on her gloves. She nodded to Du Pré and Susan Klein and she left.

"How's Bart doin'?" said Susan.

"Ah," said Du Pré, "he is doing very well. He should have been a cop or a priest, you know, there is nothing that he likes more than to help people."

"Throw folks in jail when they fuck up so he can talk to 'em," said Susan Klein. "I think I get it."

"We don't have so very much crime here," said Du Pré. "Maybe some kids, they steal something. But then we got this, these murders, and this is some different."

"It is that. Listen, would you mind waving a shovel out round the door? Damn snow slamming down, I dunno anyone can find it now."

Du Pré got up and he walked to the door and took the grain shovel leaning against the wall and he went on out. Snow splattered against the plastic and the translucent sheets bellied in the wind.

Du Pré shoveled the deep drift that had built up in the last hour away from the beaten path through the plastic sheets. The snow wasn't letting up and the tracks of Corey's big pickup were already half filled.

Du Pré saw some headlights glow in the white whirl and then the front end of Bart's Rover, thickly covered, nosed slowly up to him. Du Pré walked to the driver's window.

"And a fine spring afternoon to you," said Bart, as he rolled the window down. "Agent Ms. Banning passed me up the road a ways. I was doing about ten, she was doing about seventy. Split the difference, I guess she wasn't speeding. What's happening in the social center?"

"Just me and Susan Klein," said Du Pré. "We are just all waiting around for things to melt."

"All but the cattle," said Bart. "The calves are starting to come on. They like this weather, so they can be born and die the same day."

Du Pré nodded. He remembered all the calves he'd pulled and he could think of very few that hadn't arrived in a blizzard.

"Come on in, I will buy you a soda, coffee, something," said Du Pré.

Bart pulled round and parked and he got out and came to Du Pré, still shoveling.

"Snow'll have it back there in ten minutes," said Bart, "but the thought was nice."

Du Pré sighed. He threw one last shovelful off and they trudged back through the visqueen flaps and on into the bar.

Susan Klein set them up and they sat there in silence, sipping and waiting for nothing much. A truck ground up outside. Doors slammed.

Benetsee and Corey Banning came in. The old man was sopping wet; his ragged clothes ran water. He was smiling.

"She came by so fast she made me jump into the ditch," said the old man. "She drive like that, she come up on the rear end of a snowplow and kill herself."

"Pour some wine down this old bastard," said Corey. "I want to loosen his tongue."

Benetsee drank three very big glasses of fizzy screwtop wine. He belched and grinned. Susan Klein set a cheeseburger and fries down in front of him. He wolfed the burger down and then picked at the potatoes. She filled his glass and he emptied it in a long swallow.

"What do you see?" said Corey.

"Two pretty ladies, two men, a lot of snow," said Benetsee. "You want me to tell you who killed the people up in the mountains, who killed the people down here, all six of them, well, I can tell you that they are well liked by the coyotes."

Du Pré looked off, only half listening.

"Why's that?" said Corey.

"Coyotes don't tell me why they like them, just that they do. And you need to go now. Stay here, you get killed."

"Me?" said Corey Banning.

"Yes," said Benetsee, "but I don't know no more than that. You make this too much your fight. Lose sight of things."

Corey shrugged.

Du Pré felt the hair on the back of his neck rise.

If Benetsee said she was dead if she stayed, she would be.

If that's what the coyotes meant.

"Other people, another time," said Benetsee, "some stories, people don't go all the way to the end. You know, people die, they go away, the story leaves them."

"Madelaine, she want you to come to dinner," said Du Pré, before Corey could speak.

"Yah," said Benetsee, "I got to talk her, anyway, so I go now, you come along later." The old man rose and drifted out the door.

"What you going to do?" said Bart, looking hard at Corey.

"Stay," said Corey Banning, "until I got this wrapped and knocked. My job. Danger's part of it."

"That does it," said Bart. "I think I'll see if I can get you pulled out of here."

"Listen good, you guinea son of a bitch," said Corey. "You can try and you can even maybe get me pulled out of here. You got a long arm. And what I'll do then is resign and go right on as a PI, for one lousy dollar. If I got to pay myself the dollar. Kiss my ass, Fascelli. You piss me off."

She walked out.

"Shit," said Bart. "She would."

"Yeah," said Du Pré. "I sure wish this damn winter would quit."

❖ CHAPTER 21 ❖

"Some damn winter, this," said Du Pré.

Bart and Booger Tom and Du Pré were standing in the mud of a snowplow turnout, looking down on the lands below the bench. The Chinook wind had come, warm and thick with rain. The snows were melting, the creeks roared, the river was jammed with ice and out of its banks, and all the flat fields were flooded with water and sheets of ice. The cattle were soaked, their hair plastered; the horses snorted nervously and kept to the highest ground they could find.

"If it freeze bad," said Du Pré, "we will have some bad trouble."

"Ain't seen this since '49," said Booger Tom.

"The Gold Rush?" said Bart, sweetly.

Booger Tom looked at Bart for a long moment.

"Of course," he said. "I don't come to Montana till *after* they invented grass."

Du Pré looked down at the county road. Bill Stemple's pickup was struggling up it toward them.

"Hey, Bart," said Du Pré, "something is . . . Stemple, he would not come up to us unless he had to. Too much work he has now."

Bart went to his truck and he switched on his radio, shaking his head. He spoke into it for a moment.

"Let's go down," he said when he came back. "There's bits of cloth and I don't know what all washing out of Cooper Creek. Pieces of those idiots got killed by the avalanche. Stemple tried to get hold of me but I'd turned off my radio. The dispatcher couldn't raise me."

They drove down toward Bill Stemple, who turned off and waited.

Bart pulled up and rolled down his window.

"Howdy," said Stemple. "Listen, there's scraps of cloth floating out from under that mess of snow up the canyon there. I can't figure it. The cloth's been torn up, ripped. It don't look like the avalanche done it."

Bart nodded. "Puzzling," he said. He looked at Du Pré.

"How much cloth?" said Du Pré, shouting past Booger Tom, who was sitting in the middle of the seat.

"Damn near half a bushel," said Stemple, "strips and scraps."

"We'll be right along," said Bart.

They drove on down the hill. Stemple turned around and followed, not close. The road was either muddy or slick.

"What do you think?" said Bart, as they plowed on toward Stemple's.

Du Pré and Booger Tom shook their heads.

At the ranch they got on a pair of snow machines, Bart and Booger Tom, Du Pré and Bill Stemple, and slopped and roared up to the mouth of the canyon. Du Pré looked up at the deep, deep snow, melting down rapidly. The creek roared, high and brown.

He saw some bright red pieces of cloth float past. There were other pieces of ripstop nylon on the brown boiling water, stuck in the tangled branches of alder at the verge of the creek bottom.

Du Pré eased down the bank far enough to grab a couple scraps. He sidestepped back up the sodden bank and stood, turning the scraps around. He knitted his eyebrows.

"What?" said Bart.

Du Pré shook his head.

He walked over to Bill Stemple.

"You seen any them grizzly this winter?" he said.

"Oh, my God," said Stemple. "Not a sign. None."

"What the fuck are you talking about," said Bart, "that I can't know about?"

"Them male grizzly, they don't hibernate," said Du Pré. "I think that maybe one he was just napping when the avalanche it come down. So then he maybe get out of his den and he come on one of the people got killed. Eat them, then he just go on, under that snow. They were maybe all pretty close together. This cloth got some punctures in it, I think the holes made by bear teeth, myself."

"Hee, hee," said Booger Tom. "All winter long that damn bear there he has sack lunches under the snow. Didn't have to come out to the meat dumps."

"Oh, God," said Bill Stemple, "I shoulda thought of it. All those dead sheep we put there and a couple cows went tits up. I should have known."

"What meat dump?" said Bart. "I ain't following."

"We put them dead animal out so coyotes and bears eat them, don't bother the good stock," said Du Pré. "Worked good. Them Fish and Game people say it is illegal."

"I gather that the corpses in there are reduced to bear shit," said Bart. "Oh, they are gonna love this at USA Today. I think we have a good deal of the obnoxious press to look forward to. I suggest that we don't bring it up right away."

"No," said Du Pré, "I think you call a press conference maybe an hour from now, you do it by phone."

"Why?"

"It make such a big stink that the Governor, he will have to send people, dig around in there, otherwise we have to."

"I take your point," said Bart. "Although maybe all we have to do is put a screen across the creek here."

Benetsee say this country, this land hate these people, Du Pré thought. All my time here, I never know of anything like this now. But it did not kill me. It did not. It could have, but it held me for some time and it let me go. Up toward the light.

"Thanks," said Bart to Bill Stemple. They got on the snow machines, rode back down to the ranch.

Bart drove as quickly as he dared back down to the Sheriff's office. Du Pré went in and listened while Bart informed a news bureau of the day's startling events.

Then they drove back to the Toussaint Bar.

Benny and Susan were behind the bar, pulling beers and mixing drinks. The place was packed. The winter had been so miserable that no one had gone outdoors much, but the warm weather had come and spring and its mud and sleet weren't far away.

"It seems that a bear has been eating the unfortunates at the bottom of Cooper Canyon," said Bart.

"I know you don't drink anymore," said Susan, "so did you fall on your head?"

"Du Pré thinks the avalanche that buried the people also buried a grizzly sleeping in a cave or something. Then the bear crawled out and began munching. It's preposterous. I think he's probably right."

Benny looked at Du Pré for a long moment.

"Cooper Canyon is part of that big bear's country," he said.

"I've seen the son of a bitch a couple times. He'll go twelve hundred, maybe."

"Can he just move through the snow?" said Bart.

"Easy," said Du Pré. "They are very strong. Pick up a bull and carry it, you know."

"Jesus," said Bart.

Du Pré nodded.

This is some place now, strange time, he thought, I am perhaps not seeing something. The ranchers they have killed, the country it has killed, but who was it shot the four people up in the mountains? Shot the wolves? Me, that I don't understand.

That time they thought about it, thought about it long time. They know this country, know it as good as me, lots of people know it as good as me.

Up there, big bear with a full belly sleeps under the ice.

Just shove his way through the snow, I have seen them in their strength.

Du Pré looked down suddenly at the drink Benny had set before him.

He lifted it and he sipped.

Some of my friends I fiddle for are murderers.

Them Fish and Wildlife people they kill that bear now, they will have to, the Governor, he will make them. Bad for the tourists, not so many will come.

My state is some kind of whorehouse now, I guess. I work in it. Take nice hot towels around.

I got to go and see Benetsee.

Du Pré rolled a cigarette and he lit it and he drew deeply. He drank.

What they do now? Try to dig what is left, those people, out?

I got to see Benetsee.

"Du Pré!"

Du Pré turned. Corey Banning was standing there, snifter of brandy in her hand. Her leather jacket was open. Du Pré could see her stainless-steel nine-millimeter in its holster on her belt.

"Are you all right?" she said.

Du Pré's fingers hurt.

He looked down. The cigarette had burned down between them. He dropped it on the floor, stepped on it, reached down, and picked up the butt.

"Thinking," he said. "It is very hard for me, you know."

"Strange business," said Corey, "the bit about the bear. You sure?"

"Pretty strange," said Du Pré, "but I don't know how else that cloth get all torn up. Them avalanche break bones but they don't do that, the rocks were covered in ice, no trees to tear them up, just brush in the bottoms."

She nodded.

"Corey," said Du Pré, "I think maybe everything has some changed, you know, I never had a time like this. Someday soon maybe the winds all smell different and I look at the stars on a clear night and the Big Dipper it is gone and there is something there I don't know."

"Well," said Corey, "things should start unraveling soon."

"Huh," said Du Pré. "Like them cloth, Corey? Only it don't unravel. It was ripped right apart."

She sipped her brandy.

They both looked at the floor.

❖ CHAPTER 22 ❖

The backhoe dug at the ice jam in the creek. The brown water started flooding through. There was a heavy fine-meshed net across the creek below. It was hung from two other backhoes' buckets, one on each side of the creek. When the chunks of ice were near, the operators lifted the net, let the ice pass, and set it down again. Strips of cloth were stuck in the net.

It was early April. The snow was melting back up the canyon. Earthmoving equipment had been brought in and National Guardsmen to operate it. The big machines were painted in desert camouflage.

A front-end loader dug at the collapsed snow and lifted its bucket. The big machine backed away.

"There," said Bart. He pointed.

The tail of a snowshoe stuck up from the bucket.

The operator backed away from the snowbank and he set the bucket down.

Bart and Du Pré walked over to the big machine. They looked at the snowshoe. It was twisted and the wooden frame was broken. Du Pré looked at the tail. It had been bitten. There were teeth marks, big ones, cutting right through the hard ash.

"There," said Du Pré.

Bart shook his head. He signaled the operator, who lifted the bucket and dumped the load in front of them. The snow broke open. There was a pack still tied into the thongs, but the felt liner was gone and whatever foot might have been in it.

"Jesus," said Bart.

Du Pré shook his head.

Not much to say. So far we got not one scrap of a person but I don't know what we find, them grizzly got big strong jaws. Eat someone's head like it is an apple.

"You become Sheriff things get so interesting," said Du Pré. "I think I quit, change my name, move to Canada."

"Too late," said Bart, "or I'd join you."

Bart jammed the sharp end of a crowbar at the snow. It began to crumble. A glove appeared. Bart picked it up. He rolled the wristlet down. Some bones stuck out.

"Bingo," said Bart. "Now we call the medical examiner."

He trudged off toward a tent where there was a radio telephone.

Du Pré worked the frozen hand out of the glove. A woman's

hand, a wedding ring and diamond on her left hand, there in the snow.

Du Pré reached in his pocket and pulled out a clear plastic bag and he sealed the hand and glove in it. He looked up at the loader. The operator backed away from the face of the slide. A long red stocking cap stretched between the bucket and the snow face. The hat parted.

Du Pré slipped and slid over to the snow face. He pulled out his sheath knife and chipped away around the edges of the hat.

He pulled the hat away.

Just white packed snow is all, he thought. I wonder, that damn bear he eat everything else?

Bart waved at Du Pré from the trail. Du Pré slid back down to him, holding part of the hat.

"They said for us to leave it alone," said Bart. "Better minds and much better men than the likes of us will take it from here."

Du Pré shrugged.

He handed Bart the plastic bag with the hand and glove in it.

"Just a minute," said Bart, walking toward the tent.

He came back empty-handed.

They walked down the muddy, icy track, stepping over big lumps of snow and gravel, to Bart's truck.

The mudlug tires threw slop and gravel hard against the truck's bottom shields. They wallowed down to firmer ground and out to the dry county road, and Bart got out and so did Du Pré to unlock the front hubs.

"Where you put that hand?" said Du Pré.

"On top of the sandwiches in the cooler," said Bart.

Du Pré nodded.

"It's a clear day," said Bart. "I think I'd like to fly up and look at the mountains."

Du Pré nodded.

"I'll go, too," said Du Pré.

I want to see who might be up them mountain. No one is trapping now, no one did too much this year, too bad. But there is

someone who was up there when they set down them people and
them wolf. That guy is crazy. The rest of it I don't know we ever
know but I find out, that one.

Got to go up, got to come down, someone got to have seen
something.

They went to the Toussaint Bar for lunch and had just finished
their cheeseburgers when the Martin ranch's helicopter racketed
in and set down on the bare brown softball field across the road.
The picnic tables were still piled the way they had been in the
winter, when the fools came for the service for the martyrs for the
environment.

Du Pré and Bart ducked under the rotor wash and got in and
strapped down. Taylor Martin revved the engine and they lifted
off. It was a small, light machine, made for crop dusting and
herding cattle.

Bart sketched out where he wanted to go on the pilot's knee
pad of paper. Martin nodded and headed off toward the Wolf
Mountains, hard and bright with snow, black-green forest running down the flanks like thick spilled paint.

They flew over the nearest high basin, unbroken white save at
the edges where the trees held shadows. One tree shook and
dumped its load of snow and the white clod sank and a lynx
appeared, clutching the very top and glaring up at the noisy
machine.

The pilot flew over to the north side and along the flanks of the
mountains about a third of the way down. Some ravens were
feeding on something in a thicket. They flew a bit and settled back
down.

The pilot turned and flew over to the south side. The deep cleft
of Cooper Canyon and its barren sides and the massive slide in the
bottom appeared.

They went over a spur of the mountain to the next drainage.

Du Pré spotted some tracks.

"Skis!"

Bart leaned over and looked and he banged on the pilot's

shoulder and pointed. The helicopter sank quickly toward the double line of tracks across the white. They went into thick growth a mile or so down the mountain.

The pilot dipped down lower and he went back and forth. The spur of the mountain ended in rock.

The tracks did not come out of the lower side.

He flew up the spine of the spur slowly.

The rotors roiled the snow below; it rose like a ground blizzard.

Du Pré stared.

"Have him go back up, find where he came up now," Du Pré yelled in Bart's ear. "Why this guy, he don't go down where he come up?"

Pretty simple, that, when you run a trapline it is a long circle or a U or something, so you got the most traps.

They rose up the slope till the mountain began to rise nearly straight up, broken masses of rock hard under the sky.

He didn't come over that.

They went to the right.

Nothing.

They went to the left.

Du Pré stared again. There was a small basin just above the tree-line and the snow on it looked strange.

The wind had pretty well cleared it.

The pilot flew slowly around the edge.

Du Pré spotted some ski tracks at a place where the low trees had come in close.

"Go back down!" he yelled at Bart.

Bart scribbled on the pilot's pad.

The machine dipped and headed down, blades biting the gelid air.

They sank from winter to spring.

The pilot set down on the softball field.

Du Pré and Bart ducked out and ran and the machine rose and went off.

"The son of a bitch is still up there," said Bart.

Du Pré nodded.

"He'll wait till dark to come down," said Bart, "but he's only got so many ways he can come."

"He has a bunch of them," said Du Pré. "He get down low and hide his skis he can cut across long ways. Take time but I don't think he will care."

"We call all them ranchers, see if there is a truck or car parked someplace," said Du Pré. "But I don't think so."

Bart nodded.

"Why be up there?"

"It is not far from where the people and the wolves were killed," said Du Pré. "This guy, I think he just wanted to see it again, you know."

"Why?"

Du Pré rolled a cigarette.

"He's a very tough guy," said Du Pré. "Knows this country good, you bet."

He smoked.

"Bart," said Du Pré, "he is very proud of what he did. He just maybe wanted to see where he did it again."

"Jesus," said Bart.

They walked toward the bar.

✤ CHAPTER 23 ✤

Du Pré squinted through the cold rising light at the mountains. He was hidden on a long sloping ridge, one with a good view to both sides. Anyone coming down the mountain for four miles on either side of him would have to cross the open sometime.

He glanced quickly back and forth. The air was dead still. He waved his smoky breath away from his face.

This guy he is out here. No car waiting on him. Nobody knows of anyone who was up there and I wonder he maybe drop from the sky. Somebody drop him from the sky.

Lot of damn work and it needs someone else who has a helicopter. Now who has one and who used it yesterday morning? Guy took us has one and he didn't take us till the afternoon. That guy, Taylor Martin, he was a war hero, Vietnam, flew choppers. Been over east there, his family, long as us Du Prés been here. Big ranch there.

Du Pré stood up. He switched on his telephone and dialed.

"Yeah," Bart whispered.

"That guy we look for he is gone," said Du Pré. "I think that Taylor Martin drop him off, take us up, bring us back down, go back up and pick him up."

"You know him?" said Bart. "Why do you think that?"

"Got to be someone pretty close," said Du Pré. "Chopper can't fly that fast. It's his, he don't fly out of an airport, just out of his hangar. Sixty miles away, you know. Now, he got a brother and a couple brothers-in-law there. Some of them people shot, they are killed near that Martin ranch. That bunch of people, they are burned, you know. Hot fire, someone made a firebomb, that car. Magnesium."

"Is there a reason that we are sitting out here playing soldier?" said Bart. "I'm cold. I'm hungry. And you say he's gone."

"You maybe call Corey?" said Du Pré.

"You call her," said Bart. "She likes reaming me out so much and I have a terrible headache. She's at . . ."

Bart read off the number. Du Pré hung up and dialed.

"Agent Banning," said Corey.

"It is me," said Du Pré. "I think maybe it is those guys, that Martin ranch out east, you know. "This guy we are looking for he was dropped off by a helicopter, you know, picked up, I think, too."

"Yeah," said Corey, "I know it's them. Can't be anybody else, but we haven't got any proof."

"You talk to them?"

"Oh, yes," said Corey. "I just did my best and the bastards looked at me like I was touched and needed some home cooking. Very clannish, they are."

"How come you don't tell us this?" said Du Pré, suddenly angry.

"Well," said Corey, "I'm a manipulative female and I thought if I let you alone you'd sort of stir things up."

"You tell me, I would stir things up some time ago," said Du Pré. "Don't you do this again."

Silence.

"Damn you," said Du Pré. "Them Martins, you think they maybe shot some of those fool kids, too?"

"You're very quick, Du Pré," said Corey Banning. "Now, don't fuck up. There's too many people over there who know. It'll come apart. But you go stir the shit they'll back into a circle, horns out, and it'll be another six months before it loosens up. I got to get them before too much longer or I'll be sent more help, and you know what that means."

Du Pré shut the telephone off.

I do not like this, I had thought she was more honest than that. But maybe she is right. There is more good weather coming. More tourists and fools and the way that this goes now maybe more dead people. Me, I don't got no answers.

Hell. Shit. Damn.

Du Pré walked down to his Rover and started it and sat in it smoking until the engine warmed.

I am a brand inspector, little rancher, grandfather, and a bit part, some cheap television movie.

But I did not make it like that, it was those foolish little bastards from the flat with all their silly notions, feel like they are better for this place than we are.

Du Pré reached under the seat and pulled out a fifth of whiskey and he had a slug and sat there watching the mountains and the sun spilling down them.

Can't find Benetsee, he is not around or not around when I come to find him, old fart. Leave him meat, tobacco, wine, he still won't come.

Here I am, cold morning, looking for a guy up there who was looking for something that he left behind that frightens him now. Or maybe just wanted to see . . . oh, I am a very stupid man. Not proud, scared, and two of them to do it.

Du Pré saw a car coming up the sloppy road behind him, a rental car pasted half over with mud.

Journalists.

Du Pré had another slug of whiskey. He rolled a cigarette.

Good headline. "Officers drink and smoke while so many lie dead."

They bother me, I will piss on their shoes.

Du Pré punched some numbers into his portable telephone and he waited a moment.

"Special Agent Banning," said Corey.

"More you are awake, longer your name gets," said Du Pré. "Now I am some mad with you. You don't lie exactly, you just don't maybe tell me all the truth you know. Well, I know something now which I am not going to tell you yet. Lead me someplace. I arrest somebody, I don't let you know and see how you like it."

"I'm trying to save some lives," said Corey.

"You still aren't telling me, you know, what," said Du Pré.

"Shit," said Corey.

"There are, you know, couple newspeople driving up toward me now, so I think maybe I tell them I spend time out here, freezing my ass, while them FBI don't tell me what they know, things are now interesting."

"You bastard."

"Oh, no," said Du Pré. "My parents, they are married three, four days before I come, my mother she hold her missal out on her belly, I pound on her stomach while she said she marry Catfoot. Me, I get there just in time always."

"Shit."

"Now, now," said Du Pré, "you maybe got this nice big thick file, the Martins, you let me see it."

"Goddamn you," said Corey Banning.

"Maybe we, how you say, do lunch," said Du Pré. "Now I got to go a minute here, soon as these newspeople get stuck."

Du Pré got out and looked down the muddy road and waited till the rental car got to a steep rise. It slowed and stopped while a spray of mud flared out behind. The rear end slid slowly to the edge of the road and off; the wheels settled and dug in.

Two people got out and looked helplessly at the car. They were dressed in funny clothes with pockets all over the arms.

Du Pré had another slug of whiskey and he rolled another cigarette and he got in his Rover and turned around and drove down the hill. The two reporters stood beside the car.

He drove past them, waving.

One of them screamed something.

Du Pré stopped the Rover, got out, walked to the back where they could see him, gave them the finger, and drove on.

This whole thing is now to come together, all them strings in knots and the ends followed into the shadows.

He glanced in the rearview mirror and the mountains flamed in the sun, up high where the snow lay deep and would till July. The orange and red-pink of an abalone shell.

Du Pré stopped at the edge of the bench, where there was a turnout for the snowplows. He looked down at Stemple's ranch, the cattle in the pastures, Bill Stemple driving a tractor, unspooling a big roll of hay for his stock.

He could see all the way south to where the Missouri ran between its bluffs and gravel hills.

He looked off toward a shelf of rock in the high grass and sage. There was a pile of rocks on it, the slabs of limestone spalled off the mountains over time and time again. Piled about ten feet long and three feet high, littler slabs on top.

Plenty of holes to look through.

Two scouts could hide there and watch and there would be nothing visible if you looked up from below.

Du Pré got out and he walked to the fence and stepped through and he followed a game trail through the sage to the ledge and the pile some Indians had made so long ago.

The rock behind the pile was still wet.

Du Pré squatted down on his haunches.

He saw a cigarette filter tip.

Another.

A scrap of foil.

He got up and moved back and forth, looking at the ground.

Someone had crapped near a sagebrush.

Du Pré pulled a bag from his pocket and poked the turd into it with a stick.

He looked at a little left on the ground.

Raspberry seeds.

Somebody from right here, Du Pré thought. But me, I knew that.

❧ CHAPTER 24 ❧

I was damn close," said Corey Banning, "and you got me and here it is."

She handed Du Pré a folder filled with sheets of computer type. Ugly stuff, Du Pré hated it. Always smelled like fluorescent lights, cheap floor polish, that paper.

"How much more they find up Cooper Canyon?" said Du Pré.

"Oh, scraps," said Corey. "That goddamn Governor swears to have the bear killed, right, and now the animal rights idiots are picketing the statehouse. Anyway, folks want to die of pure dumbness and have a bear eat 'em, I don't care."

"Lot of medals, these two guys," said Du Pré. Taylor Martin and his brother Clark. Southdowns, probably, the Missouri people who came here to get away from the Civil War.

I meet these guys once, twice. Soft-voiced. Cattle, sheep, pretty big ranch. Both of them fly helicopters, both of them crash behind enemy lines, Vietnam, and both of them make it back. Volunteer a lot. Some trouble, get drunk in Saigon, beat the shit out of some MPs, lose rank, end up on the ground. Then they sign up, second tour for Clark, third for Taylor, they like it.

"Pretty good," said Du Pré. "Guys looking for the murderers are the murderers, they fly in and out. Nobody saw that some."

"I'm going out to reef on them," said Corey. "You want to come along?"

Du Pré nodded. He called Madelaine, told her where he was going.

Du Pré drove. He smoked. He reached under the seat and had some whiskey. He offered the bottle to Corey, but she shook her head.

"Not this time," she said.

"What you going to do you can't arrest them?" said Du Pré. "They don't talk to you, what?"

"Piss 'em off."

She will do that. Hope we all live through it, woman got a mouth on her like my great-uncle Hercule.

Du Pré shot down the lonely two-lane highway, swerving to miss the worst frost boils. A cock pheasant ran in front and into the sere weeds.

They drove for half an hour. Corey pointed to a pole covered in signs, each pointing to a ranch somewhere the hell and gone back in the rolling High Plains country.

Martin.

Du Pré turned and roared up a wide county road. A flock of ravens flew away from a dead deer by the side of the road. Antelope stood in the low swales in the folds of the hills, staring at the Rover as it shot past. Flights of ducks rose from marsh ponds that would be dry by July.

A fork in the road, another sign pole. Du Pré bore off to the right. Another ten miles and they found a mailbox atop a long welded chain, links the size of boot soles, "Martin" on the top. They turned off and drove up the rutted road and when they topped the second hill they saw the ranch, down in a stand of cottonwoods. Barns and sheds and three simple two-story ranch houses, railroad houses, bought as kits from Chicago factories, shipped by rail and then ox team to this place between the earth and sky, where there were no trees but cottonwoods, the lumber from them weak and useless.

Du Pré drove into the big yard. Tractors and machinery, seed bins, some chickens fluttering across the mud. A pair of blue heelers came out barking and circled behind the Rover, ready to bite the rear tires as soon as it stopped.

Du Pré sat for a moment. Corey opened her door and got out and she stood by the Rover, looking around.

A man came out of one of the machine sheds. He was wearing rubber irrigation boots and a red mackinaw and a yellow plaid hat. He walked slowly over toward Corey Banning.

"Special Agent Banning, FBI," said Corey. She held up her ID and the man came close and he looked for a long moment at the cards in the black leather case and he nodded and she put the wallet in her pocket.

Du Pré got out and he walked round to them.

"Du Pré," he said.

"The fiddler?" said the man. "You play right nice."

"I have some questions for you," said Corey. "Is there a place we can go sit?"

"How 'bout the truck here," said the man.

They got in.

Du Pré and the man sat in the front, Corey in back.

"I'm investigating the murders," said Corey, "of two Fish and Wildlife agents, two other men with them, on or about the evening of the sixteenth of November, and of two other people shot in October. Now, what is your name again?"

"Taylor Martin, ma'am," said the man, "like I told you before."

"You have a helicopter."

"Three of 'em," said Martin. "We run twelve thousand head here."

Jesus, thought Du Pré, that is one big damn bunch of cattle.

"You flew Du Pré here and Sheriff Fascelli over the Wolf Mountains yesterday?"

Martin nodded.

He wear that helmet and mask I don't know him, thought Du Pré. His hands are pretty steady there, though.

"Mind if I have a cigarette?" said Martin.

"Fine," said Corey.

Du Pré rolled one and lit it; so did Taylor Martin.

"It seems that someone was up in the Wolf Mountains, and that they could only have got in and out flying in a helicopter. You were with Du Pré and Fascelli part of that day. Where were you before and after?"

Taylor Martin blew out a long stream of blue smoke.

"Agent Banning," said Martin softly, "I shot two people who were cutting my fences and shooting my stock on the night of the twelfth of October, and then I burned them with a thermite unit I made."

"FUCKING FREEZE!" yelled Corey. She had her nine-millimeter jammed against Martin's head. "CUFF HIM!"

Du Pré took out his handcuffs and snapped them on Martin's wrists. Martin had turned slowly, so Du Pré could clip them behind his back.

"And then," he went on, "I flew up into the Wolf Mountains and I shot four men and six wolves. I chopped the slugs out of the bodies. Heads, actually, all of them, and then I flew back here."

"Christ," said Corey Banning. She was digging for her tape recorder.

"And I'll be perfectly happy to tell you everything you wish to know," said Martin.

"Call Bart and have him get a cell ready," said Corey. "I'll have to get transport for this guy, out to Billings."

"Let me out of this whatever-it-is for a minute," said Taylor Martin. "My kid brother is in the shed there and he's got a rifle on you and I'd just as soon this all ended now."

Du Pré nodded and he got out and walked around the front of the Rover and he opened the door and helped Taylor Martin out.

"Clark!" yelled Martin. "I told them. I'm going now, it's over, go and finish feeding the calves in the third lot. I'll call you when I can."

Clark Martin came out of the building. He was carrying an assault rifle in one hand.

"OK, Taylor," he said. "Good luck."

The Martin brothers laughed.

Du Pré drove back down to the county road and then he cranked up to speed and when he hit the highway he drove at ninety, light bar flashing.

When they got to the jail in Cooper Bart and Benny were there, and they hustled Martin back to a cell after taking his clothes and giving him an orange jumpsuit.

Taylor Martin rubbed his wrists and he looked amused.

Corey Banning pulled a chair up to his cell and began to fire questions at him.

Martin answered all of them which did not mention anyone else. He maintained that it was only he who had shot six people.

"That's a lot of goddamned people," said Corey.

"I killed over three hundred in Vietnam," said Martin. "I have a true talent."

"Your brother helped you."

"Nope," said Martin.

"I'm going to keep asking questions till I know everything," said Corey.

Martin shrugged. "Could I have a soda? Flavor don't matter, a smoke, too."

Du Pré walked down to the fridge and got him one.

He lit a cigarette and passed it through the bars. Taylor Martin took the smoke and nodded at Du Pré.

Martin had a slug of pop.

"Bring me a pad of paper and a pen," he said. "I'll just write down what I have to say now and sign it. Or go away."

Du Pré fetched him a pad and pen and a clipboard.

Martin began to write.

"Agent Banning," said Martin, "I will write this, and it's pretty simple, really. And while I do I'm going to say a few things to Mr. Du Pré. He will, I think, understand them rather better than you."

"You don't talk like a ranch guy," said Corey Banning.

Martin laughed. "We have a uniform speech? My, my. No, we do not. I went to Yale, ma'am. Classics. With honors. So did my youngest brother. Clark went to West Point. So did one of our brothers-in-law. Other one went to Princeton, but every family has 'em, yes?"

"Vietnam?"

"I wanted to see what being a warrior meant," said Taylor Martin. "I did and I liked it."

"Do you like killing?"

Martin shrugged.

"I'm indifferent," he said. "It's either necessary or not, you know."

"You're lying about your brother."

"Nope."

He scratched on the pad.

"Mr. Du Pré," said Martin, "your people have been round here since when? 1870? 1886?"

"Eighty-six," said Du Pré.

"The second rebellion," said Martin. "We have been where the ranch is since 1879. Now it seems that our leases for summer grazing are to be terminated, on the whim of people who have never been here at all. A purely political decision, of course. It's the property of the United States government and therefore the people of our country, of course. But it was handled very badly and when those idiots came to cut fences and shoot cattle I thought I'd make an example of them."

Scratch scratch.

"Here," said Martin, handing the confession through the bars. "You need to sign as witnesses where I marked the two X's."

"Christ," said Corey Banning. "I don't believe any of this."

"Oh, but you must," said Taylor Martin. He took a drink from his can of pop.

"Bullshit," said Corey.

"The soda washed down a cyanide capsule," said Taylor Martin. "I suppose that you'll get in trouble for not checking the inside of my mouth. Too late now."

Corey Banning looked at him, stunned.

Taylor Martin smiled and then put his hand to his eyes and fell to the cell floor and died in a matter of seconds.

Du Pré pounded on his chest for a while, but it didn't do any good.

❧ CHAPTER 25 ❧

I didn't know he was so short," said Madelaine. She was looking at the Governor, who was squelching through the mud toward a portable podium. TV crews and reporters stood in deep ranks, waiting.

"Well, I have heard steers fart," said Du Pré, "and I do not need to listen to this one sing, too. I think I will go to the bar now and have a nice drink. See there is a pretty woman there, buy her some pink wine."

"Poor guy," said Madelaine. "He can't be very happy, want a job like that."

They got into Du Pré's Rover and drove off to Toussaint in the gray spring rain.

"That Taylor Martin, why he do a thing like that?" said Madelaine.

"He was sick," said Du Pré, "some kind of cancer, maybe from that Agent Orange, they used it in Vietnam. Anyway, he confesses and then he kills himself. Now we got a confession and a dead end. Pretty smart guy, pretty tough, too."

"I wish all these people would go away," said Madelaine. "So angry, everyone, I never seen our friends and neighbors so mad."

Du Pré nodded. He shifted in the seat, scratched his neck.

"Only reason it is not much, much worse is that Bart and that Lawyer Foote they are very, very powerful people, they have kept too many of them FBI out of here. About twenty of those fools kicking in doors we have a real war. And now the Fish and Wildlife, they will let more wolves loose up there, and more wolves will get shot, and I suppose more people, too, you know. None of this, it would have happened, those people cared enough about what was here, find out a little what it is before they come."

"You are plenty mad, too, Du Pré," said Madelaine.

"Yah, well, I got to go fish dead people out of places here and there get buried alive, avalanche, I am a deputy which I swore I would never do, poor Bart is the Sheriff, we got to have a Sheriff, a rich man, otherwise we just get smashed. Lucky for us, he is here, a good guy."

"You didn't have time, make meat this fall," said Madelaine. "First time I know that happen."

Jesus, Du Pré thought, I shoot my elk, my deer, every year I am here since I was fourteen and I shoot deer before that. I shoot deer sometimes in the summer when Benetsee wants summer hides for his women relatives up in Canada, against the law but we got more deer here than we got jackrabbits. Deer carcasses, they keep the coyotes off the lambs. I don't make meat this fall, I ride herd on a bunch of mostly dead assholes should have stayed to home.

I hate these people, but kill them, no, that is wrong.

"It is a shitty mess," said Du Pré. "I would quit, you know, but I cannot do that, Bart."

"You cannot do that, you," said Madelaine. "This is plenty bad now, you know, but it will be worse, you quit. Bart quit, you quit,

Governor send in his people, lot of shooting. Our friends, neighbors, very good shots. Also, they only want to live, so much."

"Huh?"

"You know what I am saying, Du Pré," said Madelaine.

Yah, I know, I am like that, too. I get mad enough, me, I don't
care what anybody think. Kill Lucky, for sure. I almost kill that
damn Bucky Dassault, too.

"Hah," said Madelaine. "Now that damn Governor, he worried
about the tourists, you know, they will be afraid, not come to
Montana at all. Maybe they get caught in avalanche, July, big old
grizzly eat them under the snow. All those fat guys, Chamber of
Commerces, having fits. Hah."

Du Pré laughed.

"Hey," he said, "we make maybe commercial, television. You
want to die, come to Montana. We shoot you, feed you to the
bears. Everything that walks, it is here, it bites."

"Don't get too mad, Du Pré," said Madelaine. "I know you
pret' good, you don't get too mad, you get too mad, you talk,
your Madelaine, before you do something."

"Ah," said Du Pré. He parked in front of the Toussaint Bar.

"I don't want to come visit you, Deer Lodge, or the cemetery,
have to put flowers on your stone, say, Du Pré, you bastard, you
were going to call your Madelaine."

She began to cry.

Du Pré put his arms around her and he held her and stroked
her hair. She smelled of roses and mountain gentian.

"OK," said Du Pré, "I will do that. But you know, if someone is
going to be having some shots at me I will have to talk to you
maybe after."

"Well," said Madelaine, "that is all right, they shoot at you you
just kill them, you hear, so you can talk, me, later."

Du Pré rocked her.

She snuffled and then fished around in her purse and took out
a linen handkerchief and blew her nose and dabbed at her eyes.
She never wore makeup.

"Pink wine," said Madelaine, "and I feel pretty lucky, so I roll for it with Susan."

They went in. The bar was empty but for Susan Klein and old Benetsee slumped down on a stool.

Du Pré yelled.

"Old man, I look for you, weeks, you old bastard, now you are here! I think you are white bones and coyote shit. Damn you!"

Madelaine ran to the old man and hugged him.

Benetsee turned round and he grinned his old brown grin at Du Pré.

"I been, Canada," he said. "I left you note, you know, hanging on a bush, behind my house."

Shit, Du Pré thought, I never went behind his damn house. The snow was deep. I never went far enough. Never went far enough. I am afraid of the snow now a little bit. A lot. Did not want my legs all the way down in it. Deep under that snow it scared me. Made me mad enough to live but it scared me. Damn, I ought to go burrow into it, sleep in it a few nights. Damn.

Benetsee's notes, they are carved in wood, bone, stone. His notes, very hard to understand. Easy to read, very hard to understand.

The old man lifted up a big glass of fizzy screwtop wine and drank it.

"Them people pretty good meat, Old Black Claws," said Benetsee. "I see him wake up under the snow, he grumble, claw his way out, find someone. Can't believe his luck, Old Black Claws. He eat pretty good there, couple three months. Hee. Sleep some, get up, go eat. Good life."

"God," said Susan Klein.

"Yeah," said Du Pré. "They hunt him down now for sure. Old bastard. I will miss him."

"He is gone," said Benetsee.

"Gone?" said Du Pré.

Gone fucking where? Them Wolf Mountain, they are an island range, it is hundred and fifty miles to next bear country.

"Where gone?" said Du Pré.

Benetsee belched.

"North."

Susan Klein set down Madelaine's wine and Du Pré's whiskey.

"Where north?"

"He don't tell me," said Benetsee.

"Old man," said Du Pré, "your help, I need now. What you know about these people killed? Who killed them? It is not right, you know. And we can't have more, you know."

"No more," said Benetsee, "of them. They all live now. Somebody else die but I can't see who."

Old man always knows the riddles.

I don't need this. Who dies? Bart? Me? Who?

"Yah," said Benetsee, "Old Black Claws, he eats them but he don't like them much, I guess. Except for candy bars in their pockets. Hee, Pretty damn bad when a grizzly don't like eating you."

"Oh, you awful old man," said Madelaine, "those people they got mothers, fathers, you know. Lots of tears, pretty awful, can't even bury their kids. Pretty awful."

"Them whites, they like to pickle their dead people," said Benetsee. "Pretty selfish. Lots of hungry Peoples out there. They take, they don't give back."

"Oh, barf," said Susan Klein. "Way you talk I ought to go dig up someone, fry them up, serve 'em to you."

She filled Benetsee's wine glass. He drank it.

"You have a cheeseburger now," said Susan, "or no more wine."

"Is this going to stop?" said Madelaine. "This horribles?"

Benetsee nodded.

"Sure," he said. "Everything stops, you know."

Du Pré looked down at the whiskey and ice in his glass. He could see a carving in the top of the bar, someone's initials, very old and filled with black polished dirt. The bar top was more than a century old.

"Hey, Susan," said Du Pré, "looking down through his glass, "how old, this old bar here?"

"Made in Pennsylvania in 1868," said Susan, "this and the backbar. Old German woodcarvers. Shipped to Fort Benton and when that died out it was hauled to Miles City and then here. Got dates on the back of the far left door there, where the old ice blocks were kept. All zinc in it, like the ceiling here."

HDP, the carving said. My ancestor, Hercule Du Pré, the one who did cuss so very good, him, he sat here, carve his initials in this wood.

He say goddamn, shit, Balls of Christ, all that. Me, I say it, too.

✤ CHAPTER 26 ✤

Du Pré and Bart looked up the Cooper Creek Canyon. All mud and rock now, a couple bloated carcasses of mountain goats that had died when the avalanche came down.

One of the medical examiners stood next to them, puffing on a pipe. He was young, moustached, very calm.

"The bear didn't eat the lower jaws," the ME said. "Nice of him. We were able to identify all of the victims. If he had we would have been mixing and matching teeth till the next millennium."

Du Pré nodded.

Good for that Old Black Claws. Hope he walks all the way up to Canada and finds himself a nice ski hill to feed off of. Nice fat young yuppies. I send him a case of hot sauce or something. This is pretty terrible but pretty funny.

"Yeah, well," said Du Pré, "that Governor he send in his trappers and hunters and they don't find Old Black Claws, but I guess they shoot some other bear and call it even."

"Governors are like that," said the ME. "Offering a million-dollar reward for information leading to the conviction of the murderers of the people killed here last October is another example. Would you care to bet that someone is convicted?"

"No," said Du Pré.

"You're all done with this now?" said Bart. The torn ground was trampled by searchers. The ice had scraped off the brush, tearing the roots out when the moving equipment had lifted it.

"Eight death certificates," said the ME. "I suppose I'll be back here soon. For one thing, it strains credulity to think that Taylor Martin murdered six people without assistance."

"I just want to know who killed the two in my county," said Bart. "I have very modest ambitions."

"Well," said the ME, "one of them died instantly. A Magnum rifle shot through the brain, but it hit the stem. Magnum rifles are useless, of course, for shooting much of anything; they just punch a hole through. But the woman didn't die right then. Someone cut her throat. She was alive till her jugular was separated."

"There was not that much blood, that car," said Du Pré.

"There's been plenty of time to wash up," said the ME. "There are some chemicals that reveal minute quantities of blood. But without a tip you won't know where to look, and if you do get a warrant and you can find some blood there still probably won't be enough to type even if there is enough to declare it human, which I doubt."

"I wonder if we will ever know," Bart said.

"Murderers are an unremarkable lot," said the ME. "They kill when they are angry, or for money, or in a botched robbery, or jealousy. If you haven't found out anything by now I don't think you will find enough to get any convictions, since your confession will come from someone who was a part of it. You have to have corroboration. There won't be any. And there isn't any *reason* for anyone to come forward. Nobody's talked by now, I don't think anyone will."

"Very encouraging," said Bart.

"Taylor Martin's confession foxed you," said the ME. "Now you have to go *around* that. Even the vaunted FBI is at a loss. That formidable Banning woman, by the way, is dangerous."

"Eh," said Bart.

"I don't happen to be from Montana," said the ME, "and I love it here. I love the people, too. I even love the fact that they are crazy. My brother was an officer in Vietnam, and when he arrived, a fresh second lieutenant, out in the boondocks, the staff sergeant took him aside and saved his life."

"Huh?" said Bart.

"The sergeant said, son, these are Montana and Wyoming boys here. You ask them to do something, they'll probably do it. You order them, they'll kill you. Last officer ordered them lasted seven hours. My brother was polite to his men and he lived because of them. This Banning woman is from here, and she's getting pissed, and I fear she may saddle up and charge just to see what she can shake loose. Even unlawfully. I would recommend that you request her transfer."

"She talk to you?" said Bart.

"Frequently," said the ME. "She has four suspects. She's probably right, but the days when you could bung suspects into a cell, let them sit in the dark, and then use the rubber hoses are long gone. That is only done in graduate schools now. But she just may do something out of anger and it will not be the right thing."

"She is one girl who hates to lose," said Du Pré.

"Get her out of here," said the ME.

He walked off, in his rubber boots.

"What do I do about this?" said Bart.

"Huh, ah," said Du Pré, "well, we are some her friends, we maybe talk with her?"

"Worth a try. All we need now is an FBI agent getting blown away," said Bart. "I thought she was sent here to *avoid* that."

Du Pré shrugged.

This Corey Banning has been looking very tired and she is not letting us know that she knows anything even if she don't know anything.

"Maybe we let that Madelaine of mine talk, her," said Du Pré.

"OK," said Bart.

They squelched back to their four-wheelers and backed and

filled, tires sucking out of the mud, and went down the wrecked road toward Cooper.

Children were playing soccer on the softball field. The trees were in bud, cannily waiting out the several frosts between here and the summer. Du Pré saw a long flight of geese headed straight north, the lead goose homed on the polestar even in high sun.

Du Pré and Bart parked in front of the Sheriff's office and went in. Bart tried to raise Corey Banning on his phone, then called the FBI office in the trailer.

"I don't have anything to say to you, fuckhead," Bart said to whoever was on the other end of the line. "Just tell Banning we are at the Toussaint Bar and have some items of interest to discuss with her." He hung up. "I'm usually a nice man."

Du Pré nodded.

They drove down to Toussaint. Corey Banning's muddy rig was already parked out front.

"I go get Madelaine," said Du Pré to Bart, out the window of his Rover. He drove off to her place, his, too, now.

She was sitting at her beading table in the living room, picking through jars of beads, looking for the perfect shade to add to the hatband she was making for her son.

"I need you, my love," said Du Pré. "Come talk that Banning woman, she is I think about to maybe get herself in trouble."

"OK," said Madelaine, "but I don't know what I say."

"Oh," said Du Pré, "maybe just listen, you do that good for me."

"All people really need," said Madelaine. "They talk through it mostly."

Du Pré nodded.

She screwed the lid on a little jar of beads and she shrugged into her jacket and they went out and down to the bar.

Bart and Corey Banning were sitting off at a table. They weren't talking. Bart was looking a little off to the right, Corey a little off to the left. Bart got up and walked to the bar the minute Madelaine began to move toward them.

Madelaine stood for a moment. She said something in a low voice and she laughed and sat down. Corey bent to listen. Madelaine whispered. The two women got up and came round so that they could sit with their backs to the rest of the saloon. They put their heads together.

"Well," said Bart, "we're pretty worthless here. I need to run out to my place and see that old misery Booger Tom and sign some paychecks. Are you gonna go look at the spot where our two came to rest? I wonder if we missed anything last fall."

"OK," said Du Pré.

Yeah, we miss something last fall. You miss something, every time. But now maybe the water and spring it move it down to the little creek or stick it on the uphill side of a sagebrush and maybe now I see it. You can hope, anyway.

Du Pré waved to Madelaine and he went out and drove back up the bench to the turnoff above the draw where the four-wheeler and the two dead fools had been dumped fifty years ago, it seemed.

I like to see that snow go away, Du Pré thought, maybe I move, the damn desert.

Du Pré walked to the rock and then he let himself down hand by hand, grabbing on to sagebrush till he was at the spot where the two dead kids had been. The marks in the earth had mostly erased. A few chips of glass on the ground. Du Pré squatted and looked hard, looked up at the sky. A raven flew past.

Been a badger through here, couple days gone.

Smell the new grass.

Something's not right here.

That root there is too straight.

So is the other one.

I wonder.

Du Pré shuffled over to the sagebrush.

He reached down and picked up a nail. One for a horseshoe. Never been used on a horse, though.

Another. Another. Another.

Du Pré stood up. He put the nails in his pocket and he went back up the hill to his Rover and drove off.

✤ CHAPTER 27 ✤

D u Pré," said Packy, "you're nuts. I couldn't make it down that hill with this leg. And you act like I'm the only man in the damn county has a use for shoein' nails. Is this all because of that dog? Jesus, man, I found the dog thirty miles away."

"I tell that Corey Banning she is all over you like stink on shit," said Du Pré, "so you better think good and you better have some other people they know where you were that damn night, you know."

"I pulled shoes till fucking two in the morning," said Packy. "I did it three different places. You know me, I just make my rounds and send my bills out and that's it. I didn't *see* anybody. They were out or they were asleep."

"Which places you do that at?" said Du Pré.

"Stemple's. They was off in Billings, you know. Then I did some at Moore's, till about ten at night. Then I went way the hell out to the St. Francis place. I hate those bastards and they take lousy care of their stock, but I got to do what I can. I love horses."

"And they were in jail that night," said Du Pré.

"Well," said Packy, "they are a lot. But the lights were on in the house and there was a pickup there I didn't know. It was dark, I didn't look at the license plate. It took a long time to catch all the damn horses and it was after two-thirty when I finished."

Du Pré nodded.

"Packy," said Du Pré, "if you are lying even a little bit you got to tell me now, for Chrissakes. This is a very bad business. People around here they got to know some who did this. OK? Them FBI they will not go away, me and Bart we won't stop. We can't, they can't. It was wrong, that. They cut fence and shoot stock we arrest them, make them pay. But not that."

Packy raised his hands. They were covered in scars, white memories of cuts and punctures from his hard work. A couple fresh red holes.

"OK," said Du Pré, "I will do this. I will tell that Banning about the nails but not about you. She probably figure that out, you know. I got to do that that way, you know."

Du Pré rolled a cigarette and lit it and he smoked a moment.

"OK," he said, "you are at the St. Francis place, you see this pickup. Now, they got some other trucks out there. Any of them gone, you know?"

Packy shook his head. "They had a couple old beaters, didn't even license them, used 'em for hauling on the ranch. Never took 'em off of it. Then they had that canner truck."

"Oh, Jesus Christ," said Du Pré, "I forgot about that."

The St. Francis brothers bought dead animals for the dog food canners and the rendering works. They had a truck with a stain-less-steel bin on the back, one that could be steam-cleaned. Winch and tackle.

I bet that cable was long enough to let that damn car with them two dead people in it down into that gully. Careful, so it don't catch fire.

"The pickup," said Du Pré softly. "What can you remember? Light? Dark? You tell what make?"

"I don't know new trucks so good," said Packy. "It was dark and it had a low camper cap on it and that's all I remember. I was tired as hell and I hardly looked. I don't know whether the canner truck was there or not."

It damn sure wasn't there.

I find out who run that truck when the St. Francis brothers are in jail or busy sometime other way, you bet.

"OK," said Du Pré, "I think I tell that Banning now about your nails down there, in the gully."

"They weren't mine," said Packy. "Damn it, they weren't mine."

132

"We got to find out some things," said Du Pré. "You better come with me, I guess."

"Christ."

"It is better than she come for you, maybe with some them fools she got stuck down in the trailer," said Du Pré.

Packy got into Du Pré's Rover, and they drove down to the trailer park where the FBI was parked.

Corey Banning's big diesel pickup was parked out front.

Du Pré and Packy got out and walked on in. Corey and her three assistants looked up from their desks. Du Pré nodded.

"We got to talk, Corey," said Du Pré.

Corey got her coat and put it on and they went back out and sat in Du Pré's Rover. Every other second a face appeared at the trailer window.

"OK," said Du Pré, "I went back out, the place where those two people found dead, up on the bench there. I find some horseshoe nails, I go to talk to Packy, he says they are not his, he did not put them there."

Corey looked at Packy impassively.

"That night Packy say he is shoeing, I mean taking shoes off for the winter, he does horses at Stemple's, at them Moores', then goes on out to the St. Francis place. They are in jail we know. But Packy he see a pickup there, one he don't know. Don't know there, anyway. And then I ask him, other trucks the St. Francis got? He says, they got a canner truck."

"Holy Christ," said Corey Banning. "Who else drives that truck when the St. Francis brothers are in the jug?"

"Me, I don't know," said Du Pré. "I miss that, I don't sell my dead horses, I bury them, I sign off horse shipments but I don't sign off dog-food horses already dead. I live here all my life, I know them St. Francis do it, but not who does when they cannot."

Corey Banning nodded.

"Got a nice long winch on it," she said. "I don't think that they thought it would get seen. Didn't think we'd use choppers."

"No," said Du Pré, "it wasn't important. If the dead people, their truck are found, Martin wants it found."

"That's a conspiracy," said Corey Banning. "Bingo. *They* means conspiracy."

Du Pré nodded.

"Other thing, I think that these people knew that those little fools were coming, and they spotted them and they followed them. Killed them. Make a point, them."

"Uh, huh ho ho," said Corey Banning. "And who here lives in both worlds?"

"Yeah, I guess we know now," said Du Pré.

"Whaddya think, Packy?" said Corey Banning. She grinned at him.

Packy looked blank. He looked away.

"I'm scared," he said. "I'm accused of something horrible. And you think I did it."

"Nope," said Corey Banning, "I don't think you did anything bad, Packy. Not at all. Not a moment. What I think, you little fucker, is that you know something you ain't telling us. Not even something you saw. Something you heard, I think. What did you hear, Packy?"

"Hear?"

"You move around a lot, Packy," said Corey Banning, "and the weather wasn't all that bad, the fall here. Why the fuck are you out there till three in the morning?"

"I do that a lot. It was dry, I do that a lot."

Corey Banning nodded.

She looked off into the distance.

"Who drives the damn truck, Packy?"

"The canner truck?" said Packy. "I do."

"*You do*," said Du Pré. "You son of a bitch, you quit playing your fucking games with me. Damn you."

"Look," said Packy, "I didn't do it and I just don't know if that truck was there that night. That's all I said. Now I'm tired of being yelled at. Take me home, damn it."

Du Pré looked at Packy. He looked at Corey Banning.

"Let him go," said Corey. "But, Packy, you stick around. And if I ask you a question, you bastard, you give me an answer. All of it."

Packy got out of the Rover and he limped off.

Du Pré rolled a cigarette. He lit it, offered a pinch of tobacco out the window.

"Give me some, too," said Corey Banning.

She did the same, mumbling.

"These people who were killed," said Du Pré, "they belong to some group want to take the West, make it over for them. That group decide, this night, we cut fences, we shoot cows. Maybe all of them aren't killed, maybe some they chicken out, you know."

Corey Banning nodded.

"At last," she said. "Useful work for my three dear friends in the trailer. Who's a member of Earth First or whatever who is also from here?"

"I hate this," said Du Pré. "I could maybe take them being mad. Not waiting on these kids like that, I cannot take that."

Corey held out her hand for Du Pré's tobacco and they smoked for a while. Du Pré reached under the seat, had some whiskey, put it back.

"Packy," said Du Pré, "he is some scared, you know."

"He should be," said Corey Banning.

"I am scared, too," said Du Pré.

"You should be, too," said Corey Banning.

"Why, you think?" said Du Pré.

" 'Fore this is over we are all going to find out things about our people we will really wish that we did not know," she said.

✤ CHAPTER 28 ✤

I don't give a shit you don't like it," said Bart.
Both of the St. Francis brothers were standing beside their canner truck. It was a lot bigger than the two of them so Bart and Du Pré could look at it anyway.

"How much cable you got on this thing?" said Bart.

"What's it to you?" said the St. Francis on the left.

"Listen, asshole," said Bart, "if I got to go get a warrant I'll be pissed off and I'll get a nice fat one and toss your fucking house, too. Now, how goddamn many feet of cable?"

He was looking at a big winch mounted on a high frame at the rear of the truck bed, over the stainless-steel bin.

"A hundred and fifty yards."

"Pull a couple ton?"

"Yeah. We never had to, but it could."

Bart walked over to the truck and he swung up to the winch drum and he grabbed the hook and undid the brake and pulled out three feet of it.

"My, my," said Bart. "Which one of your dead horses had dark green paint on it?"

"What?" said the same St. Francis.

"I said your fucking truck is impounded. Now get me the goddamn keys."

Du Pré raised his eyebrows.

So now we are going out the other side, the fog.

I liked it better in there, but the sun, it always come up, burn that fog away.

Now I carry that other nine-millimeter, too.

Shit.

"The damn keys are in it."

"I'll call you when you can have it back. There gas in this turkey?" said Bart. He looked blood mean.

"Full tank."

"You want to flip, see who drives the hearse?" said Bart.

"Nah," said Du Pré, "you can do it."

"What if I order you to?" said Bart.

"Ah," said Du Pré, "I guess you can still drive it, you know."

"I thought so," said Bart.

He clambered down and got in the cab and started the truck. It was well tuned and settled into a rolling hum quickly.

Du Pré drove on ahead to Cooper. He unlocked the gate at the impound lot and waited. It took Bart another fifteen minutes to get there.

"I believe we will share our newfound lead with our FBI friends," said Bart.

"Good," said Du Pré. "She scream when we don't do that."

They went in and called Corey Banning's office. She wasn't there. The flunky on duty patched Bart through.

"The meat wagon from those asshole St. Francis brothers has a cable winch. There is dark green paint on the three feet of cable just above the hook. The four-wheeler pulled out of the arroyo was dark green on the bottom. I think we have our first piece of actual evidence, if I can guess what evidence is."

"Sounds good," said Corey Banning. "Cut it off and send it to the State Crime Lab boys."

"It's late in the twentieth century," said Bart. "I believe there are girls there, too, actual medical examiners and like that."

"Anything else need to go?" she said, ignoring him.

"I'd say the whole thing. The bodies may have been hauled in the bin in back. It looked spotless. But you never know."

"Very thorough. Who's going to drive it over there?"

"How about one of your guys?"

"I wouldn't really trust them with a rubber duck," said Corey, "but if you insist."

"I do."

"OK."

"Where are you, anyway?" said Bart.

"Up on the bench."

"OK," said Bart, "why are you up on the bench?"

"Following Packy around. Just want to see if I can make him run a little."

Du Pré looked idly at the speakerphone on Bart's desk.

So many damn gadgets here now today. I don't like any of them.

"Well," said Bart, "you want to come in and look at this?"

"Nah," said Corey, "I'll call one of my bozos."

"OK," said Bart.

The speakerphone sounded with shattering glass and then popping sounds and then silence and gurgling.

Bart and Du Pré looked at each other.

"Oh, my God," said Bart.

They ran out to Du Pré's Rover. He gunned the engine and switched on the light bar and they shot along the road fast enough for the rear end to wallow.

"The damn bench is only twenty miles long, fer Chrissakes," yelled Bart. "*Where* on the bench? Where's the phone, damn it, I'll call Booger Tom."

Bart dialed and waited and waited and then he shouted into the phone.

"Not there," he said, shutting it off. "Booger Tom says Packy went on toward the Stemple place when he drove away, but he didn't talk to him so he isn't sure really where he was headed."

Du Pré turned to miss a dead porcupine and then swerved back. He gunned the engine again.

"I go down below and you watch the line up there," said Du Pré. "We can see a car easy, there is no trees there."

He took a fork in the road and raced back down to the county road in the bottom flats. Bart scanned the line of road up on the bench.

They drove and drove.

"There!" Bart said, pointing.

Corey Banning's big diesel pickup was up near a gravel pile on the bench road. Du Pré roared onto a cutoff that led up to it. They flew coming up over the top. Du Pré braked hard and they skidded to a stop behind her truck.

The rear window on the driver's side was shattered.

Du Pré went to the right, Bart to the left, guns out, looking at any nearby cover.

Du Pré looked in the cab.

Corey had fallen over toward the passenger seat, most of her head blown away. Her hair was thick with clotted blood. The phone was still in her hand.

"Damn," said Du Pré. "Now the shit really hit here."

He turned away and breathed heavily.

Pile of rocks down there in the field.

Rifle barrel sticking though them.

"Get down, Bart!" Du Pré screamed. He jerked one of his nine-millimeters from his holster and squeezed off several rounds at the rocks. Keep his fucking head down, you bet.

A slug slammed into the grille of the truck and whined off.

She probably had a rifle, that truck somewhere, Du Pré thought. He squirmed backward and reached up and opened the door.

A black hole appeared, just below the handle.

Very nice assault rifle, on clips in there, couple extra stacks for it.

Du Pré pulled it out.

He slithered over far to his right and edged slowly through the rank green grass at the edge of the road.

He set the sights on the rocks and he waited.

The rifle barrel moved a little.

Right there.

I hit that it ricochet on through, if he is aiming it, it kill him maybe.

Du Pré waited.

"Du Pré!"

"Yah, Bart!"

"What do I do?"

"Stay back, don't get shot."

There. I see that damn barrel twitch a little. I know.

Wish my eyes was good like I was twenty.

The barrel moved a little.

Du Pré squeezed off six rounds.

The barrel was gone.

"OK," said Du Pré, "I am going down the hill now. You stay back, you know, I got a better gun."

Du Pré coiled around, stood up and ran downhill suddenly.

Nothing moved there.

He went down to his knees and slammed onto his belly and snaked through the sage and grass.

He edged slowly around the rocks.

A hand, outstretched.

Gun stuck up on a sagebrush.

Du Pré stood up and moved around slowly.

"Damn," he said, looking down. "I want to arrest you, Packy, and I say no to myself, and then you do this. Shit."

He looked back up the hill.

No Bart. He must be calling.

Oh, shit.

Bye, Packy.

❖ CHAPTER 29 ❖

Du Pré sat on Benetsee's porch, leaning against the woodpile. His boots were in the iris shoaled round the old man's shack. Plants here grew well and close. The old man never tended them.

Du Pré rolled a cigarette and snapped his old brass lighter till it caught. Some hairs from his moustaches turned to ash in the flames. He inhaled tobacco and rank stink. He blew the mingled smokes out.

Ah, old man, I need you, I do not know what to do. Corey Banning, FBI, gets her head blown off and I kill poor Packy and now we got a dead FBI and a dead end and we got maybe fifty FBIs headed here and not even Bart and Lawyer Foote can stop them when one of theirs been killed. Even if the killer is killed, too.

Me, I know out there all them soldiers come back from some wars, they are looking to their guns and making sure they got the ammunition, take a lot of FBIs with them, and out there in the sheds and attics of my friends and neighbors there are assault rifles and machine guns and heavier stuff, too.

The Constitution, it say the government may not stop the people from having arms. Then the government, it argue, well, no machine guns for you or heavy artillery, bombs, grenades, bazookas, even sawed-off shotguns. We government, we can have them, but not you.

My friends and neighbors some say bullshit, Christ, I got no idea what they got out there, but I got, me, in my attic that MP-40 Catfoot bring back from the Second World War, I got that Russian assault rifle I buy and take to Dave the gunsmith who files down the sear and I got twenty-twenty five thousand rounds of ammunition for them both, nine-millimeter and the long cartridges in that funny curved clip, and I got fifty pounds of dynamite and diesel fuel and fertilizer and I can easy make a great big bang I want to.

There is somewhere around here two hundred them onetime rocket grenades, stolen from that Great Falls Armory. Couple twenty-millimeter cannon not counting the ones on that old warplane, that Lightning P-38, keeps driving the FAA nuts 'cause it is not registered but it is out there fully armed. I don't know who got that.

That's just the stuff I know about.

Corey Banning's brains splattered on the dashboard.

Packy not got no face when I get through with him, them rock chips see to that.

Time of the Blood Moon. Time of Sorrow.

They hurt my Madelaine, they hurt my Jacqueline, my people, I will kill every one of the sonsofbitches myself. Me, I am sick of these assholes, we were doing pret' good before some shitheads from the flat come here and cut fence, shoot cattle, get the government put them wolf up in the mountains. It is like you are leaned over your kitchen table some Sunday morning, bunch of preachers kick your door down, bang a gong make your headache worse, go through your whole house and when they are done then they stay, how nice, we will just live here, help you. You can be just like us.

Shit. Shit. Shit. Shit.

Goddamn twentieth century.

Nineteenth wasn't so fucking wonderful either.

Hope that Bart, he can keep his temper, too, he got one, them FBIs come here now they are out for blood. Don't care whose long they get some and a promotion, bigger office.

It is all so wrong.

Never would have happened, them fools stay home, don't come here, do what they did.

Du Pré heard the bull-roarer. He went around back to the sweat lodge. The flaps were up. The sound of the cedar shake on its rawhide string bellowed and died and bellowed again.

Old Benetsee, out from the house a ways, behind the lilacs and the red willows.

Du Pré walked through the bushes. The old man was squatting in the shade. A younger man, short and stocky, was whirling the bull-roarer overhead and Benetsee was either nodding or raising a finger. When he raised the finger the younger man stood up on tiptoes and put all of his strength to the task.

Du Pré squatted down beside Benetsee and he waited. The old man would speak when he wished to and not before.

They watched the apprentice for a while. Finally Benetsee stood up. The young Indian slumped wearily and the bull-roarer flapped to silence.

"Go out to this man's car," said Benetsee. "There is some wine in it. Some tobacco. Food."

"Just wine," said Du Pré.

The young man stretched for a moment and then he walked away.

"Pret' bad things," said Benetsee.

Du Pré nodded.

"They get a lot worse," said Du Pré.

"Maybe not," said Benetsee. "Maybe I go and talk with them."

"Huh?" said Du Pré. "You remember last time? They come here, I have to jam my gun, a neck, before they remember their fucking manners. Why you think they got better, last week?"

The apprentice came back with the wine and a big canning jar. He poured Benetsee a staggering draft and set the jug down and went off out of sight behind the trees over the little creek.

"You got a very bad temper, my son," said Benetsee.

Never call me that before, Du Pré thought. I be getting some good advice now, you bet. Probably better than I want to hear.

Pretty crazy, all around here now. Watch the earth go mad, maybe. I could use a big earthquake.

"Well," said Benetsee, "maybe we go on down to Susan's, get me a cheeseburger. You know, I have two young men show up this morning, long hair, expensive clothes, they want to go on vision quest."

Du Pré waited.

"I send them, Benjamin Medicine Eagle, he does that sort of thing."

Du Pré laughed.

"What they say?"

"Nothing," said Benetsee. "I tell them, me, I do only circumcisions. Benjamin Medicine Eagle, he is their man."

Du Pré howled. He roared.

"We go now," said Benetsee. He stood up, scratched the back of his neck.

Benetsee went into his shack and he came out with the red

nylon envelope that held the eagle's wing he had taken from the fools in winter. He swung the flat red package by a loop at one end, idly.

"Ah, good," he said. "We smoke now."

Du Pré rolled and lit two cigarettes and then he drove off toward Toussaint.

There were four government car-pool cars parked out in front of the bar, and eight men standing by the front door. Susan Klein was standing in the doorway, shaking her head.

Du Pré pinned the badge on his leather jacket. He and Benetsee got out. The FBI agents turned and looked curiously. One of them came round the hood of the far right car, walking easily, a tall, very dark man.

Lot of Indian blood, him, thought Du Pré. The man glanced off to his right.

Long earlobes. Lot of Indian blood.

"Special Agent in Charge Harvey Wallace," said the agent, extending a hand to Benetsee. "How are you, Uncle?" He looked down at the ground politely, waiting.

Couple minutes now, Du Pré thought, then Benetsee speak. This FBI is Indian some. Knows to respect the old, they know things.

"You long way from your people," said Benetsee. "You go back there often."

The agent nodded.

"I'm Wallace in white world," he said, dropping into Blackfeet. "I am Weasel Fat in Indian."

"Ah," said Benetsee. "We maybe go talk to Susan, there, she is some upset, I know, maybe smooth things down. Less noisy."

"Good," said Harvey Wallace.

The two men walked over to Susan Klein, still blocking her front door. Du Pré followed. The other agents looked at him, looked away after they spotted his Sheriff's badge.

"Afternoon, ma'am," said Harvey Wallace to Susan. He turned and passed Du Pré and began to speak very quietly to the men. They got in the cars and went off in opposite directions, two cars each one.

Harvey Wallace, Du Pré thought. This is one tough son of a bitch.

Du Pré was still standing outside. Harvey Wallace walked up to him, rubbing a long finger on the side of his nose, looking at the ground.

He looked up suddenly. Very black eyes, very sad ones.

"Gabriel Du Pré," he said, "Corey Banning thought a lot of you. She respected the spot you were in, too. This is a very bad business. And I need your help."

Du Pré waited.

"We must uphold the law," said Harvey Wallace, "and I am charged with doing that and I will. And it must be done in such a way that we don't start a war."

Du Pré let out his breath.

"Do us all a favor," said Wallace, "and don't kill anybody else. Poor Packy might have led us to the killers. Might not. I know he was shooting at you, but in future, please just run. I need suspected killers and their accomplices alive. Dead, they merely pose more questions."

Du Pré nodded. Well, me, I don't back away, a fight, so good.

"Let me buy you lunch," said Harvey Wallace.

✤ CHAPTER 30 ✤

Maybe they've changed," said Bart.

Du Pré shrugged.

"All it take, one of them fuck up it all goes," said Du Pré. "They got at least an idea now, maybe they don't be such assholes, but even then some of these ranchers, pretty brushy, they don't like *anybody* mess with them."

"I like Agent Wallace," said Bart.

"Him pretty good," said Du Pré, "but that's just him. They got ten others east, twenty more north, and twenty here. All it takes, one of them piss off somebody. Our people, here, they are mighty hard to piss off. Oh, yes. Most of them, you know, you send them half a wrong look, you are very dead now."

"Foote calls this the hot rug treatment. You roll the rug out over everything and then wait, and see what scurries out the sides."

"They don't scurry, I think," said Du Pré. "I think maybe they dig them foxhole."

"Christ, I am tired," said Bart.

"October, it seems a long time ago," said Du Pré.

"It was a long time ago," said Bart. "We weren't old men last October. You know I have not thought one thing about anything but death. Sixteen of them, and then the two in the car accident. Nice, normal deaths, those were. Pleasant ones, you know. Just two drunk kids missed a turn."

"Who lives, both worlds?" said Du Pré.

"Eh?"

"That Corey Banning," said Du Pré, "she said that, we were talking, I wondered, you know, these people were shot cutting the fences that night, but Stemples, they come to me before and tell me about shot cattle, cut fence. And the St. Francis brothers. Then they are gone the night the two are killed, then the car is dumped, them in it, probably lowered down, the canner truck."

"If," said Bart.

"I never look at that ME's report on them two," said Du Pré.

"Neither did I," said Bart.

"What?"

"I don't remember that we ever got it," said Bart, "or if we did I never saw it. Things were a bit hectic."

Bart went to the telephone. Du Pré went outside to smoke and look at the spring.

Pretty time, this is. But I can't see it.

Bart slammed out of the Sheriff's building, cursing.

"He sent it to Corey," said Bart, "and she promised to give us a copy right away, save the ME time and postage. She didn't, of course."

"Ah," said Du Pré. Corey, Corey, you weren't dead I'd yell at you.

"Anyway," said Bart, "they both died of gunshot wounds. But he could not fix a time of death, at all, because their bodies were refrigerated. Not frozen, just chilled, he thought. If they were kept at just above freezing, he couldn't give us any time, and so he didn't."

"Now them Stemple got no alibi," said Du Pré.

"They don't need one, at the moment," said Bart, "and Corey interviewed them over and over."

"Ah," said Du Pré. "Well, maybe this Harvey guy give us that file."

"I'll see," said Bart. "No, we'll both see. The ME was faxing us his report. Should be here. I'll be right out."

"Well," said Du Pré, "I bet you the woman was messed with and I bet you it was those fucking St. Francis brothers. And I bet you Corey was after poor Packy 'cause she knew he knew more'n he'd tell."

Bart went in and came right back out, holding papers.

"You care to drive, Mon Sewer?"

"OK."

"Well," said Bart, "I'm right. Now if Cousin Weasel Fat will share like a bighearted guy, which I am sure he is, we can maybe do something right for once. I haven't had so much experience of that in life, I am hungry for it."

Wallace was standing in the parking lot in front of the FBI trailers. He waved as they pulled in. Du Pré slowed to a crawl so he didn't splash mud on Wallace's suit.

"Good to see you," said Wallace. "And you won't believe it, but I was going to call this afternoon and apologize and explain that my predecessor failed to take you into her confidence. I really don't know why. We are a kinder, gentler FBI these days, to our brother officers. And if you believe that horseshit you deserve what you get."

"I goddamn know it is those St. Francis brothers," said Du Pré. "They kill those fool kids, stick them in the meat cooler they got, hide their car, dump it after they know about the others."

"No," said Bart, "the time doesn't work."

"It does if they are in jail and poor Packy is stuck with it," said Du Pré. "It work just fine. He brings the damn dog back, too."

Only person I am liking in all of this is the dog, thought Du Pré. Me included.

"She had that," said Wallace, "but she needed something more, and she was after it when Packy cracked and killed her. What, I don't know. But the St. Francis brothers are slobs and fools and we will be dropping in on them at about four this morning waving warrants. They're fuckups. I like fuckups. I can't catch the good ones, they make lists and like that. Dos and don'ts. First thing, you murder someone, don't overcomplicate it. Kill 'em, get rid of the weapon, answer all questions sort of, and you're ally ally oxen free."

"OK," said Bart. "Now, I don't give a rat's ass about us getting glorious arrests. I won't run for reelection. I don't care about even a bit of the credit. But I would sure like this not to turn into a war, you know, and peace I will have, whatever it takes."

Harvey Wallace looked at Bart for a long moment.

He grinned.

He stuck out his hand.

"How nice," he said, "that you'd like to avoid mass slaughter. Now, would you care to speculate as to just how many wholly illegal automatic weapons right on up to cannon there are out there? There's one P-thirty-eight, four fifty-caliber Brownings and a twenty-millimeter cannon, and two Mustangs. The late models, also with cannon. Where, I do not know. There's all sorts of soldiers, and this state produced an uncommon lot of Lurps and SEALS and demolitions champions. They don't like governments, cops, daytime TV, fluoride in their water, Democrats, big words, and especially they don't like arrogant pricks from Washington, D.C."

Bart laughed.

"But I will have these murderers. Because if we can't find them this is going to be a sport out here, like clubbing jackrabbits and shooting gophers of an idle Sunday. We can't have that, you will admit."

Bart and Du Pré nodded.

"Nobody around here's dumb enough to do anything with the St. Francis brothers. We bust them, dead end, right? My esteemed colleagues to the east and north will perhaps find out something about the vagaries of Montana, but not much else. The Martins need not talk. The folk to the north present a united front of silence."

"It's wrong," said Bart.

"What the fuck does *that* have to do with anything?" said Wallace. "Point is, no one did it for revenge or gain, it just sort of happened, other'n the St. Francis brothers, and so no one will speak. And there's nothing in it for them, anyway. You hate someone these days, give 'em a cow. Nobody *wants* the neighbor's ranch. Can't even hope for anyone to covet enough to drop a damn dime. Nope."

"I got a thought," said Du Pré. "Them two killed on the first night? We were wondering, maybe there is a Martin kid, some kid spying on these people, tipped the Martins off, said, well, these fools all plan to cut fences, this night."

"Good," said Wallace.

"Kid is maybe an environmentalist member, you know, even helps plan it."

"Excellent," said Wallace.

"You think of it?" said Du Pré.

"We did, and the little bitch is Angela Green, one Harold Green having married a Martin sister. Big wheeze in environmental lunacies. She calls home regularly, nothing much there."

"Young kid?"

"Twenty-three."

"You talk to her?"

"Oh, we talked to her a lot. See, she gives passionate speeches about running cattle off the public lands, bringing back the buffalo, and what pigs ranchers are. Good speaker, too. I've heard her a bunch of times."

"Her parents are not mad at her?"

"Parents love their kids, even unto Murder One and such," said Harvey. "Interesting, though, how she howls and yells about destroying them but she comes here in the summer to help out. The old homestead."

"What'd she say?" said Bart.

"Oh," said Wallace, "she said her business was hers and her parents' business was theirs and now please fuck off and get out of my face."

"Uh," said Du Pré. "She sounds a real Montana girl, her."

"Right down to her custom boots," said Wallace. "And we even got to the idiots who planned this spree of cattle shooting and fence cutting that got sixteen people killed. If you count the mourners the avalanche got and the bear ate."

Bart and Du Pré waited.

"She rigorously opposed that course of action and so they went off to plan their suicides in more sympathetic surroundings."

"How would she know the date?" said Bart.

"She's a spectacularly beautiful woman," said Wallace.

"I see," said Bart.

✤ CHAPTER 31 ✤

I am sick worried, you," said Madelaine. "All this time you are getting thin, you don't smile, you smoke too much, there, you drink that whiskey, and you don't drink it for fun."

"I am sorry," said Du Pré. "This whole business, you know, the place I live blowing all apart, nothing will ever be the same now, you know. I don't see you, I don't see my daughter, grandchildren, all, I don't play the damn fiddle, I am not Du Pré anymore, you are right."

"Well," said Madelaine, "us Métis we are here, Montana, sure by 1700. That Lewis and Clark Expedition it come, we are here, we draw them map and give it to Blackfeet to give to them because we are Métis and if we give it then we are betrayers. So there has been lot of blood, you know. My great-great-great-grandfather was that Mitch Bouyer, he send the other Métis scouts away and he go down the hill, die with Custer. So it is not the first time and you are not God and you can't stop everything. I tell you you going to play that damn fiddle Susan's this afternoon for sure. Or I cry and cry and cry till you so miserable you cry, too. I do that, Du Pré. You are dying right in front of me, I will not let you."

"I feel pretty good," said Du Pré.

"Shit you feel pretty good. Your friends, enemies, neighbors, they are some of them murderers. You damn near die, avalanche, you know you toss in the night and sweat some. You lie there, I get towels, mop you off."

"Oh," said Du Pré.

"I already know you are a hero," said Madelaine. "I don't need to hear it more."

"OK," said Du Pré.

"I got your fiddle. I buy new strings for it. I put them on as good as I can. Now you tune it, you take your Madelaine, the bar, we have some drinks, I listen to you play, I even make you a nice red shirt, send away, one of them paisley scarves. You wear them, please. We go, have some good time, come back here, fuck, and you *sleep*."

Du Pré took a hot shower and he put on clean jeans and his new shirt and knotted his scarf and they drove down to the Toussaint Bar. He grabbed his old rawhide fiddle case with the porcupine-quill stars on it all worn away and he carried it in. There weren't any other cars there, odd for a Sunday afternoon.

Du Pré held the door open for Madelaine. He stepped inside.

Fifty friends sat there silently. There was a big table all covered with food, a whole pig on a huge wooden platter, one his father Catfoot had carved from a big piece of basswood he had sent off for.

Cousin LeBlanc from Canada was there with his accordion.

Cousin Beauharne from North Dakota with his guitar and harmonica and his dancing shoes. He did the old Métis dances, old as the Romans.

Bunch of people, good people.

"You get that big drink, Du Pré," said Cousin LeBlanc, "then we play that good music."

Du Pré looked round, somewhat shocked. The Stemples were there and the Moores and many other couples, some of them Du Pré thought might have had something to do with the murders. But they were here and they seemed happy.

If old Benetsee was here, I would like that, Du Pré thought, I need him very much now. What is in this that I cannot see, or don't want to? Who am I to decide this? What do I do, I don't know.

Play some music, my friends. Drink some whiskey and love my woman. Forget death for some time now and let some good things be remembered.

Du Pré felt a tug on his right sleeve. He looked over and there stood Benetsee, grinning, holding out a huge glass of whiskey and ice.

"You play them song, the voyageur," said Benetsee. "They go through that dark forest, they die in the black water, but they sing and fiddle there, Du Pré, you give me tobacco and you drink and fiddle."

Du Pré rolled them each a cigarette and lit them and he had a pull of whiskey and he put his arm on Benetsee's shoulders.

"Old man," he said, "I . . . we got to stop this now, you know, the women will have many tears and the children misfortunes. What do we do?"

"Good," said Benetsee.

"What good?"

"You always asking me what *you* to do, never us," said Benetsee. "Pretty dumb, you are."

"Hey!" said Cousin LeBlanc, "You tune that fiddle, yes, we play them paddle songs, pack carry songs, you know the one about the bet, carry them pack on the portage?"

I grow up to I'm three I know it, Du Pré thought, how many hundred-pound packs the voyageur carry, huh? Three, sometimes four, but this song they say they carry ten, half a ton, roll home on their balls, I guess.

The strong portage.

Du Pré pulled on the new strings to stretch them, ran the blob of rosin over the finger lengths. He tuned, sending the strings far sharp and letting them down to pitch.

Cousin Beauharne began to pick bass lines, Cousin LeBlanc let the bellows out, Du Pré fiddled. A young couple, Métis, Du Pré didn't know them, got out on the floor and began to dance, heel and toe, the old tapping.

We do that, the buffalo robes pegged on the ground. The decks of the little ships bring us first here, some say we were in that Gulf of St. Lawrence by 1200, maybe. Running from them damn priests and tax gatherers. Lot of cabin foundations all over the north Rockies go so far back the Cheyennes, they was still in Iowa raising pumpkins and corn.

Pretty old music, pretty old blood.

I go to Brittany sometime.

The song ended. LeBlanc and Beauharne looked at Du Pré. Gabriel drew one long note out of his fiddle and then he started a lament, one the voyageurs sang, about the women they had left behind who weren't pulling on the rope to help them back; they were sparking with the soldiers who never left the fort.

Maybe even not building them canoe so tight for their voyageurs, so that the canoe come apart, the Big Rapids, the voyageurs they drown. All the voyageur hearts in a big brass kettle, lost at the foot of the rapids, their souls like smoke underwater, forever reaching for and never rising to the light.

Pretty tough times.

More people got out on the dance floor. The young couple put arms across the shoulders of others who wanted to learn and taught them the steps quarter-time. Everybody laughed, everybody danced.

Du Pré looked up to see Jacqueline and Raymond come in. His daughter pregnant again, this would be the last, though, the doctor said. It would be twelve. She had two sets of twins.

But she laughed and she danced with her Raymond and Du Pré felt very proud, he looked at her and played one song just for her and everyone else stopped dancing but Raymond and Jacqueline.

Du Pré was running sweat. He stopped and wiped his face and set his fiddle down. LeBlanc and Beauharne went on, moving the tempo up a little every third bar. The choruses rounded and backed together.

Du Pré made his way to the bar. Madelaine was sitting on a stool, smiling like a June bride.

"It is my Du Pré," she said, "my Gabriel, not the old grouch, always mumbling, himself. Ah. You have not forgot to play that fiddle. Give my Du Pré a good red shirt and some whiskey and he will play that fiddle, hah."

Du Pré grinned. He looked down the bar and saw Bart behind it, pulling beers and mixing drinks. Harvey Wallace was at the far end, wearing jeans and boots today, smiling.

Du Pré had some whiskey and a cigarette.

He went back up to the bandstand and he picked up his fiddle and he fiddled a fisher's jig. The Métis were great fishermen. Pull them pike up, split them and smoke them, get them salmon and them big trout.

LeBlanc and Beauharne put down their instruments.

Old Benetsee shuffled up to the stage and he sat down on the front of it and he pulled a fresh-made willow flute from his jacket and he blew into it softly for a few moments, his gnarled old fingers seeking out the holes.

He played. It was a tune like no other that Du Pré had ever

heard, the scale strange, the rhythm deep and turning round and the notes soft and piercing all at once.

The old man's face was shadowed underneath his stained old hat. The red willow stem stuck down. His fingers rose and clamped again and the crowd sat silent, transfixed, breathing softly if at all.

I have never heard this old man do this, Du Pré thought, how much else is buried deep within him? I don't even know how old he is.

I do not know.

He has sometimes made me very angry.

I might as well be angry at the Red River.

Shadows or the ghosts of buffalo.

Old blood.

Help me.

❖ CHAPTER 32 ❖

We just flat may never know at all," said Bart.

Harvey Wallace sipped his coffee and he blew out a long stream of blue smoke from his mouth. He set his pipe down in the ashtray.

"Could be," he said, "but you put enough glue around, your fly steps in it. Except for one thing. This isn't a crime done by just one person for just one reason. Those fool kids came out here and stepped right down into the crack between the old time and the new. Angela Green keeps making speeches damning what her family's done for six generations, and they still send her three grand a month. So go figure. I can't indict indulgent parents."

"Is it really true that that fool Governor had a bear killed over west of Glacier? Flown here and dumped so he could claim the bear that ate the folks killed in the avalanche had been killed?"

"I don't even need to check," said Harvey Wallace. "It's true. I know in my bones. I know in my dick. I know it better than my own name. I have worked in government service lo these many years and I tell you this is true."

"Yah," said Du Pré, "that Old Black Claws he is gone, sure. I miss him, he used to come round, I am up there, see who I am. A gentleman. Other'n he eat ol' Jimmy Moore's big dray horse that one time."

"Huh?" said Bart.

"You were . . . uh . . . not here," said Du Pré. "When them grizzly are all protected, the federal government, one time, Old Black Claws he is much hungry, he come down in the late spring, climb the fence, old Moore's horse pasture, drive his big Percheron stud into the corner, break his neck, one swipe of his paw."

Du Pré took a drag of his smoke.

"Old Jimmy, he is looking out the window, he see this, he cuss some awful, pull on his boots, go to get his rifle, shoot that bear. Jimmy's wife, she say, no, you can't shoot that bear, big trouble, put you in jail. You call them Fish and Game."

"Hoo boy," said Harvey Wallace.

"So Jimmy he does and they are not there, phone ring, finally he get some kid who say, 'Are you sure it is a grizzly?'

"Jimmy, he say yes, he know what a grizzly is. Kid says, 'You sure it kill your horse? Your horse didn't just die, that bear eating it, helping clean up?'

"Jimmy, he say a bunch of things before he tear the phone out of the wall and then he get his gun but by then Old Black Claws, he has dragged the stud horse through the fence and up the canyon and so Jimmy he just shrug and say, 'Well, I guess that old bastard was hungry.' "

"Jesus," said Bart.

"Yeah," said Harvey Wallace, "kid must have watched that dumb TV show, the one with the bear eats soybeans or something."

"But why," said Bart, "would Black Claws just up and leave? Benetsee said he went north? So, how'd he get the idea?"

Du Pré shrugged. He didn't want to talk about it.

Booger Tom stomped through the front door and back through the living room to the kitchen where the three younger men were sitting.

"Goddamn lawn forcement," he said. "Ever' time I turn round there's another one a ya spoilsports. When do the preachers start stampedin' in? The company around here gets lower and lower."

"We were talking about lynching someone, for the practice," said Bart. "Watch your damn mouth."

"Any a you geniuses figger out who done all of this yet?" said Booger Tom. "Or I got to do that for you, too?"

The phone rang. Bart picked it up, listened, hung up after saying only "Christ, yeah, right there."

"What?" said Harvey.

"Oh, one of my good upstanding local citizens is holed up in his machine shed, armed to the teeth, while two of your guys, Harvey, are crouched behind their car pointing guns at the guy in the shed while he points a gun at them. Mexican standoff, but I think we had better haul ass."

"Who?" said Harvey. "What are my guys doing there, anyway?"

"Asking questions," said Bart, moving for the door.

"That does it," said Harvey. "I'll just have them mail out questionnaires from now on, prepared confessions."

Du Pré laughed.

"My guys won't shoot unless they get shot at," said Harvey.

"Not comforting," said Bart.

"Where are they?" said Du Pré.

"Well," said Bart, "Benny Klein is in his machine shed and the two FBI guys are behind their car. Susan is in the house, watching. She's so pissed I think when the FBI guys leave Benny will stay barricaded in there anyway."

Du Pré drove them rapidly toward Benny's. It wasn't that far. He turned in the driveway and saw the light blue government motor-pool car and the two agents crouched behind it.

Bart and Harvey got out and sauntered up to the agents.

"Benny!" Bart yelled. "Cut the crap and come on out. Jesus Christ, man, what the fuck are you doing?"

"I wanna be on *Sixty Minutes*," said Benny. He emerged from the shed in a filthy coverall, carrying a steel box wrench. "They hollered, I come out of the shed here with my Magnum *wrench* in hand, and they go for their guns and I dive back in the shop and here I am. Wanna have me tighten down your fucking gaskets, you morons?" He glared at the agents, who looked at the ground.

"Magnum what?" said Bart.

"The box wrench," said Benny. "Look, I don't blame them. Everybody here is wound about nine cranks too tight, you know. Susan is in the house there, probably got a bead drawn on their heads."

"Yes!" said Susan, from behind the paint shed, fifteen feet from the government car. She stepped out, carrying a pump sawed-off shotgun.

"I think that I go down the bar, have a drink," said Du Pré. "You know it is pretty bad when the former Sheriff and his wife, they are about to declare war on the U.S. government."

"Former Sheriff," sighed Harvey Wallace.

"Damn it," said one of the agents, "it was all a mistake. I saw the flash of metal and I dove."

"I'm sorry," said Benny. "I wasn't thinking how scared you are of wrenches. All this is going to lead to is some more folks getting killed, Bart. Nobody's gonna get nowhere but us who lives here. Nowhere."

"OK, guys," said Harvey Wallace, "go pull in your fellow agents. Pack it in, head for Billings, do it right now. I'll call you later. Don't even go back to check and see the door's latched."

"Suits me," said the other agent. "This is bullshit."

They drove off.

"My job just showed the first signs of creeping death," said

Harvey Wallace. "I now have to tell my superiors that our best course of action is to leave. They will not like it, but it is so."

"I'm sorry," said Bart.

"I, uh, never learned that the toes you step on today may be connected to the ass you need to kiss tomorrow," said Harvey. "And I believe that you have a means of getting to the Attorney General of the United States. Bart? It is a matter of life and death."

"I'll call lawyer Charles Foote," said Bart. "Tell him either get you guys out of here or he has to come here himself."

"He hates it that much?" said Harvey.

"He likes to say so," said Bart. He walked off with his telephone.

"Get them all out of here, I hope," said Du Pré. "I think sometime the whole air gone crazy, all you got to do is breathe it and you are nuts."

"That kind of time," said Harvey.

"Angela Green," said Du Pré.

"Only hope," said Harvey, "you get that little girl to sing a nice clear song and we are someplace. Not, forget it. It's the Martins and their allies, whoever, a few rich ranchers to the north. You know how I know that? Poor folks make threats; rich folks do things and smile. That's all, folks."

Poor folks act like people, rich folks act like governments, thought Du Pré. Damn, I thought that my own self.

"She ain't in my jurisdiction," said Bart, "and I think the next Sheriff over is in on all this, anyway."

"Probably," said Harvey.

"Christ," said Bart.

"Yeah," said Harvey, "this is a dog, sure enough. All kinds of leads but they don't go anywhere. Funny thing about conspiracies like this, what with our system of civil liberties and proof beyond a reasonable doubt, it's almost impossible to break one of 'em."

"What about the Mafia?" said Du Pré.

"Idiots," said Harvey. "They'd make more money driving trucks."

"Angela Green," said Bart.

"All you got," said Harvey.

"What exactly *have* you got?" said Bart.

"Come look at it," said Harvey, "but you just never tell anyone I let you peek at it."

❧ CHAPTER 33 ❧

I am needing your help, old man," yelled Du Pré. He sat down and waited for the old man to come.

Some shit, this, I don't believe, me, one minute that Harvey Weasel Fat gone away all nice. But Benetsee say that the killing is all through, there will be no more. I don't understand what he mean, I never have till later. What he say only make sense looking back.

I want to maybe ride horses with my Madelaine, go up in the Wolf Mountains, see maybe my grandfather's ghost, find some place there is a tree that shouldn't grow there. Look at them old mine, where someone hoped till their money it was all gone. That little place high up on Toussaint Peak, where the turquoise lies all around, chunks of it, some dark green, some blue, some almost white.

I wonder what just shoved them Wolf Mountains right up out of the plains, it is down there, though. Got very big shoulders, it.

I dream now, I am out in the snow forever on a piss-flat plain, me a little black thing struggling through the deep snow toward the horizon, flat white line, not even any damn wind, just me and nothing at all.

Maybe this is why them voyageur songs, they are all mostly sad. The ones for dancing with your women, they are not sad, but the others they are, long haul in the canoe for the Here Before Christ, them Hudson's Bay Company bastards.

Long time, much blood, we fight a war there, Selkirk Colony, we fight a war here now, and there is sadness. All them people dead and their parents crying for them and they don't understand.

Me, my Jacqueline, my Maria, Madelaine, they are dead I will not understand either.

Some shit, this.

Them damn dead fools they stay home they be alive and still be fools.

Piss me off. All of it.

Got good reasons break the law, it is still a broken law.

Du Pré wandered back to his Rover, fished around under the seat, pulled out a fifth of whiskey. He had a slug and looked up at the Wolfs, the snow on the peaks. The wind had changed and it was blowing down from them, thick with fresh pine.

I dream of flowers growing out of the eye pits of skulls, I dream of bears under the ice and snow, I dream of wolf cubs stolen and raised in cages, far from the north where they are free.

I dream of young fools knowing for a few seconds maybe how little time they had to live.

They would have been surprised. They would not have believed it.

Us people we do not believe in death. That is something, it happen to other people.

He rolled a cigarette. Far off down the road there was the jangling whine of a VW engine. It came closer. It slowed.

An old VW bus, painted with ordinary house paint, the usual peace symbols and slogans.

A long-haired young man got out. He waved limply to Du Pré and he walked up the drive to the Rover, round it, and he walked up to Du Pré and around him and on to the porch and he banged hard on the old door.

Du Pré looked off at the middle distance.

"Hey, man," the longhair said, "you know where the shaman is?"

"At the dentist's," said Du Pré, "get a tooth pulled."

"Oh," said the longhair. "Who are you?"

"I'm the other shaman," said Du Pré. "My teeth, they are all right."

"Oh, yeah, cool," said the longhair. "Lissen, I want to go on a vision quest, you dig, and I wanted to see the shaman, you know."

"Oh, yes," said Du Pré.

"This is Benjamin Medicine Eagle's place, right?"

"Oh, yes," said Du Pré, "but he is not here. I maybe can help you."

"Cool," said the longhair. "I mean, I don't know where the fucking butte is, man, where I got to go for the vision."

"It is up that canyon," said Du Pré, pointing up toward a cut in the flanks of the Wolfs. "Not very big."

Big thunderstorm coming in, just hit the mountains, though, thought Du Pré, big one, hit maybe two hours.

It was a nice warm day.

"Listen," said Du Pré, pulling up a handful of dried fallow grass, "you take this up that canyon, you see a little butte right ahead of you, you get on top and light this sweet grass, very holy grass, lie down, wait there. Maybe all night, next day, next night, too."

"Yeah," said the longhair, "I know it's tough. I seen *Dances with Wolves* ten times, you know."

"Oh, yes," said Du Pré. He had laughed so hard at the wrong times that the manager of the theater in Billings threw him out.

Good thing, too, me, I don't sometime like them Sioux, but that movie, pretty insulting, you know. Make them look like a bunch of idiots, no blood to them either.

"You can't wear no white-man stuff," said Du Pré, "no blankets. You got any furs, your truck there?"

"Furs are cruel," said the longhair.

"Well," said Du Pré, "I give you my blessing. You got to hurry now, you know, you aren't there before the sun is off that peak there, you got to wait till tomorrow."

"Thanks, man!" said the longhair.

He drove off and Du Pré watched the VW turn and go up the Forest Service road. He went to his Rover and got his binoculars and he watched the longhair take off all his clothes and then put on his shoes and walk up the trail toward the little butte stuck in the throat of the canyon.

Good place, that top of that butte. Thunderstorm hit, it is always hit by lightning, it is scorched and burnt up there, the rock.

The clouds were bunching black and rising above the Wolfs. They flashed inside, dark purple in the black.

Oh, I am a prick, Du Pré thought, but I was drove to it.

Du Pré had another draw on the bottle of whiskey.

I am never see my Madelaine, I don't see my daughter, I have not talked to my other daughter in weeks, I am losing all my life I care for.

What do I do?

Bart, me, we can't quit. We are not going to find out nothing we can use and that Harvey Weasel Fat, he can piss up a rope, stand under it while it dries, you know.

A whistle.

Falcon whistle. Prairie falcon, hunting, hunting.

Poor Corey Banning, she dive so fast she hit the rock.

What?

I need this old man now, tell me what to do. If he know. Not always he does know, maybe just them riddles.

Old Black Claws, he gone north.

Shit.

Du Pré heard some thunder, distant, deep. He walked to where he could see the whole of the Wolfs stretched out east to west, rising from the red and yellow plains. Island in the sky, there.

The clouds sent a lash of black rain down; lightning stitched the canyons, struck along the ridges.

Been up on them a couple times, that hit, the rocks blow up like grenades. Five-hundred-pound grenades.

Some movement up that little canyon.

Du Pré put the binoculars to his eyes.

The naked longhair was running flat-out down the trail toward his VW. A young grizzly was chasing him, maybe two hundred yards behind, so the bear was just having a little fun.

I call you Young Black Claws, thought Du Pré, this is very good, I am feeling some better now.

A grip on his elbow.

"Eh?" said Benetsee. "You got nothing better to do, tease some poor white fool like that? He wants to be Indian. I don't know why anybody wants be something else. What's the use? You got me wine?"

Du Pré nodded. He handed the old man his tobacco pouch and he went to the Rover and fished out a gallon jug of horrible cheap fizzy wine and he brought it back and picked up a jar out of the grass and shook out the beetles in it and he filled it and gave it to Benetsee.

The old man drained it.

He put his cigarette in his mouth and waited for Du Pré to light it.

The VW screamed past.

"Funny times," said Benetsee.

"No shit," said Du Pré. "Me, I am not laughing so much."

"This land, pretty quiet for a long time. It be quiet again," said Benetsee. "Don't do it by your time, though. You wait."

"OK," said Du Pré. "But I can't see myself no more, you know."

"OK," said Benetsee. "I wonder when you ask. You got questions."

Du Pré nodded.

"Go sleep, your grandfathers."

"They are in the little cemetery, Toussaint," said Du Pré.

"They got their holes," said Benetsee. "You go, take your blanket, you know. Give some tobacco, little sweet grass, say a prayer with that Father Van Den Heuvel, he is good man."

"OK," said Du Pré.

"OK?" said Benetsee.

❖ CHAPTER 34 ❖

A h," said Madelaine, "well, I am maybe having some hope of seeing my Du Pré maybe. I have not, nearly a year now, you know. I see . . . well, I go pray. You see your grandfathers, you say hello, your Madelaine maybe not let you back in the house some soon day."

Du Pré nodded. The jukebox was blaring and a couple of people were playing pool at Susan's. Not much else. It was an early June night warm with crickets and the scent of the tangled little roses that grew in the little draws near the water.

That Custer, his men, that is the smell they die in, that and dust, the Little Bighorn, Du Pré thought. What a dumb man, him. That Mitch Bouyer, he die with Custer. Us Métis, we die a lot, white-man quarrels, die a lot, Indian quarrels, weren't for all them sons-ofbitches we live a long goddamn time, you bet.

The door opened and Harvey Wallace padded in. He wore running shoes and old clothes and a windbreaker to hide his gun.

Ol' Harvey Weasel Fat, I am think he could paint his face I'd feel better, thought Du Pré, them Blackfeet chase you clear home. Then they wait. Chew on a little jerky. Lie in the river, breathe through a reed. Lie by the horses, covered in grass, you walk over them up them come, stab you, left thigh inside high, slash the artery, you whirl, right wrist, then your throat.

Who told me all this? I don't know.

Harvey sat down with them, a soda in his hand.

"Madelaine," he said, "how are you this fine evening? You want to dance maybe?" He spoke good Coyote French, too.

Madelaine smiled and she got up and they danced by the jukebox.

Du Pré watched, sipped his drink.

Good woman. I am such a pain in the ass, big one, lately, maybe she take up with Harvey Weasel Fat. No, she like me OK. She is just worried some.

Du Pré went to the bar, got another drink, another pink wine for Madelaine.

Harvey and Madelaine came back to the table. She sat down and had a drink of her pink wine. Harvey stood and drained his soda.

"I been a cop worse places," said Harvey.

"There are lots of them," said Du Pré. "You know, Harvey, I don't think some that we ever find out sometimes. That Bart, he is a madman, do his job good, all of it. We ask and ask but no one here say anything. Nobody is bragging. Nobody."

"Yeah," said Harvey, "well, I like to fish. Sometimes I won't even bait the hook, you know, I like to fish so much, not be disturbed."

Du Pré nodded.

"That evening rise is starting," said Harvey, "and I am going to fish on the bottom. You know, I talked to poor Packy's wife and I don't think now Packy had anything to do with anything. Just a short fuse and poor Corey lit it. Ya never know. Guy just snapped."

Du Pré nodded.

Yah, well, Packy he do whatever his sweet government tell him, he get scared, he stop it some for just a little while. Too bad, he was pretty good guy and he got kids, wife, all left and no money. I got to talk to Bart about that.

Susan and Benny came out of the back with plates. They sat at the table next to Du Pré and Madelaine, to eat dinner early before the rush started, if it ever did. When the nights were so short and the days long and the light hung in the west until nearly eleven at night the bar did a slender business.

"Lo, Harvey," said Susan. "You want something?"

"No, no," said Harvey, "you eat. If someone comes in I'll get them whatever."

Susan nodded. She had a forkful of meatloaf, the night's special.

"Harvey," said Benny, "you don't hit seventeen, you play the dealer."

Harvey nodded.

Du Pré sipped his drink, rolled a smoke. He lit it, lit Madelaine's filter tip. They smoked and held hands.

"That a message?" said Harvey.

"Line from a song I like," said Benny. "I just hope things go better now. This is awful."

"What song?" said Harvey.

"I dunno what the title is," said Benny, "but the song is about how fast them summer wages go, you know."

"Ah," said Harvey, "yeah, now I remember. I like that song, too."

"You get your fiddle, Du Pré," said Madelaine.

Du Pré went out and got it and he came back and he played it very softly while the cigarette smoke rose to the ceiling. No one came into the bar.

He played the old laments, the songs of tiredness and loneliness in the black-green forests the voyageurs paddled through, far to the north where their canoes crossed their footprints of glaciers and the rising land. Four feet a century, in a flat place the rivers ran one way for a while and then another.

The Red River of the North was mostly lakes.

Harvey left. Benny and Susan held hands, Madelaine rubbed Du Pré's knee.

They all left the bar at two in the morning. Susan never closed it early, saying that a reliable place to get a drink was a must in a small town.

Du Pré dropped Madelaine off and he drove the little ways to the Catholic cemetery out behind the little church, in its groves of Russian olives. The place was well kept, plastic flowers on some of the graves and the weeds pulled and piled in one spot for burning in the fall.

An owl hooted softly.

Great horned he is hunting. The Hush Wing. Maybe another Hush Wing, they don't care, they just eat.

Du Pré pulled his bedroll out of the truck and he carried it and his whiskey and he walked into the cemetery and he went to the place where his grandparents and parents were buried, his wife near them, too. He unrolled the blankets pinned in their canvas cover and he sat cross-legged and he looked up at the Dipper, rolling around the polestar.

The sky was clear and the stars burned fiercely, hanging low.

Light my cigarette, one of them.

He drank.

A bullbat shot past overhead. He heard them call, and then gone.

Sweet sound, them goatsuckers.

Du Pré thought of Black Claws, under the snow.

Almost get me to eat. Well, I been killed almost, bunch of times.

Pretty stars.

A coyote howled, the choirmaster.

The chorus joined him.

God's dogs, they must know everything that is important. Very smart, them coyote, too smart, they get into trouble being so smart. Good way to trap them set two traps, one where they look at it, the other where they go to think about it, a little rise nearby.

The coyotes stopped. Then a yipping.

Got a rabbit, they run that rabbit in shifts till it is worn out. Poor old jackrabbit, he don't got a thing but speed.

But they don't run, can the coyote find them?

I do all the thinking good as I can and I don't got dick. All I got is Madelaine pissed off and my friend Bart a badge he don't really want and the same shit start again soon, the summer is here.

So where am I.

Sleeping with my grandfathers in the cemetery, my father he is there, my mother, my wife. Lot of my aunts, great-aunts, friends, old people I knew as a kid, I wish that they were here, I was not old or smart enough to ask them the right questions and they knew many things, old people always do. I thought that I would when I got older but it does not seem so.

Du Pré drank.

He looked up. The Dipper had moved round another hour. Good clock, it was.

No coyotes. They are eating rabbit.

Owl eating owl.

Me, I am drinking whiskey and smoking that Bull Durham.

Wondering what the fuck I am thinking of, doing what I am doing.

Nobody else dumb enough to.

Angela Green. I talk to her.

We don't know *nothing*.

That Taylor Martin, he spit in our faces.

Du Pré fell back on his bedroll. The night was cold and the dew forming.

He crawled into his bedroll and smoked one last cigarette.

He stubbed it out, put his face in the soogans, and slept.

He woke up just before dawn when the birds began to chirp and sing, the night hunters passed, and the day hunters passed by, in the air or on the ground.

The wind brought a scent of fox piss.

Du Pré sat up. He rolled a smoke. He looked up at the Wolf Mountains.

"OK," he said.

"Thank you, grandfathers."

✤ CHAPTER 35 ✤

Well," said Benny Klein, "I guess that they thought if they held this hearing near us they'd never make it out alive."

Du Pré nodded.

The Fish and Wildlife people were dropping another batch of

wolves into the Wolf Mountains, but they didn't want to announce that anywhere *near* the Wolf Mountains.

"Yeah," said Du Pré, "well, maybe they pitch these wolves out of an airplane, parachutes on them."

The hearing was being held on the campus of Northern Montana College in a room in the library. Most of the ranchers who had come were wearing cowshit-covered boots and occupying themselves with grinding it into the rug.

"Will they ever learn?" said Benny.

Du Pré shook his head.

"I know people like this, the army," said Du Pré. "Someone tell them that Chinese women are built sideways, they believe it, rest of their life. It is not much good, this talk."

Du Pré looked round the room. He saw the young woman who had been so angry with him at the last hearing. Seemed like ten years ago.

She saw Du Pré and glared at him. She nudged another young woman near her and pointed.

The two looked hard at Du Pré.

"I don't know who that one on the right is," said Du Pré, "but the one on the left is that Angela Green. You look at her good, Benny, she is the only way we find anything out, you bet."

Angela was tall, dark-haired, and pale-eyed. She bent to whisper in her companion's ear and then they both sat down.

One of the Fish and Wildlife reps called the meeting to order, said it was open to public commentary, looked at the list in her hand, called a name, and sat down looking bored.

The decision had been made long ago. The hearing was a sop.

A rancher rose and walked to the witness stand, while most of the wolf crowd tittered.

The man spoke haltingly, shyly. He said that he saw no reason to return wolves, that they would kill stock, and that he was opposed to it. Montana was not a park.

He left the stand, walking slowly, dragging his left leg; it was an artificial one.

Which war you lose that in? Du Pré thought. Korea, that is it, I know that guy, he has the place just over the line. Bill Gustaffson, he is the brand inspector there.

Du Pré went out to smoke. There were a couple ranchers outside, too, having cigarettes. They nodded at Du Pré.

"This year the wolf bullshit," said one. "Then next year they'll raise the grazing fees and we'll be out of business."

"Aw, Wally," said the other, "we can open a tofu stand for the little bastards. We'll love it."

Wally shrugged.

Du Pré finished his cigarette and went back in.

Another rancher got off the stand.

Angela Green rose and she made her way gracefully up to the stand, and she began to speak in a low voice, pleading for the return of the predator to the ecosystem. It was meant to be. So much damage had been done, by her family, for one, and this was some way to put it right. The wolf was the symbol of wilderness. Why, in Minnesota wolves killed hardly any cattle at all. The objections of the ranchers were foolish.

She went on until the F and W rep stopped her for speaking longer than the allowed minutes.

She walked past Du Pré on her way outside, a leather cigarette case in her hand, the kind that has a lighter in it.

Du Pré followed.

They smoked on opposite sides of the walkway, each leaning up against a railing.

Du Pré looked at her. The new Levi's—old faded ones were for dudes. The custom boots, scuffed and resoled and heeled. The turquoise and silver buckle, an old one, sand-cast and soldered.

Her hands they are the hands of a horsewoman, Du Pré thought, they are big, they grew big because she worked with them when she was a girl. She is very hard.

She leaned up against the railing in a way people do when they've leaned against a lot of fences.

She locked eyes with Du Pré.

"Long ways from the county," she said pleasantly.

"Uh," said Du Pré, "well, this is what start it all last time, you know, I am looking for things."

"I'm sure you are," she said.

"You like them wolf," said Du Pré.

"Magnificent animals," she said. "Think of this beautiful country. The buffalo, the Plains Indians, the elk on the river hills, the Eden that it was."

Yeah, Du Pré thought, well, this West not a very wild place till the white man come with guns, but look at the world now. Everybody got guns they try to kill each other, you bet.

"How long your people been here?" said Du Pré.

"One and one-quarter centuries," said Angela Green. "Busy raping the land." She walked over to Du Pré. She dropped her cigarette on the sidewalk and she ground it out with her boot.

"Taylor Martin was much man and my favorite uncle," she said.

Du Pré nodded. He drew on his smoke.

"I suppose we'll see each other often," said Angela, "and if you will excuse me now, I must go fight the good fight."

She kissed Du Pré on the cheek and she walked back through the door.

OK, Du Pré thought, I am seeing now. Not too much to do now. Oh, no, that Harvey Weasel Fat, he will like this, though. Plenty Indian enough, he always like a good joke.

Even if it is killing you, if it is doing it in a funny way, you got to laugh, this earth is that sort of place.

That Angela, she wouldn't crack, not ever.

But this can't happen again.

Benny wandered out.

"Buncha assholes singing three-part harmony in there," he said. "Are we here for a reason? I mean, I ain't even a deputy. Not anymore."

"Just spend some time," said Du Pré. "But there is no reason, not anymore, no."

They got into Du Pré's Rover and turned around and drove off. Du Pré stopped at a package store and got a fifth of whiskey and some sodas and some cheese and lunch meat.

Pack of Pall Malls. They were weak, but the best next to his hand-rolled ones.

He and Benny drove and drank and drove and drank.

"Am I still a sworn officer of the law?" said Benny.

"Oh, yeah," said Du Pré. "It is like a tattoo."

Benny nodded.

Du Pré was doing a hundred and ten down a two-lane blacktop.

"We are breaking a bunch of laws."

"Four," said Du Pré. "I am drunk more than the limit, we are on duty more or less, car is full of guns, all loaded, and I am driving fifty-five miles over the speed limit."

"Oh," said Benny, "is *that* all."

They shot past a Highway Patrolman. The patrol car roared after them, lights flashing.

Du Pré switched on his light bar and radio.

"Officer Du Pré," said Du Pré into the microphone, "taking a heart for transplant to the airport."

Crackle crackle.

The patrol car dropped behind.

"Dirty, dirty," said Benny.

"Pret' good whiskey," said Du Pré. "Have some."

Benny did.

"So what do we do now?" said Benny. "You know those feds are going batshit but they can't get anywhere. They got nothing and no one to frame even."

Du Pré nodded.

"You talk to Angela Green?" said Benny.

"Oh, yes," said Du Pré.

"What's she like?"

"Oh," said Du Pré, "dumb kid, you know, how they fight their parents. She will get knocked up next, I guess maybe."

Benny nodded.

"Pretty rich family."

"If they release the wolves again this'll happen again," said Benny.

"Yah."

"What are we gonna do?"

"We got to stop them," said Du Pré.

"How?"

"Well," said Du Pré, "I will have to think about that."

❖ CHAPTER 36 ❖

Dicked," said Harvey Wallace, aka Weasel Fat, "dicked, dicked, and dicked. I told 'em, we go there, we get dicked. No other way. Won't help my career."

"Uh," said Du Pré, "well, you don't know how to do nothing else, maybe?"

"I don't like doing nothing else," said Harvey. "I like chasing bad guys and running them down and throwing them in the slammer. I like to hunt ducks even more, come to think on it. I could be a duck cop."

"OK," said Du Pré, "now, you can come long as you behave, there, it is very important, you know, you do this, I don't want no more people killed here. Maybe this is not the best idea anybody ever had but I cannot, you know, think of any better one, I am too old and dumb."

"OK," said Harvey.

"I ask you to please do this," said Du Pré. "You don't dick me."

"OK," said Harvey Weasel Fat. "Sure as my name ain't really Wallace I will not dick you. I drive you there and sit outside and I wait."

"Well," said Du Pré, "they will not, you know, come apart. We got no bullet. Gun it was fired from, guns, they are cut apart and melted down. Nobody knows nothing more than they got to. Smaller number of people in it than we thought. So there we are."

"Dicked," said Harvey.

"Dicked dicked dicked," said Madelaine. She stood in the kitchen doorway, hands on her hips, looking at Du Pré and Harvey, eyes narrowed. "You guys so dumb all you do is talk dirty, my house. I don't care you talk dirty, you be funny, though."

"OK," said Harvey.

"OK," said Du Pré. They were waiting on dinner. Being good boys.

"And you Harvey," said Madelaine, "you say dicked dicked dicked you know what you are sounding like?"

"No," said Harvey.

"You are *whining*," said Madelaine. "And you don't stop I call you Weasel Dick for couple weeks, see how you like *that*."

Harvey nodded. He looked sheepish.

Madelaine brought in the rest of the bowls and they sat down to supper. Her children wouldn't eat for an hour, but Du Pré and Harvey had other business.

Pot roast, potatoes, home-canned green beans, home-baked bread, and blackberry pie.

"Wonderful," said Harvey. "You let me wash dishes?"

"No," said Madelaine, "I don't want you guys around, you go do what you are going to do, come back, tell me, we go have some nice drinks. I listen better, your whining, I am about drunk."

"Me, Du Pré," said Harvey, "we give up our badges, we send you."

"Me," said Madelaine, "I am a woman. Dumb jobs like that, we send you guys. No way. Eat your pot roast."

"You speak pret' good Coyote French there, Harvey," said Du Pré.

"You damn Métis everywhere," said Harvey, "like ass pains and bad debts."

They finished and got up.

Madelaine kissed Du Pré. After a moment, she kissed Harvey on the cheek.

"You be back here, ten o'clock," said Madelaine.

"Maybe," said Du Pré. "I don't know."

"I know," said Madelaine. "I know what you are goin' do, too. Fine. Good idea. Be back by ten. I will want some pink wine then."

Du Pré and Harvey walked out to Harvey's government car and they got in and they drove off toward the Grange Hall fifty miles away. The building sat in the middle of the plains, miles from anything, and the Stockgrowers' Association was meeting there.

"What you got, the medicine bundle?" said Harvey.

Du Pré looked at the case in the back seat, a case made more than a century before for a double-recurve bone and Osage Orange bow. Du Pré wasn't sure where it had come from. Benetsee had given him the soft leather case, quilled and beaded and faded and cracked.

"Sacred shit," said Du Pré. "Don't think so very much, Harvey."

"OK," said Harvey.

Du Pré pulled a pint of whiskey out of his pocket and he had a drink and offered it to Harvey. Harvey shook his head.

"Afterward," said Harvey, "fine. I dunno what you got in mind, none of my business, but afterward."

Du Pré nodded. They turned onto the highway and shot hard for the east. The tires whined and birds burst up from crushed gopher carcasses mashed to the asphalt.

The sun was hot. They drove with the windows down. The blackbirds in the barrow pits chirred liquidly.

Du Pré looked to his left. He couldn't see the Wolfs, only the hayfields just past the fence. A red fox flamed in the green grass.

Du Pré rolled a smoke and lit it and he looked down to the south toward the far Missouri and the breaks, out over the buffalo country, where the cattle grazed so far from plates and tables. People back in there, too, in their Sears, Roebuck ranch houses, with

the Siberian elms screening the wind, the windmills screaking
overhead.

You can take this land but it makes you its own, he thought,
got to be here some, it gets into your blood and bone and marrow and the dust colors your bones gold.

My country, this.

They made good time. Du Pré pointed off to the right, at the
old Grange Hall red in the leafing cottonwoods. The ground
around it was thick with cars and trucks, people moving slowly to
the hall.

Harvey drove to the last row nearest the road and he switched
off the engine and he sighed.

"I'll just wait here, like you asked," he said, "but don't kill
anyone."

"Too much of that," said Du Pré.

Harvey nodded.

The last few of the ranchers were filling inside.

Du Pré got out. He opened the back door and took out the
medicine bundle and he tucked it under his arm and he walked
up to the door and he waited just a moment and then he walked
inside.

People were talking and joshing and standing and sitting.

The Martins and some of their kin looked at Du Pré for a
moment and then they went back to their conversations.

Clark Martin left his knot of family and he walked to the
podium and he rapped on it with a stick of kindling. Everyone sat
down but Du Pré. He leaned against the back wall.

"I call this meeting to order," Clark Martin said, loudly.

Du Pré slipped the MP-40 out of the bow case. He lifted it and
pressed the trigger and the machine pistol jumped in his hands.
He stitched a line of holes in the ceiling. The brass went on rat-
tling and then tinkling on the worn wooden floor.

People dived for the floor or stayed rooted in the chairs, hands
to ears. Someone sobbed. Morgan Taliaferro Martin turned and
looked at Du Pré flatly, her eyes as old as Egypt.

Du Pré looked over at Angela Green; she sat with her mouth open and one hand to her face.

"Count them holes, the ceiling," said Du Pré. "Sixteen of 'em, that's how many dead we got here. Fool kids, plain fools, Packy, and Banning. Lot of holes there. You who did this, you are so big, you go to those holes, call those kids out of them. Call Packy. Call the four people killed up in the mountains, just doing their job. Call Corey Banning. Call them out now, I see them, then I go away."

Clark Martin stared at Du Pré, eyes sleepy.

"I have pretty well figured this all out," said Du Pré. "But if I have not, I throw my badge in the ditch, I don't throw my gun, and I come for you. I don't care no more. I don't care, me."

"Mr. Du Pré," said Morgan Martin, "this is appalling. Simply awful. I'll see you prosecuted for this."

Du Pré slid the machine pistol back in the bow case.

"Night that those four were killed, up in the mountains, with the wolves, someone flew up there, in a helicopter," said Du Pré. "But there was this. There were one, maybe two people been flown up there before. Early, before them wolves and biologists were. Waited, in the snow, and then when the helicopter came back, make a lot of noise, them four people all walk toward the helicopter, wondering what it was doing there, and not looking behind them. Probably had maybe a television station's letters stuck on the side."

Du Pré picked up the bow case and he walked to the door and he turned.

"We are ver' close now," he said, "and we come to you, who did this, soon. Until then, though, you remember, there is no more of this. It is enough. Now, you have your damn meeting."

Du Pré walked out, leaving the door open. He stepped across the puddle at the foot of the steps and he opened the back door of Harvey's government car and he slid the bow case on the seat and then he shut the door and opened the front door and he got in.

He slammed the door hard.

"Sometime," said Du Pré, "you lose on that poker, you got to make lucky with them dice."

"Did I hear automatic-weapon fire in there?" said Harvey. "Of course not. Firecrackers. Somebody was celebrating. Firecrackers are illegal, too. Especially as big as those sounded. Terrible, but out of my jurisdiction. Don't suppose you'd like to tell me just what the fuck is going on."

"Kids these days," said Du Pré, "they don't respect nothin'."

Harvey turned the car around and headed back toward Toussaint.

"We can't be late to take Madelaine out for pink wine," said Harvey.

Du Pré rolled a cigarette and he lit it and rolled his window down.

"Yah," said Du Pré, "that is important for sure."

"You think that did any good?" said Harvey.

"Maybe," said Du Pré. "Depends how many people were in on this. I don't think many. We'll see."

They rode in silence for a while.

"Your Madelaine, think she'll dance again with a Blackfeet?" said Harvey.

"Oh, I am sure that she will," said Du Pré.

❖ CHAPTER 37 ❖

You sure she'll come?" said Harvey. He sipped his coffee. They were sitting in the Toussaint Bar. It was about ten in the morning. The place stank of bleach and stale beer and old cigarettes.

Du Pré shrugged.

Shit, I am tired, he thought. I am very tired of this. Also it makes me very sad.

The front door was open and thick shafts of light stabbed through it. Du Pré heard a magpie scrawk.

A truck pulled up outside and stopped. There was a diesel throb for a few minutes, then the engine died and a door slammed.

Angela Green came through the door, the light behind her. She wore a light fringed jacket and a new Stetson. She stood a moment, her eyes adjusting to the dimness. She saw Du Pré and Harvey Wallace sitting at the bar and she walked over. She dragged a stool away from the bar and put it in front of them and she sat down.

"You set them up," said Harvey.

Angela looked at him, her face blank.

"They set themselves up," she said. "All they had to do was stay home and mind their own damn business. Taylor . . . nobody knew he was going to go to war. And that's the story."

"Taylor was a mighty man," said Harvey, "but he was just the one. Took more than that, more than him."

"Taylor was plenty," said Angela. "Now, if you want to talk to me anymore, maybe you should arrest me."

"In time," said Harvey, "though I doubt it. You probably knew what would happen. Probably. But Taylor wouldn't have let you know anything for sure."

"He was always a gentleman," said Angela.

"Yeah," said Harvey, "well, you be a lady and quit spying on those idiot flatlander environmentalists. Leave them to hugging their bunnies in peace. Poor little things'll find some new cause soon anyway. When I do find anything out, though, I will happily arrest you."

Angela lit a cigarette. She looked at Harvey.

"You like this?" she said.

Harvey shrugged.

Susan Klein came out of the kitchen.

"Need something?" she said.

"Ditch," said Angela.

Susan nodded and mixed the drink and pushed it across the bar.

"How're your folks?" she said.

"Thriving," said Angela.

A plastic bag sailed through the door and plopped on the floor. Du Pré and Harvey tensed.

"Look at it," said Clark Martin. He was standing where they couldn't see him. Du Pré got up and he walked over and scooped up the bag, his gun in his right hand. The sun shone on the rutted parking lot, the blacktop, the field beyond the little park.

Du Pré carried the package back to the bar and he set it down and put his gun by it and he pulled it open. Wallets. Four wallets. He opened them. Two had Fish and Wildlife Service badges in them.

"Shit," said Harvey. He had his gun out, too.

Angela sipped her drink.

Du Pré looked at Harvey. He nodded.

They went to the doorway. Harvey ducked out in a crouch, pointing his gun.

No one there. Du Pré followed him, walking loose. They went down the steps, squinting in the sun.

Clark Martin was across the road, leaning against one of the box elder trees at the far side of the park, a hundred yards away. He had his arms folded on his chest.

Harvey padded across the road, Du Pré close behind.

"You're under arrest, Clark Martin," said Harvey.

"Stop there," said Clark. Harvey kept on walking.

"It's all there is," said Clark, "me and Taylor. Du Pré was right, Taylor dropped me up there the day before, and when he flew the chopper back they all bunched up. I came in from the trees behind. It was all over in five seconds."

Harvey stopped.

"Get your hands way, way up," he said. He swung up his nine-millimeter. Du Pré came up beside him, gun in hand, not pointing it.

"Show time," said Clark. He jerked his hand into his jacket and pulled out an automatic and he dropped into a crouch and fired.

Du Pré felt something whack him in the chest.

Harvey fired three bursts of two each. Clark Martin shuddered as bullets struck him. He fell back against the tree and tumbled around to the side and fell boneless, like a bundle of rags.

Du Pré felt his chest. It stung where he had been hit. His fingertips felt wax.

Harvey walked on the balls of his feet over to Clark Martin. He kept the gun pointed at him. He kicked Martin's pistol away with his foot and then he knelt and pulled on Martin's shoulder to roll him over. He put his knuckles to Martin's neck. He stood up.

Du Pré came up. He looked down at Clark Martin, his chest red and his eyes glazing.

Harvey scratched at his shirt. He looked at his fingernails.

"Wax," he said.

"Me, too," said Du Pré. "He was pret' quick there."

"Real slugs, I dunno we'd made it," said Harvey. "You didn't fire, did you, Du Pré?"

"No," said Du Pré.

Harvey sighed. He put his gun back in the holster.

"Let's smoke," he said.

Du Pré nodded. He rolled a couple of cigarettes. They stood there, looking down at Clark Martin.

"You figured he'd do this?" said Harvey.

"Yah," said Du Pré. "Them Martins got a lot of Indian in them."

"Could have fooled me," said Harvey. "Makes sense, though."

None of this makes much sense, Du Pré thought. Except that people thought that it did. Little bastards insult this place, everybody who lives here, now they'll be a little scared, maybe. Damn Martins, they took a chance. Didn't work out. Taylor's dead. Clark's dead. When he knew we'd find it out, he come in, make us kill him. Pretty Indian, that.

Bart's Rover roared up, light bar flashing, but no siren.

He drove right into the park, across the scrubby grass. He stopped the car and got out.

"Shit," he said.

"Well," said Harvey Weasel Fat, "it's over."

"Oh?" said Bart.

"I checked the phone records," said Harvey, "and there's nothing there. Angela Green called Montana frequently, but she never called the Martin ranch, not once. Her folks. A couple girlfriends. Taylor gave us a confession. Clark gave us the evidence. End of story."

"What evidence?" said Bart.

"Four wallets," said Harvey, "two of them from Fish and Wildlife officers."

"Why the hell did he keep those?" said Bart.

"Proof," said Harvey. "We got proof and we got a lot of suppositions. Hardly anyone else in on it, directly, anyway. Other people knew. Sort of. Maybe. When the snow finally melts up there we might find a few things, but only Clark and Taylor were actually there. 'Less someone wants to confess just for the fun of a long prison sentence, this is it, folks, this is all there is."

Bart pulled a yellow rescue blanket out of his Rover. He went to Clark Martin and covered him.

"My superiors are gonna love my report," said Harvey. "As I am the Agent in Charge, I hereby suspend myself pending investigation of this shooting. Thank you, Agent Wallace. Harvey Weasel Fat needs a drink. I'm locking this son-of-a-bitching gun in the trunk. Maybe this time they'll fire me."

Du Pré waited while Harvey shed his belt gear into the trunk of his car. Harvey turned and looked over at the park. Bart was scribbling in a notebook.

They went on into the saloon.

Angela Green was sitting at the bar, and Susan Klein was with her. Both of them were crying.

Du Pré mixed a couple of ditchwater highballs.

They took their drinks to a table in the corner.

"To brave men," said Harvey.

Du Pré nodded.

They drank.

"You know this was going to happen this way?" said Harvey.

Du Pré looked down at his glass.

"Thing about brave men," he said, "is that you can trust them."

❖ CHAPTER 38 ❖

W ell," said Madelaine, "you are coming? Yes?"
      "No, I am not goddamn coming," said Du Pré. I got to
shout, I'll shout, he thought, I will yell very loud.

"They call me, ask that you come."

Christ.

"I am not going to Clark Martin's funeral," said Du Pré. "I did
not go to Taylor's, I will not go to this."

"You are wrong."

Madelaine was dressed in black. She had a little Bible and her
rosary on the kitchen table.

A shadow went past the window. Du Pré saw Benetsee's shock
of dirty white hair bob twice, and then pass the edge of the window frame. Du Pré threw open the kitchen door.

"You old shit," he said, "now what you want? You are never
around when I need to talk to you. What you come here for?"

"Go to funeral with you," said Benetsee. "What you think? Du
Pré, you know them Martin people, eh? Taylor, Clark, they are
brave. You be brave, too."

"Christ," said Du Pré, "I don't got to have both of you, you know."

"You got both of us, sure enough," said Madelaine. "You go
get dressed now, get your fiddle. They were good warriors, now
you go play a song for them and the ravens. Huh. I don't think
this is a good time to be late."

Du Pré put on his worn clothes and he walked out to the Rover.
Madelaine and Benetsee were already sitting in it. Benetsee
grinned and chuckled.

Du Pré got in. He looked down at the console between the
front seats. Madelaine had put his fiddle there.

"I am not liking this," said Du Pré. "I sort of helped kill them both, you know."

"Shut up and drive this or I will," said Madelaine.

The day was cold and overcast; it had rained in the early morning. The backs of the cattle in the pastures steamed in the gray light. The sky hung down low and there was no wind at all.

Du Pré drove fast, not speaking. Benetsee and Madelaine chattered about good places to pick morel mushrooms. Asparagus. Logged places where stump mushrooms would grow by the hundredweight.

When Du Pré got to the turnoff that went into the Martin ranch's holdings, he stopped the Rover.

"I don't like this," said Du Pré.

Benetsee cracked him hard in the head with the knuckles of his left hand.

"This white world is not good for very much," he said. "Now, you just remember some Indian in you, I hit you till you do. Clark and Taylor are still around, won't leave till maybe next spring. You don't come and honor them, they will be hurt."

"Shit," said Du Pré. He went on down the gravel road. It was four miles in to the main ranch house. The Martins had their own graveyard, a quarter of a mile from the dozen buildings of the old homestead.

There were a couple hundred trucks and cars parked in orderly rows out in a hay meadow that shouldered over next to the creek. A straggling line of couples, families, and groups was moving toward the grove of birches where the graves lay.

"Damn," said Du Pré, "I will not take my fiddle."

"OK," said Benetsee, "I carry it for you."

Du Pré pulled off and parked and got out and walked around and he opened Madelaine's door and helped her down. Benetsee was on his own. Madelaine took his arm and tugged him along toward the birches over by the chuckling water of the little creek.

They stood at the back of the crowd and listened while the minister spoke the simple burial service. Du Pré could see Morgan Taliaferro Martin standing with the wives of Taylor and Clark, and her grandchildren. Nine of them, the biggest two boys over six feet, gangly, with dark blond hair and big hands. Du Pré saw the little girl who had laughed as she danced with her father, his big boots under her tiny feet.

Someone tugged at Du Pré's elbow. He turned his head and there was Angela Green, Benetsee grinning behind her. The old man had lit a huge twist of sweet grass. The pungent smoke swirled softly in the still air.

"You come with me," whispered Angela. "The family wants you to play a song. One for the lost sons of the voyageurs."

Du Pré nodded. Angela led him around the crowd, up by a bower thick with red-purple lilacs. The bees in the flowers buzzed sleepily. Rain was coming.

The minister stopped and Clark Martin's wife came from the family group and she laid a bundle of flowers, iris and lilacs, on the coffin. Then some men in ranch clothes picked up the coffin and lowered it down into the grave.

Du Pré checked his fiddle for tune. Pret' good.

Morgan Martin looked at him. She nodded.

Du Pré played a lament for a young voyageur lost beneath the dark waters, homeward bound to his love. The song spoke of hardship and courage and loss, and then how from this, friends, remembering him, sang to his love when they finally got home.

It was a fairly long piece, and Du Pré let the last note fade and he put his fiddle to his side and he heard a faint sound that grew and grew. It came from the forest over the creek, the drone of the bagpipes, skirling.

The piper played the first movement of "Brave Caledonia," and then rolled gently to a long drone, and then to the sad "Flowers of the Forest."

Plenty sad music, thought Du Pré. Plenty sad time.

Benetsee was behind him. Sweet-grass smoke purled out of the lilac bower.

The Martin family walked slowly away, back toward the ranch house. The crowd didn't move until they had gone up the steps and the door had closed behind them.

"The Piper in the Forest," Du Pré thought. One of my cousins does that song, plays it on the concertina.

Du Pré walked back to Madelaine. She was praying, as always, for everybody.

Du Pré waited until Madelaine lifted her head. Her eyes were bright with tears.

"Ver' nice," she said. "Now you glad you come?"

Du Pré nodded.

"Where is Benetsee?" she said.

Du Pré shrugged.

He looked round for the old man but he had gone, drifting into the dark trees. He would make his own way home.

We all got to.

"OK," said Madelaine. "We go now, the bar, get me some pink wine, maybe dance a little. You quit being so damn sad, Du Pré, everybody they do what they have to. It is over now, I think, yes?"

It is not over, Du Pré thought. A song ends. Music never does.

"Yes," he said. "We go there. I could use maybe a little whiskey."

"You don't have to be a deputy no more," said Madelaine. "Bart, he don't have to be Sheriff."

Bart was behind them a hundred yards or so, talking to Lawyer Foote.

They walked a little faster and got to the Rover before many people had begun to drive out of the hayfield. Du Pré backed up and turned and bumped out on the road. There was a truck up ahead of them, moving fast.

Angela Green.

Well, Du Pré thought, I am going to quit this deputy shit right now. No more. No more of this.

He sped down the county road toward Toussaint, the Rover sometimes going a little soft on the turns as the gravel rolled under the tires. There were no cars in front of the bar when he turned in and parked.

Susan Klein looked up briefly when they walked in, and back down at the book she was reading.

187

"How was it?" she said, when Du Pré and Madelaine came up to the bar.

"Ver' sad," said Du Pré, "but nice, too. At the end of the service a piper started to play off in the woods."

"That music, it always makes me cry," said Madelaine. "Maybe it is one of those Scots, my great-grandfather in me."

"They dumped some more wolves up there," said Susan Klein. "You'd think the dumb bastards would know when to quit."

"Eh?" said Du Pré.

"In this morning's paper," said Susan. "It's on the table there."

Du Pré looked down at the Billings newspaper's headlines. Some idiot reporter thought dropping wolves by night was just wonderful. So did the editorial writer.

Du Pré sipped his drink.

✤ CHAPTER 39 ✤

Du Pré watched the fire of the welding rod melting, through the thick, dark green visor on his face. He smelled the acrid stink of burning metal and felt the spatter of molten steel on his boots.

He flipped up his heavy face mask and looked at the weld. Good and tight and well filled. He walked two steps to the water barrel and doused it, hissing.

He ground the weld down and then he heated the spring with a torch and doused it several times to temper it.

Looking good. These things they sit here, what, maybe seventy years now and I got to expect that they get a little bad.

"Du Pré!"

Du Pré turned and looked toward the bright light of the doorway. Booger Tom was outlined in it, Benetsee standing behind his right shoulder.

"Ya kin leave off for a moment and come settle an argument," said Booger Tom.

Du Pré set the steel down and he took off the heavy leather welding coat and the mask and he put them on their pegs and he fished around in his shirt pocket for his tobacco and papers and he went outside with the little white bag in his hand.

He rolled a smoke for Benetsee and one for Booger Tom and he lit them and then rolled one for himself.

The July day was close and cloudy and promised hard short rain at sundown. Now, in the afternoon, silver sheets fell from the black clouds but the rain evaporated before it hit the ground. Thunder rumbled. A jet plane drew a white line high past the sinking sun.

Du Pré fished around in his car and found his whiskey and a half-gallon jug of screwtop white he kept there in case he ran into Benetsee.

They walked round back of the old place to the little creek and sat on log seats under the lilac bushes Du Pré had planted years before, when he and Bart had found out the sad story of Du Pré's father and Bart's brother, joined now in death, one made the other and it was all too late but for a good story, maybe.

Bart's Rover pulled in up front and some of Jacqueline's many children ran laughing toward it. He never came without something for them, and he never talked down to the kids.

"Which one a us is the biggest liar," said Booger Tom, "me or ol' Too Many Feathers here?"

Du Pré looked at the two old monsters for a long moment.

"I am just a brand inspector, deputy, fiddler," he said finally, "and that is a question for an astronomer. It is too big, me."

Benetsee laughed and he washed out an old jam jar in the creek and he poured himself wine.

Du Pré and Booger Tom passed the whiskey back and forth.

"Benetsee and me been playing cards," said Booger Tom. "We both cheat pretty good, so we're about even."

"Him, he cheat more," said Benetsee.

"I don't care which, you old shits, cheat more," said Du Pré. "I got things, you know, to think on besides that."

Benetsee cut a willow stem and he began to notch it and he twisted the red stick in his old hands and the bark spun and he slipped it free. He carved a moment and put the bark back on and fingered the holes he had made. He made a couple bigger and then he began to play, a pipe tune, old Métis song, dance on the buffalo hide pegged to the ground.

Song about people making their meat, in the fall, there, kill them buffalo, cut the meat into sheets, hang it in the sun and fire. Let it dry good, pack it away. Pound it to powder, mix with the dried chokecherry and Indian plums. Heat the marrow fat and pour it some salted over the mixed powdered meat and dried fruit. Eat it when the sun dogs ride the sky and the cold has claws reach through your chest to your heart.

Du Pré got his fiddle, he tuned it a moment, and he played a slow song some voyageur had made up on a moonless night when the lake was smooth and full of stars and the loons called far off, and then he heard the loup-garou, the werewolf, scream in the dark and he knew it smelled his blood and was following. Song prays for protection all things that are evil, when they come they cannot find you.

They heard Bart's booming laugh and the squeals of the happy kids.

Du Pré had a slug of whiskey. He rolled another smoke.

His horses curled back on each other, up to the fence, curious about who was here.

Benetsee played another tune. Du Pré listened, nodding.

He finished.

"That for Prairie Falcon Woman," he said.

Poor Corey, Du Pré thought, you did your best.

"Yeah," said Du Pré, "well, it be some quiet now, I think."

Benetsee laughed. He roared with laughter.

"Sure," said Booger Tom, "now maybe you just tell me which three of them packhorses you want and quit lyin' by not even botherin' to lie to me."

Du Pré laughed.

"OK," he said, "I want them two grullas and the big bay. I am about done with them welding anyway."

A couple of big helicopters whacked and whacked off in the distance, headed up into the Wolfs. Two smaller helicopters followed.

"There they go," said Booger Tom. "Don't learn for shit, do they?"

"I be there, a minute," said Du Pré.

He went into the shed and picked up two of the wolf traps, and he brought them out and set them down and he rolled them up in some canvas. And two more. Two more. Two more.

They weighed fifty pounds apiece, with the long chains on them.

Six wolf traps, all oiled and scraped free of rust.

"I ain't seen any of those since I was wet three places, includin' behind the ears," said Booger Tom.

Du Pré nodded.

Booger Tom and Benetsee walked back to the pasture with catch-ropes and they dropped loops over the necks of the grullas and led them out the swinging wooden gate. The tough little horses came willingly.

Booger Tom and Benetsee tied them to a post and they went to the tack shed and came out with two packsaddles and blankets and ropes and they began to pack the horses.

Madelaine came, parking her old car on the grass by the drive. She lifted saddlebags of food and such out of her trunk and walked back to the men.

Du Pré knelt by the little creek. Brook trout darted in the water's dapple.

Drink this water all my life. Tastes of fish piss. I like it.

Live under them mountain all my life.

See that rain never get to the ground every summer.

See them sun dogs in the cold black winter.

My people they were here, they are here by maybe 1700.

My great-great-grandpa he fight with little Gabriel Dumont, he come down here after the 1886 Rebellion, them Red River people, and he raise his family, pick them mussel shell for the button makers. Never know how to read and write, but he is a great fiddler. His name was Gabriel, too.

Pretty fine country.

Du Pré stood up.

"They drop them wolf off now," said Madelaine. "Got the TV crews up there, you know."

Du Pré nodded.

"Yeah, well, you know, my grandpapa he hunt down that last pair buffalo wolves with that Don Stevens," he said, "long, long time ago."

Them wolves have names.

Old Snowdrift and Lady Snowdrift, almost white wolves, them. Old Snowdrift the biggest wolf ever killed, I hear.

Du Pré went out to the pasture and he whistled and his mountain horse, old Walkin' Tom, came over, whuffling. The horse was getting old but was still sound and Du Pré had ridden him always and if he left without him the horse would grieve. Then he'd just jump the fence and come along anyway.

Du Pré opened the gate and the horse followed him back to the tack shed. Du Pré saddled him. He put the food Madelaine had brought on the grullas, helped pack the old bay with the rest.

He picked up his .270 and lashed it on to the bay's load.

Checked his saddlebags for tobacco and whiskey.

They loaded the horses into Bart's huge trailer and then Bart pulled it up to his ranch and on up the access road that led to the trail to the Wolfs, the quickest route to the pass above.

They offloaded the stock and checked the knots and Du Pré swung up and he took the rope from Booger Tom's hand. He leaned down to kiss Madelaine.

Bart stood there, still the Sheriff.

One of the big helicopters lifted off the top of the mountains, then the other. The little white ones were circling round the place they'd come up from.

"OK," said Du Pré. "Well," he said, touching his hat with his hand, "I thank you. You know, this is my land here. And I like them wolf all right. And when I am ready, they can come back."

He chirred to old Tom and the string followed along.

I got to write a song about this, he thought.

Notches

For the women who are lost in the desert

✦ CHAPTER 1 ✦

This terrible, Du Pré," said Madelaine. She was looking at the newspaper. "Person, do this, pretty far from God, yes?"

Du Pré nodded. He sipped his coffee. They were sitting in Madelaine's kitchen. The breakfast dishes were piled on the sideboard next to the sink.

Du Pré watched the cluster flies fumble clumsily against the window glass. It was spring and the fat-bodied black insects were crawling out toward the warmth. They wintered in the walls of the house.

Madelaine handed the front section of the paper to Du Pré. He looked at the headline.

FIFTH VICTIM FOUND

Du Pré sighed.

"It is a long way from here," he said. "Pretty ugly, this."

"Not so far," said Madelaine. "It is what, a hundred miles, maybe. Just up above the Wolf Mountains, here, on that Hi-Line." Highway 2, which runs fifty miles south of Canada all across Montana. North Dakota. Ends at Sault-Ste.-Marie in Michigan.

"The parents, these girls," said Madelaine. "Oh, they must weep."

Oh, yes, Du Pré thought, your little girl she quarrel with you and she run away. Someone take her and rape her and torture her and kill her and dump her body out in the sagebrush, let the coyotes and ravens eat what is left, well . . . he thought of his two daughters. His grandchildren. Anybody's children.

"People kill people, here," said Madelaine. "They got a reason. Not a good reason, there is never no good reason, kill someone."

Yes there is, Du Pré thought, but me, I will not argue this time.

195

"That Lucky," said Madelaine. "He kill all those Indian women, Canada, that Washington, D.C. What was he like, there?"

Before I kill him? thought Du Pré. Damn, him I almost forgot. No, I did not. Hit him with a stone from a slingshot, he fall and break his fucking neck so I don't got to cut his throat. Only good thing he did, me.

Du Pré sipped his coffee.

"Hey, Du Pré," said Madelaine. "I lose my voice? You gone deaf? I ask you this question, you hear me? What this Lucky was like?"

"Him, he was a bastard," said Du Pré. "He don't look crazy, though. Good thing he break his neck, he go to trial, they say him crazy, he be out by now. Give him Social Security or something."

My Madelaine, she does not think there are bad people in this world. Just people who are far from God. I wish she was right.

Madelaine was fiddling with the thick braid of black hair she wore, shot with silver now. Her face was smooth and unlined. She was still a little asleep. Du Pré lifted his coffee, and he smelled her on his hand. He remembered her in the night.

Du Pré looked at her, smiling a little.

"Eh, Du Pré," said Madelaine. "You want to go back to bed, now, you look at me like that. It is on your forehead. No. I got to go to the church. See Father Van Den Heuvel. No, Du Pré, you are a big boy, you wait till tonight."

Du Pré grinned.

"OK," said Madelaine. "This afternoon maybe, but not now, no."

Du Pré stood up and he went around the table.

"I bite you," said Madelaine. "I am not fooling you. Men. You are supposed, not want that so much, you get to be a grandfather."

Du Pré rubbed her shoulders through the thick silk bathrobe she wore.

"I am not explaining, Father Van Den Heuvel, I am late, our meeting, I am fucking that Du Pré. We are not even married."

We would be, Du Pré thought, you were not waiting on that fool Church say, OK, your husband, he is dead, you can marry Du Pré now. Eight years I wait for her to get word from those priests, something is stuck in the works.

Du Pré looked out the kitchen window toward the fields that lay right at the edge of the little town. Stout rows of winter wheat rose green above the brown earth. Tough plants, that winter wheat, stayed green right under the snow. Got a jump on growing in the spring.

Du Pré made a grab for Madelaine's ass when she got up. She slapped his hand and smiled at him, wagged her finger.

"I take care of you, later," said Madelaine, heading off to the bath.

Du Pré heard the water start. He got another cup of coffee and he brought it back to the table.

The newspaper. He hadn't read the article.

He didn't want to read the article.

Something itched in the back of his mind.

Me, I am going to get tangled up in this, he thought.

A warm wet scent of flowers and herbs bloomed in the kitchen. The potpourri that Madelaine made and put into the soap that she made from fat and ashes and berries. Métis' soap. Kind of soap Madelaine's old aunties, grandmothers made.

She always smelled wonderful.

Du Pré lifted his coffee cup again and sniffed his hand, smelled his woman.

This afternoon, he thought, it is a long time till this afternoon.

Du Pré looked at the photograph. Some people carrying a black body bag out of the sagebrush.

The body had been found by a rancher. The man had been driving along and a hubcap had fallen off and sailed out into the sagebrush. On the open range. The rancher backed the car up and he walked out into the sagebrush and he found the body. It was badly decomposed, the paper said. Evidence indicated that the murderer was the same person who had killed four other young women and left their bodies in places where they might lie for a long time, or forever.

Damn, thought Du Pré, there maybe are a lot more dead girls out there. Maybe, hah. There are plenty dead girls out there. This guy, he has been doing this for a long time. Like that guy Bundy, he killed . . . sixty women? Maybe more.

Serial killers, always men.

Hunters. But they don't eat what they kill.

Damn, this guy, he is driving in places which don't got so much traffic and someone has seen this guy, seen what he drives.

They see this guy, what he drives, don't think nothing of it.

Cut it out, Du Pré thought, you are not a part of this. No part. Ah, shit, I better go and see Benetsee. See what he dreams.

The shower stopped. Du Pré went to the hallway and he stood there. Madelaine came out, naked, wringing the water out of her hair with a heavy towel. Du Pré looked at her.

This afternoon.

I cancel, all them appointments.

The telephone rang. Madelaine picked it up in the bedroom.

"Hey, Du Pré," she called. "It is that Benny Klein."

Benny Klein, the Sheriff. One of Du Pré's friends. His wife owned the bar in Toussaint.

Du Pré didn't want to pick up the telephone.

He went to the living room.

"Yah," said Du Pré.

"Du Pré?" said Benny. His voice was distorted. So he was calling the dispatch office and they patched him onto the telephone line.

"Yah, it is me," said Du Pré.

"You see this morning's paper?" he said.

"Yah," said Du Pré. I don't want this, I want to fuck my Madelaine this afternoon, maybe take her to the bar, buy her a pink wine, a cheeseburger. Maybe we dance.

"Well," said Benny, "I got another one and this one is ours."

How do I know this? Du Pré thought.

"Shit," said Du Pré.

"If I sound funny," said Benny Klein, "it's because I just threw up."

"Where are you?" said Du Pré.

"The old highway," said Benny, "about a mile past the Grange Hall on Palmer Creek. You know the one?"

"Yah," said Du Pré.

"This is bad," said Benny.

"Look," said Du Pré. "You stay there and I will come. You call anyone else?"

"Not yet," said Benny. "Who would I call?"

"The coroner."

"He quit," said Benny. "So I'm the coroner."

Benny is a brave man who does not like dead bodies or bad people at all and he is afraid of much but he still does what he said he would do. Be a sheriff. He is a brave man. He hates it.

He still does it.

"Ah," said Du Pré. "You call your dispatcher, have her call the State."

"I shoulda done that already," said Benny, "I'm just upset."

"I be there, right away," said Du Pré.

Benny rang off.

Du Pré walked back down the hallway. Madelaine was sitting at her little vanity, putting lipstick on. She was still naked.

"Hey," said Du Pré from the doorway. "I got to go. Benny wants me."

"He find a girl's body," said Madelaine. "I knew he would. Poor girl."

"I am sorry," said Du Pré.

"No," said Madelaine, "You are not sorry, Du Pré, you are my good Métis man. I know you."

Du Pré shrugged.

"You make my babies safe," said Madelaine. "You make every-body safe again, Du Pré."

"I don't know," said Du Pré.

"I do," said Madelaine.

✤ CHAPTER 2 ✤

Du Pré shot down the old highway, driving ninety. His old police cruiser was still plenty fast, and he had very good tires on it. The lights and siren were gone. He tried to remember if this was the fourth or the third one that he had owned.

That Bart, Du Pré thought, my rich friend, he try to give me a Land Rover. I find out they are sixty thousand dollars, I tell him no good Métis drive a car cost more than three houses cost here. So he find me this. It is faster than all the others.

Du Pré saw the old Grange Hall ahead. White clapboard, a little building, smaller even than a schoolhouse. Some schoolhouses.

Du Pré glanced left and right. He saw Benny's four-wheel drive pickup off on some benchland a half mile or so away from the road. Du Pré slowed down. He saw a pair of ruts that went down into the barrow pit and up the other side and into the scrub. The ruts had been driven in recently.

Du Pré turned and the heavy police cruiser wallowed down and up and then he floored it. He kept an eye on the center of the tracks, looking for boulders, but this wasn't that kind of country. The rocks were up higher.

Then he hit one and he felt the transmission heave.

"Shit!" he snarled. He slowed down. The transmission whined. He smelled hot coolant.

Fuck me, Du Pré thought. Fuck me to death. Damn.

Benny Klein was sitting on the tailgate of his pickup. Du Pré parked the cruiser and he got out and walked to the sheriff. Benny was white and he was sweating even though the day was not warm.

"OK," said Du Pré.

"Over there," said Benny. He pointed toward some silvered boards piled haphazardly and clotted with the yellow skeletons of weeds from the last year.

An old lambing shed, maybe, who knew?

Du Pré walked slowly toward the pile of wood. A magpie floated past, headed for the creek a mile away.

Du Pré smelled the rotten flesh. Dead people, they smell deader than anything else. You smell a real dead person, you are smelling yourself someday, you never forget it.

She was lying facedown on a patch of yellow earth. The coyotes had eaten parts of her. Her legs were chewed. She was naked. She was swollen and greenish brown.

Du Pré squatted down on his haunches. He rolled a cigarette. He lit it with the rope shepherd's lighter his daughter Jacqueline had sent him from Spain, when she and her Raymond had gone there for a vacation.

Left me with all them babies, Du Pré thought, Madelaine not help me, Madelaine's daughters, I *die*.

Fourteen kids they got now. I don't think she is through yet.

Jesus.

Du Pré watched some maggots writhing under the dead girl's skin.

A gold chain glittered on her left ankle.

She had been blond.

Du Pré stood up and he walked around the body, a circle about six feet away. He brought the ground to his eyes, like he was tracking. He saw bombardier beetles struggling through the grass. Some tiny shards of green glass shone against the ocher earth.

Couple paper towels, slumped against a sagebrush. Been here a while. Yellow stains on them.

Du Pré circled out another two feet. The sagebrush was sparse here and clumps of grama grass spotted the harsh earth.

Rusty piece of barbwire, sticking out of the earth.

Du Pré ground his cigarette out under his bootheel.

He circled.

He stopped the fourth time he'd walked slowly around, counter-clockwise.

He looked back at the road.

He rolled another cigarette and he walked back to Benny, still sitting on the tailgate of the truck.

"Who finds her?" said Du Pré.

"One of the Salyer kids," said Benny. "Hunting gophers."

That kid not going to sleep so good, next month of nights.

"Your dispatcher, she call the State?"

Du Pré detested the dispatcher, who was a stupid bitch.

"Yeah," said Benny. "They're on their way. Probably be here, an hour. Said not to disturb anything."

Du Pré snorted. Same old shit.

"This not good," he said.

"No," said Benny. "It ain't. This animal is doing this, dumping the bodies. I just thought, shit, I bet there's a lot more. A lot more."

Du Pré sighed.

He glanced over toward a movement just out of his line of vision. A magpie had flown up from the sagebrush a couple hundred yards away.

"We never had anything like this before," said Benny.

Du Pré nodded.

A white pickup roared past on the road. The driver waved. Du Pré and Benny waved back.

In the night, Du Pré thought, a man could drive here, cut his lights, carry the bodies here in maybe ten, fifteen minutes, drive away, not turn his lights on till he was back on the highway. Have to have a lot of gas, couldn't afford to be seen buying any.

Benny's radio began to squawk.

Benny stood up and walked around to his cab and reached in and got the microphone. He listened for a while.

"Of course I'll stay here," he said, angrily. "What the hell do you think I am gonna do? Go play cards?"

"Well," the dispatcher's whiny voice said, "they asked me to call you."

"We actually wipe our butts and everything here, Iris," said

Benny. "Those bastards are not going to be pleasant to have around."

"I was just trying to do my job . . ." whined Iris.

"OK, OK," said Benny. He clicked the microphone off.

"Poor Iris," said Benny. "Husband up and left, she's got six kids and two of them got in trouble and sent to Pine Hills."

Du Pré looked at Benny.

"Me," he said, "I don't be surprised her husband left, her kids are in jail. She is . . ."

"I know," said Benny.

Du Pré shrugged.

Benny walked morosely back to the tailgate and he sat down.

"Could I have a smoke?" said Benny.

Du Pré rolled him one.

"I don't need this shit," said Benny.

Du Pré nodded. It is your shit, though, Benny, you are the sheriff.

"That poor girl."

Du Pré stretched. He glanced off to his left.

Another magpie, same place.

Shit.

"OK," said Du Pré. "I think there is another one over there, so, Benny, why don't you just sit here, smoke."

"Oh, God," said Benny.

Du Pré got up and he started off toward the dark smear of sage that ran across his vision, there must be a slab of rock under it that caught water and held it.

Another magpie.

Shit.

Du Pré kept glancing down at the ground at his feet.

He was moving fast now, dancing through the sagebrush.

Du Pré heard drums in his head.

He smelled the smell of dead people, dead long enough to rot.

Du Pré looked hard.

He saw them then.

Two of them.

Du Pré looked hard and he drifted to his right, circling.

Two bodies, naked, laid out one atop the other, crossed.

Du Pré closed in. He rolled a smoke and lit it, to cut the smell.

He wished he'd brought a bottle with him from his car.

A sudden whiff of skunk. Du Pré saw the black-and-white creature waddling away.

These were awfully small women. Girls, really.

They had both been blond. The magpies and the scavengers had been at their faces. Flies buzzed around the eyepits. Their bellies were hugely swollen and the skin glazed with dirt.

These were fresher than the other, Du Pré thought, few days old.

Du Pré stopped.

He spat on the ground.

He moved away and he began to circle.

Him, Du Pré thought, he maybe leave more here.

Him, he like this place.

Why?

✤ CHAPTER 3 ✤

Right here," said Susan Klein. She was pale and angry. She shook her head. She rubbed the bartop with a towel.

The Toussaint Saloon was packed with people who were all talking at once in little groups. They were drinking but not much. They ordered drinks and then forgot them. The telephone was tied up with people who were checking on their families and friends. They did this over and over.

"It's something that happens somewhere else," said Susan Klein. "In the cities. It doesn't happen here."

Madelaine reached across the bar and she put her hand on top of Susan's. Madelaine looked down at the scarred wood.

Bart Fascelli was sucking down his second soda. His left arm was in a sling. Once again, he had hurt himself working on his gigantic diesel shovel. It did not come naturally to him.

"Bad man like that don't leave those girls nothin'," said Madelaine. "Kill them, dump them like old guts in the brush for the coyotes to eat."

Du Pré was standing on the other side of Bart, sipping a whiskey. He kept looking off somewhere else. Far away. A far country.

"I don't suppose it would do any good to post a reward?" said Bart, looking from Susan and Madelaine to Du Pré. Bart was rich. Very rich. He had money, at least, to offer.

Du Pré shrugged.

"I didn't think so," said Bart.

"It is maybe a good idea," said Du Pré. "Except this guy is not a thief or a guy does things with other people, you know. He just does this alone, you know. People now will be watching all the time, you bet, I hope they don't just shoot every stranger. This is not funny."

Benny Klein came in, looking tired and worn and sick.

He came up to his wife and he leaned up against the bar. He didn't say anything. After a moment, Susan reached over and touched his face.

"Benny," she said softly, "calm down. Have a beer. Come on, now."

Du Pré looked in the mirror. The four of them, the two women near poor Benny, who liked evil even less than he liked violence. Bart looking off and far away.

I hope he don't say he is afraid of me again, Du Pré thought. I hope this bastard gets caught today. But I don't think that he will.

Du Pré's thoughts flicked back and forth like a hunter's eyes on a landscape. He sighed and sipped his whiskey.

Susan Klein was pulling beers and mixing drinks, her face sad.

I been here plenty, thought Du Pré, playing my fiddle. Happy times with my friends and neighbors, drinking and laughing and dancing. Maybe we get to do that. But we have to wait on someone with a dead heart to let us.

"Gabriel," said Bart. He had come up behind Du Pré.

"Unh," said Du Pré.

"What do you think, now?" said Bart. He was looking levelly into Du Pré's eyes.

Du Pré shrugged.

He rolled a cigarette. He lit it.

"Plenty bad, what I think," said Du Pré. "Maybe I call that Harvey Wallace, you remember?"

"Oh, yes," said Bart.

"He is with them FBI," Du Pré went on. "Maybe he have something he can tell us."

"Good," said Bart.

"I also try to find Benetsee," said Du Pré. "But he is gone. He tell me he is going to Canada, see some of his people. But I don't know what he meant, how long he is gone, you know."

"I'm trying to think of something I can do," said Bart.

"You are doing it," said Du Pré. "You can spend your money later."

Bart laughed.

"It's the first thing that I think of," he said, "you know how I am."

Du Pré looked up at the tin ceiling. Yes, Bart, I know how you are and you got more money than most countries got. It almost killed you, all that money. But it did not.

You are my friend.

My father kill your brother, long time ago.

Life, it is very strange.

Du Pré stubbed his smoke out in the ashtray. Light flashed against the ceiling, someone had opened the door.

Clouds moved, Du Pré thought. He glanced over to see who had come in.

A middle-aged couple in new heavy jackets and the sort of shoes that city people buy to go to the country in were standing inside the door, and they looked uncomfortable.

The man took the woman's arm and led her toward the bar, he bent over and was speaking softly close to her ear. She looked at the floor and she dabbed at her eyes with a handkerchief.

Susan Klein had seen the couple and she had come out from the bar, moving very quickly.

Du Pré looked at her, standing in front of them, her face grave. They talked in low tones. Susan glanced over at Du Pré.

She said one more thing to them and then she led them over to where Du Pré was sitting. Du Pré got up.

"This is Mr. and Mrs. Kamp," said Susan Klein to Du Pré. "They are the parents . . . of a missing girl. They wanted to talk . . . to you . . ."

Missing girl, Du Pré thought. Oh, yes, they are missing, they just up and left for hell.

The woman looked up at Du Pré. She was a tiny creature, her eyes huge in her sad face.

"Shannon was . . ." she began.

"Our daughter," the man cut in. "She ran away a year ago . . . we never heard from her again."

"We just want to know . . ." the woman said.

Du Pré nodded. "The police, they call you?"

"No," said the man. "They haven't . . . they said they haven't been able to identify any of the victims . . ."

The woman had pulled a photograph from the pocket of her coat. It was an ordinary yearbook photograph, the kind kids in high school pass around.

"She looked like this," said the woman. "Isn't she pretty?"

Du Pré took the photograph. He stared at it.

If one of them was your daughter, I would not know it, he thought, their faces had been chewed almost off, they had rotted, there was nothing there that looked like a pretty girl, like this picture.

"The police won't let us look at the bodies," said the woman.

No shit, thought Du Pré, you look at what we are finding out there you will not sleep again, this lifetime.

"She was so pretty . . ." the woman said, again.

"Could you tell us anything?" said the man. "She had a birth-mark on her back."

Du Pré thought of the green-brown bloated mess lying in the sagebrush, the birds pecking at it.

"I don't know," said Du Pré, lamely. "I wish I could help, you know, but you will have to wait for the police."

"But you found them," said the man. He was getting angry.

Du Pré nodded.

"Why can't you tell us about Shannon?" said the woman.

Du Pré felt his temper rise. Then it cooled. Crazy question, these are people crazy with grief, he thought, they are mad.

"It's a conspiracy," said the man.

Yes, Du Pré thought, it is.

"Do you know what it is like, to lose a child and not even really know what happened to her?" said the woman.

Du Pré nodded.

"Why won't you help us?" said the man.

"He is helping you," said Susan Klein.

"Bastards," said the woman.

Susan narrowed her eyes. She stalked out the front door of the bar. She was gone only a couple of minutes. When she came back, she had a manila envelope in her hand.

"Oh, God, Susan," said Benny.

"My husband is trying to find this animal," said Susan Klein to the couple. "So is Gabriel, and about five hundred other cops. Cops are people. Pretty good people."

She pulled a big glossy black-and-white photo from the enve-lope.

"Is this your daughter?" said Susan, eyes blazing.

The couple looked at the photo.

"What is it?" said the woman.

"It's what Gabriel found," said Susan. "They don't look like what you see in a funeral parlor when the cops find them. They look like this."

"Oh my God," said the man. "That's a body."

"People aren't good keepers," said Susan Klein.

"I don't understand," said the woman.

"Good," said Susan Klein, slipping the photo back in the envelope. "Now, mister, I suggest that you take your wife and get the
hell out of my bar and don't come back for a while."

"Why?" said the woman.

"Come on, Grace," said the man, pulling on his wife's arm.

She went with him, shaking her head.

They went out.

Susan Klein went back behind the bar.

Du Pré looked at her.

She was lighting a cigarette with a butane lighter.

It took her four tries. Her hands were shaking. Badly.

❖ CHAPTER 4 ❖

They have to do it that way," said Harvey Wallace, whose Indian
name was Weasel Fat. He was Blackfeet, and FBI.

"Shit," said Du Pré. "It was some surprising, you know, they
come here and they want to question me, you know. Then this
guy of yours, he says, Mr. Du Pré, we know you are killing these
girls, we want to help you."

"Yeah," said Harvey Wallace/Weasel Fat. "Well, that is the way
that they do things."

"They ever *catch* anybody," said Du Pré into the telephone. He
was so mad he was shouting.

"Fairly often," said Harvey. "We catch bad guys pretty often.
You'd be surprised. I know I look like a dickhead, but even I have
caught bad guys. Jury even agreed."

"I am sorry," said Du Pré. "I am pret' mad, say things."

"Don't blame you," said Harvey, "now, he'll probably come on back and want you to take a polygraph."

"Lie detector?" said Du Pré. "Jesus Christ."

"Yeah," said Harvey. "Please take it."

"Why the fuck I take that?" said Du Pré.

"Well," said Harvey. "If you pass it, then you're out of it altogether."

"Harvey," said Du Pré, "I am out of it now."

"No," said Harvey. "You aren't. Tell you a story. Ten years ago, we had a case, guy was killing little girls, you know, like five years old. Cops are stumped. We come in. We don't get squat. Couple more little girls get found. There's no thread."

Du Pré rolled a cigarette with one hand. He'd taken two years off when he was sixteen and he had done nothing much but try to roll cigarettes with one hand. Like his Papa, Catfoot, did. Got so he could do it pretty good. Two years.

"I come in on it and I look over all the reports. Nothin'. I can't see anything. Case drags on a year. Three more little girls. The people in this city are ready to lynch all the incompetent bastards in the FBI."

Du Pré struck a match with his thumbnail. Some of the match's phosphorus stuck under his thumbnail, burning. It hurt like hell. Du Pré glared at the pain.

"I can't see a fucking thing. Hundreds of leads followed, a few suspects but nothing worth spit, they all got good alibis, nothing, not one fucking thing. So I send all the reports to Statistical Analysis. They put the data into the computer. The computer notices that there is this one cop who is around more than he should be, it's not his case but he's around it a lot."

"You give him the pollywog, whatever," said Du Pré, "And it's him?"

"Not quite," said Harvey. "I have him take the polygraph and he's lying about something. But he didn't kill the little girls. Polygraph says so, so does a bunch of other things."

Du Pré sucked on his burnt thumb.

"I am curious," said Harvey. "So I grill this poor bastard over a

nice hot flame, woulda put burning toothpicks under his fingernails, skinned him slowly, it is the way of my people."

Them Blackfeet, mean fuckers, thought Du Pré, looking at his
thumb.

"Well," said Harvey, "after working his kidneys over with a
rubber hose and threatening to fry up his pet guppies for lunch,
he finally breaks and tells me about the report he didn't file.
Seems he was working and a call got routed to him, the dicks on
the case were all out. Some little old lady had seen something suspicious. Ho-hum, little old ladies drive us nuts."

Du Pré clenched his teeth. His thumb hurt like hell.

"Well, this poor cop was going through a bad divorce and he'd
gobbled too many Valiums and he was kinda addled, and he
scrambled everything he jotted down and then he went home
and slept it off and when he came back the next day he couldn't
make fuck-all out of his notes so he trashed them."

Du Pré farted.

"Case goes on, the cop is obsessed with this little old lady who
called in when he was all fucked up, but he can't find her. It's the
one time he's ever done this. He's ashamed. The little old lady had
given him the license plate number of a car."

Du Pré waited.

"Finally I say, look, here's what you do. Go back and work out
from the places where the little girls were found. See if any little
old ladies croaked after the day you were too fucked up to take
the call."

"By midafternoon the cop's got a name of an old lady who
stroked out three days after one of the bodies was discovered. He
goes to look at the house. House has a clear view though it's
pretty far off. Goes up to the house. It's sealed, pending probate.
He gets a court order and gets in. What do you think he finds?"

"This old lady," said Du Pré, "she has this telescope, she looks
out the window with. She writes things down. There is a note by
the telephone, got description of a guy, a car, the license plate
number, the time, and everything."

"Exactly," said Harvey. "How'd you guess that?"

"I never heard you speak more than fifty words at once, all the time I know you," said Du Pré. "So I figure it has to be a real story and so that is how a real story would work out."

"Indeed it did," said Harvey. "Picked the guy up, grilled him, sent in Come-to-Jesus Wilkins, and the guy confessed just like that."

"Come-to-Jesus?" said Du Pré.

"FBI agent who, so help me, can go into a room with a raving sociopath and convince the motherfucker that he ought to do the best thing. Come-to-Jesus, get it off his chest and straight with the Lord. I saw him do it once with a wacko who ate everyone he killed."

Du Pré snorted.

"So," said Harvey Wallace/Weasel Fat, "I'd appreciate it if as a personal favor to me you would take the polygraph."

"Fuck," said Du Pré.

"Fine," said Harvey. "Just after you take the polygraph. Now, after you take the polygraph I can be more helpful than I can before."

"Shit," said Du Pré.

"Du Pré," said Harvey, "humor me. This is almost the twenty-first century and gadgets rule us."

"You think I maybe done this?" said Du Pré.

"Don't be an asshole," said Harvey. "Of course not. But once you take it then all the guys in the agency who live and die by the damn things are stalemated and they cause less trouble. I won't be assigned to that case. Wish I could be. I keep telling them they are fools and they keep promoting me."

"OK," said Du Pré. "You gonna have Benny take it? He is so upset he probably flunk it."

"You don't worry about that," said Harvey. "Benny's the Sheriff and he's not the problem. You are. You have no official status."

"Oh," said Du Pré.

"Which means I can't talk to you much," said Harvey.

"I am going, this murderer, I am going to find him," said Du Pré.

"Probably," said Harvey. "Benny won't. You might."

"OK," said Du Pré, "I get him to deputize me?"

"Yup," said Harvey.

"Then what?" said Du Pré.

"I send Agent Pidgeon to see you."

"Why?" said Du Pré.

"She's a specialist in serial killers," said Harvey.

"She?" said Du Pré.

"Yeah," said Harvey. "We quit binding their feet, taught 'em how to read, write, things like that. Nothing to be done about it now, we got 'em."

"How long she been doing this?" said Du Pré.

"Couple years," said Harvey. "She got her doctorate in psychology and then she joined the FBI. Nice young woman. Beautiful, too. Ambitious. Great knockers. Smart. If she heard me tell you she had great knockers, I'd be jailed for sexual harassment. Lose my job."

"Why she pick serial killers?" said Du Pré.

"You'd have to ask her," said Harvey. "I'd be afraid to, myself."

"OK," said Du Pré. "I go to this polygraph."

"It makes things simpler," said Harvey.

"Who do I call?" said Du Pré.

"Oh," said Harvey, "I already did."

"Prick," said Du Pré. "You know I say yes, huh?"

"Yup," said Harvey. "I need you on this one, we do anyway."

"OK," said Du Pré.

"Bodies are dumped out in the sagebrush," said Harvey. "Very few FBI guys know much about sagebrush."

"Yah," said Du Pré. "I am trying to find Benetsee."

"That would have been my next question," said Harvey.

"He is in Canada," said Du Pré.

"I'll send you some money," said Harvey. "You buy him some wine and tobacco and meat."

"Oh," said Du Pré, "I take care of it."

"Thanks," said Harvey.

"Yeah," said Du Pré.

✣ CHAPTER 5 ✣

D u Pré!" said Madelaine. "You ask him to ask you them question I give you."

"Yah," said Du Pré. "He ask me I am fucking twelve women, like you keep telling me I am, I say no, the machine, it says I am lying."

"OK," said Madelaine. "I thought so."

"It is fourteen, anyway," said Du Pré. "My dick, it is huge and it is very hungry. Twelve women, they do not quite do it for me, you know."

"OK," said Madelaine. "I fix that. You don't be telling me, you have a headache, you hear."

Du Pré nodded and grinned at her.

"Now on, you don't got time, fuck more than me," said Madelaine.

"Love is holy," said Father Van Den Heuvel. "And never more so than when the two of you discuss it."

The three of them were sitting at Madelaine's kitchen table having lunch. Elk and vegetable soup and Madelaine's good bread and home-canned corn and peppers.

The big, clumsy Belgian Jesuit had splotches of elk soup and kernels of corn down his cassock.

Been a while since he knock himself out shutting his head in his car door, Du Pré thought, he should maybe do that pretty soon again.

Three times the good priest had been found lying by his car, out cold. He was the clumsiest human being Du Pré had ever known. He was not allowed to split wood anymore. He had split his own foot so badly he was two years on crutches.

It was maybe the only congregation in the world which laid

214

bets on whether or not the priest would drop the Host during Communion.

There was half a foot of snow outside on the ground. Even though it was the first week of June, it was Montana, and it seemed to snow at least every other year in early June. Late June.

"It ever snow here in July?" said Father Van Den Heuvel. "I think it has snowed every other month."

"Yah," said Du Pré. "We got two feet once, Fourth of July."

"Ah," said Father Van Den Heuvel, "God's love is wonderful."

"It is sad, them girls, no one know who they are," said Madelaine.

Only one of the three bodies could be identified. Father Van Den Heuvel had buried the unknown two this morning. The county had paid for the coffins.

"Poor children," said the big priest. "I wonder where their families are."

"Lots of runaway kids," said Madelaine.

The pathologists had said that the two bodies that Du Pré had found were approximately sixteen. Dental work had been of minimal quality. One of the girls had a tattoo, the kind made in jails with pen inks and dull needles. A skull with a cross sticking out of it.

On the web of skin between thumb and forefinger of her left hand. The girl may have done it herself.

"How come they bury them so quick?" said Madelaine.

"They get their samples and that is that," said Du Pré.

Modern times.

Don't want to pay the cold storage on them, Du Pré thought. These are not kids from nice homes. People who have some power, money. These kids, they will be forgotten. They always were forgotten. Their parents never even knew that they were there, I bet.

Only Du Pré and Madelaine and Benny had come to the interment.

Benny left immediately.

Father Van Den Heuvel had said his few words and then he and Du Pré and Benny had let the coffins down. They were very light.

"Du Pré!" Madelaine said. "I want you to promise these two little girls that you will find who did this to them. They got no one else to speak for them, you know."

"Yah," said Du Pré.

"You promise them."

"They don't got names," said Du Pré, "so I say, OK, you are my people, I find this bastard."

Madelaine reached up and touched Du Pré on his cheek.

"Everybody is our people," said Madelaine. "We are Métis."

Du Pré nodded. That was true. The Mixed Bloods. That is pretty much everybody.

Long time ago, my people who were in France come to the New World and they marry my people who were already here. Then we really catch hell. Whites call us Indian, Indians call us whites. English, they hang us, steal our land. Send us all across Canada, move them furs for the Hudson's Bay Company. The Here Before Christ. Most places they were, too.

Long time ago.

They come down here after them English crush the Red River Rebellion, got nothing, bunches of children.

Had each other, my people did.

These poor girls, they have no one at all.

They got my Madelaine, who would feed all the world. Wipe all the tears.

They got me, too, I guess.

I find this bastard.

Du Pré rolled a cigarette while he waited for Father Van Den Heuvel to come back from taking a leak. The old police cruiser, light bar and sirens taken off, decals off the doors, still runs good. Runs fast.

There were a lot of cigarette burns on the backseat, where smokes Du Pré had flicked out the window flew back in.

Du Pré rolled a cigarette and he offered it to Father Van Den Heuvel. The big priest nodded and he took it. He had never tried to roll his own smoke. He couldn't do it.

"I must go," said the big priest. "I have to drive to Miles City and see Mrs. LeBlanc. She is dying."

"I send her something?" said Madelaine.

"She can't eat," said Father Van Den Heuvel.

Madelaine dug around and she found a St. Christopher medal.

Father Van Den Heuvel put it in his pocket.

Madelaine walked him out to his car. Du Pré had some more coffee.

Tomorrow, I got to go sign off, some cattle. His son-in-law, Raymond, did most of the brand inspections now, but Du Pré did what Raymond could not do. Cattle business was not too good. Hate someone, give them a cow. Cattle business was mostly not too good.

Du Pré heard the priest's car drive off. Madelaine came back.

"You sure like, devil that poor priest," said Du Pré.

"Poo," said Madelaine. "Him like it. He is a nice man."

Du Pré laughed.

"Devil me, too," he said.

Madelaine stood in front of him, hand on her hip.

"Fourteen, huh?" she said. "You come on now, I show you some damn fourteen."

After, Du Pré sat on the edge of the bed, smoking. Madelaine was in the shower. Du Pré could smell the potpourri soap she made, the smell of the steam from the hot water. The door to the bathroom was open and he could see her shape through the glass door of the shower.

Fourteen, huh? Du Pré thought, I got as much trouble I need, just this Madelaine. She fuck good. I am a lucky man.

Where is old Benetsee? My old coyote friend. Him, he got things to tell me that I need to hear.

Who is, this man does these things. What does he hide behind? Where is he going? I want to kill him, where do I wait.

Thing about good hunters, they wait well. Don't bother them, they dream, don't move.

When Madelaine came out of the bathroom in her robe, toweling her thick long dark hair, Du Pré went in and he showered quickly. He dried himself and he got dressed and he went out to the kitchen.

"I am going to Benetsee's," he said.

Madelaine nodded. "Him not back."

Du Pré shrugged.

"Leave him a note," said Madelaine.

"Don't know, him read," said Du Pré.

"Then you leave him note he don't have to read," said Madelaine. "You leave him a loaf of my good bread."

She went to the kitchen and she wrapped up a loaf of bread in foil and she put it in a plastic bag.

"His dogs all dead?" she said.

Du Pré nodded. Dogs got old, they died.

"We get him another dog," said Madelaine.

"OK," said Du Pré. He did not ever argue with Madelaine. She had taught him not to do that.

"Old man," said Madelaine. "I pray for him."

"You pray for everybody," said Du Pré.

"Don't pray for your fourteen other women," said Madelaine.

"Them don't need it," said Du Pré.

"I find you, another woman, you need it," said Madelaine.

"OK," said Du Pré.

"You find that man," said Madelaine.

✤ CHAPTER 6 ✤

Du Pré and Madelaine watched the fancydancers circling on the floor of the high-school gymnasium. Men with huge feather bustles and fans and headdresses and legpieces and all of them as proud as fighting cocks. Fancydancers. Roosters.

Wolf Point, Montana. It felt cold here even if it was hot.

"Let's go, look at the things the traders have," said Madelaine. There were tables and booths all up and down the halls of the schools. Jewelry, clothing, crafts, one man even had some buffalo robes.

They walked down the steps of the bleachers and out into the lobby. Madelaine looked around at the displays of junk jewelry, most of it bad turquoise and cheap silverplate, made in Southeast Asia.

She spotted an old man in a ribbon shirt who didn't have very much. Just a black cloth, worn velvet, sprawled on a card table and a few pieces set on it. The old man stood with his arms folded. He had big rings on each finger and thumb and bracelets and a necklace of silver rattlesnakes with turquoise eyes.

Madelaine stopped in front of the table.

"How far are you from your people?" she said.

"Long ways," said the man. He smiled. He had no front teeth.

Madelaine bent over to look. She picked up a bracelet which had a huge cabochon of black-spotted turquoise set in a mass of silver. She turned the bracelet around. She squinted at the back of the setting.

"I like this," she said. "Will you sell it?"

"Thousand dollars," said the old man.

Madelaine nodded.

"He say a thousand dollars."

"He does, eh?" said Du Pré, who hated shopping.

Madelaine smiled at him.

"You trade this for a good fiddle?" she said.

"Mebbe," said the old man. "If I can play it as well as your man the first time I pick it up."

Du Pré snorted.

"Five hundred," said Madelaine.

"OK," said the old man, smiling. "I give this to you, five hundred and half his fiddle. I got a saw in my truck."

Du Pré nodded. He wondered if he had seven hundred dollars on him, since that was where Madelaine and this toothless old man were headed, after they had got through threatening to saw Du Pré's fiddle in half. He probably did.

They stood there for a moment. A band of teenage Indian kids ran past laughing. They all had on black satin jackets with red feather fans on the backs. They were headed outside to smoke.

Inside the drummers and singers were making music. The sound was very old and eerie. It had been going on here in America for thousands of years. Du Pré looked through the open doors and he saw the fancydancers speeding up, through the crowd of people drifting past. Sometimes the fancydancers danced for hours. Some dropped dead of heart attacks. It was an exhausting dance.

"Seven hundred dollars," said Madelaine.

Du Pré dug out his wallet. He looked in one of the side pockets where he kept his hundred-dollar bills. There were two wads in it. He usually only carried one. He fished out the wad, quartered, that didn't look familiar. There were seven hundred-dollar bills in it. He handed them to Madelaine.

The old man was fitting the bracelet to Madelaine's wrist, squeezing the soft silver with his strong old hands.

Du Pré handed him the money. The old man didn't count it, he just tucked it in his shirt pocket.

Du Pré looked back at the fancydancers. They were rocking back and forth as they circled, dipping forward and arching their backs.

Du Pré ached looking at them.

The drums went faster, the singers ululated.

"Thanks, Du Pré," said Madelaine.

"Uh," said Du Pré. "There is this seven hundred dollars there I don't know I got."

"Oh, how is that?" said Madelaine. "One of your women you fucking tip you, you were so good one night?"

"No," said Du Pré. "One I am fucking put it in my wallet, though."

"Well," said Madelaine. "Maybe, who knows."

Du Pré laughed.

There was food being served in the cafeteria. They went in. There were pots of buffalo stew and fry bread and chokecherry syrup. Cost two dollars. They took their food to a table and Du Pré went to buy some soft drinks.

"They don't got pink wine," said Du Pré, setting down the paper cups.

"No shit they don't," said Madelaine. "They don't allow no alcohol at all here. Too much trouble."

"I got whiskey in my truck," said Du Pré.

"They find it they beat the shit out of you," said Madelaine.

Some of the young men, who were the security people, came in, and they looked pretty tough.

"Probably," said Du Pré.

"Well," said Madelaine. "There are some of your Turtle Mountain people."

Du Pré glanced over. He waved at the Turtle Mountain people, in their bright red shirts and cowboy hats and boots.

"We play some tonight," said Du Pré.

It started to rain outside, sudden slashing rain with a lot of wind. The sheet of glass in the windows flexed and shimmered.

The buffalo stew didn't have enough salt in it. Du Pré got up and he went to get some.

He found some little packets of salt. He took ten.

He went back. Madelaine was looking at her new bracelet.

"It is very pretty," he said.

"Yes," said Madelaine. "Me, I like this."

They ate their food. Pretty bland. Du Pré wished he had some pepper sauce.

"You want to smoke," said Madelaine, "you will have to go outside. Me, I will go and look around, these other traders."

Du Pré laughed.

"You want money?" he said.

Madelaine shook her head. "I got my nice thing," she said. "You go and smoke."

Du Pré carried the used bowls and plates and plastic forks to a trash can and he dumped them in. Madelaine grinned at him and she went off down a side hall rowed both sides with tables.

Du Pré made his way out front. The sidewalk was thick with cigarette butts.

The rain had stopped as suddenly as it had begun. The sun was shining down in golden shafts through the black clouds. The air was fresh and smelled of lightning.

Du Pré rolled a cigarette and he lit it and he drew the smoke deep into his lungs. He blew out a long blue-gray stream. He sighed. It tasted good.

Knots of people stood around, smoking and chatting. Little kids shrieked and ran and jumped. Their parents were inside, shrieking and running and jumping, some of them anyway.

Young bloods in ribbon shirts with fancy hairdos an-nounced their tribe by their clothes and paints and bad attitudes of young warriors.

Du Pré snorted. Backbone of the tribe is the women, they give life, strength of the tribe is the warriors, their humility.

These boys, they got some to go, Du Pré thought. Spend a little less time, front of the mirror, little more time helping the old people.

Du Pré glanced off at a little copse of blue spruce in the middle of the lawn. There was a sculpture made of stainless steel to one side.

An old man dressed in ragged clothes was leaning against the sculpture.

It was Benetsee.

"Damn," said Du Pré. He threw his cigarette on the ground and he began to walk toward the old man.

"Hey!" Du Pré yelled.

Benetsee moved. He was shuffling, fast enough, toward the lit-tle stand of spruces.

Du Pré got to the lawn and he started to run.

Benetsee went behind the trees.

Du Pré cursed.

He ran flat out, his cowboy boots slipping at each stride with a jerk, leather soles on wet grass.

Du Pré tried to turn and his feet shot out from under him and he fell full-length.

He slid a good fifteen feet. He was all wet on his right side. He could smell the crushed grass. His jeans would be stained. The elbow of his shirt.

Du Pré got up and he walked on, his side stitched a little, he had pulled some muscles in his chest.

Du Pré went around behind the spruces.

No one there. Of course.

Du Pré heard feet running toward him.

A couple of the young security men came around the spruces, one on each side.

"Hey, man," said one. "Everything all right? We saw you running."

"Oh, yes," said Du Pré. "It is all right."

The three of them looked at each other for a moment.

Du Pré shrugged and he walked back toward the gym.

✦ CHAPTER 7 ✦

Them powwows all the same," said Madelaine. "Same people doin' same things. I go to 'em, but I don't miss leavin' them." Madelaine grinned at Du Pré. She had her left hand on the dashboard of the car. The turquoise bracelet burned sea blue in the sunlight.

Du Pré glanced over at the fence line crossing a little feeder seep. A prairie falcon gripped a post, wings half-extended.

They were doing about eighty on a narrow two-lane blacktop road. Every once in a while, they passed a little white cross mounted on a steel fencepost. The crosses marked spots where people had died in car wrecks. On Memorial Day, family would often put plastic flowers on the crosses.

"I had some good times with them Turtle Mountain people," said Du Pré. "Them good people."

"That guitar player, him Daby, is a dirty old man," said Madelaine. "He grab my ass, you know."

"Um," said Du Pré. Well, he thought, you can eat old Daby for your lunch, the old bastard won't try that again, I am sure. Maybe he drive, Turtle Mountain, ice bag in his lap, keep the hurt from his nuts getting ripped off down a little.

"He play pretty good guitar, though," Madelaine said.

She don't rip his nuts off. She tell him, you play pretty good, I don't rip your plums off this one time, you know. Second time, I take 'em, fry them, eat them. Turtle Mountain oysters.

"I tell him, mind your manners, I fry up some Turtle Mountain oysters," said Madelaine. "Him don't like that."

They crested a long sloping hill and looked down suddenly into a swaled bottom, thick with cattails and loud with Canada geese. The car windows were shut but the geese honked loudly enough so they could be heard easily. Du Pré glanced over and saw young geese, in their yellow down, following their parents.

The car bottomed out as it crossed a little bridge and then shot up the rising road. A pheasant flew suddenly.

Above the water's reach to the roots hanging down into the earth, the sagebrush reappeared.

They got to Toussaint in two hours. It was a bright and sunny day and the Wolf Mountains to the north gleamed with fresh snow up high.

"You want some pink wine?" said Du Pré.

"No," said Madelaine. "I need to go home. I am a little worried about Lourdes."

Lourdes was Madelaine's eldest daughter. A good student, quiet and shy, when she grew up she would be a stately woman. She had her father's big bones and blade nose.

Du Pré nodded. Lourdes had just turned fifteen and she was

the most rebellious of Madelaine's children, in a quiet, firm way. No scenes. No calls from the police. If she drank or smoked dope she did so very quietly. Du Pré didn't think that she did.

Lourdes liked to control everything around her.

Lourdes was a frightened, intelligent girl.

Du Pré drove up to Madelaine's house. The front door was open. The radio was turned up very loud. Bad rock and roll music.

It was all pretty bad, Du Pré thought.

Du Pré parked and he got out and opened the trunk and he got their nylon suitcases. He took one in each hand and he walked up toward the house.

"Du Pré!" Madelaine yelled. Her voice was a little hysterical.

Du Pré came in. He set the bags down.

Madelaine was standing by the telephone, which sat on a little Parsons table Du Pré had made for her, out of some walnut he had found in an abandoned bar.

Madelaine was holding a piece of ruled notebook paper. The sort that is bound with wire. One margin was all tiny holes, now ripped out when the page had been taken from the book.

"Lourdes, she run away."

Du Pré nodded. Neither of his two girls had ever run away, but, then, neither of his two girls got any crap from Du Pré, who knew better. My Jacqueline and my Maria, they know who they are. Father Pussycat, they call me. I give up early on.

"She say where she run away to?" said Du Pré.

"It is not running away you let your poor mother know where you are visiting," said Madelaine. "That's just visiting."

"She got a boyfriend?" said Du Pré.

"Yeah," said Madelaine. "She is hanging out with that poor Dassault boy, Sean. That asshole old man of his, name him that."

Bucky Dassault was one of Du Pré's pet hates. The man was wholly dishonest. He'd come out of Deer Lodge Prison on parole from a statutory rape conviction. While he was in there, he had taken extension courses and qualified as an alcohol and drug counselor. That didn't work out well, so he became Benjamin

Medicine Eagle, New Age Shaman, and he took out ads in New Age magazines and he made a lot of money. His wife had the good sense to divorce him after only three kids. Sean was around, but the other boy and the girl were in juvenile custodial programs.

"So we ask Sean, where is Lourdes?" said Du Pré.

"No shit," said Madelaine.

"OK," said Du Pré. "I go and find the little prick and talk with him, you maybe make some phone calls."

"You don't hurt him," said Madelaine. "He's a pretty good kid, don't have much at home, you know. You can scare him some, but you don't hurt him, Du Pré."

Du Pré nodded. He wasn't going to hurt poor Sean in the first place, but then Madelaine mothered even people she hated.

Du Pré went out and he got in the car and he drove down to the bar and he got out and he went in.

Susan Klein was standing behind the bar. Her husband Benny was out in front.

Sean Dassault was sitting on a barstool, cringing.

"She mad about something," he whined. He turned and looked and saw Du Pré and he jumped off the stool and tried to run.

Benny Klein held his arm.

"You want to kill him or can I?" said Benny.

"Oohhhhh," wailed Sean.

"Sean," said Du Pré, "you quit bawling, some stuck pig, there. We are worried about Lourdes."

Sean looked at Du Pré warily.

"She pregnant?" said Du Pré.

Sean turned red and shook his head.

Bingo, thought Du Pré. Little bastards act just like we did. Now we know better, spoil their fun.

"You know where she go?"

"She was going to Seattle," said Sean.

"How is she getting, this Seattle, Sean?" said Du Pré.

"She going to hitchhike," said Sean.

"Where from?" said Du Pré.

"Going up to the Hi-Line," said Sean.

"Who give her a ride there?" said Du Pré. "Or . . . wait a minute, she was running, the track meet in Cut Bank?"

"She don't go, she tell them she is sick, first thing on Saturday morning."

Me and Madelaine, we are at the powwow. Smart kid.

"Who give her the ride there?" said Du Pré.

"I did," Sean sniffled.

Oh, good, thought Du Pré, Lourdes has the balls to hitchhike a thousand miles, and you, you little pile of shit, won't go along to protect her. Not that you could so much, but the thought is nice.

"Why don't you go?" said Du Pré.

"I am eighteen," said Sean miserably.

Right, thought Du Pré, that is statutory rape, even if you don't touch them, here. OK, this kid is at least not wanting to see Deer Lodge first minute he is eligible, go there.

"You try to talk her out of it?"

"Hah," said Sean. "She don't never do what I say."

"You take her yesterday morning?" said Du Pré.

Sean nodded.

"Drop her off, Raster Creek, first place got a little rest stop?"

Sean nodded.

"You wait to see, she gets a ride?"

Sean shook his head.

"Why not?" said Du Pré.

"She don't want me to," Sean said.

"We got girls dead in the sagebrush," said Du Pré, "and you, you little fucker, you don't at least wait, see who picks her up?"

Sean shook his head miserably.

"You pussy-whipped little bastard," said Du Pré. "Good thing I don't not promise my Madelaine that I won't hurt you."

"She tell me, go away," said Sean.

"Madelaine, she skin you out, whole hide," said Du Pré. "She wipe her ass with your brain. You want good advice, grow a foot, turn blond, move away. Jesus."

Sean snuffled.

"Sean," said Susan Klein, "you fucked up big time."

"Well," said Du Pré, "since you are gonna die so soon, you maybe better go find Father Van Den Heuvel."

"Oh," said Sean.

"It is important," said Du Pré.

"Oh," said Sean.

"Madelaine, she will not kill you while there is a priest looking," said Du Pré. "He quit looking at you, you dead."

Sean looked at Du Pré, and Susan, and Benny. He snuffled and wiped his nose on a bar napkin.

He went out the side door and headed for the little Catholic Church.

Du Pré rolled a smoke.

"Poor little fucker," he said.

✤ CHAPTER 8 ✤

God damn you Harvey Weasel Fat, I thought me and you were friends!" Madelaine said not very sweetly into the telephone. Du Pré couldn't hear Harvey defend himself.

"You talkin' like a man got a velvet mouth," said Madelaine. "Why you don't help me?"

Harvey, he is not doing so good, thought Du Pré.

"I got a daughter out there bein' fucked by truck drivers if she isn't dead," said Madelaine. "You goddamn right I am upset. You bastards so busy burning down churches full of dumb people you got no time for a poor woman who's worried?"

She really is mad, thought Du Pré. Mothers, they go nuts, their kids give them mental illness.

"What you care some pussy white man give you a bunch of dumb rules?" said Madelaine. "You Indian or what?"

Poor Harvey, thought Du Pré, he forget it is the women in the tribe do all the torturing. Nothing they like better, saw off nuts with a dull rock.

"Well, I thank you," said Madelaine, "you skinny Blackfeet prick."

Madelaine slammed the phone down.

"Asshole," she said.

Du Pré went to her and he took her in his arms and she began to cry softly. She buried her head in his chest. She put her hands to her face and she rocked a little, keening.

"What I do wrong?" said Madelaine. "I love that Lourdes, I know she is not having such a good time, you know? What I do wrong?"

Du Pré had an attack of smarts and he didn't say one damn thing.

"Damn," said Madelaine. She sniffled. She pulled away and went to the roll of paper towels in the kitchen and she ripped one off and blew her nose and wiped her eyes. She went off to the bathroom. Du Pré heard the water running in the sink.

She will be better now, Du Pré thought, not OK but better.

That damn little bitch Lourdes. She got to know how worried this will make her mother.

Not to mention me. That guy, he is out there, eating runaways.

Dumping their poor bodies in the sagebrush.

That guy, he had a mother, too. We all get one.

Where is he?

Madelaine came out of the bathroom. Her eyes were swollen but a little clearer. Her black eyebrows were knotted and her hands were clenched tight.

"You call them Missoula police?" she said.

"Yes," said Du Pré. Also Kalispell, Spokane, Seattle.

This would be plenty bad enough without what else we got, Du Pré thought. She ought to be crazy.

There was a knock at the door. Du Pré went to it.

Father Van Den Heuvel and Bart.

Du Pré motioned them in.

"You want some coffee," said Madelaine, looking up at them. "I get you some. You sit."

They sat.

Madelaine put water on the stove and they heard the coffee grinder, a heavy cast-iron one maybe a hundred years old, crank.

"I have a plane here," said Bart.

Du Pré nodded. Sometimes it was good to have a rich friend.

"Not much to do but wait and pray," said Father Van Den Heuvel.

No shit, thought Du Pré.

The three men sat and waited, motionless and silent. Madelaine brought coffee for everybody and they drank it.

"How is that Sean?" said Madelaine suddenly.

She looked at Father Van Den Heuvel.

"Upset," said the big priest. "He doesn't feel he did the right thing."

"Where he is?" said Madelaine.

"Uh," said the priest. "He's . . ."

"He's hidin' out at your place," said Madelaine. "I better go and see him. Poor little guy. My Lourdes wrap him around his own dick just like that. Him, he is not match for her, for sure. It is not his fault. I better go tell him that."

Du Pré looked away and smiled.

"I'll go and get him," said Bart.

"I will go with you," said Madelaine. "I . . . you two stay here, you answer the phone."

Du Pré and Father Van Den Heuvel nodded.

Madelaine grabbed her purse and she and Bart went out.

"It's terrible," said the priest. "Poor Madelaine. Poor Lourdes."

"She is a good girl," said Du Pré. "Just strong-willed like her mother. She be all right."

They sat.

Du Pré heard the grind of a big truck moving from a stop up to a slow speed.

It was coming around the corner of the main street and heading up toward Madelaine's.

"That Lourdes, I think that she is here," said Du Pré. He got up and he went outside.

A big black eighteen-wheeler, bright with chrome, flames painted on the hood, tinted windows. It ground slowly up the dirt street and it came up to Du Pré and stopped.

The passenger door opened and Lourdes stepped down on the fender and then to the running board. She pulled a duffel bag after her. She dropped the duffel bag on the ground and then she jumped down.

Lourdes looked at Du Pré.

"Momma here, yes?" she said, warily.

"Bart take her to talk to that dumb boyfriend of yours," said Du Pré. "Me, I don't like to be Sean this moment."

"He is a dumb shit," said Lourdes.

"Yeah, well," said Du Pré. "He is not a very happy dumb shit this time, you bet."

Lourdes shrugged.

A young man dressed all in black, cowboy hat, boots, belt with a big turquoise-and-silver buckle, rings, watch, bracelet, came round from the far side of the big truck. He was blond and moustached and bearded. He stood by the front of his truck, loose and relaxed.

"This your friend, here?" said Du Pré.

"She don't like me so good," said the trucker. "I give her a choice, she could either tell me how to get where she lived, or I could hand her off to the juvie cops. She bitched about it some, but here we are."

Du Pré looked at the guy. The man was smiling a little and his bright blue eyes were twinkling.

All right, thought Du Pré, we got very lucky this time.

He walked over to the trucker and he stuck out his hand. The trucker shook it.

"Du Pré."

"Challis.

"Found her at a truck stop in Spokane," said Challis. "I was . . . well, I just thought I'd bring her here. Didn't know if I bought her a bus ticket she'd use it. And them juvie cops can be kinda nasty."

Du Pré nodded.

"You headed, Chicago?" said Du Pré.

Challis shook his head.

"Seattle," he said.

Well, thought Du Pré, here is some gent, he turn around and drive seven, eight hundred miles take a dumb kid home. Turn around, drive back.

Du Pré glanced over. Lourdes and the priest had gone into the house.

"I thank you," said Du Pré.

"Happy to," said Challis. He pulled a pack of smokes from his shirt pocket and he lit one.

"Uh," said Du Pré. "You spend a lot, diesel, can I give you some money?"

"Nope," said Challis. "All taken care of."

"Her mother will want to thank you," said Du Pré. "She be back in a minute."

"Well," said Challis. "Her mother comes back she'll be takin' a chunk outta the kid's ass, don't need me. I'll be on my way presently."

The man's soft drawl was Montana's own.

"Coffee?" said Du Pré.

"Nope," said Challis. "I just stretch a little here. Got to highball make the freight run there pretty close to time. I called, told 'em I had a little trouble, I'd be along presently. The thing ain't full of hearts ready to transplant, so I suppose folks will get on a couple days later."

They smoked.

"Pret' good of you," said Du Pré.

"Oh," said Challis. "Not really. I had a kid sister, she took off a few years ago. Shelly. That was her name."

Du Pré waited, knowing.

"Finally found her last year. What was left of her, anyway. She was a nice kid. Little wild. Loved children. Would've made a good mother."

Du Pré nodded.

"We got this bastard now," Challis went on. "I wonder maybe he was the one killed Shelly."

Du Pré nodded.

"You're Gabriel Du Pré," said Challis. "I hear you maybe are looking for the same man I'd like to meet."

Du Pré looked at Challis. The blue eyes were gray now and cold as the moon.

"Here's my card," said Challis, handing one to Du Pré. "Number on it's the cellular phone. Got a tape machine, everything. You just call me any old time. I run the Hi-Line pretty much. Sometimes Chicago to Seattle on the interstate. Haulin' goods. Lookin' for something."

Du Pré nodded.

Challis dropped his cigarette in the dirt. He ground it out with his boot and he got up in his cab and the big diesel thrummbbbed and the huge truck moved away.

You damn bet I call you, Du Pré thought.

Bart's Rover was coming up the street.

❧ CHAPTER 9 ❧

That's very good news," said Harvey Wallace. "I didn't care to have any more phone time with your Madelaine. Lovely woman. I don't like having her mad at me."

"Yeah," said Du Pré. "It is always better, life, when Madelaine is not mad at you."

Du Pré was sitting out on the porch of Bart's house using a

portable telephone. He didn't know how it worked. He didn't want to.

"Reason I called, though, is Agent Pidgeon is going to be out your way, her with the gorgeous knockers, asking questions about this swell guy you have dropping the bodies in the sagebrush. Agent Pidgeon is personally very pissed off at that guy. She tells me no man can quite understand how pissed off she is on account of we are not the prey of these predators. She has a point."

Du Pré rolled a smoke with his left hand. He licked the paper.

"So I told her to call you *after* she calls Benny," said Harvey.

"OK," said Du Pré. "I don't got much to tell her, though."

"Benetsee ever show up?" said Harvey.

"No," said Du Pré. "I thought I saw him, at a powwow, over by some trees, but when I get there he is gone."

"They are like that," said Harvey. He meant medicine people.

"Yeah," said Du Pré. "Me, I give a lot to talk to Benetsee about his dreams about now."

"Well . . ." said Harvey.

"One more thing," said Du Pré. "I just think of it. This trucker, he is a nice guy, bring Lourdes back OK. I like him. He say that he had a little sister, they found her dead after she had been missing a long time. He tell me, call him, I need anything. He drives the Hi-Line and some Chicago, Seattle stuff."

"Oh, great," said Harvey. "We got an avenging angel in a big rig."

"He tell me his name, Challis."

"What does he look like?" said Harvey, sharply.

"Blond, six feet, blue eyes, middle thirties maybe," said Du Pré. "Got tattoos on his hands and forearms, I don't remember what they were."

"Oh, yeah," said Harvey. "I know Rolly Challis."

"Shelly and Rolly?" said Du Pré.

"Makes you wonder why more kids don't off their parents," said Harvey. "But Rolly is no laughing matter. I almost busted him, but he done got clean away. I would dearly love to bust him. Can't, though."

"OK," said Du Pré. "Why you want to bust him."

"There was a time . . . look, the guy robbed banks. Damn good at it, too. Never hurt a soul. Most of those assholes are so stupid they can't piss and whistle at the same time. Not Rolly. Never worked with anyone else, so we couldn't get an accomplice to rat him out. Didn't leave us anything nice, like fingerprints or blood or hair. Tell you about one of them. Little dink town called Bigfork, it's gone to yuppies now, up on Flathead Lake? They had a little bank there. There was never any money to speak of in that damned bank but one time a year. They grow a lot of cherries up there, and the bank had to have cash to take care of the checks that the growers wrote the pickers. Cherry season lasts a week, maybe ten days. They had about a quarter mil in small unmarked there, that one fucking Friday, and some guy in a ski mask comes in and takes it. Soft voice, Montana drawl, big gun—I'd bet Rolly didn't even load the damn thing—in and out in five minutes with a couple garbage bags full of twenties. He run everybody into one corner and loaded up, leaving the dye packet bombs. Pretty smooth. Out the door, into a car he'd stolen just ten minutes before, they find the car an hour later on a Forest Service road and the bandit is solid gone."

"Oh," said Du Pré.

"Now," said Harvey, "I don't want you to get the impression that I hate Rolly or anything. He's a pretty nice guy, never did any of the things the assholes do. Just robbed banks some until he got a stake together and then he quit. I think. I got no proof. Or his ass would be in Walla Walla, but there it is. Actually, it could be a lot worse. Guy has brains and balls."

Du Pré laughed. Then so did Harvey.

"I like him," said Harvey. "Dropped by, asked him a few questions once, he looked me in the eye and lied and we both knew it. Now, there wasn't a thing I could do, unless he decided to get clean with Jesus and confess, but Rolly ain't the religious type and he just wouldn't help me throw his ass in the pen for twenty years."

"Yeah," said Du Pré. "Well, neither would I."

"So he made us look like assholes," said Harvey. "Big fucking deal."

They chatted a few more minutes and Du Pré hung up.

Agent Pidgeon, Du Pré thought. My Madelaine, she will like this.

Du Pré looked off toward the lower pasture. Forty head of horses were running flat out across the rolling yellow grass. There was a lot of green in it, there was still water and it was still raining some.

Good horses. Booger Tom had bought them over time. He pretty much ran the place, to lose money, so Bart could take some tax write-offs. Booger Tom said there was just nothin' in the world easier than losing money in the cattle business.

And Bart about had a cow himself when Booger Tom made money. Quite a lot of money, in the cattle business. The perverse old bastard.

"I never been able to do nothing right," said Tom, straight-faced, when Bart complained. "There it is. So shoot me."

Then Booger Tom had said he didn't like cows all that much and he was sure he could lose money in the horse business.

"You made seven hundred fucking thousand dollars!" Bart had yelled, "Which cost me *three million!*"

"You want to lose money or not?" said Booger Tom, and he grinned.

Du Pré chuckled. He looked again and saw Booger Tom on a big roan gelding chasing the horses. Man was probably seventy-five and he rode like a rider. No effort.

Du Pré went in the house and he got a drink of water and some ham from the fridge and an apple and he ate out on the porch. He picked his teeth with a sliver. He looked down at the deck he had built and noticed a few of the pegs had started and were fair. Water in the punch holes. He'd have to pound them down. Reglue them. Maybe just cut them off, they had lasted a couple years and a few were always not quite right.

Du Pré went to the tool barn and he got a hammer and he came back and whacked the pegs down flush with the redwood.

It was a beautiful cool, sunny day.

A golden eagle hung high in the sky, drifting.

Now, Du Pré thought, where that god damned Benetsee is? I need to talk to him.

Du Pré heard a siren, far off. It faded. Came back. Faded.

The hills were muffling it.

Headed this way.

Why? Someone is sick.

Du Pré looked down toward Cooper.

He saw flashing blue lights crest a hill and dip out of sight.

Shit.

Benny's car.

Du Pré went into the house and he got a canvas jacket and he filled a water bottle and put some jerked meat in his pocket. He went out to his car and he started it and turned around and headed down the long county road toward Benny.

Du Pré stopped in a snowplow turnout and he waited.

Two minutes later Benny's car came flying over the crest of the near hill. Du Pré leaned against his old cruiser. He smoked.

Benny saw him and he slowed and turned in.

Du Pré walked to Benny's car. He saw Benny's white face through the window. Benny fumbled with the electric window openers for a moment, too upset to do small things properly.

"Du Pré . . ." said Benny.

"We got another one?" said Du Pré.

"Yeah," said Benny.

"Well," said Du Pré. "Why don't you call me?"

"I needed some time to think," said Benny. Or not think, just drive.

"Where?" said Du Pré.

"Dry wash near town," said Benny. "Cooper, I mean."

"OK," said Du Pré.

"Been there a while," said Benny. "That little Morse girl who disappeared five, six years ago?"

Du Pré nodded. He remembered that one well. The child was five or six, had gone out to play a little more at dusk. No one ever saw her again. She might have been taken by a mountain lion, there were some fresh tracks in the area. That was all that anyone could come up with. The cat ate all of her.

Mountain lions did that. Ate children, skulls, everything.

The child was the daughter of a schoolteacher. The schoolteacher had stayed another year and then had moved away. Du Pré didn't know where she went.

"OK," said Du Pré. "We go there."

Benny turned around and Du Pré got in his car and he pulled up behind Benny.

Benny roared off, a crazy speed for the bad road.

The two of them shot down toward Cooper.

Benny slowed near town and he pulled off the road into a big pasture which had a rutted track going cross it to a slash in the earth a half mile away.

Another Sheriff's car was there, lights slowly flashing.

Benny and Du Pré drove slowly over the rocks and ruts up to the other car. They parked and got out.

Du Pré walked up to the edge of the dry wash.

Benny's deputy was down in the bottom, near a rusted fifty-five-gallon drum.

He was on his hands and knees, vomiting.

✤ CHAPTER 10 ✤

I hate these motherfuckers," said Agent Pidgeon.

She was looking at the photographs of little Karen Morse. What the killer had left of little Karen. Among other things, he had skinned the child and carefully rolled the skin up in salt and tied the package with the ribbons the little girl had had in her hair.

Du Pré looked at the FBI agent. She was six feet tall, slender, with big tits and a narrow waist and legs, legs, legs. Heart-shaped face and big brown eyes. Long pale brown hair. Caramel. She had some Indian blood in her, long earlobes. Thick gold earrings. A nice stainless steel Sig Sauer combat nine-millimeter in a holster hung low under her arm. She had her fitted jacket off. She was smoking.

"Skeleton was in the bottom of the barrel, this was wrapped up and just lying off in the brush, right?" said Agent Pidgeon. "We'll go out there tomorrow."

You and me and Madelaine go out there tomorrow, thought Du Pré, is how that will work, until Madelaine and you have a little talk. Not that you would want anything to do with a Métis grandfather, but what I think don't mean shit here, yes.

"Uh," said Benny. "Ma'am, do you want to get some dinner?"

"S'pose so," said Agent Pidgeon. "Keep up my strength. Thanks. I get a little jacked, I see things like this."

"Yeah," said Benny. "I know what you mean."

"Fuck," said Agent Pidgeon.

Benny's glance kept returning to Agent Pidgeon's tits. He was helpless before their magnificence.

"Yeah, right, food," said Agent Pidgeon. She slipped her jacket on and she picked up her attaché case.

The rest of her luggage was piled out in the front of the Sheriff's office. Three suitcases and a couple big aluminum trunks.

"You screen the crime scene?" she said. "Run everything through a sieve?"

"No," said Benny.

Agent Pidgeon nodded.

"Well," she said. "Maybe there's nothing there. You . . . I dunno. Look, I don't mean to stalk in here, be a hotshot asshole from the FBI. But maybe he dropped something. Maybe there's a piece of jewelry. Some damn thing. You got Boy Scouts? Let them help out?"

"Help out how?" said Benny.

"We could dig up all the earth around the site," said Agent Pidgeon, "and run it through a screen."

"Oh," said Benny. "I guess so."

Agent Pidgeon looked at Benny. She looked at Du Pré. She shrugged.

"Yeah," she said. "I am a little hungry."

When they went out the door of the Sheriff's office they saw the tan government sedan that Pidgeon had been driving being towed to the garage. Pidgeon had driven at such a rate of speed from Billings that the car had blown up twenty miles down the highway. One rod and piston had gone right through the side of the engine.

Du Pré had been closer, so he fetched her after she called Benny's office on the phone.

When he had pulled up to the steaming car, off in the barrow pit, he noticed all the luggage piled neatly by the roadside. Agent Pidgeon was sitting on one of the suitcases, legs nicely crossed, smoking a cigarette and looking like an ad for some filter-tip brand.

"You Indian?" she said, when Du Pré had loaded her luggage, with her help, and loaded her, and driven off.

"Métis," said Du Pré, "French, Scottish, Cree, Chippewa—we are the Mixed Bloods."

"Hum," said Agent Pidgeon, "I'm a Redbone myself. Black, Cherokee, white, Mexican, French. . . ."

"Oh," said Du Pré. "You are Louisiana."

"Some of my folks were," said Pidgeon. "Me, I'm pure California surfin' girl. Grew up in Coronado. Drink Dos Equis, get tan. Wear gold chains."

"How you get to the FBI?" said Du Pré.

"They needed me," said Agent Pidgeon. "I'm so many nice minority groups. Besides, after Georgetown Law School I was pretty well convinced that I would be a lot happier putting scum in jail than I would be keeping them out of it. Did a stint in the D.C. Public Defender's Office. That'll do it for ya."

"Oh," said Du Pré.

"I am not a nice person," said Agent Pidgeon.

"Uh," said Du Pré.

"You seem like a smart man," said Agent Pidgeon.

"Huh?" said Du Pré.

"Yup," said Agent Pidgeon.

Du Pré shrugged. He rolled himself a cigarette with his left hand as he was shooting down the highway at eighty.

Agent Pidgeon looked at him doing it.

Du Pré lit his cigarette.

"Let me try that," said Agent Pidgeon.

Du Pré handed her the papers and the little bag of Bull Durham.

"You are a psychologist?" said Du Pré.

"What do you think?" said Agent Pidgeon.

"That Georgetown is a pretty good law school, yes?" said Du Pré.

"They think so," said Agent Pidgeon.

"Where you get your psychology degree?"

"Columbia," said Agent Pidgeon. "They thought they were a pretty good psychology school, they said so."

Du Pré laughed.

"OK," said Agent Pidgeon. "What matters to me is we catch this guy and send him up forever or fry the fucker, either one'll do. If we do that, then they were good schools, if not, they ain't shit."

Du Pré roared.

"Harvey said I'd like you," said Agent Pidgeon. "He also said you were a good guy and not to beat up on Benny Klein, who is a good guy, too, but not that much of a cop."

"Benny, he is a small rancher," said Du Pré. "He is maybe too kind a man to do this well."

"I imagine he does fine," Agent Pidgeon had said.

Du Pré thought about all this while he drove Agent Pidgeon to the bar in Toussaint, which had the only real food in the area.

There were a few people in the bar. Agent Pidgeon looked around the shabby big room, at the mangy deer and elk heads and the ratty bear skin nailed to one wall. She nodded.

She walked over to the bar and leaned over to Susan Klein and she said a few words and then she fished a little gift out of her attaché case. Susan laughed and took it and she turned it around in her hand and then she took the ribbon and paper off it. She lifted the lid of the little box and took out a pair of silver earrings, big circles of metal with strands of beads hanging in the center hole.

Du Pré looked on and he grinned. That Harvey Weasel Fat, always sucking up to them women. Smart man, that Harvey.

The door opened behind Du Pré and Madelaine came in with Lourdes in tow. They were laughing. They hugged Du Pré.

"That is that Agent Pidgeon," said Madelaine, hissing into Du Pré's ear. "Some set of tits she got, there. I think maybe I watch the two of you pret' good."

"She don't want some broke-down Métis," said Du Pré.

"Good thing, too," said Madelaine.

Agent Pidgeon had turned around and she was looking at Du Pré and Madelaine and Lourdes. She came over.

"Madelaine?" said Agent Pidgeon. "Harvey said that you were the best thing about Du Pré, here. And this is Lourdes?"

"Yes. Yes."

"Um," said Agent Pidgeon. "We could get a table."

They found an empty table with four chairs and they sat. Susan Klein came over.

"I know what they want, dear," she said. "How about you?"

"Red wine?" said Pidgeon.

"Cabernet?" said Susan. "It's pretty good. What I drink."

"Wonderful."

"Steaks are good," said Susan. "The special is gone, sorry."

"Rare," said Pidgeon.

"OK," said Susan. She went off.

"Harvey sends his love," said Pidgeon.

"Ah, he is such a good dancer," said Madelaine.

Du Pré looked at the ceiling.

"Nice man, too," said Madelaine.

"Harvey?" said Pidgeon. "Harvey maybe changes he comes out here. Back there he's a giant pain in the ass. Always staring at my tits and wondering when I am going to get what he needs out of the computer."

"He is a guy," said Madelaine. "They got only the two heads, think with the little one, they all belong, hospitals."

"Mama!" said Lourdes.

"My daughter, she wants me in a cage," said Madelaine.

Lourdes was blushing.

Why she run away? thought Du Pré. He hadn't been told.

"Lourdes," said Pidgeon. "This Challis guy who brought you back here? How did he pick you up?"

Lourdes looked down at her lap. Her lower lip quivered.

Pidgeon reached over and she patted Lourdes's hand.

"It's OK, honey," she said, "as long as you're all right."

Du Pré looked at Lourdes.

I wonder any of us know any of us, he thought.

❖ CHAPTER 11 ❖

Du Pré threw a shovelful of earth scraped from the hard ground near the barrel against the sieve. Booger Tom played a hose that ran from a spray tank on a big flatbed truck against the earth. The soil ran yellow from the screen. Gravels gleamed.

Nothing.

They had been doing this for three days.

They had found one post from an earring for a pierced ear.

Little Karen Morse had not had pierced ears.

Du Pré thought about the skinned child. She had been white-blond.

Five years old.

He threw another shovelful of earth against the sloping screen.

Bart and a couple of the ranch hands were walking slowly on each side of the rutted track that led back to the dry wash, stooping to look at anything out of the ordinary. There were a few condoms left by kids who had pulled off here to fuck. Beer cans and bottles, a couple bright paper bags that once held potato chips.

Booger Tom had spotted a hank of the child's hair stuck on a sagebrush a hundred feet away.

"Moved wrong," said Booger Tom. Tracking, you looked for what should not be there and was, or what should be there and was not.

Tracking.

Du Pré shoved the tip of the shovel's blade toward a thick old sagebrush trunk. The earth parted easily. Something gleamed.

A chain, the sort that made a bracelet. The links were bent flat. Du Pré whistled.

He dropped down on his hands and knees and he stared hard at the chain peeking out from the broken earth.

A green gemstone sparkled.

"What you got, there?" said Booger Tom. He had come after he shut off the hose.

"A chain," said Du Pré. He took a pencil from his pocket and he put it through the loop of chain and he tugged it away from the earth that held it.

Several clods came up with it. Du Pré saw a knife blade, a stainless-steel one, short and wide.

"I'll get some bags," said Booger Tom. He limped off toward the cab of the truck.

Du Pré waited and he stared.

When Tom came back Du Pré dropped the bracelet into the first of the locking plastic bags. He took a pair of folding pliers from his pocket and he jabbed the needlenose points around the knife blade and pulled the knife away from the soil.

Buried about three inches deep, Du Pré thought. Scratch this earth and it breaks up like dry bread.

Du Pré looked at the knife. Stainless-steel, three-inch blade, double-sided. Black plastic handle. He looked at the brand name but it had been ground off.

Du Pré grunted. He dropped the knife in a plastic bag and sealed it.

He tugged a ring out of the dirt.

The metal was discolored, the gem a piece of dime-store glass.

The sort of trinket a poor girl would buy for herself.

Du Pré stood up. He picked up the shovel and pushed it into the ground. The soil broke easily.

He carried the shovelful to the sieve. He tossed it on the screen.

Booger Tom hosed it down.

Five earrings.

Thin cheap silver chain gone to greenish black.

A penny.

Du Pré put them all in the same bag.

Du Pré and Tom worked the spot carefully, shoveling around the trunk of the sagebrush.

They found one small brass key, of the size for a jewelry box.

Nothing else.

Agent Pidgeon arrived in the tan government car. Wally the mechanic had stuck a new used engine in it. It took him about half a day.

"Paydirt," said Pidgeon, holding up the bags. "There won't be anything else. This guy is very careful."

Bart and the ranch hands were standing near. They'd walked the whole half mile of road without seeing a thing that could be useful.

"It's him," said Pidgeon. "He dumps the bodies and he buries a knife and some effects nearby. The effects usually don't square with the bodies. I expect he buries the trophies from the last killing with the next, and so forth. Only keeps the most current mementos."

"Trophies?" said Du Pré.

Pidgeon nodded. "Souvenirs," she said, "of his triumphs. Young women are the enemy. When he kills one, he wins. My profile is fairly standard. This guy is white, unmarried, thirty-five to forty. He's compulsive about cleanliness. He's quiet. He's not very skilled socially, and feels very clumsy around women. He probably doesn't drink or smoke and certainly never takes street drugs. He is, on the surface, very religious, though all his talk of it is about sin and atonement—he's providing atonement for these poor women. He's physically very strong, because he fears weakness of any kind. He's probably been in some trouble with the law as a juvenile."

"What kind of trouble?" said Du Pré.

"Arson, petty theft, violence to kids younger than he is. He would have tortured animals and killed them though he may never have been caught at it. May never have been caught with the other. Probably came from a poor and violent home. Single parent, most likely his mother. She can't, for whatever reason, offer love. I bet this guy has a young sister who he thinks got all the love."

Pidgeon lit a cigarette.

"He kills with a knife thrust to the juncture of the spine and the skull. That's why he uses these short blades. The victim is bound. He may have intercourse with the body. Probably can't, can't get it up at any time. If he goes with a prostitute, she'll maybe suck him off, but he'll do so rarely. If she can't manage to get him off, he'll kill her even if he has to wait."

"Sweet guy," said Booger Tom.

"Fellow Americans," said Agent Pidgeon. "About forty of 'em plying their trade at any given time. We maybe catch half of them."

"Like that Ted Bundy?" said Du Pré.

"Dunno," said Pidgeon. "But I suspect this guy is a lot smarter than Bundy. I suspect this guy is very smart indeed, and he has the instincts of a wild creature."

"Why smart?" said Du Pré.

"Um," said Pidgeon. "He does some of the things that various of these types do, but never so much they provide us with a weakness. Like the trophies. He keeps a few. There is probably a number he allows himself. He never keeps the knife he kills with. The knives have always been so thoroughly cleaned there aren't any residues on them. He always uses this kind of knife. The handle is tight and impermeable plastic. Blood can't seep in between the blade and the handle. He hides the bodies where they will be undiscovered for a long time. He isn't taunting us directly. He's not playing chicken with us. He doesn't want to get caught."

"You're damn right there," said Booger Tom.

"No," said Pidgeon. "They mostly do. See, most of them get crazier and crazier and more and more careless. They've been able to milk the system for bennies, con the shrinks. They want to get caught and be famous. They think they're unique. Living National Treasures, you bet."

"Social workers done this," said Tom.

"Yeah, right," said Pidgeon.

"Well," said Tom. "Ever' time ya turn around someone is getting off scot-free because his mother pulled the tit too quick or something."

"Whatever," said Pidgeon. "This guy worries me, though. They all worry me, but this guy really worries me."

"OK," said Du Pré. "But why?"

"He's very smart," said Pidgeon. "He's probably an autodidact. He reads a lot. High IQ. If he works, it's at a highly skilled job where he doesn't have much to do with people. He doesn't have close friends, but people will think of him as a friend. He'll be thoughtful and ingratiating. He'll wear clothes in muted tones. He doesn't talk a lot and when he does it will be about inoffensive subjects. He won't argue with anyone. He won't get into rows in bars. He doesn't vote. He has a driver's license and a Social Security card, but no charge cards. He always pays cash and in small bills. He doesn't save receipts. He most likely cuts the labels out of his clothes. He wears jogging shoes, or the heavier walking shoes, in dark brown or green. Black is too much of a statement. He wears glasses, probably black frames, heavy ones, with ordinary lenses. No bombardier glasses for this boy. May not even need them. He's clean-shaven. He gets his hair cut short regularly. He may still live with his mother, or, if she's dead, with a sister or other female relation. He always makes his bed. Unlike most of you guys, when he does his laundry he bleaches his whites and keeps them separate. He cleans up after himself. He knows a lot about women and he hates them if they are young and pretty and innocent or if he thinks they are whores."

"How you know all this?" said Tom.

"I read fucking tea leaves," said Pidgeon.

"I thought so," said Booger Tom.

"Let's go get a drink," said Pidgeon. "I'm buying. Thank you for all this stuff."

"I'll take the rig back and meet you to town," said Booger Tom.

"Du Pré?" said Pidgeon.

"My car is in Toussaint," said Du Pré. "I come out with Tom, he had to come to town to get a belt for the truck."

"Ride with me," said Pidgeon. "I need to talk to you anyway."

"Social workers and fairy shrinks," said Booger Tom.

"Fuck off, you old bastard," said Agent Pidgeon.

✤ CHAPTER 12 ✤

She is some pistol," said Du Pré, into the telephone.

"Oh, yes," said Harvey Wallace. "I would dearly love to make a dozen little Redbone Blackfeet with her, but Angela would object and she's Sioux and you know what they do to unfaithful husbands."

"You are married?" said Du Pré.

"Twenty-seven years," said Harvey. "Six kids. Lovely wife. Two dogs. Home in the burbs. A station wagon and a Jeep Cherokee."

"Oh," said Du Pré.

"Yeah," said Harvey. "I'm hopelessly middle-class. And I don't like buffalo meat. Or horse meat. Or chokecherry jam. Makes my teeth hurt. Moccasins make my feet hurt. Poor-ass Indian."

"Uh," said Du Pré. "Well, she did tell me a lot about this guy, she thinks she knows this stuff about him."

"If she says the guy does this or that, he does this or that," said Harvey. "She's a damn fine psychologist and then on top of that she's intuitive as hell."

"What's intuitive?" said Du Pré.

"Senses things without thinking them through."

"Yeah," said Du Pré, "she is a woman, you bet."

"Whatever," said Harvey. "Under law, there is no difference between the brains of men and the brains of women."

"Laws are pretty much bullshit," said Du Pré.

"I wish you would quit talking like that," said Harvey. "I have a sick feeling that if you find the guy he's gonna have more holes in him than a fucking colander and then we'll have to arrest you and try you and toss you in Walla Walla. For a long time."

Du Pré said nothing.

"Benetsee back?" said Harvey.

"No," said Du Pré. "I do not know where he is." The old bastard, may he drop slowly through all the levels of hell, frying while he falls.

"Shit," said Harvey. "Agent Pidgeon needs to meet him."

"Me, I need to talk to him," said Du Pré. "But I can't find out where he has gone."

"He's his own guy, for sure," said Harvey. "Well, Agent Pidgeon did call from Billings and she raised merry hell down there with the cops who screwed up some evidence."

"I like her," said Du Pré.

"She's a good one," said Harvey. "By the way, you talk to Challis at all? He's on my mind some."

"No," said Du Pré, "I have not."

"Well," said Harvey. "No more bodies turn up there, I hope, you can maybe work on what you got. I wish to Christ we knew more about time."

"Yeah," said Du Pré, not quite knowing what Harvey meant.

"When this guy is dumping them. Time we find them, they've been out there for months, usually. Your three were under the snow until late, it was a late spring."

"Four," said Du Pré.

"I haven't forgotten," said Harvey. "Poor little Karen was skinned and her skeleton was fleshed out. All sorts of knife marks on the bones."

"Jesus," said Du Pré.

"I want this guy alive, Du Pré," said Harvey. "I have heard bad rumors about you. Some guy up in New York State."

"Ah," said Du Pré.

"Ah?" said Harvey. "OK, I'll go now. Don't make me sad, my man, I beg of you."

"OK," said Du Pré.

"Enough of this bullshit," said Harvey. "I'm calling Madelaine."

Du Pré hung up.

He went outside on the porch again.

Harvey and Pidgeon are not telling me everything, Du Pré thought, they play to win. I kill this asshole, they will try to get me.

Him call Madelaine, she tell him her Du Pré do what he is gonna do, which, for Madelaine, would be kill this bastard anyway.

Then everybody's babies safe from him.

Lots of others out there, though.

Forty of them, any given time.

Pret' bad people.

I wish Benetsee would show up.

Du Pré rolled a cigarette. He whistled a little in between drags. This afternoon he would go to the bar in Toussaint and fiddle with a couple of cousins down from Canada.

Big family, mine, Du Pré thought. Indian family. These cousins they are from people come down here with my great-great-grandfather, then they go to North Dakota and back up to Canada. Always in the Red River country. I like that country, sings in my bones.

Goes to Hudson's Bay.

Wonder how them whales are doing.

Wonder that Hydro-Quebec kill that River of the Whale yet. Damn it. I should ask Bart, he sends money to fight that.

The fields of winter wheat were ripening now. July. They were going to red-gold and that hard red wheat was getting ready for the harvest. Ring good on the shovel, that hard red wheat.

Du Pré remembered threshing, the combine crews, everybody itching from the chaff. The streams of dark red winter wheat shooting out of the pipes and into the trucks lumbering along on the side of the combines. Sell all the hard red wheat you could grow, anybody. Make pasta, them good noodles. One-fifth protein. Come from Russia, that hard red wheat.

The Dukhobors brought it, I hear.

Du Pré liked the Dukhobors, a pacifist Russian sect. If a Dukhobor got really mad with you, they undressed. I will not fight you, I am naked before your violence, but I am mad at you.

The Mennonites, during the First World War they came and got the men and hung them from handcuffs on a pipe till their shoulders dislocated, because they wouldn't fight.

The Hutterites. Good farmers, shrewd traders.

Good people, just don't have much truck with the rest of the world. Who can blame them?

Du Pré flicked his smoke out into the yard. The grass was meadow grass, already drying and yellowing and going dormant.

Du Pré got his fiddle and he went to his old cruiser and he got in and turned around and went down the long drive.

That Bart he is off digging a big irrigation ditch with Popsicle, his lime green diesel shovel. One we find the answer to his brother's death with. Find a lot of things. Find out more truth than maybe we want to know. That is the thing about truth, there is only too much or not enough.

Du Pré drove slowly, windows down, listening to the meadowlarks trill. Big yellow-breasted birds got a black wishbone on their chests. He glanced over and saw a brilliant bluebird, winged sapphire, sitting on the fence post its house was nailed to.

Got to get the hole the right size in the house or you got starlings. Yuppie birds, maybe. Lots of squawk and sharp elbows. No
taste.

Du Pré was in no hurry. It took him an hour to go the twenty
miles to town. He went to Madelaine's.

He parked and went in the front door.

"Du Pré!" Madelaine called. "There is a box for you there!"

Du Pré looked at the box on the coffee table. Shirt box.

Madelaine, she make me another shirt.

"OK," said Du Pré. "I see, shirt box."

"Smarty," said Madelaine from the bathroom. "You look in
that, see how your woman love you."

Du Pré lifted off the top.

Bright red shirt with black piping and fiddles over the pockets
made of porcupine quills. The shirt was heavy silk. Du Pré picked
it up. A red silk Métis sash was folded underneath. Fiddles on that,
too, and DU PRÉ on the back in black beads. Very fine beads. Two
circlets on each side with coyotes howling at yellow moons on
them. Du Pré felt something crinkle in the sash's pocket, on an
end that hung down. He fished out a dollar bill.

Bad luck to give an empty purse.

Madelaine came out of the bathroom. She was wearing a heavy
turquoise silk/satin shirt with yellow flowers embroidered on it
in fine beads, a long yellow skirt, and yellow cowboy boots. Her
rings were all turquoise and silver and coral.

Her hair was in two long braids. Beaver fur wrapped around
them.

"You play that good music, eh?" said Madelaine.

Du Pré nodded. He was shrugging into the shirt. He put his
fiddle rosin in the pocket of the sash and he stuck the other end
through the loops on his jeans.

He drove down to the bar. Two old cars with North Dakota
plates stood outside. Cousins.

Du Pré was a little late and his cousins were picking and
singing already. He tuned his fiddle and then joined them.

They played the old voyageur stuff, the longing songs of men far from their women, thinking that maybe they would not see them again.

Long time ago, on the lakes bordered by the deep black woods.
The Company of Gentlemen Adventurers of Hudson's Bay.
The Métis voyageurs.
Red River.

✤ CHAPTER 13 ✤

Round midnight Du Pré and his cousins were playing very tight and the crowd had thinned to those who simply loved the music. The whoopers had gotten drunk and left. Madelaine was looking at Du Pré with her bright and saucy black eyes and she would smile when he looked at her.

Got plans for you, her face said.

Du Pré grinned and rosined his bow.

There is nothing left of us but songs and stories finally, Du Pré thought.

Even maybe when the earth is ice again and the Red River sleeps for a long time. Missouri, she used to flow to Hudson's Bay, but ice come and now she goes to the Gulf of Mexico.

I am a man, but we are not very big.

" 'Baptiste's Lament'!" said Sonny, the accordion player.

Du Pré nodded. The song was about a young voyageur who misses his love and he sees her in the moon on the water, smiling. And when he gets home she is dead, and he drowns when he sees her in the moon on the water again, swimming down after her, singing.

Sad song.

They took a break. Du Pré was leaning up against the bar kissing Madelaine when Susan Klein tapped him on the shoulder and handed him the telephone. Du Pré looked at Susan. She shrugged.

"Eh," said Du Pré.

"Du Pré," said a soft drawling voice.

"Who is this?" said Du Pré.

"Rolly Challis," said the soft voice. "I'm in Browning. I'll be at Raster Creek in four hours. Could you meet me there?"

Five in the fucking morning.

"Sure," said Du Pré. "You got something."

"Maybe," said Rolly. "Some things I need to talk over with you anyway. Sorry about the time but that's my run. I can take a couple hours there, highball later."

"Yah," said Du Pré, "I be there."

The phone clicked.

"Girlfriend?" said Madelaine.

"Yah," said Du Pré, "She meet me at five in the morning. I got time for you before, maybe after. I am busy man, you know."

Madelaine smiled suddenly. She reached up and took Du Pré's right earlobe in her teeth and she bit it softly.

"You see that man brought my Lourdes back?" she hissed. Du Pré's ear was a little wet. "You thank him for me. No, I will not go, but sometime I like to thank him, smile at him with my face."

Du Pré nodded.

Sonny and Bassman were chatting with a couple pretty women from Cooper. Everybody looked happy. Be even happier later.

"That Sonny, he better not get tangled up with that La Fant woman," said Madelaine. "She is some twister. She take guys, make them crazy. She likes to watch them fight about her."

Du Pré shrugged. My cousin, he is forty, I never hardly know him he is not fighting over some crazy woman. He like it, help get his dick up, I guess.

"That Bassman," Madelaine went on. "He is talking sweet to Alyse. She is nice, have a bad time, men. She picks bad men."

Bassman, he collect women all over the place. Someday they all have nice lunch, together, there, get up a posse, go cut off Bassman's balls and then hang him from a tree, sit down, drink beer while he bleeds to death dangling.

My cousins want to play that way, I am not their mother, thought Du Pré, I am just a cousin. Fools.

Sonny and Bassman got back up on the little stage, grinning like dogs in a field of fresh cow shit.

Heat.

"I go now," said Du Pré. "Do some songs then we go."

"Poor Du Pré," laughed Madelaine. "You get no sleep tonight. I do while you are gone. You get back, you get no sleep then either."

"I stand it somehow," said Du Pré. He picked his fiddle up off the top of the bar and he walked to the stage and he got up and stood and listened to the rhythms Bassman was pulling out of his fretless electric bass. Some backbeat, there.

Play across the creek, Du Pré thought, sail my hat over.

He shot little icy notes into the smoky air.

People got up and they began to dance.

Madelaine came to the stage and she danced in front of Du Pré, running her tongue tip around her lips.

I hope I don't drop the beat, fucked up by my hard-on, thought Du Pré, my woman is messing with me. Some fun.

They played and people danced and they left in couples. The bar was emptied by the last song, except for a few people.

Du Pré cased up his fiddle. He shook hands with his cousins and he nodded and smiled at their women and he took Madelaine home.

After, they lay pearled with sweat, the window open and the cool night air flowing over their hot bodies.

"I got to go," said Du Pré.

"I got plans, you, you get back," murmured Madelaine.

Du Pré got up and he pulled on his clothes and boots and he went out to his old cruiser. The glass was thick with dew. Bullbats flew overhead, catching insects in the single pole light by the street. The little brown bats would be down by the water, eating mosquitoes.

Du Pré started the cruiser and he let it warm while he took an old towel and wiped the thick stippled water from the windshield. He got in and he rolled three cigarettes and laid them on the dashboard, and then a fourth he stuck in his mouth and he lit. He pulled a bottle of Canadian whiskey from under the seat and he had a stiff drink.

Keep me awake. Run on whiskey, pussy, and music. Not a bad life that I got. I say that, my Madelaine belt me in the mouth.

Du Pré turned around and he headed for the little two-lane black-top that snaked around the foothills of the Wolf Mountains to the west of the range. It led up to the Hi-Line and came into the main stem at Raster Creek.

I did not know what Raster meant, Du Pré thought, so I ask Booger Tom. The old man snorted and said it was a corruption of "arrastra," the Spanish millwheel of heavy stone drawn round and round by burros to crush ore for roasting.

Du Pré had seen a couple of the huge stones up in the Wolfs. The Spanish had got this far north?

Why not?

The road was wet, black and snaking north into the night. Du Pré put the car up to ninety and he shot along under the blurry moon. High cloud, lot of water in the air.

The country changed. Du Pré could smell a different soil, some sour thing in the water. Several times deer froze in the headlights. Du Pré braked hard and got down to a crawl till he was past them. They might move off the road, but they might run back if the headlights blinded them.

He got to Raster Creek at a quarter to five. He got out and he sat on the warm hood of his car, smoking and drinking whiskey.

At five minutes to five he heard a big rig to the west. The truck was moving damned fast. The headlights rose ahead of the big diesel and then they blazed into view and the drive began to ring down the gears and slow the huge, heavy machine.

Big black eighteen-wheeler.

Rolly Challis brought the truck into the parking lot of the rest stop at a crawl. He stopped and the lights went out and Du Pré heard the air brakes hiss and lock and then the cab opened and Rolly dropped down, freehanded, his foot touched lightly on the rubber plate on the running board and then he was on the ground and walking quickly toward Du Pré.

Du Pré slid off the hood of his car and he walked toward Rolly.

They stopped two feet from each other.

Rolly grinned and he held out his hand.

Du Pré grinned and he shook it.

"How is Lourdes?" said Rolly.

"Oh," said Du Pré, "she is all right. She scared herself pret' good. She really ask you you want a piece of ass, Spokane?"

"Uh," said Rolly. "No, not exactly. She asked me if I would like to have her suck my *penis*. She had trouble pronouncing 'penis.' Sort of choked on it, you know. So I said, 'Little girl, you are a long damn way from home and in a lot of trouble. How 'bout you tell me what's up over breakfast.' I didn't think she had a lot of time in giving blow jobs to truckers. Poor kid."

Little Lourdes, Du Pré thought. Kids, these days. I will not tell Madelaine, who would shit bobcats.

This Rolly, he is a funny man. Probably, he rob a bank, leave them all laughing.

Du Pré put the bottle of whiskey forward. Rolly shook his head.

"Thank you, though," he said.

They stood there. The sun was rising in the east, the sky was a pink curtain halfway up to heaven.

"I don't have much," said Rolly. "But I thought I'd best talk to you about it. I been driving back and forth for seven years on this route and down on the Interstate. One thing I never did, though, is look at where the bodies of the girls were dumped."

Rolly pulled a map from his back pocket. He stuck a small flashlight in his teeth. He went to Du Pré's cruiser and he unfolded the map. It was the western half of the United States.

There were many black X's on the map.

From Seattle to Minnesota.

From Amarillo to Calgary, Alberta.

257

Du Pré squinted.

The big picture.

One wide band across America, up high, the Pacific to the Great Lakes.

One wide band running north and south, along the front of the Rockies and east to the hundredth meridian.

Du Pré blinked.

"Jesus," he said. "There are maybe two of them."

"I believe so," said Rolly. He folded the map and he started to walk back to his truck.

"You go now?" said Du Pré, surprised.

"Yup," said Rolly. "When you talk to ol' Harvey Wallace, there, give him my best. Ask him about time. We need to know when the bodies were dumped."

"Yah," said Du Pré.

Rolly swung up into the cab and he moved out toward the rising sun.

✤ CHAPTER 14 ✤

Ineed to learn how to say 'No' better," said Bart. He looked tired. The huge lowboy trailer that had tires running nearly the entire length of it, on both sides, triple tires, sat in its spot. The giant diesel shovel, boom tucked, sat on it.

"Big job, eh?" said Du Pré.

"Biggest I have done," said Bart. "I should have another operator for Popsicle, there, but I kinda hate to hand her off to anyone."

Du Pré snorted. Bart loved his diesel shovel. Bart had, Du Pré had heard, hundreds of millions of dollars. He would have been much happier if he had been born poor. But he wasn't. It almost killed him. Du Pré remembered Bart's drunken, bloated red face the first time he had seen him. Sticking out the window of the too-big house. Booger Tom had burned the house down on Bart's orders.

Long time ago.

Bart, he had gotten drunk a few times, gotten sick, but the times got farther apart and there hadn't been one in over three years.

Du Pré nodded.

Bart, he is doing good. Wish he could find him a woman, but when he does he spends too much money on them and they feel bought and go away.

The day was already bright and hot. The eagle was high on the updraft from the fields of wheat that reached from the foothills of the Wolf Mountains behind the ranch house clear out south to where the rain fell so scantily the soil held water enough only for sagebrush.

"Wheat's up," said Booger Tom. The old man had come round the side of the house. He moved slowly now, his many injuries from a life of hard riding were coming due. Arthritis. Bones broken many times. Hands gnarled and twisted like the roots of willows.

Old cowboy, tough enough.

"I can see it's up," said Bart. "I keep telling you I want to *lose* money. I get half of the crop, if it's five-dollar wheat this year then I lose . . . oh, fuck it. Numbers, all it is."

"I keep tryin'," said Booger Tom. "Tryin' hard."

"I think," said Bart, "that the old bastard is pulling my dick."

"Give the damn wheat to charity," said Booger Tom. "Give it to them damn Rooshians."

"Yah, yah," said Bart. He went inside.

"It don't rain, then maybe harvest in a couple weeks," said Booger Tom. "Them combine crews are about a week behind."

Du Pré thought about the contract harvesters. Started down in Texas and worked north, on the road five or six months out of the year. Chaff and dust and itch and long hours. But damn good money. Good people, worked very hard.

Then, a hailstorm could come up and knock all the kernels off the heads and you got nothin'. Don't pay to comb the field.

Farming.

Ranching, you got your cows, looking for a place to hide, or your sheep, looking for a place to die.

People here, they got to be tough some.

Bart appeared at the screen door.

"Du Pré," he said, "phone. Harvey Wallace."

Du Pré flicked his butt out on the yard and he went inside and he picked up the portable phone and went back out. It crackled a little, not too bad.

"Mornin'," said Harvey.

"Yah," said Du Pré. "Nice out here. How is that Washington, D.C?"

"Foul," said Harvey. "Sticky, full of slimy politicians and government titsuckers like me. The founding fathers hated the idea of democracy. They stuck it out in a swamp and waited for the mosquitoes to give everybody yellow fever and kill it off. I take it my man Rolly put you up to this?"

"Yah," said Du Pré.

"Well," said Harvey. "We are all low-rent riverboat gamblers here, you know, and you want to peek at our hand."

"How is that Pidgeon?" said Du Pré.

"Her of the gorgeous knockers and mean mouth?" said Harvey. "Thriving. I relayed your request to her and you know what she did?"

"Uh," said Du Pré.

"Pulled out a computer printout and said she knew you were bright and would get around to this."

"Christ," said Du Pré. "There are what, one hundred fifty of them crosses on that map? One hundred fifty?"

"A lot," said Harvey. "I doubt that all of them can be credited to one or two accounts."

"How long you know there are two of them?" said Du Pré.

"Gabriel," said Harvey, "quit spitting at me. I don't know there are two. I know there are a lot of dead bodies. I thought I would let you just run and see what you came up with. If I had told you everything we think we know, that's what you would have looked for."

"Uh," said Du Pré. "Yah, well, I do not know either. It makes me sick, all those girls, this guy, these guys, years they do this. No one sees them."

"The Green River Killer out in Washington?" said Harvey. "Killed as many as ninety. Then stopped. He died or moved away. We doubt we will ever know. I have a collage of the faces of the murdered women. It is on the wall of my office. To remind me that there is evil in the world."

"These girls," said Du Pré. "Not many of them, you know, we find out who they are."

"There are a hundred thousand runaway teenagers at least out there at any given moment," said Harvey. "Some parents are just glad that they are gone. Some parents don't have one single photograph of their child. Not one. Nothing. Some of them never report anything. They don't care. Kids are gone, not eating, taking money for booze or drugs. There are some real pieces of shit in the world. Lots of them."

"That Pidgeon," said Du Pré. "How come she has not called me?"

"She's in Europe," said Harvey, "helping out Scotland Yard. They have some bastard dismembering prostitutes around Edinburgh. Jock the Ripper, of course."

Du Pré snorted.

"We have some information," said Harvey. "But in so many cases the bodies weren't discovered until they were nothing but bones. Can't get a real good fix on that."

"How many skinned?" said Du Pré.

"Nineteen," said Harvey, "or maybe more, we just haven't found the skins."

"This guy is pretty smart," said Du Pré.

"Very smart," said Harvey. "We may never catch him."

Du Pré snorted.

"We're gonna try good, though," said Harvey. "Where is that god damned Benetsee?"

"Dunno," said Du Pré.

"He ever gone this long before?" said Harvey.

"No," said Du Pré.

"You know how to get hold of him in Canada?"

"No," said Du Pré, "I ask people, who are from there, but, one thing, I don't even know what tribe he is. I guess maybe Cree but them Cree they don't talk, each other's business at all. Very close. Anybody publish anything about their religion, they sue them. They don't want them fool New Age people bothering them."

"Like Bear Butte," said Harvey.

"Yah," said Du Pré.

Bear Butte was sacred, a vision place to many Plains tribes. So now men's movement groups and New Age idiots went there, did what they thought were Indian ceremonies. How they like it, we have a Sun Dance in the cathedral, there in Washington? We don't do that. Leave Bear Butte alone. Leave us alone.

Du Pré snorted. Here I am, bad Catholic, worse Indian. I guess I am more religious than I know.

"Shit," said Harvey. "We even tried some psychics. Not helpful. Or maybe we just can't unravel their babble. I dunno. I'd try reading animal guts like the Romans I thought'd help."

"Oh," said Du Pré, "I am forgetting, Rolly, he say to tell you hello."

Harvey laughed long.

"That son of a bitch," he said. "I can't help but like the guy. Though I'd never admit it, like every other American, when Banker Bob takes it in the shorts but good I can't help but feel a little better."

"Him got something else," said Du Pré.

"What?" said Harvey, suddenly collected.

"I don't know," said Du Pré. "I have just this hunch, you know, that he was going to tell me something else and then he changed his mind."

"Damn," said Harvey.

"One other thing," said Du Pré. "That Rolly he is a killer."

"Killed who?" said Harvey.

"Dunno he did," said Du Pré, "yet."

"You're right there," said Harvey.

"So maybe he think he get close he just do that, see if this stops," said Du Pré.

"That has worried me," said Harvey.

"Uh," said Du Pré. "He got them eyes, you know."

"Oh, yes," said Harvey.

"Maybe I am wrong," said Du Pré.

"Nope," said Harvey. "Another thing worries me."

"Uh," said Du Pré.

"You got those eyes, too, Gabriel. Remember, I'll bust your ass."

"Thanks," said Du Pré.

Harvey hung up.

❧ CHAPTER 15 ❧

Du Pré stood by the silvered pile of boards still marked with the yellow tape that the investigators had used to cordon the area off. The dirt under where the single body had been found was turned and mounded. There were bootprints on the loose soil and the marks of the feet of horses and cattle.

A coyote had scratched at the earth, perhaps scenting the meat that had rotted here. But not much. Then the coyote trotted on toward the slash of pale green where a tiny plume of water ran through the soil, coming out as a small spring miles away.

Du Pré looked up. The eagle was a speck so high in the sky that he never could have seen it had he not known exactly where to look.

That eagle, Du Pré thought, he must like it up there some. Nothing to eat, and by the time he dive the thing he is after would be ten feet under the ground.

Du Pré remembered nearly forty years before, when he was hunting with his father, Catfoot, that they had come to the edge of a meadow covered three feet deep in snow, hoping for elk on the far side. But what they saw was a deer with an eagle on its back. The big golden bird had its talons sunk in the deer's back near the neck and the eagle was flapping its wings and the deer, tongue lolling from exhaustion, was trying to run to safety but there was none.

The eagle let go and lifted and the deer stood quivering, and then the eagle's mate stooped and grasped and the deer leaped forward again.

Du Pré and his father went on. When they came back hours later, pulling the gutted carcass of a dry cow elk, the eagles were feasting on the deer.

"Them do that," said Catfoot. "Eagle, him smart bird, the gold ones. Them balds not so smart. They just steal from smaller birds."

Du Pré looked down at his feet. They seemed far away. There was a sprig of sagebrush caught in the cracked sole of his boot.

Du Pré tried to fly up with the bird, to think what this land looked like from high in the air. He could have got someone to fly him but he wasn't sure what he was looking for.

Du Pré closed his eyes.

Old house was here. Had a well, must be there, where the water ran underground.

The tracks of the tires come in here, ranchers, hunters, they go from the road off into the sagebrush past this old house that is gone, taken by the wind, to the place where there is a little saddle. Rock on either side of it is in shelves six feet high, so that is the way that you have to go to get on out into the prairie.

High plains.

Desert.

All the prophets came from the desert.

It is the place of clarity.

I have spent too much time with that Bart and his books.

This is all Red River.

The road went west, the snaking ribbon of green that followed the fractured invisible rock beneath went north. They crossed right here.

The two bodies crossed one on another were over there. Under the left arm of the cross.

Christ's right hand was on the left arm of the cross.

Du Pré shook his head.

He walked a spiraling path around the spot where the first body was found. The spiral was tight. He could see clearly ten feet or so on a side. Twenty feet wide, the ribbon of earth in his eyes unspooled.

There.

Du Pré saw some tiny leaves, little plants which had just taken root in the turned earth. Not very much turned earth. That much could be cut open here with a knife. A little trench scraped.

Filled and patted and tamped.

But the seeds knew the air and water there were enough.

They sprouted, and then . . .

There wasn't enough water.

The plant was dwarfed.

Not dead, dormant. Take a few years here, where a single season would be enough if there was enough water.

Du Pré pulled the folding tool from his belt and he opened it and selected a long file with a square tip and he locked it in place and he shut the handle.

He dug at the earth beneath the little plant.

Nothing anywhere here like that little plant.

Du Pré felt it. He wiggled the tip of the file and clods of earth broke apart.

Stainless steel gleamed.

Du Pré dug the knife out.

Short, triangular blade, black plastic handle with the brand marker scraped off.

Gleam of metal.

Gold.

Du Pré lifted out an engagement ring. Small diamond, but the gold was good, probably eighteen-carat.

Hopeful ring. We don't got much money starting out here, but some time, I get you a better one.

Du Pré pulled a plastic bag from his pocket and he dropped the knife and ring into it and snapped it shut, punched a little hole in the side of the bag with the file and squeezed out the air and put the bag in the pocket of his canvas jacket.

He dug around the spot, as far as the earth was disturbed.

Little piece of duct tape.

Little agate ring, silver mounting.

Two gold post earrings.

Du Pré felt the root of the sagebrush. End of the little trench.

Fucker might buy them damn knives by the gross, Du Pré thought. Hah. He buy one here, one there.

But I bet that he got a lot of them to hand. Neatly laid out in nice rows.

Duct tape.

Right hand of Christ.

I am getting something here.

Du Pré turned and he looked back through the sagebrush to the place where the woman's body had lain.

Clear view.

Knife blade pointing directly to the spot.

Du Pré got up and he walked down the line of sight, looking to the left and right.

Only place you can see this far in to where the body was.

What is it?

Old path?

No sagebrush here.

Why?

Du Pré tried to remember if the other knife blade had been pointing at the body.

Well, he thought, it would have been.

Everything this guy does he has got a reason for doing. I do not know what them reasons are but they will be there.

Tracks.

This guy lines things up.

He gets upset when something is out of place.

He gets really upset when he has a plan and it don't work out.

He is thinking God's plan is not doing well, women are fucking it up maybe.

This guy is trying to fix things.

Everything.

Du Pré looked back up at the eagle. Now there were two.

He walked over toward the spot where he had seen the magpie fly up so long ago. Less than a month but a long time ago.

He looked left to right. He kept looking back.

The two bodies under the right arm of Christ on the cross.

Left arm of the cross.

Everything depends on where you are standing.

He came to the spot. There wasn't so much evidence of scarring and turned earth here. They were not so thorough.

The girls had those inky jailhouse tattoos. So who cared?

Just trash in the brush.

Du Pré wondered if they had been killed at the same time.

He wondered if they were maybe sisters.

They were now.

Du Pré rolled a smoke and he lit it.

No knife here.

I know that there is no knife here.

Him, he did not do this.

These two were someone else.

They know about each other.

One of them kills north.

Other one kills east.

I am high above them looking down.

If I can bring them together, then maybe . . .

Where is Benetsee.

Where is Benetsee.

Du Pré began to whistle a tune that he realized he had never heard before. It was pretty and sad.

Try it on the fiddle.

Get it right.

The Women are Lost in the Desert.

Du Pré walked back to his old cruiser, whistling.

❦ CHAPTER 16 ❦

I don't pay that much attention to that sort of thing," said Father Van Den Heuvel. "I know that it exists and of course it probably does around here but I spend my time in pastoral duties and so forth. Why do you ask?"

Du Pré shrugged.

"I think maybe this guy have something to do with those people," said Du Pré. "The guy who is killing these girls."

"Why do you think that?" said Father Van Den Heuvel. "I perhaps could help you if I knew your thoughts."

Du Pré sucked his teeth. He rolled a cigarette.

They were sitting on the front porch of the little house Van Den Heuvel lived in. It had been willed to the church by an old woman of great faith who had pitied the priests stuck in one bare room with a tiny kitchen and bath.

"It may be that I am wrong," said Du Pré, "but that Agent Pidgeon said that this man probably felt he was doing the work of God. Killing these bad women. That he hates but he has to find a way to make his hating all right, you know. He hates because God wants him to."

"Ah," said Father Van Den Heuvel, "yes. The primitive people who join such ignorant sects are good haters, all of them. I have seen advertisements in the Billings paper for evangelists who hate practically everyone. Especially those who practice and accept abortion. The Mother Church abhors the practice, of course, but we stop short of recommending that those who disagree with us be killed outright."

Lately you have, thought Du Pré. Lot of the history of the Church it was saying just that. Remember the Huguenots, lot of them fled here.

"OK," said Du Pré. "What would be at the right hand of Jesus, when He is on the Cross?"

"Interesting question," said Father Van Den Heuvel. "I will have to think about that."

"Um," said Du Pré. "I am going down to that Miles City and go to one of those churches, I want to see the people in it."

Van Den Heuvel nodded.

"Hmm," said Van Den Heuvel. "I wish I could join you. The Devil's work must be, to succeed, plausible enough."

"I don't think that I go there with a Jesuit," said Du Pré. "I do not want to hurt your feelings."

"Yes," said the big priest.

Du Pré rose and he left. He got in his cruiser and he went to town and gassed the car at the little grocery, laundromat, and service station, waving at the kid through the window.

Write it down, whatever it is.

Du Pré drove on. He saw the boy coming out to read the charge on the pumps.

Wednesday night.

Madelaine had said he was dumb enough to want to listen to some redneck preacher rant she would go, Mass, pray for him.

"I got cousins got sent to school run by those people," she said. "They did not do so well. Made them hate that they were Indians, those people, them evangelists, usually molested the kids, too. Pret' sick bad people. I don't like them so good."

Du Pré didn't either, but, then he never had known very many.

Me with my priests and old ones like Benetsee, like Mrs. High Back Bone, who come here and gathered herbs with my mother.

Mrs. High Back Bone was maybe Assiniboine, funny old lady, had a laugh, very warm, round fat face. Medicine person, people come to her, she cure them, cure them of broken hearts even. Cure them, stomach cancer and bad lungs.

Du Pré had been bitten by a rattlesnake and Mrs. High Back Bone had chewed some leaves and put it on the bites and Du Pré felt the poison leave his body. The paste of green leaves turned black. She washed it off and touched the wounds. The next morning Du Pré had two little white spots where the fangs had gone in. Never felt sick.

The cruiser shot along at ninety. Du Pré had a little whiskey. Driving bored him and if he was a little drunk and relaxed sometimes he could think up songs as he crossed the far empty places that Montana was mostly made of.

Some day some pissant cop is gonna bust me for drunk, Du Pré thought, damn social workers everywhere.

Du Pré crested a long hill and he hit the brakes hard. There was a tractor and a hay baler behind it wallowing from side to side on the narrow ribbon of asphalt and another car coming as fast as Du Pré had been. The rancher on the tractor tossed a beer can over his shoulder and the can bounced out from under the hay baler and Du Pré's right front tire crunched it.

The car in the other lane shot past, wheels clear out on the verge, damn near over the edge. Young cowboy in an old Cadillac.

Du Pré glanced round the baler, saw the road was clear, and in a minute he was doing eighty again and then ninety down a long perfectly clear road.

He got to Miles City at five. He found a restaurant that had a lot of men in cowboy hats in it and he ate some prime rib and had a couple glasses of whiskey in coffee cups.

"We don't have a liquor license," said the waitress. "S'pose we oughta get one?"

Du Pré laughed. He sprayed a little whiskey into his moustache.

I go there protected by the Demon Rum, there, he thought. I think that I know what I will find anyway.

At a quarter to seven Du Pré drove off to an evangelical church which advertised by printing portions of its pastor's sermons. Du Pré found the ad in the Miles City paper. The pastor thought the world's ills were the work of "godless liberals."

Du Pré found the ratty building. The sign out front held cheap plastic letters and over the 7 P.M. it said EVENING SERVICE. Du Pré went in when people began to arrive. Fat women and sad-looking children, men skinny and bowed by hard work. They were dressed in cheap clothes. Du Pré took a seat in the back. The congregation, about forty people, constantly turned and looked at him.

I am maybe a little dark in the skin, be here, Du Pré thought.

The amounts of the last two collections were posted on a placard hanging in front of the pulpit.

Someone started a tape of organ music. The congregation began to sing a hymn. It was awful.

Du Pré got up and walked out.

We got poor people, Toussaint, he thought, but these are poorer people yet. They don't even got themselves.

Du Pré felt sorry for them.

But they could be plenty mean.

Du Pré drove up to the downtown of Miles City. He liked the place. Still had old bars. Still had a lot of cattle people. The Bucking Horse Sale was some party. He had not been here for it for ten years. Too many people.

But it was still the West. Not like the mountains, all yuppies and ski hills and homes built on winter range so it killed off the deer and elk. All of them drive those silly four-wheel drive things, denim seat covers. Funny boots.

Du Pré went in a big old high-ceilinged saloon and he got a drink and he walked around it looking at the pictures on the walls. Signed pictures. Tom Mix and Art Acord and Hoot Gibson. Monty Montana and Yakima Canutt. Casey Tibbs the rodeo champion. Will James, who had been born . . . what? Nepthele Dumont, something like that, French-Canadian. Drank himself to death. Du Pré's grandfather had known James, they spoke in Coyote French, though James was from Quebec.

Du Pré stopped before a little watercolor in a heavy gilt frame that was bolted to the wall.

Charley Russell. Him and Du Pré's great-grandfather had been great friends, drank together till Charley quit. Charley had painted Du Pré's great-grandfather many times, the Métis with the carbine with the stock all full of brass tacks. Métis moccasins and Red River hat, sash. Charley wore a Métis sash every day of his life, even wore it with a tuxedo.

That Red River, she reach far.

Du Pré had another drink.

He went out to his cruiser and he headed back home.

I guess I just want to be with myself and think.

It was still light and Du Pré was within a hundred miles of Toussaint before it got dark enough to bother with the headlights.

He shot along.

A coyote ran in front of him and disappeared in the shadows.

Du Pré laughed.

Couple miles farther on, another.

Du Pré laughed.

Du Pré wound up a long rise that ended on a bench of stone that once must have been a tall butte.

There was a turnout at the top and Du Pré pulled over and he got out and he fished the whiskey bottle out from under the seat and he rolled a cigarette and he sat on the warm hood of his car. The night air was chilling down fast.

The coyotes suddenly started to sing. First one, then more, then a whole chorus.

Gettin' ready to hunt.

Just like Du Pré.

Du Pré howled once.

A coyote howled back.

Benetsee?

✤ CHAPTER 17 ✤

The night was black except for the silver starlight which made soft ghosts of the sage and Siberian elms that crept up to Benetsee's cabin. Du Pré turned off in the driveway and he could smell woodsmoke.

Ah, the old bastard is back. Never know where he goes, Canada, the moon, China, maybe. The fucking North Pole.

Du Pré parked by the falling-down front porch. He went to the door and he knocked.

Nothing.

He looked in the window. A kerosene lamp was burning low.

The old dogs had all finally died. Du Pré missed them, woofing and wheezing and trying to do dog work to the last, even when they could barely get up anymore.

Du Pré had tried to give Benetsee a blue heeler pup, but the old man said no, he would not live long enough and so the dog would be sad because its master would be gone.

The smell of smoke was pretty thick. Du Pré knocked again.

Nothing. He went around back to where Benetsee's sweat lodge was.

Big fire gone down to coals now, the pit where the stones were heated before being carried to the steam pit in the sweat lodge. The flaps were down on the lodge and tendrils of steam rose from the seams and curled in the night air.

In there, he is praying.

Or fucking a goat, maybe.

So I wait.

Du Pré went back to his car and he opened the trunk and rummaged around and found a bottle of the cheap awful screwtop wine that Benetsee liked so much. He carried that and his whiskey and tobacco back to the sweat lodge and he sat on a stump smoking and drinking whiskey and looking up at the stars. A green streak of fire shot across the black and it bloomed and faded in seconds.

Meteor.

Another.

Another.

Du Pré wondered why they burned with green fire, little yellow, but mostly green.

He had a slug of whiskey.

Du Pré heard some singing coming from the sweat lodge.

The lodge would be cooling and soon the old man would crawl out, wearing only his loincloth, and he would dance in the cool night air while the sweat rolled off him in streams.

Du Pré rolled a cigarette for the old fart.

I got plenty question for him, thought Du Pré.

The flap of canvas over the door shook and then a hand poked a stick up into it and opened the door all the way. Steam rose in the night air.

A young man emerged, naked, carrying a dipper.

He stopped when he saw Du Pré, reached back in the lodge and brought out a towel which he wrapped around his waist.

Du Pré waited for Benetsee.

He didn't come.

The young man stood with his arms raised to heaven, his lips moving but making no sound.

Then he went around behind the lodge and he pulled his clothes from the branches of the blue spruces and he dressed.

Du Pré smoked.

That old fucker, he thought, he is not even *here*.

"Good evening," said the young man, coming toward Du Pré. He was dressed in jeans and boots and a worn Western shirt. He had a belt buckle made of black metal and bear claws. A turquoise and buffalo-bone choker around his neck.

"I come to see Benetsee," said Du Pré. "Would you like some wine?"

"I don't drink anymore," said the young man. "Thank you, though."

Du Pré nodded. Res Indian here.

"Where is Benetsee?" said Du Pré.

"He gone to North Dakota," said the young man. "You are Du Pré."

"Yes," said Du Pré.

"He say you catch these guys he come back then."

"WHAT?!" said Du Pré.

"Don't yell," said the young man, "the spirits are still here, they do not like yelling. You know that."

"I got to talk to Benetsee," said Du Pré.

"Look," said the young man, "I am telling you what he told me to tell you, I don't know about nothin' else."

"Shit," said Du Pré.

"I am here to take care of his place and do . . . some things," the young man said. "I don't be telling Benetsee what he may do."

"Who," said Du Pré, "the fuck are you?"

"I don't got a name yet," the young man said. "I had one but Benetsee said it wasn't my name so I . . ."

"Christ," said Du Pré.

"Well," said the young man, "he said you'd help me I needed it."

"Yah," said Du Pré, "look, I am sorry. I am wanting to talk to that old bastard and it made me mad he was not here."

"He is not coming till you catch those guys," said the young man.

"You told me that," said Du Pré.

"I am sorry," said the young man.

"It is all right," said Du Pré. "Maybe I just kick that old fucker's ass I see him."

The young man said nothing.

"You got food," said Du Pré.

"No," said the young man, "I been fasting and praying, and Benetsee . . ."

"Come on then," said Du Pré. "My Madelaine always likes, feed people. When you eat, last time?"

"Long time ago," said the young man.

Du Pré got up from the stump. He picked up the wine and whiskey and the cigarette he had rolled for Benetsee. He stopped.

"You smoke?" he said.

"Sure," said the young man.

Du Pré lit the cigarette and gave it to him. They walked to his old cruiser and got in and they sat there a moment and then Du Pré started the engine and he drove to Toussaint and up to Madelaine's. The lights were all off.

Du Pré opened the door and went in. The young man followed him to the kitchen. Du Pré set down his whiskey bottle and he opened the refrigerator and he got out some cheese and a pot of venison stew and some green beans.

Jug of milk.

Du Pré put the stew on the stove to heat and the green beans he dumped in a pan and turned the gas on under them.

"Hey," said Madelaine from the doorway. "You are back late. Who is your friend, here?"

"Guy at Benetsee's," said Du Pré. "Hasn't eaten in days. He is very hungry."

Madelaine came out into the kitchen wearing her robe. She was rubbing her eyes against the light.

"What is your name, I am Madelaine," she said.

"I don't got a name," said the young man. "Benetsee say the name I had is no good, he will help me find another when I am ready."

"You don't got a name," said Madelaine.

"That damn Benetsee he is some joker, you know," said Du Pré. The young man nodded.

"He learn from them coyotes," said the young man. "They are jokers, them God's dogs."

"Where is Benetsee?" said Madelaine.

"He say he is not coming back till I catch those guys," said Du Pré.

"Guys?" said Madelaine.

"There are two of them," said Du Pré.

"Three," said the young man.

"Christ," said Du Pré, "I could have asked you."

"You say you want to talk, Benetsee," said the young man. "I got to learn to listen pret' good."

"Benetsee say you help me?"

The young man nodded.

"He tell you to tell me things?"

More nods.

The stew was bubbling. Du Pré took it off the stove. He stuck a ladle in it and handed the young man a bowl.

"Eat," he said.

Du Pré and Madelaine watched while the young man ate all of the stew and all of the green beans. A pound of cheese. A pint of ice cream. Drank a bunch of coffee.

Du Pré rolled him a cigarette.

They smoked.

"There are *three* killers?" said Du Pré.

The young man shook his head.

"Two," said the young man. "Third guy, he is . . . it is over, when they are all together."

"OK," said Du Pré.

"Good food," said the young man. "I thank you."

"You eat here plenty," said Madelaine, looking at him carefully.

"Who is there, Mama?" said Lourdes from the dark little hall that led to the bedrooms in the back of the house.

"You come here," said Madelaine. "You meet this young man got no name."

Lourdes came out of the dark.

She looked at the floor.

The young man folded his hands in his lap and his face closed up.

✤ CHAPTER 18 ✤

Again?" said Du Pré. He was in the Toussaint Bar. Agent Pidgeon was on the other end of the line. She was yelling.

"Again? Again?" she yelled. "You sexist pig asshole! What do you mean, again? Just because I'm a woman the fucking cheap-ass government surrey they give me blew up again? Fuck you, Du Pré."

"Um," said Du Pré. "I am just wondering, you know, that it blew up again."

"Fucking did," said Agent Pidgeon.

"So where are you this blown-up thing?"

"Maybe forty miles south of Toussaint."

"You calling from a ranch?"

"No," said Agent Pidgeon. "This guy stopped, he's got a phone in his van. So I am using that."

"What guy?" said Du Pré.

"He does something with the combine crews. Mechanic, I guess. Lot of fucking tools here."

"OK," said Du Pré. "I be there. You are on the highway."

"Yup," said Agent Pidgeon. "Left side of it, way you're coming."

"I be there, half an hour," said Du Pré.

"It's forty fucking miles," said Agent Pidgeon.

"Maybe less," said Du Pré.

He kept the cruiser flat out, the speed close to 120 where he could see far enough ahead.

Hope no fucking deer decides to jump out of them bushes, Du Pré thought. A magpie splattered on the windshield.

Agent Pidgeon was looking at her watch and nodding grimly when Du Pré roared up.

"Twenty-one minutes," she said. "What an asshole."

She was sitting on her suitcases. No aluminum trunks this time.

"Where is your friend?" said Du Pré.

"Simpson?" said Agent Pidgeon. "He had to go on, said he had a down rig somewhere south of here."

Du Pré shrugged. Leave a defenseless woman alone out here. Agent Pidgeon was naked but for her Sig Sauer nine-millimeter and God Knows What unarmed combat training she had in and out of the FBI.

Du Pré piled her luggage in the backseat. He got in and Pidgeon opened the passenger door and she slid in, and pushed her skirt back up her long thighs. Her foot clunked against a bottle.

Du Pré reached over and picked up the bottle of whiskey. He had a nice long swallow. He rolled a cigarette.

Three minutes later they were shooting along at 120 miles an hour. Agent Pidgeon was moving her mouth a lot but Du Pré couldn't hear what she was saying because of the wind rushing through the open windows and the screaming engine.

Du Pré didn't need to hear what she was saying.

He slowed down a couple miles from Toussaint and he drove on in to the bar and he got out and walked inside and left Agent Pidgeon sitting in the car calling him all of the names she could think of, which was quite a few names.

By the time that Agent Pidgeon had run down enough to get out of the car Du Pré was halfway through his second whiskey.

"I need to rent the little trailer," said Agent Pidgeon to Susan Klein. Susan had two small trailers that she rented by the day or week.

"Both rented, honey," said Susan. "Harvesttime."

"Shit," said Agent Pidgeon.

"You can stay at Bart's," said Du Pré.

"I haven't got a car," wailed Pidgeon.

"You would you didn't keep blowing them up," said Du Pré.

"OK," said Pidgeon. "The damsel-in-distress don't mean shit to you."

"Stay out at Bart's," said Susan. "He's a nice guy and he has a bunch of cars."

"It's against regulations," said Pidgeon.

"Oh, fuck you," said Susan.

And they all laughed.

Du Pré turned away and then he looked back at Susan, whose face had gone troubled.

Pidgeon was still laughing but it was not laughter. She began to scream.

Susan raced around the bar and she grabbed Pidgeon and held her, and the FBI agent broke down to gasping sobs and floods of tears.

Du Pré went to the phone and he called Madelaine.

Du Pré came back and Susan Klein looked at him and she jerked her head toward the row of liquor bottles ranked below the big mirror behind the bar. Du Pré went back and he pulled a fifth of brandy out and he put some in a snifter and he slid it across.

Pidgeon took the snifter in both hands. She was shaking so badly that Susan Klein was holding her on the barstool. Pidgeon lifted the glass and she took a sip. Another.

She snuffled.

Du Pré fished out his handkerchief and thought better of it and he took the box of tissues from the cupboard by the cash register and he handed it over.

Pidgeon sipped.

She slumped so deep she seemed boneless.

Madelaine came bustling through the door.

She glanced at Du Pré and then she went to Pidgeon and she hugged her and said something very low.

Pidgeon nodded.

"We take her to my place," Madelaine said. "Me and Susan, you maybe watch the bar."

Du Pré nodded. "I bring her luggage."

Madelaine and Susan led Pidgeon out the front door. In a minute, Du Pré heard them drive off.

Du Pré whistled. He washed some coffee cups and a couple of beer glasses that had tomato juice stuck to the sides.

The bar was empty.

Du Pré flicked on the television.

He poured himself a whiskey and water and he rolled a cigarette and he watched a dumb commercial for snowmobiles. In . . . July? No, July was maybe two days away.

The news came on.

The announcer, a woman with bright red hair, said that the body of a missing schoolteacher, lost since the Sunday before, had been found near Sheridan, Wyoming. The woman had been abducted, police thought, in Billings, and there was no comment to reporters' questions.

Was this the work of the Hi-Line Killer?

Oh, thought Du Pré, now they got a *name* for the bastard, next they have a TV movie.

Hi-Line Killer.

I find that fucker.

Yes.

"Du Pré?" said a soft voice at Du Pré's elbow. Du Pré started.

The young man who lived at Benetsee's was standing there.

Du Pré hadn't heard him come in.

He never heard Benetsee, either.

"Yah," said Du Pré. He was pissed. He heard *everything*.

"Your friend, the lady who is upset?" said the young man. His face was earnest and he was eager to say what he had to say.

"Yah," said Du Pré.

"Would she have some pictures of the bodies where they were found?" said the young man. "I maybe look at them, I could maybe help."

Du Pré looked at him.

Fucking little joker, I want Benetsee, not your sorry ass.

But he come from Benetsee.

Who is not coming.

"OK," said Du Pré. "I don't know when she feel well enough to see you, though."

"She is fine now," said the young man. "Look, I just walk up there."

"OK," said Du Pré. "That Madelaine, she fix you something to eat."

"I maybe take some brandy for that Pidgeon," said the young man. Du Pré handed him the bottle.

He watched him go to the door, walking soft as a cat, his feet on a line, balanced, coiled. He slipped out, barely opening the heavy plank door.

Slipped into the light, Du Pré thought, he is here, he is not here.

I just give away Susan's brandy.

Du Pré stuffed a twenty in the till.

A couple ranchers from the benchlands came in, red and sweaty. They had several cold glasses of beer each. They went out again, arguing about the tractor being broken down and why it was.

Du Pré watched the television. He hoped to hell no one ordered a hamburger. He'd never cooked one here.

Susan Klein came in. She bustled up to the bar and around behind it.

"Pidgeon's much better," she said.

Du Pré nodded.

"She sort of lost it thinking about all the women this bastard has killed, and just before you picked her up she heard about another body found down by Sheridan. A young schoolteacher, she was only twenty-two."

Probably looked about sixteen, Du Pré thought. My age, they look sixteen until they are maybe thirty-five. Kids.

"You go on up there," said Susan. "That young Indian guy is there. He brought up some brandy."

Du Pré nodded.

"He wants to look at some pictures," said Susan Klein. "The pictures are in her stuff, there."

Du Pré took a go-cup of whiskey and a fresh bag of Bull Durham and some fried pork rinds.

Du Pré drove up to Madelaine's.

Pictures.

Young-Man-Who-Has-No-Name wanted to look at them.

I would like that, too, Du Pré thought.

❧ CHAPTER 19 ❧

The young man sat at the kitchen table. He had three large black-and-white photographs on the white enamel top.

There was a big clear glass of iced water in his hand.

The young man bent his head and he looked through the glass at the photographs. He cocked his head this way and that, like a bird, using one eye and then the other.

Du Pré and Madelaine and Pidgeon leaned against the kitchen counters. Du Pré and Pidgeon were smoking.

The young man moved to another photograph.

He stared down through the ice, water, and glass. He moved the glass in little bits of motion.

Pidgeon was red-eyed but calm. Her strong jaw was set.

They waited.

The young man kept on looking, photograph to photograph, intent and out of time.

Pidgeon jerked her head toward the door and looked at Du Pré.

He followed her out to the back porch, past the boots and coats waiting on another winter. Pidgeon opened the screen door and she went down the three steps to the yard and over to some chairs under a willow tree.

She sat down and lit a cigarette. She sucked the smoke deep into her lungs and blew out a long blue stream, eyes closed.

Du Pré took another chair and he rolled a smoke.

"Thanks," said Pidgeon.

"Yah," said Du Pré.

"I haven't lost it like that for a while. Not supposed to let this stuff get to you. It gets to you. Those poor women. They come to me in my dreams. I was raised by kind and loving parents. Ozzie 'n' Harriet kinda family, you know. I think of those poor runaway girls screaming while this bastard rapes and tortures and kills them. I hate him. I am not supposed to. Not professional."

"It don't seem very professional not give a shit," said Du Pré.

"Harvey really likes you," said Pidgeon. "Said you're one of them Montana cowboys that's more'n half-Indian. Crazy fuckers, what Harvey says, but you can trust them. He told me about . . . the Martins, and that guy Lucky . . . and how you and Bart came to be such good friends."

Du Pré shrugged.

"Tell me about Benetsee," she said.

"Him," said Du Pré, "he is an old man, been around here long as anybody. Good friend to my grandfather, my father, me. Old drunk, he is, sometimes. Dreamer. Medicine Person, holy person. Funny man, though some time he make jokes on me I want to kill him."

"He's Métis?"

"Dunno," said Du Pré. "We are all over, you know, some of us act real white, live whiteside. Some of us been doing that generations, don't even know we are Métis anymore. Some of us live on the reservations, are more Indian. Lots of us around. Whites call us Indian. Indians call us white. Catch shit, everywhere. Been like that for three hundred years. More. Some say we were here before Columbus."

"How?" said Pidgeon.

"Seapeoples," said Du Pré. "Celts, you know, Breton French, Irish, Scots, maybe sail here, their little fishing smacks, long time. Catch the cod, dry it, take it to Portugal, sell it for bacãlao. We are the voyageurs, most of the Mountain Men, they were Métis. Got French names, Scottish names, look Indian."

"What's the name of the guy with the ice water, in there?" said Agent Pidgeon.

"He don't got one," said Du Pré. "I guess he had one but Benetsee say it is the wrong one. So he is waiting for a name."

"I see," said Pidgeon. "Is he an apprentice?"

"Dunno," said Du Pré. "That Benetsee, when I say he joke, it is true. Be like that Benetsee, hide in the bushes, watch us listen to some guy don't know shit."

Pidgeon looked at him startled.

"I am being pissy," said Du Pré. "Benetsee not do that, this guy is maybe some relation of his, wants to learn from Benetsee. You can't decide to be a Medicine Person. It just happens. Happen to anybody. Happens to whites, once in a while. They see things maybe."

"Anything that will help," said Pidgeon, "will help."

Madelaine came out, carrying a little tray with three cups of coffee on it. She set it on a low-cut cottonwood stump and she took a chair that Du Pré pulled up for her.

"Him something," said Madelaine. "I don't know what he is seeing, but he is seeing something."

"He was telling me about Benetsee," said Pidgeon. "I wish that I could meet him."

"Oh." Madelaine laughed. "He will be here sometime."

Du Pré pulled out the map of the West with all the marks on it where the bodies had been found, dozens and dozens.

He unfolded it. The paper was getting beaten and soft. He carried it in his hip pocket, always. There were two more like it at Bart's.

Madelaine looked once at it and she looked away. Her lips moved a little. Hail Mary.

"First off," said Pidgeon, "this guy may have been doing this for as long as twenty years."

She was pointing to the crop of x's stippled up the Front Range of the Rockies. The old Great North Trail.

"And this one," she said, pointing to the trail that began near Puget Sound, "may have been doing this for fifteen. Ten, more likely. Hard crimes to solve. That bastard Bundy may have killed ninety women. We'll never know."

Green River Killer. Ted Bundy. Hi-Line Killer. What they call this asshole come out from Seattle?

Bastards. They die some, soon.

Du Pré was getting angry looking at it.

"They are not all him," said Du Pré. "Not all them two."

"No," said Pidgeon. "Of course not. But enough of them are. The Bureau has been on this for three years. Before that, we weren't welcome. The killer spread the damage across so many jurisdictions and we can't in law come in on this sort of thing till we're asked. Nobody asked. When they did ask—Sheriff down in southern Colorado, in fact—the crimes led both directions. Christ, what a mess. This guy knew what he was doing. He'd drop bodies in places where jurisdictions overlapped. Then nobody wanted the cases."

Madelaine got up and she took the coffee cups and she went into the house with the tray.

"I'm going to Sheridan," said Pidgeon, "soon's we wangle a request from the cops there. Could you come?"

"What I do there?" said Du Pré.

"Think," said Pidgeon.

"Take the guy in there," said Du Pré.

"Hmm," said Pidgeon. "I'll think about that."

"Me," said Du Pré, "I live here, I know here, what I can maybe do I do here. Don't want to go, you know."

Pidgeon nodded.

"What else can you tell me, maybe, about this guy," said Du Pré.

"Oh," said Pidgeon. "I don't favor getting too cute and specific. Trouble with that is that then that's what you are looking for. Profiles are pretty good up to a point. After that, they can blind you."

Pidgeon got up and went into the house.

Du Pré smoked.

The sun was warm. He looked up for the eagle but he couldn't see it, he scanned the sky for a black speck.

Nothing.

Pidgeon came back out.

"He left," said Pidgeon.

"Huh?" said Du Pré.

"Yup," said Pidgeon. "Told Madelaine that the little girl was the work of one man and that the other three were the work of another."

Du Pré nodded.

"That there is witchcraft around the killer of the little girl."

Witchcraft? What the fuck he mean by that? Du Pré thought, we got green-skinned hags boiling up lizards here? Witchcraft.

"You're going to Sheridan," said Pidgeon.

OK, thought Du Pré, my Madelaine is in this.

"Day after tomorrow, I guess."

Du Pré nodded.

"Bart's flying us down and back," said Pidgeon.

My Madelaine she has been on the telephone. World is cranking around all right, she has seen to it.

"That OK," said Pidgeon, "with you?"

Du Pré nodded.

"Good," said Pidgeon. "I guess I'll be staying here."

Du Pré nodded.

"Du Pré!" Madelaine yelled through the kitchen window. "You got a phone call here!"

Du Pré got up and he went to the steps and he tripped and fell going up, catching himself on the jamb.

Madelaine was looking sad.

She handed him the phone.

"Du Pré?" said Benny Klein.

"Yah," said Du Pré.

"Another."

"Shit. Where are you."

"Blaine's Cut."

Years ago some crazy old man had cut a road through rock.

Charged a quarter to use it. The only way to get up to the top of a dry riverbed, left over from when the glaciers melted.

And then up into the Wolf Mountains, so the miners paid.

It was maybe fifteen miles away.

Right next to Bart's land.

"I be there," said Du Pré.

Pidgeon was sitting in his cruiser when he got there.

✤ CHAPTER 20 ✤

Now I spend the rest of my life looking at crosses in the earth and remembering, Du Pré thought. I ever find this guy I kill him for what he has done to what I see every day.

Du Pré was about six feet up the left wall of Blaine's Cut, looking at what at first glance seemed to be a tree root sticking out of a wide cleft in the fragile rock. It was a human foot, with dark brown skin, dried and mummified. The toenails were dark yellow-brown.

There was a vertical cut in the rock about ten feet to Du Pré's right.

Left arm of the cross, right hand of Christ.

Du Pré looked in the cleft. He squinted. The body had been in a duffel bag. The canvas had rotted and the edges of the tears were white. Insects crawled over the dried corpse. It didn't look like anything human.

Du Pré dropped back down to the ground.

"No telling how long that's been there," said Benny.

"Years," said Pidgeon. "Who found it?"

"Kid out shooting his .22," said Benny. "Shot at the foot. Toenail fell off. Smart kid. He took one look at the toenail and he ran like hell. Got his dad and the old man come and crawled up there and then he called me. No telling how many people just walked right by this, you know."

"I dunno how I'll get the body out of there," said Benny.

"You'll have to hook it out," said Pidgeon, "and it'll probably break up. Pretty dry and brittle. Where's the toenail?"

Benny handed her a glassine envelope. Pidgeon looked at it for a long time.

"Got a little red polish on it," said Pidgeon.

Du Pré nodded.

Pidgeon was looking up at the top of the cut. The sagebrush hung over the sheer edge a little. She made a clicking sound with her tongue.

"What's up there?" said Pidgeon.

Du Pré nodded and he started up the cut so he could get up top and look. Pidgeon was wearing lady penny loafers with little gold chains over the arch of the foot.

Du Pré found a steep path that cut back and forth twice in rising ten feet to the top of the limestone shelf. He went up it. He had to grab a sagebrush at the top and hoist himself over the crumbling lip of yellow-gray rock and earth.

Du Pré looked off to the west. A rutted track looped and meandered back and forth through the dry tough benchland, one that avoided the rocks that stuck up high enough to grab a transmission. Grass grew in the ruts. Sparse yellow blades. They had been flattened. Someone had driven up here recently. He walked back along the lip toward the vertical cleft that split the formation.

Water. Du Pré rolled a smoke. Water and mountains fight, water it always win. Takes a long time, though. People, we don't got that much time. Old stories.

Du Pré stood and thought of dead women lying alone in the dirt, eyes pecked out by birds, skunks chewing their faces.

He went to the cleft and he looked down. Pidgeon and Benny were looking up at him.

Du Pré glanced around.

"No more bodies up here," he said, spreading his hands, palms up.

Benny called him a son of a bitch.

This is not funny, Benny, thought Du Pré. No, it is not funny.

One spur of the rutted track came to within fifty feet of Du Pré. He walked over to it, a circle wide enough for a pickup truck to turn around in. He walked around it slowly. Couple old beer cans. Deer hunters, antelope hunters. Du Pré glanced up. A half dozen antelope were running up the long slope of the next short hill.

Them prairie scooters. Move some. Good meat.

Du Pré stopped and he breathed deeply and he set his mind to lock out sounds and the wind and all that was not in his first sight. To bring the ground up to his eyes, see what was on it that shouldn't be there.

At the place he had begun, when he returned to it after a time spent walking slowly, he glanced toward the center of the loop and he saw something circular.

No circles out here but eyes.

Du Pré walked over to the small circle in the yellow earth. He bent down and he looked a long time.

Socket. From a socket wrench set. Expensive kind, that black metal. Little yellow mud on the top, hard to see.

Du Pré rubbed the dirt from the outside of the socket.

$\%_{16}$.

Made in America.

Snap-On Tool Corporation.

Du Pré had seen their trucks. They went around to where mechanics worked and they had a huge assortment of tools. Gave credit till payday.

$\%_{16}$.

Du Pré put the socket in his pocket and he went back to the lip of the cut and he looked down at Pidgeon and Benny.

"Nothing here much," said Du Pré.

Socket probably rolled out of somebody's pickup they open the door. That is how I lose mine. When I figure out how I lose my sunglasses, I will be better, you bet.

Du Pré walked back down to the narrow steep path and he

dropped off the edge and he landed and flexed his knees to absorb the shock and he took tiny steps quickly till he was at the bottom and could lengthen his stride.

"Had some maybe antelope hunters, deer hunters up there," he said, "Beer cans. Found this, it maybe roll out of somebody's truck."

Du Pré handed the socket to Pidgeon.

She looked at it and nodded.

"Shit," said Benny. "I have lost more a them damn things, you know, the box bounces open and they fly out and roll out the door when you open it. And there goes another three, four bucks. For the good ones, anyway."

"This is a professional's tool?" said Pidgeon.

"Yah," said Du Pré. "But you got, remember, all the ranchers here have to be pret' good mechanics, pret' good welders, pret' good carpenters, all them things . . ."

"Pretty good psychics, too," said Benny, "and gamblers. Cattle business is like a damn séance. Always has been, I guess, when you deal in live things you never know what's going to happen."

"OK," said Pidgeon. "Now, you gonna drag the bones out of the rocks, there?"

Benny nodded miserably.

"I do it," said Du Pré. "You got a something I can use?"

Benny went to his truck and he got a boathook out and a black body bag. He brought them back.

"I got a ladder, too," he said.

He fetched it.

Du Pré put the ladder up against the rock, to the left of the dried corpse jammed in the horizontal cleft. He went up the ladder and he picked up the boathook and he reached in and jiggled the hook for a purchase and he pulled.

The whole bundle moved, and very easily.

Du Pré inched it toward him.

Smell of stale old corruption. Some startled mice scurried off from their nests under the rotted canvas bag.

Du Pré got the bundle out to the edge of the rock face. He dropped the boathook and he grasped the bundle and he slid it forward and let it fall.

He squinted and looked in.

Couple lumps of something there.

"Benny!" said Du Pré. "You hand me that boathook again, maybe?"

Benny did.

Du Pré pulled and scraped the lumps out.

Looked like old hide, all balled up.

One lump had some brown hair on it, fairly long.

An ear.

Christ, Du Pré thought, this is the skin of her face.

Du Pré dropped it over the side. And another brown gob.

He looked in. The rock floor of the cleft was clean. There were stains, dark ones, where the bundle had sat.

I wonder how that foot got out there.

Skunk shit there, a foot from my nose, all dried and black.

Coyotes could make it in here, too.

They chew and drag. Wonder they did not drag the whole thing off.

Du Pré went down the ladder. Benny was zipping up the black body bag. He carried it to his truck. Du Pré followed with the ladder and the boathook.

"Where," said Pidgeon, "in the name of God did you find a boathook in this fucking desert?"

"Navy recruiter," said Benny, solemnly. "Busted him for speeding. He didn't have any money, so the judge took this."

He is some better, now, thought Du Pré!

"Thanks," said Benny.

"You send that to Helena?" said Du Pré.

"I drive it to Helena," said Benny.

Du Pré nodded.

"The north–south guy," said Pidgeon.

Du Pré nodded.

❧ CHAPTER 21 ❧

Du Pré drove into Toussaint past combine crews harvesting the hard red wheat. The giant machines marched slowly across the golden fields, trucks grinding along beside them, receiving thick streams of hulled grain. One combine, two trucks. When one truck was full it would pull ahead, the second would move up under the spout, and the first would head for the metal storage bins standing at the ranch houses.

Lotta damn noodles, Du Pré thought, wish I liked noodles better.

He drove into the little town and to the bar. He parked and walked inside. There were a lot of strangers in the bar, drinking beers and eating and playing the video poker machines.

The combines ran twenty-four hours when the weather was good. All night, with giant spotlights hung on the cabs focused on the wheat. The whole year's work on the fields brought in, the bank's notes paid off. Everyone hoped. Maybe something left over. Wheat was up.

The off-duty crews were using part of their twelve-hour break to let off a little steam. They talked in soft Texas accents. They had started down in Texas three months before, working their way north with the ripening grain.

The pool table was busy. Quarters piled beside the coin slot. The players waited. Money was bet on these games, and on the poker games that went on round the clock, too.

Boomers. Make it, spend it right away.

Du Pré grinned. He liked these people.

They never caused much trouble, and anyway they would

never fight in a bar. They needed that bar, and being 86'd from it would make life very hard indeed. They fought across the street in the parking lot.

Susan Klein was scurrying fast behind the bar, drawing beers, mixing drinks, and somehow getting hamburgers and french fries done right and on plates.

She got a good timer in her head, Du Pré thought. He went round the bar and he made himself a whiskey ditch and he dropped a twenty on the ledge of the cash register.

The owners of the equipment sat at corner tables, writing checks, lending money to crew members till payday, and then they'd leave a day or two ahead of the crews, on to the next place of work, and see to all arrangements. The owners were weathered men in their sixties, in light straw cowboy hats and custom boots with lone stars on the front of them.

Susan caught up for a moment. She ran a couple of bar napkins across her forehead. The place was hot. The day was hot and there were a lot of people there and the grill was going.

"Looks good," said Susan. "If the weather lasts another week, the wheat will be in. No problems."

Other years, it had rained, and the grain had to wait for the sun. Put up damp, it would mold. Running grain dryers was expensive. There weren't enough of them. Not needed until they were needed, and then too much grain for the ones at hand.

The big parking lot across the street was filled with the motor homes that the crews lived in. In past years, the ranchers put the crews up in bunkhouses, but since farm and ranch hands had been replaced pretty much by machinery, the bunkhouses had rotted or burned down.

Combine gypsies.

Voyageurs.

Du Pré sipped his drink.

"Could you maybe do some music tonight?" said Susan. "Crews switch at nine or ten, so if you started at seven or so then both shifts could hear you."

Du Pré nodded.

"Thanks," said Susan.

Du Pré thought about who he could get to back him up.

Couple kids. Ranch kids, one played pretty good rhythm guitar and the other pretty good bass.

Wish my cousins were here, they got some music in them.

The kids are OK, just too young.

And they like the old songs. Guitar player he wants to fiddle, I give him one lesson, a tape of simple stuff, say, when you can do all this perfectly then I give you another. Me, I don't listen to you practice at all. I listen to myself practice is bad enough.

Du Pré called the boys, who weren't in but their mothers said they thought they would, which meant that they would.

These ranch women pret' tough.

Du Pré laughed.

A young man in faded denims and worn boots and a battered hat yee-hawed. Du Pré glanced at the point register at the top of the video poker machine's screen. Past five hundred and climbing, so the kid had hit a Royal Flush, Ordered. Ten to ace, left to right. That was eight hundred bucks.

Susan laughed and she went in the back to get the money. The young man brought the slip of paper to the bar and he waited, grinning.

Susan glanced at the little slip of paper. She handed over the eight hundred-dollar bills.

"Drinks for the house!" the young man yelled.

Everybody whooped, even Du Pré.

"Buy me a few new clothes and get my truck some new tires," said the young cowboy. "Then I'll put ten times this back into them damn machines figuring I am going to win big again. You don't, I know, but it is some way to pass the time."

Du Pré glanced at his hand. Wedding band. He was a long way from his wife. Probably missed her a lot.

Du Pré went out and he drove up to Madelaine's. She was in the kitchen, kneading bread dough. Wednesday. Baking day. Madelaine had a baking day, two cleaning days, two sewing days, a day to relax, and one day she prayed more or less all day. Unless she went to bed with Du Pré, or he offered to buy her pink wine and dance to the music on the jukebox with her.

She liked that two-step.

No Métis music, that. She danced the reels and clogs, too, but she really liked the two-step. Liked Nashville music. Cheating hearts, drunks, trucks, prison, railroad trains.

Her father had worked all of his life on the Great Northern Railroad, even though it wasn't called that any more after Burlington bought it.

Line that Jim Hill built, Du Pré thought, then the Catholics, they buy railroad cars that are chapels, run them on to a siding, say to the Métis, hey, François and Helene, you come get married by a priest, you bring your twelve children to watch.

Métis who come down here after Red River Rebellion, they don't talk to priests much. Priests betray Louis Riel, so the English hang him. Little Gabriel Dumont, Louis Riel's little general, brother to my great-great-grandfather, he come down here and he die fifty years later he still had not once talked to a priest. Wouldn't be buried in Catholic earth, either.

Red River.

"I play some music tonight," said Du Pré.

"Good," said Madelaine. "I be your . . . what . . . gropey?"

"Huh?" said Du Pré.

"Gropey," said Madelaine. "One them women follow musicians around, you know, want to fuck them."

"Oh," said Du Pré. "I got ten, twelve, more of them. You just be my Madelaine."

Madelaine looked at Du Pré. She smiled. She pegged a big lump of sticky dough at him. Missed. Hit St. Francis on the wall behind Du Pré.

"Damn," said Madelaine. "What kind of man are you, not save that poor saint? Damn. Poor St. Francis."

Du Pré laughed.

That evening it was still hot at six-thirty. Du Pré got into his cruiser and he drove down to the bar and he went in. Benny was setting up the little stage.

The two kids showed up, all scrubbed and eager. They were so young that they really couldn't legally play in the bar, if anyone cared to think about it.

Good kids, Du Pré thought, they never make much musicians, but they want to a lot.

News that Du Pré was playing his fiddle always brought some people down to the bar. Not so many this night, because everyone was working so hard. But there were fifty people in the room when Du Pré and his sidemen started. The harvest crews listened respectfully. Susan Klein shut down the pool table when Du Pré played. No arguments.

Madelaine came in after nine.

The night crews went out and the day crews straggled in, dusty and hot and tired and covered in bits of wheat hulls. They perked up after a lot of beer and some food.

Du Pré played some reels and some jigs.

People danced, some of them pretty well.

A couple of the Texans were really good.

Du Pré took a break after a long hour.

He bought Madelaine some pink wine.

"Everybody they think they make out pret' good this year," said Madelaine.

Du Pré nodded. Everybody always hoped that it would be a good year, wheat's up, no rain at harvesttime.

After Du Pré quit he and Madelaine danced to the jukebox. Late, till the bar closed.

✤ CHAPTER 22 ✤

Christ," yelled Pidgeon. "Do you have to drive like this?" Du Pré laughed. The countryside was shooting by very rapidly. They were north of the Yellowstone River and south of the Missouri. The Big Dry. Where the last wild buffalo in America were slaughtered by a Smithsonian expedition.

Du Pré's great-grandfather had watched from a nearby butte.

The expedition moved on and Du Pré's grandpère had butchered out the three cows and he had smoked the meat and taken it back to his family. It was the last of the buffalo for the Métis.

Beef is pret' good, though, Du Pré thought.

"You fucker," yelled Pidgeon.

Du Pré looked over and he grinned.

"Drive that fifty-five you never get anywhere," said Du Pré, at the top of his lungs. "Big place, this Montana."

Pidgeon tried to light a cigarette but she couldn't get the flame on her butane lighter to keep going long enough to do it. Du Pré took the cigarette from her and he lit it with his old Zippo and handed it back.

Pidgeon smoked and looked out the window.

Du Pré slowed down to eighty-five to humor her.

"How fast were we going?" she said.

"About right," said Du Pré. From the bench he could see the Interstate along the south bank of the Yellowstone River. It was heavy with traffic and it looked very busy in the calm and empty landscape.

They crossed over the river and went up an on-ramp and headed west.

South at Hardin, on the Crow Reservation, headed for Sheridan.

Du Pré drove at sixty-five. You could drive like hell on the two lane but the superhighways were heavily patrolled.

This schoolteacher, she was from Billings.

Dumped near Sheridan.

Missing for two days.

First one we got that's fairly fresh, Du Pré thought.

He's around.

I find him.

"I think we'll get some cooperation," said Pidgeon, "but you never know. The Bureau didn't try to spare anyone's feelings till recently."

No shit, thought Du Pré.

"So I talked to the Sheriff and he's meeting us at the Denny's at the north exit into the town."

Du Pré nodded.

Find your way around America by hamburger.

Bad hamburgers, too.

They came to the exit for the Little Bighorn Battlefield. Eleven Métis, they die there. That Mitch Bouyer, he is leading the scouts, he try to send his friends away. He knows how many Sioux, Cheyenne, all them Plains people are down there.

Custer sends his favorite Crow scout, Half Yellow Face, away.

Mitch, he die there. Lonesome Charley Reynolds, the old trapper, he die there, too.

That Custer, he is a bastard.

Them Indian, they have their Day of Greasy Grass.

"My heart has quit pounding," said Pidgeon. "You can speed up now. I know it hurts you to obey the law."

"Me," said Du Pré, "I obey all them good laws."

"Right," said Pidgeon.

She was dressed in jeans and hiking boots and a cotton shirt and a photographer's vest. Her gun, ID, handcuffs, and such were in the pockets. She carried a camera and many rolls of film. Little tape recorder.

"There have been three other bodies left near Sheridan in the last ten years," said Pidgeon, "all young women, all mutilated, none identified. All of them treated as isolated cases. Since they were dumped years apart, I suppose."

"Me," said Du Pré, "I never know that so much of this happens." Pidgeon nodded.

"I got into this," she said, "because of a term paper. How many women were killed and dumped and no one ever charged in their murders. Over the last twenty years, there have been thousands. *Thousands.* I couldn't believe it."

"Pret' hard to find, people who do it," said Du Pré. "They are not part of any place. Come in, kidnap someone, kill them, leave them somewhere else. Don't go back. Or kill them poor whores. They got to get in cars with men. Can't attract too much attention, cops bust them."

"These are young girls mostly," said Pidgeon, "of lower-class origin. I have heard them called trailer trash. Money's pretty damned important in this country."

Du Pré nodded. Pretty important everywhere.

"Was Bart pissed when you said you didn't want to take the offer of a plane from him?" said Pidgeon.

"No," said Du Pré, "I am trying to help him, he is too generous, some people take him for much money. He wants to help, he is a rich boy, I want him to know I like him even though he has got a lot of money."

Pidgeon snorted.

"He is a good guy."

"I like him," said Pidgeon. "He has such a sad, sweet face. A middle-aged boy who is sort of bewildered by all the trouble the world causes itself and him personally."

"Yah," said Du Pré.

They rode silently the rest of the way to Sheridan. Du Pré got off at the first exit. He could see the Denny's sign from the highway.

"We're early," said Pidgeon.

Du Pré parked the cruiser. He took off his hat and wiped his forehead and he rubbed his eyes and he yawned.

He leaned back for a moment, eyes shut.

"Hey, Du Pré," said Pidgeon. "Guess what? The Denny's is being robbed. Hey, hey."

Du Pré sat upright in a hurry.

"No sudden movements," said Pidgeon. "That car, across from the door out in the street? The one that is running? With the kid at the wheel who is smoking like hell and staring at the front door. And I notice that though Denny's is open and there are cars in the lot, I can't see anybody in there. Bet they are all lying on the floor."

Du Pré looked. Nobody was stirring in there.

"What you going to do?" said Du Pré.

"Have fun," said Pidgeon. "It's important in life, you know, to have fun. It's important. Most folks don't."

This Pidgeon, she reminds me some of that poor Corey Banning, thought Du Pré. FBI lady poor Packy killed. Some shit, that. Wolves. Balls.

Pidgeon had slid her gun out of its pocket.

She lit a cigarette.

"Oh," said Pidgeon. "Tell you what. It is so against every Bureau regulation, do what I would like to do, that I'm gonna let you do it. Here." She racked the slide and handed the Sig Sauer to Du Pré.

"What I don't like to?" said Du Pré.

"I'll tell Madelaine you wussed out," said Pidgeon. "Oh, don't kill anybody."

"OK," said Du Pré. He got out and he tucked the automatic in his waistband at his back. He walked across the little parking lot and down to the sidewalk beyond the decorative planting. The kid in the car glanced at him. Just a cowboy.

The kid went back to staring at the front door of the Denny's.

Du Pré crossed the sidewalk and he went in front of the car and he stepped out into the traffic lane.

When a truck passed, Du Pré sprinted.

He walked up to the open driver's window and he squatted down and put the barrel of the gun against the kid's head.

"Don' move," said Du Pré.

The kid shuddered.

Du Pré reached in the window and he turned off the car and pulled the keys out of the ignition and he stuck them in his pocket. He was out of sight, behind the driver.

"How many friends you got in there," said Du Pré, jamming the gun against the kid's head.

"Two," whispered the kid.

"OK," said Du Pré. "What guns they got?"

"Couple pistols. Twenty-twos."

"That's very good," said Du Pré.

Two young men came flying out of the Denny's doors. They were each carrying paper sacks in one hand and little Saturday Night Specials in the other. They ran like hell for the car.

When they were twenty feet away Du Pré stood up and he fired one round into the sky.

"Down on the ground," he said, lowering the gun.

One kid froze. The other stumbled and tripped and he went face-first into the side of the car.

Crump.

The other kid dropped the sack and his gun and he put his hands on the top of his head.

Du Pré opened the driver's door.

"You get out now," he said.

The kid did.

Du Pré prodded him around to the sidewalk. The kid who had hit the car was on his knees, holding his face, and blood welled between his hands.

Du Pré heard a siren.

Two cop cars came, lights flashing.

The cops screeched to a stop.

Du Pré waited, gun on the three young men.

✤ CHAPTER 23 ✤

Oh, this is good," said the Sheriff. He was a big, paunchy man with silver hair brushed back and squinted blue eyes.

Du Pré and Pidgeon were standing with him in the Denny's parking lot. The thugs were on their way to the jail.

The manager was being carted away in an ambulance. He'd been so scared he'd had a heart attack.

The people in the restaurant were all over the parking lot jabbering at each other.

"Well, thanks," said the Sheriff. "We know these boys. Two of them got out of the State Pen last week. Guess they weren't reehabilitated."

He spat the word.

Cops know better.

"They were not very good at it," said Du Pré.

The Sheriff looked at Du Pré. "Most of these assholes got IQs lower'n room temperature," he said. "They ain't rocket scientists. Once in a while there's a bad guy has a brain but I don't see many. 'Bout two in the last ten years, you don't count the forgers and scam artists. Holdup guys and burglars ain't too swift."

Pidgeon was standing with them. She had on big aviator sunglasses with very dark lenses.

"We're being rude, ma'am," said the Sheriff suddenly. "I apologize."

"Not at all," said Pidgeon. "Could we go somewhere and talk, though? I have to fly out of Billings late tonight."

"Surely," said the Sheriff. "There's a saloon a couple blocks away has decent food and no jukebox. How's that?"

He drove them to it. A simple old brick building with MINT CLUB on a sign and no beer neon in the windows. The place was clean and old and a little shabby. Several old ranchers sat at the bar drinking red beers and chatting.

The Sheriff led them to a little back room with one banquette and one table in it. He threw his hat on the table and slid in one side of the banquette.

The barmaid came in.

"What'll you have?" said the Sheriff.

"Cheeseburger," said Pidgeon, "glass of soda."

Du Pré and the Sheriff ordered fries with theirs.

"I don't know that I can tell you much," said the Sheriff. "I mean I don't know more'n the skinny little ME's report and a bit about the site."

"Can you fax the full reports to me in DC?" said Pidgeon.

"Sure," said the Sheriff. "When I get 'em."

Pidgeon gave him a card.

"Well," said the Sheriff. "Poor Susannah Granger. She taught typing and some home economics at the school in Billings. It was her first year. She graduated from Bozeman, Montana State. Strict Christian. Didn't drink or smoke or run around. She had alcohol in her system, she was strangled to unconsciousness and then had her jugular cut, very carefully. The killer left her in the brush, legs splayed and a . . . uh."

"She had something shoved up her vagina or anus?" said Pidgeon.

"A stick up each one," said the Sheriff.

Pidgeon nodded. The little tape recorder sat there in front of her.

Their food arrived. Pidgeon picked at her cheeseburger.

Du Pré and the Sheriff ate like pigs.

"So you wanted to see where the body was found?" said the Sheriff.

"Changed my mind," said Pidgeon. "Du Pré and me, we need to go on to Billings."

Du Pré shrugged.

The Sheriff drove them back to Du Pré's car.

"I'd like copies of the photos of the scene," said Pidgeon. "How was the body found?"

"Pilot," said the Sheriff. "He was just logging some hours for his license and he looked down and saw her."

Du Pré wheeled back out to the expressway and he headed north.

"This is the first one that is fresh and not a young kid who is just in some sort of trouble," said Pidgeon. "The bastard's losing it."

"OK," said Du Pré.

"When a killer's pattern changes, even slightly, there is something going on with them. There's something in Billings. Something else. Susannah lived with an aunt."

They rode on to Billings. When they got there Pidgeon made several calls from a phone booth. She came back to the car with a map in her hand.

"She'll see us," said Pidgeon.

She read the directions to Du Pré. They ended at a trailer court. The trailers were neatly kept, and most had little redwood decks built on the back sides.

"Number twenty-eight," said Pidgeon. "That's it, where that blue car with the abortion-is-murder bumper sticker is."

Du Pré pulled in behind it.

"Wait here," said Pidgeon. "You'd just scare her."

Pidgeon got out and she went to the front door and knocked. The door opened. Du Pré saw a fat woman in a pantsuit. A blue one. Pidgeon went inside.

Du Pré rolled a smoke. He reached under the seat and he found his whiskey and he had a good long drink. It was getting late. He was hungry. He had some more whiskey.

He looked across the drive. There was a little compact car sitting there. Blue. It wasn't in any parking space by any trailer.

Woman must have a kid or something, Du Pré thought. It was closest to the trailer owned by the murdered woman's aunt.

Du Pré had another cigarette.

He waited another half hour before Pidgeon came back. She was excited.

"OK," she said. "Susannah was at a prayer meeting the night she was taken. After the meeting she did the church's books—so it was past midnight when she left for home. Never got here. Then, this morning the police call and say they have her car, it was abandoned about a mile from here. Off on the side of the stem road. Not much traffic there at that time of night. There aren't any fast-food places around. The stem road isn't a main drag, you can get into or across town faster other ways. So they towed it here."

Du Pré looked at the little compact car.

"OK," he said. "So what we do."

"I want to see if that car starts," said Pidgeon.

She held up a key.

Du Pré took it and he went over and got in and stuck the key in the ignition and he turned it and the starter motor turned over but the engine didn't catch. He looked at the fuel gauge. Dead empty.

No gas.

Susannah Granger had pulled over because her little car was out of gas. It was dark.

And somebody came along.

"Where this car when it was found?" said Du Pré.

"Dunno," said Pidgeon, "but I can call and find out. I've talked to the cop handled the case here."

Du Pré drove back out to the stem road and found a telephone booth.

Pidgeon was on the phone for ten minutes.

Du Pré had a smoke and some more whiskey.

"OK," said Pidgeon. "I got to get to the airport but I want you to find where the hell this place is, Spurgin Road."

"We are on it," said Du Pré.

"Oh," said Pidgeon.

"What is the number?"

"One seven five four five," said Pidgeon.

"It is about a half mile toward the airport," said Du Pré.

When they got to the place, Du Pré pointed it out. A dirt parking lot in front of a long metal building.

WELDING SUPPLIES.

OK.

So she was coming home, he thought, and she pulled off there
when she ran out of gas.

Du Pré went on, up to the rimrocks above the city, to the airport.

He helped Pidgeon carry her luggage in and check it.

"Thanks, Du Pré," she said. She kissed him on the cheek.

"You come back," he said.

"You find those pricks," said Pidgeon. "You know how to get
ahold of me. Or Harvey."

"You tell Harvey hello," said Du Pré. "Maybe he come out, we
go hunt or something."

"Harvey hates the great outdoors," said Pidgeon. "He'll go out
in it, but not for fun."

Du Pré laughed.

"But I will," said Pidgeon. "You give my love to Madelaine."

Du Pré nodded. Pidgeon went on up to the departure lounge.

He drove back down to where the car had been found. It was
dark now. He got out of his cruiser and he switched on a powerful flashlight. He scanned the ground where a car might have
rolled to a stop with no power.

It had rained here, three, four days before. Old mud puddles,
dried now. Du Pré saw a piece of paper stuck in pale clay.

Folded many times.

Du Pré tugged it free.

FREE WILL EVANGELICAL CHURCH

A printed service.

Du Pré opened the pamphlet and he looked at the second
page. He walked over toward his car and held the program in the
headlights.

"solo . . . Susannah Granger . . ."

So she was a singer. In the church.

Wouldn't sing for God no more.

✦ CHAPTER 24 ✦

Du Pré sat on the hood of his car. It was four in the morning. He was up on the Hi-Line at Raster Creek, waiting for Rolly Challis. Who said he would be there at four-fifteen.

Du Pré rolled a smoke.

Guy drives this road so much he knows to the minute where he will be anywhere along it, Du Pré thought.

Looking for whoever killed little Shelly Challis.

Du Pré had some coffee from a steel thermos.

He glanced at his watch.

He heard the thrummm of Rolly's big black eighteen-wheeler.

Du Pré was looking at the second hand on his watch when Rolly came to a stop and hit the air brakes to hold the rig.

A minute early.

Damn.

Rolly stepped down from the cab. He walked on the balls of his feet, stretching his arms and back.

"Lo, Du Pré," he said. He held out his hand.

"Yah," said Du Pré. "Well, I don't see the papers much. Your guy he doing any good work out there, eh?"

"Maybe," said Rolly, "but nothing's turned up. Guy dumps the bodies in places where they are found by accident. I guess that there are some more. Real hell for the families, was for ours."

Du Pré waved the steel thermos.

Rolly shook his head.

"We had another down, Sheridan," said Du Pré.

Rolly nodded.

"You know about it," said Du Pré.

"Yeah," said Rolly. "Schoolteacher, young. Saw a picture, now an attractive young woman. Christer."

"Yeah," said Du Pré. "Fundamentalist. But she is maybe older than most this guy kills on the old Great North Trail."

"We got two. Well, I want 'em both," said Rolly. "Hard to find, though. Thought I might be getting close, case in eastern Washington, but it turned out the girl was raped and murdered by her uncle."

Jesus, Du Pré thought.

Well, there is that damn Bucky Dassault, now that Benjamin Medicine Eagle. Never murdered anybody, though. I hate him anyway.

They smoked.

"I call him the Gatherer," said Rolly. "He . . . it seems that he picks a place and then in a matter of a month or so he'll kill four, five, maybe more, and leave them hidden there, and then move on. Prostitutes. Runaway kids trying to survive. Woman's always got her Universal Credit Card . . . sometimes end up dead."

Du Pré nodded. Poor Lourdes. She was always such a sad kid. She always was unhappy. Madelaine tried what she knew, make Lourdes happy.

Nobody can make anybody happy.

Who refuses to be happy.

Me, I sound like them bullshit therapists, TV.

I quit watching TV.

There.

"I'll be along, then," said Rolly. "Thing I guess we'd better do is not quit."

They shook hands.

Du Pré drank coffee and smoked. The dawn was blood pink in the east.

Traffic started to move. A few big trucks, then the huge wallowing motor homes and the cars of people headed east or west.

Du Pré got into his old cruiser and he started it and he wheeled around the rest-stop parking lot and he headed back down south toward Toussaint.

The air was dry and cool.

Mule deer moved from their watering holes to where they would lie up in the day's head. The bucks had horns covered in velvet. Antelope flashed their white butts and sped away from the road at fifty miles an hour. The hawks cruised low, looking for rodents out too late in the light. A badger waddled across the road, steely muscles bunched and close to the ground.

Du Pré cruised at ninety.

There was no one at all on the road.

Soon he could see the Wolf Mountains whitecapped and dark-flanked in the rising light. The snow on the peaks blazed pale pink and gold.

Du Pré shot past a marsh and ducks exploded skyward.

The road rose before him, climbing a long slope.

He smelled something hot.

A steamy billow of scent came through the vents.

Du Pré glanced in the rearview mirror. He was trailing white steam.

He put the transmission in neutral and he turned off the ignition.

Now that damn engine heat up and seize, if it is gonna do that.

Only got two hundred thousand miles on it.

Piece of Detroit shit, anyway.

Du Pré waited for the bass clunk that would mean the engine was eating itself.

It didn't come.

He rolled to a stop, pulling off on a field access road, barely fifteen feet across.

An eighteen-wheeler roared past, close enough to rock the old cruiser on its springs.

Shit, Du Pré thought.

I hate these damn cars. I like horses. Things get tough, you can always eat your horse.

Maybe I eat this fucker. Pound of chopped steel a day, wash it down with whiskey. Maybe pound three times a day. Eat it, a year maybe.

Fucker.

A motor home sailed past. A dachshund was sticking its head out a window. The nasty little dog yapped.

Du Pré dragged the fifth of whiskey out from under the seat.

Go find a telephone, call that Bart. He can borrow Morris's tow truck, come get me.

I hate this.

Du Pré drank savagely.

Several vans with Minnesota plates shot past. They were driving close together. Take a vacation in a mob.

Du Pré had another slug. He tucked the bottle back under the seat and he rolled a smoke and got out and looked down the road.

Nothing.

Hang out my damn thumb. Me, I always look like some train robber or cattle thief. Me, I wouldn't pick up me.

Shit.

Du Pré got out and he waited to lift his thumb.

He heard a car behind him slow down.

A dark green longbed van with deeply tinted windows came to a stop across the road, on another access path.

The driver's door opened and a man got out. He was wearing mechanic's overalls. He was weathered red. Sandy, curly hair, going bald on top.

"Little trouble, there?" he said, walking across the road. "Name's Simpson."

"Me, Du Pré. I blew out a hose," said Du Pré. They shook hands.

"Let me take a look," the man said. "I work on cars a lot. Old cop cruiser. Plymouth. Good engine."

Du Pré shrugged. He popped the hood latch and he lifted the hood and stuck the jackleg in the socket.

Soaking steam rose up for a moment. The air reeked of antifreeze.

The man bent over and looked. He took out a pocketknife and he cut the blown hose away near the engine and he reached in the end of the hose and jiggled his forefinger.

"OK," he said. "Just a minute. . . ."

He grimaced a little, then pulled.

"Got a little piece of gasket, jammed your thermostat," he said. "You probably are OK. Didn't seize?"

"Didn't hear anything," said Du Pré.

"I got a hose'll fit that," said the man. "Got some coolant, too."

In five minutes the cruiser was purring. The man was fiddling with the adjustment on the carburetor.

"I pay you?" said Du Pré.

The man shrugged.

"Don't have to," he said. "The Lord tells us to succor the traveler."

Du Pré handed him forty dollars.

"I want to, give you this," said Du Pré. "Them hose, antifreeze cost some money, you have to replace them. You in Toussaint, I buy you a drink."

"I am near there," the man said. "I work on the combines and the trucks. Got to keep everything running. If the combines aren't working, the threshers lose money."

"You got a garage?" said Du Pré.

"Oh, no," said the man. "I have what I need in the van. I repair them right in the fields. Oh, once in a great while a whole engine will blow and that's more than I can manage, but not often. Last time was six years ago."

Du Pré nodded.

"Well," said the man, "I better go. Got a call up a ways here."

He walked across the road and got in the van and he pulled out and went down the road to the north.

Du Pré drove south, at ninety. The engine was running very well.

Pretty lucky, there, Du Pré thought.

Didn't have to call that Bart.

Bart, he would have made fun of me.

✦ CHAPTER 25 ✦

I'm worried about you, Gabriel," said Bart. They were sitting at the bar in Toussaint. Susan Klein was in the cooler, making up an order. There was no one else in the place. The day outside was beautiful. The old drunks had come and gone, with their morning skinful, and the lunch crowd had yet to arrive.

"Unh?" said Du Pré. He was looking in the mirror, at the smoky and rippled images of the moldering big-game heads on the walls and the neon bleeding in the beer signs.

"You get this look," said Bart. "You can't just kill these people. Harvey's worried. He tells me he'll have to bust you, and since you were warned, he won't be feeling any too bad about it."

"Yah," said Du Pré. "Well, I am not worried."

Bart looked away. He shook his head.

"Interesting requests," he said. He was looking at a short piece of white paper, words in Du Pré's meticulous penmanship.

"Them FBI can't do this anyway," said Du Pré. "Me, I would just like to know where they go, maybe, I find a car I like to know that about."

"OK," said Bart. "I'll have them FedExed here."

Du Pré peeled five hundred dollars off the roll he carried and he handed it to Bart.

Bart started to open his mouth and then he took it.

"Good thing that you do for little Lourdes," said Du Pré.

Bart shrugged.

"I have money, Du Pré," he said. "I don't have a lot of wisdom."

Lourdes was spending the rest of the summer with a maiden aunt of Bart's, in Chicago. She was taking some classes at the Art Institute.

313

"Well," Bart had said to Lourdes, "I think you'd like to see a big city. Chicago's a big city. It ain't Seattle, but it'll have to do."

Lourdes had cried, packed a little bag, and flown out the next day.

"She want' to do *art*?" said Madelaine. "How come she don't say so to me?"

"You're her mother," said Bart.

"OK," said Madelaine. "Maybe you try it for a while."

"Poor Lourdes," said Bart. "Aunt Marella is very old-country."

"That mean that Lourdes is very safe," said Madelaine. "Me, I like that."

Du Pré cleared his throat.

"Um," said Du Pré. "How old are you, you have your first . . ."

"I am fifteen," said Madelaine.

"OK," said Du Pré. "I shut up now."

"Very smart man," said Madelaine.

"Harvey'll be here the day after tomorrow," said Bart. "He said he did want to come but he couldn't really justify it since he is just supervising Pidgeon. So I sent a plane for him."

"Unh," said Du Pré. "We go to the bar now."

Madelaine was building up a good head of steam. She would sometime in the next hour make Du Pré pay dearly for his impertinence, if Du Pré was stupid enough to wait for the explosion.

I wonder she is OK now, thought Du Pré. He diddled his drink. It was watery and the ice was about gone, but then, it was early in the day.

"I think I go on out to Benetsee's," said Du Pré. "That old man, he got to come back sometime."

"Oh," said Bart, "I don't know, he could just stay away and send you notes by coyote."

Du Pré laughed. He finished his drink and he got up and he went out to his old cruiser and he got in and started it and drove slowly out toward Benetsee's cabin.

He turned up the rutted, grassed-over drive and he thumped along over some sticks of firewood fallen off the truck that brought the last load in. The weeds thinned out when he got to the cabin. A half dozen fat Merino sheep guarded by a small sheepdog were cropping the growth.

Du Pré parked and he got out and he walked around the ramshackle cabin to the backyard where the sweat lodge stood. The doorflap was up and the fires cold.

Young-Man-Who-Has-No-Name was standing by the little brook, arms wrapped around, hands on his shoulders. He was praying. Du Pré sat on a big round of ponderosa that was a splitting block for the firewood, and he waited until the young man moved.

"You got a name yet?" said Du Pré.

The young man shook his head and he smiled.

"I don't miss it," he said. "You can be named for what is not there as well as for what is."

Du Pré walked over to where the young man stood. He looked at the brook. It was boiling with little trout. The fish were clotted together and dashing around a tiny pool.

A kingfisher's blue feather floated in the air.

OK, Du Pré thought, I don't even want to know.

"You hear from that Benetsee?" said Du Pré.

The young man nodded.

"He be back in the fall," he said. "Early fall maybe. Anyway he come he say before the first snow."

First fucking snow here maybe tomorrow, thought Du Pré, I been snowed on Fourth of July, end of July, first part of August. I been stuck up in the Wolfs a week once. Blizzard on the twentieth of August. First snow. Why he don't say when the sun shines sometimes?

"Your Madelaine send me some good food," said the young man. "She is a ver' good woman."

Du Pré nodded. Madelaine, she feed all the earth, wipe all of its tears, she could. But she fix about half of this county one way and another.

"Good you are here," said the young man. "That Jacqueline, she say I come to supper, maybe you come, too?"

Du Pré nodded. His daughter Jacqueline and her Raymond and their . . . fourteen children. Well, anyway the doctor say, no more, damn it. I tied your tubes. Next set of twins, you die, for sure.

Madelaine had talked with Jacqueline a long time when Jacqueline was in the hospital, last pair of babies almost kill her. At last, she nod and cry.

My son-in-law Raymond, he is looking very relieved these days. Feed all them kids, not too bad. Remember all the names of the kids these kids have, that is pret' bad. Me, I can't remember but about half my grandchildren. Names.

I only have the two before my wife, she dies.

Du Pré felt a tight feeling in this throat. He remembered his wife dying, her eyes burning bright, her dark hair sweaty, on the pillow.

Two little girls, my Jacqueline, my Maria, standing with me, I got hold of each little hand.

My wife she smile at us and she sigh long time and she is gone.

My girls they turn out pret' good. They take good care of me.

"I want to talk, that old bastard," said Du Pré, suddenly angry.

The young man stood smiling. He had very deep, gentle eyes. The world amused him, or he pitied it.

"Well," said Du Pré, "I don't guess I go and find him."

"Benetsee," laughed the young man, "he don't want to be found, he does not be found. Try to catch a coyote, a bucket?"

Du Pré laughed.

"He say to tell you that he thinks of you," said the young man. "How stupid you are. He wishes he could help that, but there is no cure."

Du Pré nodded.

"Tell him," said Du Pré, "I say, listen, old bastard, you go fuck a lame three-legged coyote, got clap."

The young man laughed. It was a laugh that rippled like water. A deep merriment.

"How you meet him?" said Du Pré.

The young man looked off at a magpie flying past.

"I am working, Calgary, and he . . . he come . . . tell me, quit what you are doing, wrong blood for it, so I do, and I am here."

"What work you doing?" said Du Pré.

The young man pursed his lips. He looked pained.

"Teaching," he said.

"OK," said Du Pré. "What you teaching?"

"Computers," said the young man.

"Christ," said Du Pré. "I thought you were a fucking longhair."

"Oh," said the young man. "Well, no, not then."

"He stick his head out of your computer?"

The young man shook his head.

"Christ," said Du Pré.

"Me," said the young man, "I don't talk about that. It was pretty scary, how it happened."

Du Pré heard a car come up the drive. It parked. The door chunked.

"Du Pré!" said Bart.

Du Pré turned.

"You'd better come."

"I need that damn Benetsee . . ." Du Pré said. He looked angrily at the young man.

"He say you don't," said the young man.

"God damn him," said Du Pré.

"Du Pré!" said Bart. He looked anguished, drained.

Du Pré walked to Bart.

"Where?" he said.

"Up on the Hi-Line," said Bart. "They just found her. It's out of the county, but you'd better go."

Du Pré felt a knot in his gut.

"It's the oldest Morissette girl," said Bart. "Her mother thought the kid had run away to Billings. She did it several times before."

Little Barbara Morissette.

Madelaine's niece.

The family lived in Toussaint.

Three houses from Madelaine.

❖ CHAPTER 26 ❖

Damned bad," said Sheriff Paton. "I been on this job thirty year and I never . . . animal did this dies. He dies. That's all."

There were three of Paton's deputies there. They all looked like they wanted very much to kill someone.

Little Barbara Morissette was lying on her back, naked, her legs spread, a tree branch shoved up her crotch.

And then her killer had sawed off her head and stuck it in a slash in her belly.

Nightmare.

Du Pré felt his eyes burn. He remembered the little auburn-haired girl. A sweet child. Musical.

Dead young woman.

Fifteen? Sixteen?

Madelaine will be praying.

Me, I am sick and mad.

Jesus.

Du Pré looked around the rest stop behind him. The girl was off in the brush behind the parking lot. She'd been there a little while. Not very long. Maybe left there last night.

Du Pré looked at the ground. No drag marks.

The Morissette girl was slender, small. A strong man could carry her easily.

Over his shoulder.

Cut her here.

The ground was black with old blood.

Green and blue bottleflies buzzed lazily around, laying eggs.

The cross, the notch, the place where they meet, Du Pré thought. On the Hi-Line.

They know about each other.

They have to.

Are they proud? Jealous? They get angry? When they get angry, does it make them stupid?

It makes me stupid.

I got to breathe right.

Think.

Damn Benetsee, I need his dreams.

Have to make do with my own. I quit whining now.

"Damn," said Sheriff Paton. "I ain't gonna sleep a while, here."

Du Pré looked at him. Tall man, thin, weathered to wrinkles and washed-out blue eyes behind bifocals. Wore a big hogleg. Probably a .44 Magnum. Light load. Probably killed a few in his time. Kind of Sheriff calls the crook, who he knows, and says, yeah, well, either you come on in or I come and get you. And that ain't gonna make my mood any too good.

They come right in, you bet.

The FBI arrived. Several vans filled with technicians and equipment.

One car which had Pidgeon in it and two men.

Pidgeon waved at Du Pré. She stuck her hands in the pocket of her light jacket and she came over. She stared for a long time at poor little Barbara Morissette.

She bent over to look closer.

She was biting her lower lip with her straight white teeth.

The crew of technicians assembled. They talked in hushed voices. Cameras. Measuring tapes. Black attaché cases. The technicians put on light blue coveralls.

Pidgeon came over to Du Pré and Sheriff Paton.

"Special Agent Pidgeon, FBI," said Pidgeon. She stuck out her hand. Paton took it and grasped it firmly. He looked into her eyes and he nodded.

"Yes, ma'am," he said.

Pidgeon smiled.

"When was she found?" she said.

" 'Fore daylight," said Paton. "Couple of . . . tourists was headed back here with a sleeping bag to, uh, take a nap. Stumbled over her."

Oh, thought Du Pré, there is one sex life shot for a while.

Pidgeon nodded.

"You know about this guy?" she said.

"Yup," said Paton. "We've had, oh, six, I guess, twenty year. Don't know if they was all his. Bastard."

"We'll find him," said Pidgeon.

"I expect you will," said Paton. "Now, you need anything you call Myra—she's the dispatcher—and I told her to arrange it. Myra lets me run for election and get shot at once in a while, but she runs the department. Always has.

"I'm the coroner, too," said Sheriff Paton. "I done all I have to. Pronounced her dead. Filled out a form. Some job. You find this S.O.B."

"We will," said Pidgeon.

"Um," said Sheriff Paton. "I'd best go. Got a wreck to sort out up the road."

"We passed it," said Pidgeon, "It looked pretty bad."

"Eighteen-wheeler hits a passenger car it's always pretty bad," said Paton. "Only this one flipped and killed the truck driver, too. Don't usually do that. I expect we'll find he was on pocket rockets. Long road. They gobble them speed pills, try to do fourteen–fifteen hundred miles in a straight twenty-four hours."

"Yeah," said Pidgeon.

"Can't blame 'em," said Paton. "Tryin' to make a livin'. It's not easy. I got a boy does that. Hope I don't have to scrape him off the side of this damn highway."

A couple big diesel trucks roared past.

The Sheriff walked away slowly. Loose. A little sad.

"She is my Madelaine's niece," said Du Pré. "My Madelaine, this girl's mother don't like each other much. But she will go crazy, it is someone her family, anyway."

"At least someone cares about her," said Pidgeon. "Most of 'em, no one gives a damn. But I was in Seattle, and I talked to a couple prostitutes who were scared, of course, and grieving for their friends. I hate this."

"How is that Harvey?" said Du Pré.

"Pain in the ass. Worried about you. He's gonna chew on you a lot when he sees you. He'd about just as soon kill these assholes with a shovel himself. You know, we're pretty good. We nail most bad guys, take a little time. But the serial killers are very hard to catch. And of serial killers, of course, the really intelligent ones are the worst and the hardest to catch. That little fuck Bundy wasn't all that smart, but he did some real damage. Green River Killer, not a trace. The Chain Killer, not a trace. There's a guy down South, burns his victims in the swamps. Does it when the swamps are burning. Not a trace."

"These guys leave some traces," said Du Pré.

"Yeah," said Pidgeon. "We just don't know which traces are theirs. This could take years, Du Pré."

Du Pré shook his head.

"Be over before the snow flies," he said.

Pidgeon looked at him.

"Well," said Pidgeon, "I guess I'll go watch the wizards there for a while, see what they find."

Du Pré looked down at his feet. There was a little scrap of clear plastic, the kind that packages some small object. He bent down and picked it up. Pretty heavy plastic.

"What you got there?" said Pidgeon.

"Piece of plastic," said Du Pré.

"All kinds of crap blows over here from the highway and the rest stop," said Pidgeon. "I want it though. We'll see how long it's been in the sun, at least."

They walked over to where the technicians were working. Two of them were zipping up a heavy yellow body bag. They rolled the filled bag onto a stretcher and carried it off to a morgue wagon.

A couple of blue-suited men were minutely examining the ground that the body had lain on.

They kept their faces close, but didn't put their hands down on the bloody earth.

One of the two slipped a dentist's pick from his pocket and he prised something up out of the dirt. He lifted it and dropped it in a little plastic bag, already numbered. He straightened up and made some notes.

"This one is the Hi-Line Killer," said Du Pré.

"Um," said Pidgeon.

Or maybe not, Du Pré thought. Maybe it is Come-to-Jesus, trying to look like the Hi-Line Killer.

Maybe they tease each other with dead young women. See, I got her before you did.

I got to think like them sometime and I don't want to.

Got to find out what their dreams are.

Be in those dreams.

Maybe I get close and make them run.

Hunt them like the coyote hunts. One coyote, chase until he is tired, run that rabbit in a circle, then the other one take over, and so on, till that rabbit is run to death.

Something like that.

Young-Man-Who-Has-No-Name. Old Benetsee, he is some coyote himself.

Always joking.

Tells coyote stories.

God's dogs. They must know everything. Me, I always told everything to my dog and I don't hardly know nothing.

"Du Pré," said Pidgeon, "you please give my love to Madelaine."

"You be down?" said Du Pré.

"No," said Pidgeon, "I'm going with little Barbara, talk to her when they do the autopsy. I do that when I can."

"What do you say?" said Du Pré. "When you are there?"

"I'll say, Barbara, I'm so sorry. I need your help now. I promise you I will find this man. And he won't do this to anyone else after I do."

"Good," said Du Pré. "I tell my Madelaine that."

✤ CHAPTER 27 ✤

I don't know how he gets that damn plane down on that rotten little piece of runway you think is an airport," said Harvey. "Christ, my asshole was in my throat. I ate my worry beads. I thought of my orphaned children and beautiful, impoverished widow. I thought of the asshole who would follow after me with my beautiful, impoverished widow. I hated him. Christ."

Du Pré laughed. Harvey had always hated flying. He was a worrier.

The little jet had screamed in and the pilot had set it down and reversed the thrust of the engines. Du Pré well remembered being thrown against the seat belt. Sometimes there were cows, sheep, and horses in the field at the end of the runway. Sometimes they were on the runway since the rancher who owned the pasture at the end of it was careless about the fencing.

Small jet hit a cow, that is all, Du Pré thought. It would fold up pretty good.

Harvey Wallace, tall and thin and lean and dark and sardonic. Also Harvey Weasel Fat, a Blackfeet boy made good.

Mean bastards them Blackfeet, Du Pré thought, sit out there on the prairie without any cover. Have to be mean. Remember them Athapascans, Du Pré thought, some of them old songs, they describe the Athapascans come down that Great North Trail. They come from the north slope of the Himalayas. They are mean bastards. Them slaves, them Apaches, them Navajos, them Haida. Cannibals and fighters.

Come down the Great North Trail, from Asia over them Bering Straits, down the inside of the Rockies. Not so long ago. Them

Haida trade with Japan and China. They leave them Queen Char-
lotte Islands, go across the North Pacific, some woman singer
with a song tells them how to get there sings that song. Get home,
sing the song backwards.

Mean bastards. Run us Cree the hell east. Run the Sioux south
and east. We get guns from the whites and come back.

Things were not so peaceful then.

"Du Pré," said Harvey, "what you been thinkin'?"

Du Pré started. He had forgotten that Harvey was there. Standing next to his bag.

"I am sorry," said Du Pré. He picked up Harvey's bag.

They walked to Du Pré's old cruiser.

The little jet had turned around and the pilot had jammed the
little plane down the runway and into the air and the roaring
shriek was fading.

"How is Madelaine?" said Harvey.

"Not so good," said Du Pré. "Her cousin's girl, you know. Madelaine, she is helping her cousin, the sorrow. We are having a wake."

Harvey nodded.

"Songs, some old dances, the brothers and sisters of Barbara
they are very sad. Mother is sad. Madelaine don't much like her
cousin—never mention her name, I know her only as Mrs. Morissette. Morissette, him killed working on railroad, eight, ten years
ago."

Harvey nodded.

"Madelaine probably dance with you, though," said Du Pré.

"Dance with a Blackfeet," said Harvey.

"My Madelaine, she is very liberal woman," said Du Pré. "I
think she even dance with a Mormon."

"That's pretty liberal," said Harvey. "OK, what'd Pidgeon
think?"

Du Pré shrugged. He didn't know what Pidgeon thought.

"It is either that Hi-Line guy or the other one or someone trying to make us think it is him," said Du Pré. "How anyone know
anything?"

Harvey nodded.

They walked to Du Pré's old cruiser. Grasshoppers whirred past. A few of the dusty locusts, black wings with yellow borders.

Du Pré stuck Harvey's bag in the backseat.

They got in.

Du Pré started the car and he turned it around and headed for Toussaint. They were at the little airfield in Cooper. Bart had paid to have the runway lengthened so small private jets could land.

Du Pré rolled a cigarette. He lit it.

Harvey picked up the little cardboard box on the seat.

"Very nice," he said. "When you get these?"

"Couple days," said Du Pré.

"Well," said Harvey, "you stick the beeper on a car and this receiver will tell you right where the car is, up to fifty miles. Tell you if it is moving, where, and if it's headed to you how long it will be before it gets there."

"Always wanted one," said Du Pré.

Twelve big grain trucks passed them heading toward the elevators in Cooper. There was a railroad spur there, and huge towering metal silos to hold the grain. Some ranchers were selling the wheat right from the fields, some were storing it and hoping that the price would rise and not fall.

Du Pré parked in front of the Toussaint bar. There were a lot of cars, mostly old and shabby, parked around.

"The wake is here?" said Harvey.

"Yah," said Du Pré. "Can't have booze at the schools and so it is here. We don't got too many buildings, rent."

Toussaint had maybe fifty houses and those were mostly trailers. Poor little town. Lots of Métis. Poor people.

There were a few more expensive houses, not many.

Harvey and Du Pré got out. They went on in.

The place was packed.

Over in one corner Mrs. Morissette was sitting, receiving people who were bearing condolences. There was a trestle table filled with casseroles and salads and Susan had a huge joint of beef set under a heat lamp on a serving table. A rancher stood near it, ready to slice off the meat.

"You hungry?" said Du Pré.

"Starved," said Harvey. "I can't eat before I fly. After, I am ravenous. I escaped the fiery splat once more."

Susan poured Du Pré a drink. She looked at Harvey.

"Hmmmm," he said. "Bloody Mary?"

Susan nodded. Du Pré tilted his head toward the book she kept tabs in. She would write the drinks down.

Damn, Du Pré thought, I must pay my tab, can't remember when I did that last.

Harvey went off to get a plate of food.

"Susan," said Du Pré, "I pay my tab?"

"You got money on it," said Susan.

"Damn Bart?" said Du Pré.

"Lips are sealed, Gabriel," said Susan. "I think you still got a thousand in credit."

Bart, sure enough.

"Look," said Susan, "Bart's frustrated. He wants to do something about all this horror. He just came in and slapped the money down and he cleared off all the tabs. People he doesn't even know."

"Well," said Du Pré, "I guess he don't know all the people make the money for him, either."

Susan laughed.

"Benny's coming along pretty quick," she said. "Had a fight out on one of the ranches, some pair of kids with a combine crew got into it. One kid hit the other with a wrench."

Du Pré nodded.

"One got hit had to be taken to the hospital, then flown down to Billings. Head injury. Don't know how bad, but it must be pretty bad. Anyway. Benny had to arrest the other one and book him."

So he can sit on his ass, jail, wonder if it is manslaughter or just assault he is guilty of. Everybody wonder that until the guy in the hospital either makes it or he does not.

Mrs. Morissette began to shriek. Several women went to her and they held her. She wailed.

That bitch don't even really mean it, Du Pré thought.

Madelaine looked over at Du Pré, then up to the ceiling.

OK, thought Du Pré, I am right, once.

Harvey was sitting at a table far away from the knot around Mrs. Morissette. He was eating like he hadn't for days.

Him probably not eat for days. Pretty brave guy, fly when it do that to him, Du Pré thought, me, I just have the shits bad for three days before I got to fly. It don't bother me.

I don't like this twentieth century. Won't like that twenty-first one, either. I am sure of it.

Madelaine left the little group and she came over and she put her arms around Du Pré and she kissed him.

"You bring back that ugly Blackfeet," said Madelaine.

"Had to," said Du Pré. "I was the only car there."

"You think his dick is as big as I hear?" said Madelaine.

Du Pré shrugged.

"OK," said Madelaine. "I just wondered."

Du Pré shrugged.

"Maybe I dance with him," she went on.

Du Pré smelled the wine on Madelaine's breath.

She is some upset, he thought.

She is angry, me, because she is angry about poor little Barbara Morissette.

That son of a bitch doing this, he is spoiling a lot.

Du Pré sipped his drink.

✤ CHAPTER 28 ✤

Booger Tom squinted at the hot noon sun riding high across the sky. The sky was white with dust and heat. The light was tight and tough. It bleached out all the colors and the clouds of chaff blowing off the big combines glinted like flakes of metal in the air.

"One hot bastard," said Booger Tom.

Du Pré nodded. He had spent a lot of time harvesting and he didn't remember it fondly. The Saturdays in the bars after he had been paid off were fun, other than the two times he had been arrested along with the rest of the crew.

Some of them tough little Montana towns did that. Peel your summer wages in fines for disorderly conduct and run you out of the county.

Summer wages.

"I never did this," said Harvey. "I was always brown-nosing so I could go to summer school. I hate the outdoors. It's dirty. Bugs fuck in it. Not a good address."

Booger Tom looked at Harvey and he grinned.

"Got to get you up on a horse," he said.

"A horse?" said Harvey, eyes wide in horror.

"Yeah," said Booger Tom. "Like the ones you done rode in the rodeo. Quit pissin' on my boots, callin' it a rainstorm. I know who you are."

"Who is he?" said Du Pré.

"He rodeoed some," said Booger Tom. "Pretty good, too."

"I hated it," said Harvey.

Du Pré laughed.

"Well," said Harvey, "I nodded a scholarship so I could go to college and rodeo . . ."

"Got ya laid more often than football," said Booger Tom. "I know you bastards all of my life."

The big combines were rolling on, blades slowly pushing the stalks of grain into the cutters.

Then one of them jerked abruptly.

They could hear a deep whannnnggggg over the roar of the engines.

The combine stopped.

Steam shot out of the engine.

"Shit," said Booger Tom. He was looking off toward the west. The sky was clear. "It's gonna rain round midnight. Shit. Got to get that damn grain in."

Someone from the combine crew was loping over the huge

field to a pickup truck. They climbed in the cab and picked up the radio mike and talked.

"Damn downtime costs one-fifty an hour," said Booger Tom.

"Lawyers cost more than that," said Harvey.

Booger Tom snorted.

"So what are we doing today?" said Harvey. "I get to meet that guy who's out at Benetsee's?"

"Sure," said Du Pré. "We maybe get some lunch and then we can go, sure."

He led Harvey and Booger Tom into Bart's house.

The refrigerator was chock full of smoked salmon, pâté, caviar, and salad stuff. Some good wines, white ones, chilled. Bart didn't drink but he knew what went with what.

"My my," said Harvey. "Two months of my pitiful salary is sitting in that refrigerator. Those are *two-kilogram* tins of Beluga. Cherkassy. I never even heard of Cherkassy. The salmon comes from England, I bet."

"Iceland," said Du Pré.

"Oh," said Harvey, "great. Any capers?"

Du Pré sighed and he opened a cupboard and took out a tall narrow bottle.

"The guys at the office will never believe this," said Harvey. "I think I saw an open bottle of Graves in there."

Du Pré fished it out.

"I think I'll have a baloney sandwich," said Booger Tom.

"I get a hamburger later," said Du Pré.

"Barbarians," said Harvey, dipping a water biscuit into the caviar.

"Fish slime," said Booger Tom.

"The two of you can fuck off and go outside you don't like it," said Harvey, "but I will eat like a hog in peace. Or death."

"C'mon, Du Pré," said Booger Tom. "I got some ham and . . . you know, *food* over to my place."

They went out the back door and toward Booger Tom's little cabin. It was the oldest building on the ranch, perhaps a century old.

Tom opened the sagging door and he and Du Pré went in to a boar's nest. Saddles on trees, horsehair ropes and hackamores, racks of guns, and the stink of old unwashed socks.

"Awful, ain't it?" said Tom. He led Du Pré back outside and to a small brown clapboard building twenty feet away.

A little cookhouse.

It was spotless. A pump by the sink, a big old Clarion woodstove. A stainless steel monitor top refrigerator.

Tom brought out ham and mustard and he took bread out of a breadsafe and plates—battered blue enameled tin ones—out of the standing cupboard.

They ate in the shade behind the cookhouse, under the hanging runners of a weeping willow. A little creek purled by the picnic table.

"Fish eggs," said Booger Tom. "And Frog piss."

Du Pré laughed. So much for Bart's two-hundred-dollar-a-bottle wine. Frog piss.

"He's all right, that Harvey," said Tom. "I remember him from Rapid City, maybe. Took a dive into a chute to try to save a rider who'd gone under a Brahma. Saved the guy, too. Broke Harvey's arm, though, put him out of the money."

Du Pré nodded.

Tom dug four beers out of the creek and they each had two of them.

"Beer's a better kind of cold out of a crick," said Tom.

They ate and drank and smoked.

The day stayed hot.

They ambled back to Bart's.

Du Pré looked out in the field. The combine had a couple men on it, and there was another man in mechanic's coveralls leaned into the engine compartment. He reached a hand back and another man handed him a tool.

Du Pré looked at the dark green van.

The guy who saved my ass, up north, there. Simpson.

Everything was dusty. The van was spotless. The dark windows gleamed.

Du Pré rolled a cigarette.

"You be careful with that," said Booger Tom.

Du Pré nodded. He smoked the cigarette and then he crushed it with his bootheel.

"Think I'll walk out there, see what they are doing," he said.

"Too damn hot," said Booger Tom. "I'll let you."

"Tell Harvey I be right back," said Du Pré.

Du Pré climbed through the fence across the road and he walked through the chaff and broken stalks toward the down combine. The other one had kept going. Two idle trucks sat at the edge of the field. The drivers were sleeping in the shade.

Du Pré boots crackled on the dry stalks. The stalks were slippery. He had to lean a little forward and walk on the balls of his feet to keep his balance.

A magpie flew past, low.

Only damn bird I ever saw tail was longer than it is, maybe a peacock, thought Du Pré.

Simpson pulled his head out of the engine compartment of the combine. He pulled a red rag from his coveralls and he wiped the sweat from his forehead. He said something to the man who had handed him the tool and the man went back to the van and he opened the rear doors and he climbed inside. He was in there for only a moment and then he got out carrying a red metal case and a paper sack.

Simpson took the case and he opened it and selected a socket and he took something out of the paper sack and he leaned back in the engine compartment.

He stayed hunched over for ten minutes.

Du Pré could see him straining as he heaved on the wrench.

He came out and wiped his forehead again.

Du Pré was standing very near.

He watched as Simpson made some minor adjustments.

Simpson signaled the driver to try it.

The starter ground and the engine caught and the exhaust stack belched black smoke.

The driver revved the engine.

Simpson reached back in the engine compartment and then he stood back and nodded and he closed the cover. Flipped the latches on.

The driver gave him a thumbs-up.

Simpson and his assistant took the tools back to the van. Simpson got in and he waited for the assistant to hand him tools. He stowed them.

The assistant walked away.

Simpson got out. He saw Du Pré and he waved and smiled.

He went round to the driver's door of the van and he got in and he drove off.

Du Pré watched him go.

Du Pré walked slowly back to Bart's house. The trip back seemed a lot shorter.

Harvey was sitting on the porch, drinking a glass of white wine.

"What's up?" he said to Du Pré.

Du Pré shrugged.

❧ CHAPTER 29 ❧

We did that," said Harvey. "We hired psychics. What we may or may not have found out I couldn't really tell you. Sometimes we'd think that they'd been helpful, but, then, we'd run probability studies and it could as easily have been chance. You know, the old cop method. You spread enough glue around and your fly will step in it. You look at enough evidence, ten thousand things, and you find one thing that starts a chain of deductions. My math isn't good. We hired mathematicians. The Bureau doesn't like to talk about it. Truth is, though, that serial killers are the same and not the same, and that they are largely fairly stupid and survive a while because they are unpredictable. The ones worry me are the smart ones. About as many, proportionately, as there are very smart people. Not many. Not many. And it's hard enough to catch the dumb ones. Maybe we never caught a smart one. Maybe we just never did."

"Yah," said Du Pré. "Well, how 'bout astrologers?"

"Oh, yes," said Harvey.

"I am kidding," said Du Pré.

"I'm not," said Harvey. "We did. I remember one woman . . . I liked her. She was very humble and sweet and smart. She said it was a mistake to think that astrology delivered truth as it was a mistake to think that the Bible does. The truths in both were poetic. They were both ways of looking at the world that was not rational. That astrology was a means of interpreting lives and fates. But that to try to jam it into a box was foolish. She said in her world, the serial killers and certain other people—we call them sociopaths—were called 'elementals.' They were all by themselves. They were unable to grasp that there was anything in all the world but them. That the world existed to please them. And that they could charm but never love. They are all pretty charming. I thought she was nuts, until I remembered that I never had one of these assholes in hand but that they tried to charm me. Tried to explain away what had happened. Even to convince me that what had happened actually didn't. *And for them it didn't happen.*"

"Shit," said Du Pré. "Your damn elementals just sound like most teenage kids."

"That's a bit harsh," said Harvey.

Du Pré shrugged.

Harvey looked away.

"All right," he said. "Teenage kids are like that, but only some of the time. They learn. They grow up. Sociopaths don't."

"You know," said Du Pré, "trouble with words like that is that if you can pronounce them you think you know what they mean.

And if you think that you know what they mean, you think that you know something."

"Jesus," said Harvey. "You studying philosophy these days?"

"No," said Du Pré. "I am just talking bullshit."

They were sitting at a picnic table at Raster Creek, waiting on Rolly Challis.

"Here I am, a good FBI man, talking bullshit with a loose cannon who I will probably have to arrest later on waiting on a bank robber I couldn't catch," said Harvey, grinning. "The smile is just for jollies."

"Harvey," said Du Pré, "how many these dead women we talking about? Eh? Lot of them. Me, I just am going to make it stop. I don't embarrass you. You worry too much."

"I don't worry too much," said Harvey. "I know you two fuckers."

"What I do make you feel like this?" said Du Pré. "I only shoot that asshole shooting at me. Remember? I shoot me, too."

"Oh," said Harvey. "The brand inspection that went wrong."

"Yeah," said Du Pré. "I shoot me in the belly while I am being such a badass gunfighter. Then I shoot at guy who is shooting at me and I am lucky and he is not. I shoot him right through the heart. I don't even look at him, Harvey, I am just hoping to spoil his aim or something."

"I wasn't thinking about that," said Harvey.

"Lucky, he fall and break his neck," said Du Pré. "I am not there."

"Whatever," said Harvey wearily.

"OK," said Du Pré. "This Simpson he fit that list that Pidgeon sent."

"Sure," said Harvey. "So does any other compulsive guy keeps his rig neat and does a good job and who is a very loud Christian."

"But we don't know the times so good," said Du Pré.

"Bodies lie out there months or years, no shit," said Harvey.

"Hi-Line Killer," said Du Pré, "he travels this Highway 2."

"He's got to be a truck driver," said Harvey.

"Maybe a salesman," said Du Pré.

"Big route," said Harvey. "It's two thousand miles one way."

"I think that is Rolly," said Du Pré. A big truck was coming up the far side of the hill to the west.

The square black cab lifted into view.

Rolly.

Du Pré and Harvey sat silent. The big truck was moving fast. Then Rolly began to slow it down. He choked back his speed and rolled into the parking area and stopped. The air brakes hissed and set and the big diesel popped at lowest idle.

Rolly sat in the cab for a couple minutes. When he dropped like a gymnast to the ground he had on his big black hat. He grinned at Du Pré and Harvey, and sauntered up.

"Mornin', Du Pré," he said, eyes twinkling, "and Agent Wallace."

"Rolly," said Harvey, "don't be a prick. I have a headache."

"I got aspirin in the truck," said Rolly.

"No," said Harvey. "It's bad for my stomach."

Rolly grinned and he shook with silent laughter.

"You got something," he said suddenly.

"We always hope that we do," said Harvey.

Rolly nodded. He moved his chew of snoose a little in his cheek. "I been thinking wrong all this time," said Rolly. "You know I thought it had to be a truck driver on the Hi-Line, here. But now I don't think so."

Harvey looked at him.

"The places where the bodies were dumped," said Rolly. "A truck would be too conspicuous. Have to leave it by the side of the road. It would be reported. Too obvious. Nope, it's got to be someone else. Could be a salesman, or even some guy just likes to drive back and forth."

"We checked all that," said Harvey. "Looked for radiuses. There aren't all that many places on the Hi-Line to gas up. Asked if there was anyone who fit that. Just a driver, always coming through. Course, we got a lot of names and leads, but they were all salesmen. Checked out all of the salesmen and none of their routes and times fit all the bodies. This guy at least pretty well displays

his victims. We find some of them the morning after. No names
came up in the soup."

"You've been working?" said Rolly.

"Fuck you, Challis," said Harvey. "I am ready for any sugges-
tions."

"Guy's thought of about everything," said Rolly. "He'd think of
showing up at gas stations too often. Cafés. He'd be real careful."

"No shit," said Harvey.

"You got a profile?" said Rolly.

"Pidgeon's sure the guy's pissed. Abused child. He displays his
victims. He may well have a juvenile record, but probably nothing
else."

"What I hear," said Rolly, "is that the guy strangles. Often uses
drugs. Lorazepam and alcohol. Big doses. Big deal. You can get
benzodiazepines on the street like you can get peanuts in a ball-
park. Booze is easy."

Harvey nodded.

"Pinch is the gas," said Rolly.

Harvey nodded.

"Guy's got a van," said Harvey, "and that van has a couple fifty-
five-gallon drums in the rear. Plus the tank."

Harvey looked at him.

"Fifteen hundred miles," he said.

"He'll get it filled," said Rolly. "Has to. Oh, he can get a tank
easy enough, that's four hundred or so. But where does he go for
a big fill? Got to be a farm. Got some cover anyway."

"We thought of it," said Harvey, "but thought it was too far-
fetched. I think what we thought of it was we couldn't figure out
how to find a hundred-gallon fill, one hundred thirty, when the
guy didn't want us to find it."

"Or five, six fills in a big city, those gasamat places, move
around. Kids in the booths are minimum wage and they don't
stay long."

"And he wouldn't fuck with the license plates," said Harvey.

"Have to buy a lot of tires," said Rolly.

"Yeah," said Harvey. "Every fifty thousand miles he would.

That's a dozen full circles. He probably doesn't do that many full circles."

"More bodies the closer you get to Yakima," said Rolly. "He favors the lee side of the Cascades."

"We're getting pretty specific," said Harvey.

"Yeah," said Rolly. "But what else works?"

Du Pré rolled a smoke. He looked off toward the south. The Wolf Mountains were down there, but the earth's curve covered them.

I got that Simpson, Du Pré thought, it is him. But this guy, I got to hunt him. How do you hunt, the old way? You dream the deer and the deer come. You dream the buffalo and they come. You got to call them, then they come.

When we were trapping, did we dream the wolf? The marten? Them fisher cat? What they all do, that we dream them.

Du Pré rolled a cigarette.

Damn Benetsee.

I go to talk to Young-Man-Who-Has-No-Name.

Dream what it is that you hunt.

Du Pré lit his cigarette.

"I have one of those?" said Rolly.

Du Pré nodded.

❖ CHAPTER 30 ❖

Du Pré woke in the night. Madelaine was sleeping hard, her breath soft and steady. She had an arm flung out, hanging off the bed. She often slept like that.

Du Pré slipped out of bed and he wrapped a robe around his body and he padded out to the back porch. The air was thick and smelled of lightning. Then there was a great flash above and the rain lashed down. Huge drops thick together. Lightning flashed.

Du Pré saw a cat dash across the grass and dive under the garden shed.

He was half-asleep. The images burned in his brain from the faded flashes and he thought he saw Benetsee faint, white-haired, in the misty shadows among the elms and willows by the little creek.

Du Pré went out the back door and he squelched across the grass in his bare feet. He was soaked halfway there. He stepped into the line of trees and stopped on the bank of the little spring creek.

The lightning flashed so close overhead he crouched.

He was chilled. He went back to the house and he took the sopping robe off and he hung it on the back porch and he walked softly naked to the bathroom and he toweled himself off and he went to the kitchen and he rolled a cigarette and he sat there smoking. He was wide-awake after his cold shower.

He sighed. He poured some whiskey in a tumbler and ran tap water in the whiskey until it was very pale and then he drank the ditch down all at once. It bloomed in his stomach, hot.

Good that they got all the wheat in tonight, Du Pré thought. Now the crews will go a little east, some maybe north to Alberta.

The weather had been fine.

It was four in the morning. The crews would have closed the bar in Toussaint.

The tracking beeper Harvey had brought him from Washington lay on the kitchen table. Du Pré dressed, pocketed the beeper, and he went out and walked down toward the bar. He stumbled once in a pothole. His cowboy boots were slick on the gumbo. He came through the trees in the little park across from the bar. The motor homes were all dark, compressors whirring.

Simpson's van was parked in the light from the spot on the front of the bar. Du Pré made his way round. He listened for dogs, but didn't hear any.

When he got to the van he peeled the sheet of plastic from the beeper, exposing the sticky base. It was modeled to look like a gob of mud. Du Pré reached high inside a back wheelwell and stuck the little electronic device to the clean metal.

Damn Simpson, he probably scrub this by hand with his bifocals on, Du Pré thought. Maybe not.

He backed away and went back to Madelaine's and he undressed and got into bed. He dozed for an hour and then he got up and made himself some breakfast and he ate and then he went out and got in his old cruiser. He switched on the tracking unit and a small green light came on. It showed Simpson's van within six hundred yards of Madelaine's, directly to the east. Du Pré nodded. The sun was rising that way.

OK.

Du Pré drove downtown and he parked beside the bar and he put the tracking unit on the transmission case and he lay down and he dozed.

The people in the motor homes came to life. Doors opened and shut. Engines caught. A couple of the motor homes lumbered out of the parking lot and went to the main street and then turned and headed out to the highway.

Simpson's van was still there in the campground across from the bar.

Du Pré waited.

For an hour.

Simpson finally came out of the motor home he shared with two other men. One of the men joked with him through the door. Simpson was carrying a cup of coffee, a road cup, one with a narrow top and a wide base.

He got in his van and he carefully warmed it up. He checked the windshield wipers. He leaned out and fiddled with the rearview mirror.

Then he drove briskly out and turned toward the highway.

Du Pré waited for a few minutes. Then he followed. If Simpson went west, he was headed north. If east, east. South, south, but Du Pré didn't think he would head that way.

Du Pré followed down to the intersection where Simpson would go either north or east. He went east.

There was no place to turn off that made any sense for the next hundred miles. Du Pré stayed twenty miles back. The green light was east of him. Simpson traveled at sixty-five miles an hour, exactly.

The liquid crystal display barely altered at all. Nothing out here. Once Simpson slowed down to thirty-five.

He find one cow on that road, thought Du Pré. About twenty miles he is either going to Miles City, or Plentywood.

Simpson took the road to Miles City. Du Pré followed five or six miles back. Simpson kept on at sixty-five.

Longest damn time I ever take, get to Miles City, Du Pré thought. Course I am not carrying a dead body I don't want found, so I am careless with the law.

Simpson stopped at the north edge of Miles City and he got gas. Du Pré waited by the road until Simpson moved again and then he drove on into town. Simpson was maybe a mile away, stopped. Du Pré got a tankful and he checked the oil and the belts on the engine and he shook his head when he spotted the hose that Simpson had stuck in his engine a few days before.

Me, I wonder he got an expensive set of black steel sockets, Du Pré thought.

Got maybe a folding rubber sheet in the back. Thick one. Blood-proof.

Got a box of small knives with leaf blades sunk in black plastic handles. Made in Taiwan.

Maybe got a box of earrings, rings, bracelets.

Crucifixes.

Maybe a map, got marks on it.

Take it out to jerk off to, those lonely nights.

I hope that I am right, Du Pré thought.

I don't like them Christer sons of bitches anyway, they spend their time howling about love and meaning death.

Du Pré pissed and he went back out to his cruiser and he drove on into Miles City and he had a good lunch at a saloon, a prime rib sandwich and some beer, a good salad he made up himself from the offerings on a big steel cart.

He rolled a smoke and had it and then another. Had another beer.

He paid and left and he drove toward the place that the green light said Simpson's van was parked at. It was in front of a church, a low cinder-block building. There was a big banner hanging from a side-wall which said REVIVAL MEETING TONIGHT.

Du Pré drove out to the airport and he found a rental-car place had two little old sedans in the lot. There was no one in the office. A sign on the counter said, "If you want a car, call 788-9081." A telephone sat next to the sign.

A woman answered Du Pré's call.

"I need to rent a car," he said.

"Sure," she said. "I'll be right on down soon's as I get the kids out the door to school. Lunch. About half hour."

"OK," said Du Pré.

"If you want a beer there's some in a little icebox under the counter," she said. "Just lift up the passage gate and go on round."

"Thanks," said Du Pré.

He found the beer and he sat and waited outside in the shade, smoking and sipping beer. The woman came and she rented him a little brown Colt for twenty-five dollars.

"Just gas it up before you bring it back, please," she said, "or leave a few bucks if you don't have time. Leave the keys on the counter."

Du Pré nodded.

He went on into town in the little car. He stopped at a discount store and he bought a white straw hat and some big sunglasses and a loud silly shirt, one with huge tropical flowers on it in horrible colors.

I don't look like no Métis, Du Pré thought, driving back by the church. I am not buying those sandals. Maybe I go, though, to this revival meeting.

He went back to the discount store and he bought some cheap baggy cotton pants in a pale tan and some dirty-looking running shoes.

Full service, Du Pré thought, they get your shoes dirty, too.

He bought some tailor-made cigarettes. A butane lighter. His shepherd's lighter was unusual, length of rope and a striker.

I am some deep undercover, Du Pré thought. Feel like an ass-hole.

Bitch bitch bitch.

There was a big tent at the back of the church. Du Pré parked a ways away and he went to the tent and looked in.

Simpson and three other men were sawing boards and nailing together a stage. They worked quickly and competently.

Du Pré nodded.

He went to a motel and he rented a room and he slept for five hours.

The green light on the tracking unit hadn't moved.

He went to the revival meeting at seven.

There were a hundred people there.

Simpson sat in the front row of folding chairs. He was well dressed, in a dark suit and shoes, a white shirt and a dark tie. His hair was pomaded.

The congregation sang loud hymns.

There was a choir. One of the singers was a pretty blond girl, blooming with what beauty she would have before going to fat and bad makeup in five years time.

Du Pré looked at Simpson.

Simpson stared at the girl.

He was wearing tinted glasses.

But his head never moved.

❖ CHAPTER 31 ❖

Du Pré sat in the sweat lodge. It was pitch-dark. The steam was so hot and close his lungs cleared of the tobacco he smoked. He coughed once. He inhaled deeply. The paint on his face clogged his pores. Sweat ran from his skin in streams.

He was alone. He dipped a little water from the bowl with a piece of curved birch bark and he sprinkled it on the red-hot stones. They glowed very dimly, and gave no light. They floated in his eyes. He could not really say where up and down were. He was sitting, but he felt so light he could have been sitting on the tight canvas of the ceiling.

Young-Man-Who-Has-No-Name sat outside. He was drumming. The strokes and rhythms multiplied.

No one man could do all that, Du Pré thought, I am a musician. He is drumming in straight time, nine-five time, thirteen-five time, backbeats. I have listened to drumming my whole life, I never heard this.

Young-Man-Who-Has-No-Name began to sing. The wailing ululations, prayers and offerings.

Du Pré's blood sang.

He bowed his head and he wept. His tears fell with his sweat.

I ask for many things. I ask for strength and cunning. I ask for courage. I ask for a warrior's heart. The heart of a warrior is his humility, the strength of the tribe is the warrior's humility. We are very small on this earth but we have our place.

Du Pré breathed.

He cleared his mind and he let the drumming and singing flow into his breath and blood.

He dreamed.

He woke slowly. His back was cold. He was lying on his back. He could feel the rough stems of grass against his skin. He looked up. The stars were out, a fingernail moon.

"Uh, Du Pré," said Benetsee.

Du Pré's eyes shot wide-open.

"You don't move or I don't talk to you," said Benetsee.

Du Pré froze.

That old shit, he thought, here he is. Play his damn games with me.

Fucker.

"You doin' ver' good," said Benetsee.

Du Pré waited.

"You keep doin' that."

A wind came up. The willows sighed.

Du Pré waited.

He heard an owl call softly.

Felt wings brush his face.

Hush Wings. Owl's a good hunter. At night. Blind in the sun, the sport of starlings, then.

Du Pré heard the coyotes start to howl, the hunting chorus. The yips died away.

He sat up and he looked around.

Young-Man-Who-Has-No-Name was sitting with his legs tucked under him, head bowed. He held a bundle wrapped in marten skins.

Du Pré stood up. He went to the plank table he had piled his clothes on before he went into the sweat lodge. He toweled off and he dressed. His socks were damp and his boots were hard to get on. He rolled a smoke and he lit it and he looked up at the stars.

Far away, he thought, they don't need to bother with us. We can find our way around the world with them, though.

Du Pré glanced at Benetsee's praying apprentice.

Young-Man-Who-Has-No-Name hadn't moved.

Du Pré walked round the cabin to his cruiser and he reached in and got his whiskey and he had a little. He went back.

The young man was sitting on the table. He was smiling.

"OK," said Du Pré. "Where is that Benetsee?"

"I am in Canada, you fool," said the young man.

But it was Benetsee's old cracked voice.

Du Pré looked at him.

"Shit," he said.

He went to his car and got in and he drove. He didn't care where to. He drove west, out on dirt roads that wound through the rolling giant High Plains. He didn't know where he was going. He didn't care.

He came to a side road that cut across a hayfield set beneath a sheer scarp. Old pishkun. Buffalo Jump.

Du Pré took the road right up to the place where the boulders that had been spilled off the front lip were piled.

He got out and looked up at the rim.

There was just enough starlight to see faint dapples of lighter color. The grass that tongued up the watercourses.

Water and rock, water always wins in the end.

Du Pré stared hard.

He saw shadows, giant ones, tumbling through the air. The ghosts of buffalo bellowing as they fell. The hunters danced in triumph on the lip. The shaman lay broken on the rocks below. This was done once a generation, one time, use the pishkun. Plenty of meat. The shaman led them over the edge. He was singing.

The women butchered and dried meat and they danced.

The ground was black with blood.

The wolves and bears smelled the meat and they came.

Ravens, magpies, badgers, skunks, the vultures and the insects.

The eagles.

Up top there were some pits where eagle-catchers had lain hidden, a prairie chicken tethered close against the crisscrossed sticks above them. The eagle swooped and grasped the grouse in its talons and the eagle-catcher reached up and grabbed the eagle's legs and pulled down so that the eagle couldn't reach the hands with its beak.

It did not work that well, I bet, thought Du Pré.

Them shamans they are missing some fingers them eagles cut right off.

Shaman's bones right here, down in the rocks, under the grass.

Du Pré had hundreds of arrowheads and spearpoints and scrapers. He had been finding them since he was a child.

Gopher mounds were good places, new cuts where a stream was changing course, any place where a bulldozer churned the earth.

Du Pré sat and he smoked and he looked up at the scarp.

That is that kind of hunting. Me, I cannot stampede them Christers over a cliff. They do that for themselves.

What am I hunting?
A bad man.
What does he hunt.
Stupid young women.
Where does he go to feed.
To church.
Where does he go to drink?
No bars, they are sinful.
Where does he sleep?

Du Pré blew up. He got out of his car and he yelled and his voice boomed against the cliffs and rang back. Birds chirred, wakened. He kicked the door of his cruiser and he dented it. He grabbed his 9mm and he fired a whole clip at a boulder and the last round whanged off in a banshee scream, flattened to a disc of lead and copper.

"I find you bastards and I cut your fucking hearts out and I eat them. I eat them! You can wander in the damn dark with no hearts."

He sat on the hood of his cruiser.

He rolled a smoke and lit it and inhaled and he coughed and coughed.

My throat is raw from that yelling, Du Pré thought. I have some whiskey. I am drinking too much. Too much is when you like it too much. Better not do it so much, it don't damp no fires. Make them hotter.

Madelaine is half-crazy with fear, her babies get killed, this man.

Du Pré had some whiskey.

He looked up at the rim three hundred feet above.

He dropped the bottle on the ground.

He got a canteen from the trunk and he put it on, the strap over his shoulder, diagonal to his body.

He began to walk up the trail he could see, a white snake moving among the sagebrush.

He scrambled and cursed up the steep places. Put his hands where he shouldn't, rattlesnakes might lie up there on the warm rocks.

Fucking snake bite me I am so mad it die.

Hunt these guys.

Can't kill them, that Harvey is not kidding.

Neither am I.

Du Pré tore his hand open on a sharp rock. He sucked blood from the deep gash. He looked down. Obsidian spearpoint sticking out of the yellow earth, thin and settled between two rocks. Du Pré tugged at it. It would not come. He pulled his folding tool from his belt and got the screwdriver blade out and he dug away.

Stuck through a bone. Clear through it.

Buffalo rib bone. Bull die all the way up here.

Why they bother to kill it?

Du Pré looked up at the rim. He was centered under it.

Shaman was under it, that's why.

Du Pré got hold of the rib bone and he heaved. It came free. The rib suddenly split open and the spearpoint fell. Du Pré caught it in the air.

Du Pré held the black volcanic glass up to his eyes.

The stars glittered in the conchoidal fractures.

Knapper, he move around the edge with an elk tine.

Du Pré sat a moment.

He looked down at his cruiser. A coyote was walking past the front of it, and the coyote stopped and pissed.

"Yes, my friend," laughed Du Pré.

Benetsee.

❖ CHAPTER 32 ❖

Du Pré was eating breakfast with his left hand. His right palm had thirty stitches in it and it hurt like hell. He mashed a piece of ham apart with his fork and he put it in his mouth.

Madelaine sat across the table. She had eaten a bite of an egg. She was smoking one of the tailor-made cigarettes Du Pré had bought in Miles City. She was drinking coffee. Her eyes had dark circles under them and she was edgy.

"You are not talking to your Madelaine these days, Du Pré," she said. "You go off someplace, come back with them funny clothes, go off again, come back with your hand cut open bad. You don't say nothin'. You know who this guy is. I know it. You don't talk to me."

Damn right, Du Pré thought, you go on the warpath and cut off that Simpson's balls I let you know who I think it is, he is. Then Harvey he get to arrest you. I don't think so.

"What you find where you went?" She was looking at him very hard.

"Not much," said Du Pré. He bent his head and he strained to crush another piece of ham away from the steak.

"You are not talking to me, Du Pré," said Madelaine.

Christ, thought Du Pré, I had better lie some, I guess. But she will know I am lying.

Du Pré shrugged.

Madelaine dashed her coffee in his face.

"You know this guy is!" she yelled. Then she threw a plate of corn muffins at him and she jumped up and began to fire all of the dishes in the drainer.

Du Pré dropped down below the table.

348

She pegged crockery at him between the legs.

"Jesus, Mama!" said Cyril, her youngest. "You are crazy!"

"Fucking bastard Métis son of a bitch cocksucker," screamed Madelaine.

Du Pré hunkered. If he ran she'd chase him. Might as well confine the damage to the one room.

Cyril ran off.

Du Pré wished him a long life in a dark hole.

Madelaine nailed Du Pré on the left knee with a big crockery bowl.

"Ah!" said Du Pré. "I am dead. You have killed me!"

"My fucking cousin's baby she is dead with her head cut off and you won't talk to me!" yelled Madelaine. She was down to silverware.

Du Pré tried to remember if there were any big sharp knives in the drainer. He couldn't.

A big sharp knife stuck in the floor in front of his leg. It thunked when it hit and it quivered.

"Jesus!" said Du Pré. "I am finding this guy, you know, you want to kill me before I do?"

"Bastard!" yelled Madelaine.

"People, people," said Father Van Den Heuvel, rushing in the front door. "Please! Madelaine! Gabriel!"

The big priest slipped on the hall runner and he crashed into the glass-fronted cabinet that held Madelaine's collection of porcelain. The sound of the collision was awful.

"Oh," said Madelaine.

"Oh," said Du Pré.

"SHIT!" said Father Van Den Heuvel.

Madelaine was still.

Then she began to laugh, low and throaty. She went on.

Du Pré peeked over the top of the table at her. She was looking at him and laughing and shaking her head.

Father Van Den Heuvel crunched to his feet. He began to brush little white shards of porcelain from his cassock.

"Men," said Madelaine. Her voice was thick with amused contempt.

Du Pré stood up and he looked around the kitchen at all the damage. Couple holes in the plaster walls he would now get to patch. Have to drive Madelaine all the damn way to Billings, get new crockery. He measured the distance between where the knife hit and where his nuts had been sitting. Less than a foot.

Du Pré was a very smart man. He kept his mouth shut.

"I'm . . . very . . . sorry," stammered the priest. He had little bits of glass and porcelain on his black robe.

"Shit . . . heads," said Madelaine, laughing.

Du Pré nodded vigorously and kept quiet.

"I'll buy you some new . . ." said the priest lamely.

"Oh, no," said Madelaine. "You do not. You were trying to help. Me, I lose my temper, God punish me. He also forgive me right away, you guys are such assholes. I watch you, years, you do these things, mostly us women we just smile and shrug. You can't help it, them two heads, always thinkin' with the little one. Priests, too. Father crap you talk. Me, I pray to Mother of God. He needs one. Fucking fools. You men. Bah."

When Madelaine got mad her eyes flashed crimson on the black irises. Lots of Assiniboine blood in her. Women famous for their beauty, famous for their tempers, famous for being very warlike.

Wonder them damn Assiniboines don't run about everybody up a tree, Du Pré thought, women like these in the camp. Jesus.

"Well," said Father Van Den Heuvel, "now that we are all calm . . ."

"Me, I am not calm," said Madelaine. "I am not calm. You are just so sorry I cannot help but laugh. My niece she is lying dead, head cut off and stuck in her belly. No, I am not calm a little. Fucking Du Pré he go off looking, that guy, some guy, he don't find nothing, dumb shit he still come home. You know what we do, days of the carts?"

Du Pré kept his mouth shut.

"Carts?" said Father Van Den Heuvel.

"Long time," said Madelaine. "You guys you aren't much around, come, help make a baby, we send you off, be a voyageur, a hunter, 'cept for those of you supposed to be ten miles away from the camp make sure nothing get to us and our babies."

Du Pré nodded.

"So I am mad," said Madelaine.

Du Pré nodded.

"Du Pré he knows something and he will not tell me. He will not tell me because he does not want, scare this guy. He rather scare me instead. Don't let me know, maybe use one of my babies as some bait."

Du Pré shook his head.

"Shit," said Madelaine. "You lie to me, Du Pré. I cut your damn dick off right then."

Du Pré looked at the ceiling.

"We must be gentle with each other," said the priest.

"You shove up your ass, gentle with each other," said Madelaine. "That damn Du Pré know someone he think maybe do this and he won't tell me so it don't scare the guy off. He don't trust me."

No shit, thought Du Pré, you take a shotgun to him, be sure that it not come from his direction. No shit I don't tell you.

"Uh," said Father Van Den Heuvel. "We could go and get a cup of coffee and maybe talk."

"Priest," said Madelaine, "I want shit out of you I squeeze your head. My baby Lourdes we are talking, my baby Simone. You think more people save this damn Du Pré's sorry ass I think maybe you squeeze your own head. Now, you are nice man, but you are not much help. Why don't you go, talk to someone, listens. I got no time."

"Uh," said Father Van Den Heuvel.

"You go," said Du Pré. "You go on. She is right."

"Please," said the priest. "No more of this."

"More of what?" said Madelaine. "I bust up some, cheap Kmart plates, bowls, you wipe out all my porcelain, some my great-grandmother's. Some help."

"I'll go," said Father Van Den Heuvel.

"In some time I be sorry I am mean to you," said Madelaine, "but now I am not sorry. Go talk, someone else. Go fuck a goddamn goat. Go fuck a goddamn goat in your church, there, I got to talk, this Métis piece of shit."

Du Pré held his hands up, palms to the sky. He looked at the priest and he shrugged.

"You got to go," said Du Pré. "Me, I maybe die but you cannot help that either."

"He give you that Extreme Unction," said Madelaine.

"I . . ." said the priest. He was almost gasping.

"It will be all right," said Du Pré. "People, they die all the time. It is very common thing for them to do."

"I say I am sorry, I won't throw nothing more at Du Pré. I not cut his damn nuts off. I am sorry my Jesus. I lose my temper, I come say your fucking Hail Marys and I repent a lot when I fucking well want to repent," said Madelaine. "But you better go now."

The big priest crunched away on the bones of Madelaine's porcelain. The door shut gently.

They heard a yelp when he tripped and fell off the porch.

They waited.

The car door slammed. The car started.

"Him," said Madelaine. "At least he don't shut his head in it this time."

Du Pré nodded.

"I find the guy, I am following him," said Du Pré.

"He in my kitchen, here?" said Madelaine.

"I got to go," said Du Pré.

"Yah," said Madelaine. "You better, better not come back he is dead, you hear me?"

Du Pré nodded.

"My babies," said Madelaine.

Du Pré left.

❖ CHAPTER 33 ❖

Du Pré was sleeping on a high ridge that reached out west from the Wolf Mountains. He'd found a place with several stone peekaboos, piles of flat plates of shale left long ago by other hunters. They could look through the gaps between the stones and not show any movement. From the ridge, Du Pré could see maybe seventy miles north and a hundred west and fifty south. To the east the Wolf Mountains rose, stacked in an east-west line, blue flanks of pine and spruce and fir, the rock above the timber-line gray as the sea, some snow on the peaks every month of the year.

A mule deer, curious, had come to look at him. The deer slipped on some shattered yellow mudstones and it leaped in panic and sent down a shower of rock from the ledge it climbed in one bound. Du Pré awoke, his gun in his hand.

There was a flash of green light. A meteor streaked yellow-green across the sky, north to south. The bright trail faded quickly. Du Pré shut his eyes and the dancing spot where the last yellow flash as the meteor evaporated utterly burned a moment behind his eyes.

It was cold. The wind was still. The air was dry.

My people come down from Red River in the fall, Du Pré thought, to get that winter meat. Drive them little two-wheeled Red River carts, cottonwood rounds for wheels, not a piece of metal in them, they carry the parfleches, we drive the buffalo into corrals and kill them, dry the meat, the leader of the hunt he makes sure everybody got all their winter meat before he take any. Go on home. Them Sioux, Assiniboine, Blackfeet, sometimes the Crows they try to steal our horses, steal our women, kill the men, drive us away from the buffalo. We don't go. We got them Hudson's Bay Company muskets.

Trail is right over there ten miles. No Red River carts, long time. I can still hear them, the night. Screek screek screek, you hear them axles, twenty miles across the prairies. No grease on them, time to time, they catch fire. Métis men, they piss on them, keep them cool. Not so much water here.

Red River.

Benetsee and Madelaine they tell me things, better listen.

That Bart, I go to him, say, I need someone, keep on that Simpson's trail, keep real close. So that Bart, he look at me, see his chance. If he got someone close, I don't kill that damn Simpson.

Some reporter, Bart's newspapers, he is with that crew, big story in the Sunday paper, "Do You Know Where Your Noodles Come From?"

That Hi-Line Killer, him I got to find.

Dream that deer and the deer come.

Dream that killer and he leave me a track.

Sick bastard.

Du Pré slid out of his bedroll and he walked a few feet away and he pissed. The stream steamed in the cold night air.

OK, my Madelaine, I am out, the country, keep him away from you, your babies. Like we used to do. Don't paint my face, though.

It was four in the morning. The dawn would come in an hour, a first faint rim of pink in the east.

Du Pré rolled up his blankets and sougans in his henskin and he fastened the clips and he tossed it to his shoulder and he walked down to where his old cruiser was parked. He dropped the bedroll into the trunk and he set the bag with his whiskey and tobacco and spare nine-millimeter clips and ammunition and jerky and chocolate on the front seat. He had turned the car around when he had parked it. He drove down the rutted stony trail to the county road, followed that to a small two-lane blacktop. The road was narrow and poorly surfaced. Du Pré sped along at seventy-five, wallowing around the worst potholes.

He got to Raster Creek's rest area when the light was rising to full day. He parked the cruiser and went into the john and came back out and he walked slowly back to where little Barbara Morissette had lain, her head stuck in her belly and the flies dancing around the blood and wounds.

He took his time.

Some guy, walked back here, maybe yesterday, the afternoon. Du Pré got down on his haunches and he looked at the faint print of a bootsole, a hiking boot with five stars up the center of the sole.

He counted the ant tracks across the earth. Into the faint depression and on toward whatever it was that the ants were working on. A bombardier beetle had scuttled across. Four and one. He looked over at the anthill twenty feet away.

Yah, he thought, maybe twenty-four hours. Less, I think. Yesterday afternoon, late. No dew, no rain. Who are you?

He looked ahead at the line of tracks going straight to where little Barbara had lain. No dog tracks, the guy wasn't pumping his pooch out. He was going right there. No reason to go right there. No reason . . .

Du Pré went on. He saw a folded piece of yellow paper, one the size of a deck of cards. Thirty feet ahead.

Du Pré moved slower than he had.

Same tracks. Don't miss nothing now.

The piece of paper had got stuck against a sagebrush. Little wind did that. Yesterday late afternoon, when the wind always comes up from the west.

Du Pré moved slowly.

When he got to the paper he squatted and he reached out and picked it up gently and he turned it over in his fingers. The paper was crushed and shiny and on one side there was a faint stain, a brown one. Guy folded it, stuck it in his hip pocket between his wallet and his ass. Sat on it. Sweated in it. Tamped it down good.

Du Pré looked up at a hawk that had floated between Du Pré and the rising sun. The shadow had flitted across his face. The hawk was hovering. It plunged and Du Pré heard a squeak, cut off.

Du Pré unfolded the paper. Heavy, yellow stock. Printed with an announcement for a model airplane show. In Fargo, North Dakota. In two days.

Du Pré looked at the other side.

A name. An address. In Renton, Washington.

Du Pré looked at it for a long time.

He refolded the paper and he put it in his pocket and he went on toward little Barbara Morissette's killing ground.

Du Pré saw the cheap pair of girl's underwear cast on the ground where Barbara had lain. He went forward quickly and he picked up the panties and he saw the stains on them. He looked down and there were the spread prints of the bootsoles and the little gouge where a heavy belt buckle had hit to the left of the left foot when the man had dropped his pants to jerk off.

Only this guy, Du Pré thought, is him. Nobody else been back here. Just this guy. He was here, not long ago.

Du Pré walked back quickly to his cruiser. He stuffed the panties into the trash receptacle, down under a bag of cans and cigarette butts. He took out the yellow piece of paper and he stared at it for a long time.

Then he struck a farmer's match and he burned it and he ground the black ash to smears on the yellow earth.

OK, I come now.

Du Pré looked toward the sun in the east. It was shining red through low haze.

Du Pré got in his cruiser. He rolled a smoke and he had a little whiskey. He was thirsty. He got some big glasses of cold water from a blue-and-white thermal jug. He ate a little jerky.

He drove on east. Fast. He got to a junction and he angled off south a little. He drove like hell. He got to the Interstate and he got on and he slowed down twenty miles an hour.

He stopped and got gas just over the line in North Dakota. He passed the place where the Yellowstone and Missouri Rivers joined:

Used to be a big trading post there.

Take them furs in, get bad whiskey. Trade beads, knives, brass pots and vermilion, needles and thread, flour, tobacco.

Voyageurs, some of them take the boats down to St. Louis, New Orleans. Float down, haul them damn boats back up on a rope over your shoulder. Long damn walk. Takes two years, the trip back.

Du Pré turned off on a secondary highway and he headed toward the Turtle Mountain Reservation.

Been many times, this country, he thought.

See them cousins of mine.

Talk to Bassman.

Du Pré called Bassman's house from a pay phone at a gas station.

The number was temporarily out of service.

'Nother poor Métis, can't pay his phone bill.

Du Pré drove on to Bassman's house. His first wife had got drunk and died in a car wreck five years ago. Bassman had remarried quickly and the kids from the first and second marriages were all playing in the yard, a year or so between their ages. Except that there wasn't a four-year-old, since Bassman had taken ten months or a year to find that new wife. The kids were running around and laughing and the older ones were watching out for the younger ones. A couple disreputable yellow dogs barked when Du Pré pulled in and he parked.

Bassman came out the front door. He was wearing a tattered red T-shirt, jeans, and moccasins. His hair was braided. This month, he was Indian. Next month, maybe, he cut his hair short and wear a long-sleeved Western shirt, hide the needle tracks on his arms. Bassman had spent ten years in LA, mostly not very good ones.

Du Pré liked him a lot.

"Du Pré," said Bassman, "you come on in here, now, you eat?"

"Yah," said Du Pré.

"You look tired. Sleep?"

Du Pré shook his head.

"Ah," said Bassman, coming down to the cluttered yard. "You need a car got them good North Dakota license plates."

Du Pré nodded. Moccasin telegraph still worked pretty good.

"I got you a good one," said Bassman.

They drove over to where it was. Pretty new van, good engine, good tires. Dark blue. Curtain behind the bucket seats.

"Keys in it," said Bassman, carrying Du Pré's bedroll. "All gassed, you need anything, Fargo, you call that Le Bon. Toussaint Le Bon. He fiddles some good as you."

Du Pré nodded. He lifted his bag from the front seat of the cruiser.

He walked to the van and he got in and he tossed his bag on the floor behind.

He rolled down the window.

Bassman handed him a paper bag. It had something small and heavy in it. It rattled a little.

Du Pré looked at Bassman.

Bassman nodded.

❧ CHAPTER 34 ❧

Du Pré was filthy. He hadn't shaved and he reeked of sweat and cheap wine.

The fairgrounds had a big crowd of people in it, all come to see the model airplane show. The little planes zoomed and snarled and dived and the operators stood in little knots watching the competition.

Du Pré had taken one pass through the parking area and he found the truck he was looking for. A van, long-bed, dusty from the long drive. The rear tires were larger than the ones on the front. They were radials and they were deformed. The van was heavier in the rear than it should be. Du Pré glanced in the rear window. The floor was elevated a foot and a half from the original. Du Pré walked around the driver's side. There was an extra gas cap and it was mounted high, back of the driver's door. The other was behind a locking flap.

Washington plates.

Du Pré straightened up and he walked to a trash bin and tossed in the bottle of cheap wine in its brown paper bag. He walked to the van Bassman had found for him and he got in and he shaved and washed up and put on the loud tropical shirt that he had bought in Miles City and the pants and running shoes. He scribbled on a piece of paper and tucked it in the pocket of his shirt. He went to the registry booth and handed the paper to a woman, who was looking at someone else. Du Pré slid away rapidly. He went back to the van with the Washington plates and past it to a pile of railroad ties left for some future coral construction and he sat down and rolled a smoke.

The public address system bellowed the name that he had found on the yellow sheet of paper, and said that there was some trouble with his van.

In three minutes a tall, thin man with the long arms and ropy muscles of a stevedore or a choker setter came loping across the parking lot. He had long stringy blond hair. He wore jeans and running shoes and a sweatshirt. The sweatshirt hung down over his belt.

Du Pré looked at him.

Well, well.

Du Pré waited till the man had given up in the matter of his car and a problem and he went back toward the field where the little planes were taking off and landing.

Du Pré sauntered after him.

The man joined two others who were fussing over a model Piper Cub, checking the actions of the little joystick on the control box with the flaps and ailerons on the model plane.

One of the two men squatting on the ground spun the propeller with his finger and the little engine caught and the plane quivered while the tiny motor spat and banged.

The man Du Pré was after stood back. He wasn't with these two, just watching.

One of the two took the plane out to the dirt runway and held it while the operator revved the engine and then gave the thumbs-up. The man holding the plane let go and the little plane dashed down the dirt and lifted easily into the air and it flew almost straight up.

When the little plane came down the man Du Pré was after made some remark and the two men at the control box looked at him and they didn't laugh. The man colored and he turned quickly and walked away toward a black building that had rest rooms in it.

He was in there a long time.

When he came out he blinked at the bright sun for a while. He went off toward one of the fair barns.

Du Pré followed him as he went around the displays of kits and engines and paints, fabrics and plans, the skeletal assemblies of models awaiting the silk coverings and the coats of varnish.

The man paused at a booth that held replicas of WW II fighters. The details were fine and well-wrought and the man spent an hour talking with the builder. The builder was getting exasperated with him, because he would not move out of the way and let others look, too. Finally the seller had enough and told the man to move on.

This guy is not right, Du Pré thought.

I knew that.

The man spent the next two hours wandering and staring at the displays. Du Pré did, too, following at a distance.

The crowd began to stream through the door and out to the field. The public address system announced a dogfight between an American plane and a Japanese Zero. Du Pré went, too, staying a hundred feet or so behind the man he was after. The man stopped.

Du Pré moved back on a line between the man and the van with the Washington plates.

The dogfight started. The little planes snarled and climbed and went through corkscrews and did Immelmann turns and they each fired little fake machine guns.

The crowd watched the planes and Du Pré watched the man.

The man began to move back toward Du Pré.

Du Pré rolled a cigarette.

He passed thirty feet from Du Pré and he went between the parked cars toward his own van. He was hurrying.

Du Pré followed.

The crowd was all staring up at the two little planes.

When the man got to his van he went around to the back and he was opening the door to get in when Du Pré stepped out and shot him twice in the head with a small twenty-two pistol that had a perforated silencer made out of aluminum pipe on the end of it.

The gun went phut phut and the man Du Pré was after straightened up and then he fell into the van. He was dead. Du Pré shoved his legs in and he tossed the gun after him and he peeled off the plastic painting glove he had on his right hand and he stuffed it in his pocket. He shut the door and he wiped the handle with his kerchief.

Du Pré walked through the parked cars to the van he had borrowed and he got in and he drove slowly away.

The crowd sent up a loud cheer. The Zero was trailing a plume of black smoke.

Du Pré turned out of the fairgrounds and he got on the expressway and drove and drove until he felt hungry. He stopped in Bismarck and went to a good restaurant and he ate a big steak and two slices of apple pie with ice cream.

Du Pré got gas and he stopped at a liquor store and got a pint of bourbon and he drove till three in the morning. When he pulled into Bassman's yard the lights came on briefly in the house and then Bassman came out with a couple men that Du Pré had met years before but he couldn't remember whether or not they played music.

One of the men got in the van and he helped pass out Du Pré's stuff and Du Pré stuck his bedroll back in the trunk of the cruiser and then he took his bag and set that on the driver's seat.

The two men with Bassman left in the van Du Pré had used.

Bassman brought out a big plate of sausages and cheese and cold cuts and vegetables and a jug of cheap wine and they ate silently sitting on Bassman's little porch with the half-moon up above.

Du Pré got his fiddle and Bassman got a guitar out of the house and they sat and played some old music.

They played "Baptiste's Lament." They played some shanties and some meat songs. They played a couple songs the voyageurs sang after they had carried the heavy packs of furs around a hard portage.

After a while, they just sat and drank and smoked.

"I will be over, there," said Bassman. "Maybe a month, we play that good music, that bar. Me, I like that woman who own it. You know, she give us each a hundred dollars last time we play there?"

Du Pré nodded. Susan wouldn't insult him by offering to pay him, but she knew that Bassman and musicians like him never had any money. They spent it all on pretty women and booze and silk shirts and strings for their instruments.

"Yeah," said Du Pré. "She is a good person."

"Your Madelaine, she is well?" said Bassman. His eyes were twinkling.

"She is plenty good," said Du Pré.

"She dance real good," said Bassman.

"Yes," said Du Pré.

"When you maybe come back here to Turtle Mountain," said Bassman, "we maybe play some music, the bars here."

"I like that," said Du Pré.

"You play that good Métis music," said Bassman. "You know them young people used to think we were shit, they are coming around now, saying, hey, you teach me the old music. I thought they all would maybe like that Michael Jackson or something. But they are working good at it. I got a couple kids, one of them plays the fiddle, they be pret' good ten years or so."

"Take a long time," said Du Pré.

He looked up at the stars, at the Drinking Gourd that pointed to the Pole Star.

Long time ago, my grandpère he give me a little fiddle, I am maybe eight or something. I make noise. My grandpère he smile and say I do good. Catfoot, he play and I drive him crazy.

They teach me a long time. Get me a couple more fiddles.

One I got now was grandpère's. Had to get a little work done on it but it sounds right.

Play them old songs.

Didn't play really well until my wife she die. I play all right before she die, but better after, I am very sad.

Maybe you got to lose something big, play well.

What have I lost, maybe?

Du Pré put his fiddle in the case.

"I got to go home," he said.

Bassman nodded. He held out his hand.

"You come back, Du Pré," he said. "We play that good music."

✤ CHAPTER 35 ✤

Rolly Challis looked at the little black receiving unit. Du Pré stood with his arms folded and he waited.

"Looks good," said Rolly. "If you can do your end. Three days. Day after tomorrow after tomorrow. Works out good. I can make it to Spokane and then on and back, no problem."

Du Pré nodded.

Rolly grinned at him and he got up in his big black semi and pulled out on Highway 2 and headed west.

Du Pré went to a picnic table and he sat on it for a while and had a smoke and then he got in his cruiser and headed south.

The Wolf Mountains rose on his left.

Shit hit the fan pret' soon, Du Pré thought. Maybe. All I need, them FBI got somebody following that asshole I killed in Fargo. They are not maybe that smart.

Oh, bullshit, I would have been arrested, my way out of the fairgrounds. There is no one there. I would have seen them.

Not my kind of work.

It is now.

If that was the guy. If not, he still maybe should not jerk off over where little Barbara she is left dead, her head in her belly.

Tracks. That was the track, yes.

That Harvey, he add it up, be all over me like stink on shit anyway. I can hear him. Me, I just ask him he want another drink, otherwise, you fuck off maybe.

One more.

That Madelaine, I miss her but I am not going home until I am done. She is not, any mood, half the job done.

I think.

When did this all start?

Red River.

You are a poor Métis, you had better take care, your life.

Live my life under them Wolf Mountains. On these High Plains. On what was Red River.

Sometimes, I wish my people beat them English. Have our own country.

English they are pret' smart and mean as hell, nobody beat them.

Du Pré reached under the seat and he took the bottle and he had a snort. The whiskey made him cough a little. It burned good.

Du Pré rocketed down the highway. It was a clear late summer day and the air was clean. It had rained some in the night. Enough to knock the dust down. The western horizon was gray with more.

When Du Pré got to Toussaint it was early in the day. He parked in front of the bar and he went on in. The place smelled of bleach and cleanser and polish. Susan kept it scrubbed. She had hired two women to help her three days a week plus Sunday morning.

She looked up when Du Pré came in, and then she ducked down again.

Du Pré leaned over the counter.

She was inside one of the coolers, scrubbing.

"Make yourself whatever," she said.

Du Pré came round the bar and mixed himself a ditch.

"Your pal Harvey," she said, "called for you. He sounded pissed."

"Them Blackfeet, they are pissed all their life," said Du Pré.

"Yeah," said Susan. "Well, he was so pissed he said that he was going to be here soon to be pissed at you personally."

"Check I give him, it bounce," said Du Pré.

"Yeah," said Susan. "You been gone a while. Madelaine has come in here looking for you a couple a times."

The cooler made her voice big.

"She got a gun, knife, she come in?" said Du Pré.

"No," said Susan. "You ain't been pronging one of those women make the eyes at you when you play, have you?"

"Which women?" said Du Pré.

"Damn near all of them, you Métis son of a bitch," said Susan. "I didn't love Benny so much I'd jump your bones myself. You are a pretty man and you play real good."

"I don't love nobody, Madelaine," said Du Pré.

"I thought so," said Susan Klein, "but, then, you are a guy, and you guys got such strange notions of what you can do and live."

"I help you any?" said Du Pré.

"Guys," said Susan, "cannot clean anything for sour owlshit. You lugs are like bears with furniture. Benny tries to help me clean. He does the bathroom. He really works at it. Always looks worse than before he tried. You guys are pathetic."

Du Pré nodded at himself in the mirror.

"What'd you and Madelaine fight about?" said Susan.

"I don't know," said Du Pré.

"I bet you don't," said Susan. "I really do." She got out of the cooler and she stood up. She was flushed and sweaty. She had a blue bandanna around her head. Her work shirt was stained dark under the arms.

"You oughta call her," said Susan.

Du Pré looked down at his drink.

"OK," said Susan. "I will." She went to the phone and she dialed.

Du Pré sat on a barstool. He felt sick.

Madelaine came right away. She walked up to the bar and she slid up on a stool and Susan poured her a glass of the sweet, bubbly pink wine she liked. Then Susan went off through the door to the storeroom in back.

"Hey, Du Pré," said Madelaine, "you been gone, long time, don't call your Madelaine. What is her name, this new one."

Du Pré looked at her.

She dropped her eyes.

"OK," she said. "I am sorry. I am sorry for all of this."

"Well," said Du Pré, "I am not liking it much."

"Where you been?" she said.

Du Pré shrugged.

"Oh," said Madelaine, "you did that."

Du Pré looked at the mirror. He felt like he was going to puke.

"Is this, over?" said Madelaine.

Du Pré shook his head.

"OK," said Madelaine. "I don't ask you no more dumb questions."

Du Pré felt sick. He ran to the men's room. The door was open. The place was freshly mopped. He puked in the toilet, bent over and heaving. He retched and retched till he was pale and shaking and running sweat. He stood over the sink for a while, his hands on it, then he ran cold water and he scrubbed his face and splashed it on his neck. He dried off with wads of paper towels.

He went back out.

Madelaine was standing there, she was holding a bottle of the whiskey that he liked.

"You come home," said Madelaine. "You have not been eating

right. You need a bath, maybe three. You come home, let your Madelaine take care of you. You come now."

Du Pré went out and he opened the door of the cruiser for her and she got in and he drove to her place.

Madelaine led him inside. She made him a hot strong toddy with lemon and sugar and whiskey and he drank it down all at once. She cooked some mild sausage and rice. He ate. He had two more toddies.

He went off and stood in the shower for an hour, the steaming water sluicing over him.

Never wash this off, he thought.

What am I ashamed of?

He got angry. The water turned cooler. Du Pré shut off the valves and he got out and toweled himself and he went to Madelaine's room. There were clean clothes on the bed. He got dressed and he went out to the kitchen. The back door was open. He went out and found Madelaine sitting at the picnic table under the little bower covered with hop vines. She had a pitcher of pale brown liquid and ice with her.

She was rolling Du Pré some cigarettes.

Du Pré went and he sat down beside her.

He lit a smoke.

"OK," said Madelaine. "Now you are mad at yourself some, kill that guy."

"What guy?" said Du Pré, angrily.

"I only say this once," said Madelaine. "I never talk about that guy you killed again. You going to kill the other one, too. Thank you, they killing people's babies, have, long time."

Du Pré poured himself a drink. He drank. His mouth tasted all right again.

"You are a good man, Du Pré. You maybe have to do bad things because of bad men, these cops, they never catch these guys, you know. They have not, how long, twenty years?"

Du Pré lit another cigarette.

"You are a real gentle man, Du Pré," said Madelaine. "You

don't like this at all. If you did, I would not love you. I would not. Men who like it are not right, you know."

Du Pré sipped his drink.

"But you do what you have to," said Madelaine. "I am proud of you and I don't talk, this, again."

Du Pré nodded.

"You going to be a long time, getting over," said Madelaine. "Don't get over all of it, ever. Life, it is not nice. Sometimes."

Du Pré looked at her.

"Now," said Madelaine, "that Blackfeet Harvey he is pissed, he is coming here. I not say anything, you don't, that is all.

"So you get some rest now. I fix you a good supper."

Du Pré nodded.

He went in to sleep.

He lay there a long time before he drifted off.

✦ CHAPTER 36 ✦

Harvey and Pidgeon sat on one side of the table and Du Pré sat on the other. They had legal tablets in front of them and tape recorders. They were wearing Bureau drag.

Du Pré was in faded denim and he had a sack of Bull Durham and some papers and his shepherd's lighter.

"No smoking," said Harvey.

"Kiss my ass," said Du Pré.

"This isn't funny, guys," said Pidgeon.

"It's not a formal interrogation," said Harvey.

"No shit," said Pidgeon.

"You piss me off, Du Pré," said Harvey.

"You guys want me to leave so you can just lock antlers and have a good old time pawing the fucking earth I will," said Pidgeon.

"Humor me," said Harvey.

"Kiss my ass," said Pidgeon.

"Look, Pidgeon," said Harvey, "I need to do this. Our leading suspect ends up dead in fucking Fargo, North Dakota, with small slugs in his head. Looks like a standard biker hit. But nobody was mad at him. Our snitches don't have a clue. Old Larry had nothing but friends, all of whom thought he was weird. You ever deal with this fucker across the table before?"

"Perfect gentleman," said Pidgeon.

"Du Pré," said Harvey, "you will answer my questions."

"No," said Du Pré.

"I oughta demand you take another lie detector test," said Harvey.

"Kiss my ass," said Du Pré.

"Look, Harvey," said Pidgeon, "we got things like rules, you know, the old indictment, the arrest, the eyewitness, the evidence, all that shit. You get something, we could do this, but you got nothing and we all know it. If fucking Du Pré waxed the cocksucker he did a nice clean job. What? You just want to come out here, shoot some grouse or something?"

"I am your superior," snarled Harvey.

"Be still my pattering itty-bitty heart," said Pidgeon. "You want to rag on Gabriel you go right ahead, you want to fire me just try it. I'll have you up on harassment charges, your hand on my ass and all."

"I have never put my hand on your ass," said Harvey.

"I got some bad news for you," said Pidgeon. "Jury takes one look at my ass and they just will not believe any guy could help himself. Little perjury on my part, Harvey, it's a tough world out there. Now, we are all just mammals tryin' to make it in a hostile universe but, really, you want to get on Du Pré's ass maybe you just oughta go out, the parking lot and duke it out. I will take these here tape recorders, but the good news is I am destroying these tapes." She stuffed both of them in her attaché case, after taking the cassettes out and putting them in her bra. She rebuttoned her white silk blouse. High.

Harvey broke a pencil in half.

"I don't think he's gettin' enough at home," said Pidgeon. "As a psychologist, I can tell you the world runs on pussy or the lack of it."

"Pidgeon," said Harvey, "enough. You're a bad little girl. Act your fucking age."

"Studies have shown," said Pidgeon, "that they show things. This is a perfect example of what it is. Now, what have we *really* got . . . ?"

"This bastard Simpson," said Harvey.

"Oh, yes," said Pidgeon. "Now, we're talkin'. I like Simpson. He is a *fave*. I give him the *big ten*. Wish I had some *evidence*, though."

"Oh, that," said Harvey.

"Yeah," said Pidgeon. "I mean, I just can't see a judge, no matter how stupid, giving us a warrant. Can't see a grand jury of all them good citizens listening to us say, Simpson's a *fave*, the murdering bastard of all time. We all think so. Don't have a single shred of evidence, though, you'll have to take our hunches."

"However," said Harvey, "I would like Du Pré to know that if, say, the fave Simpson should be hit by lightning, I cannot help myself. I will wonder if Du Pré was sitting there next to the switch."

"Oh, 'tis true," said Pidgeon. "We got spy satellites hovering overhead and they take nifty photos. Get a snapshot of old Du Pré punching the fave Simpson's ticket, we will have to fry our friend here. We got little microphones in Simpson's jockstrap. We got undercover agents cleverly disguised as spare tires in that van of his. We got him *locked*."

Du Pré rolled a smoke.

"Pidgeon," said Harvey, "you really ought to be nicer. It's a good thing to be nice. I am nice, too. I am nicely trying to explain to this fucking prairie nigger across the table here that I am worried that I will have to arrest him and send him to Walla Walla."

"Prairie nigger?" said Pidgeon. "I think that means Indian? My Cherokee blood cries out for justice. Shame on you. We got a Blackfeet, a Creek Cherokee White Negro, a Cree Chippewa Frog.

All in this room, right here. Du Pré, Harvey's gone round the bend. His cake fell. His elevator is stuck between floors. His bread ain't baked. His deck is short of jacks. Racial slurs. Tsk tsk."

Harvey reached over and he got Du Pré's tobacco and papers and he rolled a smoke.

"Me too," said Pidgeon. She took Harvey's.

"So," said Harvey, "I ever tell you about Du Pré and his machine gun?"

"No," said Pidgeon. "You have seen this machine gun?"

"No," said Harvey. "I heard it once."

"Harvey," said Pidgeon, "if you didn't *see* the fucking machine gun, or pick up brass can be *matched* to it, or *slugs*, all you did was hear it, maybe all you heard was regrettable flatulence."

"Look," said Du Pré, "I am wanting to maybe go back down to the bar and maybe play some pool or something."

"Hooray," said Pidgeon.

"Think we're ready for prime time?" said Harvey.

Du Pré grinned.

"Of course we are, Harvey," said Pidgeon, "but first, let us tell the good Mr. Du Pré that Simpson is indeed about to be arrested, by God, and real soon."

Du Pré sat up.

"So we'd just as soon he didn't fuck us up," said Harvey.

"It would be nice," said Pidgeon.

"You got something?" said Du Pré.

"*That*," said Harvey, "we can't talk about."

"Nope," said Pidgeon. "We can't, at all."

"How good it is?" said Du Pré.

"Fair," said Harvey.

"So, hands off," said Pidgeon. "I mean it."

Du Pré shrugged.

"Really," said Harvey.

Du Pré stood up.

"I got shoot some pool," he said. "Keeps my eye in."

"Bully idea," said Pidgeon.

"Cheeseburger," said Harvey.

They left the trailer behind Susan Klein's Toussaint Bar and they went in the back door. The day was chilly enough so that Susan had lit a small fire in the woodstove. Pidgeon tossed the cassettes in on the red coals.

Du Pré got a drink and he went over to the pool table and he put two quarters in the slots and dropped the balls out of the belly. He racked and set them and he took the cueball and went to the other end and he set the ball and broke the rack smoothly. Two balls went in.

Harvey was talking to Susan Klein.

Pidgeon was squinting down a cue. She nodded finally and she put five dollars on the side of the table and looked at Du Pré.

Du Pré nodded and he matched her bet.

Pidgeon nodded and ran all the stripes into pockets without pause and then she picked one for the eight ball and sank it.

She picked up the two fives.

Du Pré nodded.

She put them back down.

Du Pré nodded.

She broke and nothing went in.

Du Pré ran six and then he fluffed a bank shot.

Pidgeon mercilessly cleared the table.

When the bet topped two hundred and Du Pré still hadn't come close to winning, Pidgeon grinned and nodded again.

There were ten or so people standing around looking on now. Making side bets. Harvey had money but not one taker on his player. Pidgeon, of course.

"How about five hundred?" said Pidgeon.

Du Pré nodded.

Du Pré chalked his cue tip and he smiled and then he bent down and ran the table.

He picked up the thousand dollars.

Pidgeon nodded.

She kissed him on the cheek.

"It was him," she whispered. "We found all sorts of stuff in the van."

✤ CHAPTER 37 ✤

He's headed south," said the voice.
Du Pré hung the telephone up.

That Simpson, back home to Texas again.

Like hell.

Bart sipped his tea. He was wearing irrigation boots and over-alls with black grease stripes on them. He'd been working on Popsicle, his giant diesel shovel.

"Thanks," said Du Pré to Bart.

Bart shrugged and he turned and he looked out the window at the Wolf Mountains.

Du Pré went outside and he got into his cruiser and he drove over to the gas tanks and he filled his car up. He checked the oil and the coolant.

He looked at the hose Simpson had put in his cruiser, it seemed a long damn time ago.

Du Pré picked up the little magic telephone. He dialed.

Rolly answered.

"That load you wanted," said Du Pré, "you be five miles maybe west of where we talk, I call you when it is ready."

Rolly broke the connection without another word.

"This be over soon," Du Pré murmured. His head ached a little and he felt his joints move with little stitches of pain. The day was damp.

I got the arthritis, too, Du Pré thought, don't seem so very long ago that I was a young guy, didn't have so much pains.

Du Pré totted up his broken bones, his bad sprains, the gun-shot wound to the stomach. Just a surface wound, but the gun had been touching his shirt and pieces of the shirt and little blue flecks of powder and denim were stuck in his skin forever by the blast.

Cows, they kick me a lot, horses throw me, then, they get concerned, come back, stand on me while I am unconscious. Hope that I am all right.

I am grandfather. A bunch of times.

Little Gabriel Dumont, poor Louis Riel's general, him, his wife, they have no children. Gabriel, him very sad about that, but he take all the Métis for his, he take care of them. After the priests betray poor Louis and the English hang him, Gabriel come down here. He never speak to them priests again. He is buried, unmarked grave, down on the Musselshell.

Me, I want an unmarked grave, thought Du Pré.

That Du Pré, he is buried out there, we don't know. That Du Pré, he did what he had to.

Du Pré got in his old cruiser and he drove over to Benetsee's shack. There was a thin tendril of blue-gray smoke coming out of the rusty stovepipe and the front door of the cabin was open.

Du Pré got out and he went up the rickety steps to the little porch. There was firewood piled on both sides. The path to the door was thick with wood chips and the early yellow leaves from the cottonwoods near the creek.

Got that first frost, Du Pré thought.

Winter.

Young-Man-Who-Has-No-Name was sitting at the table, writing a letter. He wrote swiftly and gracefully. Du Pré could see, even upside down, that his script was lovely.

"Good morning," said the young man.

"Uh," said Du Pré. "You hear from that Benetsee?"

"Yes," said the young man. "He said to tell you you do very well. He is proud of you."

Du Pré nodded. Hearing that felt very good.

"That all?" said Du Pré.

The young man nodded. He went back to his letter.

Du Pré left. He drove over to the little highway that skirted the west end of the Wolfs and he headed up the road to the north. Many of the trees and the weeds in the roadside ditches had begun to turn color. The aspens were bright orange, always the first trees to turn. Flocks of common blackbirds whirled in the sky, hundreds at a time, gathering for the move south.

Them hummingbirds, they are already gone, Du Pré thought.

We don't got much of anything but winter up here.

It was getting on to dusk. Du Pré pulled off beside the road and he opened his cooler and he took out some sandwiches and a plastic container of potato salad. He ate and he drank cold tea.

He reached under the seat and took out a tracking unit, set it on the dashboard and switched it on. Nothing.

That Simpson don't come down this way he went to Miles City, hunting that girl in the choir, and Harvey has a couple people on that, Du Pré thought. But I don't think he do that. I think that that Simpson, he come down straight now. He will come here, maybe 10 P.M.

Du Pré slipped the fifth of whiskey out from under the seat and he had a slug and he rolled a smoke and then he started the cruiser and he got back on the old road and he headed north. The little highway that stobbed down from Canada to hit Highway 2 was perhaps twenty miles east of the campground at Raster Creek.

He got to come down that way, turn left, turn right, Du Pré thought.

One or the other.

The little highway ended at Raster Creek. Du Pré put the cruiser out of sight behind a screen of alders and he waited. He rolled a smoke and he got out and he wandered over the empty parking lot. A couple of semis barreled past, headed west. A pickup truck. Not much traffic this night.

He sipped a little whiskey. He watched the stars. He glanced, from time to time, at the tracking unit on the dashboard.

Suddenly, the green dot appeared, headed south on the little road from Canada. The liquid crystal display read 47 miles. Du Pré watched the dot. It was coming south. Simpson was traveling at a good rate. When he got to the T-junction, he turned right. Headed west. Right for Du Pré.

Du Pré started the cruiser. He waited until Simpson was five miles away and then he drove out on the highway and he parked by the entrance to the rest stop. He reached under the backseat and he took out a flare and when the tracking unit said Simpson was a mile away he lit the flare and he dropped it on the road.

And now we pray no fucking cop comes along, Du Pré thought. Du Pré hunkered down out of sight and he racked a round into the chamber of his nine-millimeter and he waited. He could see the light from Simpson's headlights on the top of the closest hill.

Simpson slowed down and moved out on the center line. He crept up to the flare and pulled in behind Du Pré's cruiser and he stopped and his door opened.

He stepped out.

He walked forward.

Du Pré stood up. He leveled the nine-millimeter at Simpson, who was only fifteen feet away.

"Ho, Simpson," said Du Pré, "I kill you now, you know. You killed little Barbara Morissette, eh? Kill a lot of others. All up, down the highway, Texas to here."

Simpson froze. He said nothing.

Du Pré walked forward.

"You're crazy," said Simpson.

"Maybe I look, your van," said Du Pré. "Got little knives, stainless steel, black plastic handles? Little box, got earrings, maybe? Watches? Pieces of skin?"

Simpson was looking steadily at Du Pré.

"Let's look, your van," said Du Pré. He waved his gun and Simpson backed up toward the open door of his van.

"Let's look maybe," said Du Pré.

Du Pré's finger tripped the magazine release on his pistol. The magazine popped out and it landed on the asphalt with a metallic thump.

Simpson dived into his van and he slammed it into drive and

he drove straight at Du Pré. Du Pré rolled away, toward the barrow pit.

Simpson swerved and he headed west, the van accelerating rapidly.

Du Pré watched the van crest the next hill.

He bent down and he picked up the magazine.

He put it back in the gun.

He picked up the burning flare and he carried it to the barrow pit and he doused it in a puddle.

A bright yellow light flared up to the west.

Du Pré heard a distant explosion.

He nodded and he got in his cruiser and he drove south toward home. When he got to the dirt road that led out to the pishkun he turned off and drove very slowly, the headlights throwing the rocks sticking up out of the thin soil into high relief.

It took the better part of an hour for Du Pré to grind up to the base of the tall cliff. He took the tracking unit and he scrambled up the steep trail to the top. He took the little black box apart and he dropped the pieces down rock fissures. Someday the ice would tear the rocks away from the cliff face. Some day, long time. He kept the batteries.

Du Pré took the whiskey out of his jacket pocket and he had some and he rolled a smoke and he looked up at the stars and then he looked out to the west where the plains rolled on, dark red and black with pale blotches where the grass was thick.

Long time, Du Pré thought, some people say this was a sea, went all the way from the Arctic Ocean to the Gulf of Mexico.

Long time.

Du Pré felt the rock he was sitting on get colder. He stood up and he walked around till his butt wasn't so chilled.

Long time.

Du Pré felt very tired.

He struggled back down the trail and he got in his cruiser and he sat there for a while, smoking and drinking. There was enough water in the air to dew. It was damp and chilly out.

Du Pré took his bedroll out of the trunk and he carried it to a patch of thick grass by a dead spring.

He slept a long time.

The sun's heat brought him awake.

He stood up and he walked a couple steps and he pissed.

He stretched and yawned.

The plains went on west forever.

✤ CHAPTER 38 ✤

Du Pré looked at the crumpled burnt van. It had been crushed and then the gas tank had exploded and some of the glass that had stayed in the frames had melted to globs.

Harvey Wallace and Pidgeon were standing near the wrecked semi. It had flipped about three hundred yards away and the cab had been flattened down to the doorline. The trailer was on its side.

Du Pré walked over toward Harvey and Pidgeon.

Harvey glared at Du Pré and he walked away quickly.

Pidgeon looked at Du Pré for a long moment.

"Rolly was alive," she said. "They flew him out. Where he is, I don't know."

Du Pré nodded. I lie to Rolly, I kill the one who killed his little sister. But the only two know that are me and maybe Pidgeon, and now who cares?

"Harvey'll get over it," said Pidgeon. "He's just ticked. He's sure you set this up but, of course, no way to prove it."

Du Pré shrugged.

A wrecker with a lowboy tilt-trailer behind pulled off the highway and it bounced over the ground to the smashed van. The driver backed the trailer up and he got out and put a cable on the van and he set the trailer bed down and he began to winch the burned hulk up onto the oak planks.

"Go through that with a very fine comb," said Pidgeon. "I expect we will find a few things. Simpson, and I don't know how, was alive enough to have started to crawl out when the fire started. He burned to death."

Du Pré nodded.

Good. Hope it hurt bad.

"Now," said Pidgeon, "I expect there will be just two hundred and some odd murder cases open forever. We won't ever really know. Thing about it is, you talk to these bastards, you never really know either. They ain't human, Du Pré. I don't know what they are."

Pidgeon took a filter cigarette from a pigskin case and she lit it. The little breeze ruffled her long auburn hair.

An accident records van pulled up and technicians got out and began to walk back up the highway, looking for the black skid marks.

"You be around some?" said Du Pré.

Pidgeon shook her head. "Got some charmer down in Alabama who skins his victims. Alive. Got another in western Pennsylvania, strangles and then beheads. Got a lot of them, Du Pré. This is over. And, it's never over. Harvey and me, we'll stop in Toussaint on our way down to Billings, but not for long. It's what we do, you know."

Du Pré nodded.

"Harvey's calmed down some," said Pidgeon. "I can tell by the way he stands. You want to talk to him, maybe it's a good time."

Du Pré glanced over at Harvey, who had his hands in his pockets. He was looking off in the far distance.

He walked over and stood by his friend.

Harvey glanced at him and went on looking far away.

"Pidgeon say you maybe stop in Toussaint, your way back," said Du Pré.

"Yeah," said Harvey.

"Well," said Du Pré. "I think I go, maybe, we have something to eat you get there."

"We will," sighed Harvey. "Du Pré, just keep your fucking mouth shut, will you?"

He went back to looking far off.

Du Pré turned his cruiser around and he headed back to Toussaint. It was late afternoon when he got there. The bar had several trucks and cars parked in front of it.

Du Pré went in.

Benny Klein was standing at the bar, having a beer. Susan was pulling a draft pitcher for a couple cowboys.

Du Pré walked up and he stood next to Benny.

"Afternoon," said Benny, twinkling. "Heard about some wreck up on the Hi-Line. You know anything?"

"Semi hit this van," said Du Pré.

"Messy," said Benny.

Madelaine came out of the women's john.

Du Pré looked at her.

He nodded, once.

Madelaine smiled. She smiled and her white teeth shone. She came to Du Pré and she put her arms around him and she hugged him swaying a little.

"Come sit," she said. "I get you a drink." She went behind the bar.

Du Pré saw her beaded purse on one of the little tables by the far wall. He went and sat with his back to the room.

"That Lourdes she will be back in two days," said Madelaine. "She like that Chicago. I talk to Bart's Aunt Marella. She is a good lady. She said Bart, he thinks she is his maiden aunt but he is so drunk both times that she is married he don't remember. She got two daughters, one about Lourdes's age. Bart, he don't remember they are his cousins."

"Yah," said Du Pré. "Well, that Bart he drink some there for some long time, you know."

"It is over, yes?" said Madelaine.

Du Pré nodded.

"Du Pré," said Madelaine, "you drink some whiskey, we eat some food, you get your fiddle and make some music. It is our life, yes."

Du Pré drank a little. Madelaine dragged him out to the dance floor and she danced and then Du Pré did, too. There were a couple good dance tunes on the jukebox, a record Du Pré had brought from Canada.

They danced to "Boiling Cabbage." They danced heel-and-toe to "The Water Road."

Susan Klein brought Du Pré a big steak and some more whiskey.

Du Pré ate like a pig.

Madelaine leaned over and she smiled.

"You that," she said. "My babies they are safe now."

The bar filled up.

Bassman showed up and some more of Du Pré's cousins from Canada and from Turtle Mountain, the old Red River country. There were maybe ten good musicians and they all played, sitting in and leaving, dancing and drinking.

Du Pré stopped fiddling for a minute and he went to the john and he came back out and he ran right into Benetsee, who was standing at the back of the crowd with Young-Man-Who-Has-No-Name.

The old man was as solid as a tree trunk rooted in earth.

Du Pré grabbed his shoulder and he turned him around.

Benetsee was laughing.

"You old bastard," said Du Pré, "what are you here now for, eh?"

"Come in, drink some wine," said Benetsee, his black eyes laughing. "You got some tobacco? Some manners?"

Du Pré nodded and he rolled a thick smoke for the old man.

He lit the cigarette and he passed it to Benetsee.

"Pret' good," the old man said.

He smoked happily.

Susan Klein brought him a beer mug full of the awful cheap white wine that he liked. She kissed him on the cheek.

"Damn," said Benetsee. "Wine, pretty women they are kissing me. I like this place."

Young-Man-Who-Has-No-Name laughed.

"I call this one 'Pelon' now," said Benetsee.

"What him call him?" said Du Pré.

"I don't care," said Benetsee.

"Pelon," said the young man.

"I got to talk, you," said Du Pré.

Benetsee shook his head.

"We sweat some soon," he said. "I am here, drink wine, kiss pretty women, and maybe I play the flute."

Du Pré nodded.

He went back up and he fiddled with Bassman and some guitar pickers and a guy he didn't know who played pret' good accordion.

Pidgeon and Harvey came in and they stood by the door. When Du Pré looked at them Pidgeon tossed her head a little.

Du Pré finished the song and he stepped down from the little stage and he made his way through the crowd to them. Pidgeon and Harvey went outside and Du Pré followed.

It was cool and pleasant out in the night air. It was very hot in the bar.

"We're on our way," said Pidgeon. "Just wanted to say hello."

Harvey stood there.

"Challis is in the hospital in Billings," said Pidgeon. "He was hurt pretty badly. They had to take out his spleen and he had a collapsed lung, some fractures, pretty smashed up."

"OK," said Du Pré.

"It's been real nice," said Pidgeon. She shook hands with Du Pré.

Du Pré turned to Harvey.

Harvey hit him, hard, in the jaw.

Du Pré flew over the handrail and he landed on his head in the dirt.

He struggled to his feet.

"Don't fuck with me again," said Harvey.

"Harvey!" said Pidgeon.

They walked off to a tan government pool car.

Du Pré sat up. He rubbed his jaw.

He looked up. Madelaine was standing there.

She put her hand to her mouth and she ululated.

Victory's song.

Harvey drove off without looking back.

Du Pré and Madelaine waved anyway.

✤ CHAPTER 39 ✤

Du Pré stopped for a minute in the parking lot of the hospital. He looked up at the blank glass windows and he shook his head and he went on. Madelaine held his arm tighter.

She pulled him to a halt fifty feet from the front doors.

"Your wife die here, Du Pré," she said. "Old hurts, they leave scars. It is all right. I love you."

Du Pré looked at her a moment. She know what is bothering me, he thought, when I do not know.

He smiled a little and he nodded. They went on in.

The front desk clerk directed them toward the right floor.

"Critical care may not let you see him," the clerk said. "I can call for you."

Du Pré nodded. He walked Madelaine around in a circle while they waited.

"You can go up," said the clerk, "but they may ask you to leave if they feel the patient is tiring or getting agitated."

Du Pré and Madelaine went to the elevator and up to the floor. The doors opened and the smell of illness and disinfectants surrounded them.

Du Pré winced. Madelaine gripped his arm a little harder.

A nurse led them down to Rolly's room. She opened the door

very gently, putting out a hand to make Du Pré and Madelaine wait. She went in very quietly.

They heard her voice, then Rolly's, strong and deep.

She came back out and motioned them to go on in.

Rolly was propped up on pillows, the bed cranked high. His head was a turban of bandages and a weight hung off a frame at the foot of the bed, a cable running to the end of a cast.

His left arm was gone.

But his blue eyes twinkled out of his swollen face. Purple, green, and black bruises lay across all his skin. The bridge of his nose had a metal form taped to it.

"Mr. Du Pré and Miss Madelaine," said Rolly, laughing. "Ain't this some shit? I need a jukebox and a barstool and a beer. Pool table ain't so much of a concern anymore, I guess."

"You like pool?" said Du Pré.

"Can't remember," said Rolly. "It was a long damn time ago."

Rolly handed a note to Du Pré. His right hand had a patch of adhesive across the back of it. Du Pré unfolded the note.

"Be careful, the cops have been here some and the flowers ain't mine."

Du Pré nudged Madelaine and she glanced at the note and then at Rolly and she nodded.

"How long you be here?" said Du Pré.

"Couple weeks," said Rolly. "Got to come back, get fitted for an arm. You know, they got ones now that are part electronic. What they call 'em, bionic?"

Du Pré shrugged. He watched very little television.

"What else they cut off?" said Madelaine.

"Just the arm," said Rolly. "They thought about cutting off the leg but I told 'em I'd have to kill 'em."

"Hmm," said Madelaine. "After you get out of here where you go? You be a while, getting better, you know."

"Uh," said Rolly, "Well, your pal Bart called and he give me a choice, go someplace or come up to Toussaint and get to know Booger Tom and him better. So I guess that's what I'll do."

"Ah," said Madelaine.

"Good," said Du Pré. "She have someone, put that good soup down. Fuss over. Me, I am scared to death I get sick."

"What is wrong, my soup?" said Madelaine.

"Not enough salt," said Du Pré.

"Salt's bad, your heart," said Madelaine.

"These days," Rolly laughed, "if it tastes good at all, it's downright toxic."

Du Pré nodded and laughed.

"You need us, do anything?" said Madelaine.

Rolly grinned. "Know any hookers wear nurse's uniforms?" he said.

Du Pré laughed.

"OK," said Madelaine. "Anything else?"

"All I got to do is wait and sleep," said Rolly. "I rode a long ways on a big horse."

Madelaine tugged a flat pint of whiskey out of her purse and she showed it to Rolly. He held out his hand. She gave it to him and he slipped it under the bedclothes.

The nurse who had shown them in opened the door.

"Five minutes," she said. "He has a doctor coming."

She shut the door.

Madelaine got a small oblong plastic pill container from her purse, the sort that has seven compartments. She went to the sink and she ran a thin stream of water and she grabbed several paper towels from the dispenser as she moved the box back and forth under the stream. She dumped out the excess.

She went and sat on the bed and she put her forefinger into the paint and she lifted it up and put a crimson slash on each side of his mouth. She put black and yellow in zigzags on his cheeks. A stripe of blue from his lower lip down under his chin.

Madelaine nodded. She took out a mirror and she held it up to Rolly, and he looked at himself and he nodded.

"Thank you," he said.

"OK," said Du Pré. "We see you, Toussaint."

Rolly stuck his thumb up.

They all laughed.

Madelaine and Du Pré made good time to the elevator, getting in just as the doors closed. They were walking across the parking lot in a matter of two or three minutes.

"That damn nurse she shit rusty pickles she see him," said Du Pré.

"Yah," said Madelaine. "Me, I want a beer."

Du Pré looked at her. She didn't drink beer very often. Very hot days and this was a cool one.

They got into the old cruiser and Madelaine pointed downtown and Du Pré nodded and he drove down to the poor part of Billings, where the Indians on drunks and the hobos and the mentally ill pushed their homes in shopping carts down the pitted sidewalks.

"There," said Madelaine, pointing at a shabby sign above a little bar. The windows were glazed with dirt. A wino was sleeping curled up in the stairwell next to the front door.

Du Pré laughed.

So did Madelaine.

"Maybe I ask you a better place, start looking for Rolly's hooker," said Madelaine. "You, know them probably, yes?"

"Oh, yes," said Du Pré. "Me, I spend much time here, you bet."

They got out and they went into the bar. A very tired-looking middle-aged woman was slumped on a stool behind the bar, a cigarette hanging from her lip. She was watching a soap opera on the little television on a shelf behind her.

Du Pré ordered bottle beers for both of them. He went off to the john to take a leak. The floor was swimming in water from a broken seal at the base of the toilet. Du Pré used the toilet anyway.

By the time he came back out Madelaine was talking into the telephone on the bar. The woman behind the bar looked cheerful.

Spread a little money around, Du Pré thought, it is like the sun.

Madelaine turned away from Du Pré when he slid back up on the barstool. She listened for another moment.

"Yah, well," she said. "You do this, hundred up front, another you come back with a note from him, uh?"

Madelaine put the phone back in the cradle.

They drank beer for a half hour.

A good-looking hooker came in and she walked right up to Madelaine.

Madelaine nodded. The hooker was wearing a crisp nurse's uniform.

"Four forty-two," said Madelaine, handing her a hundred-dollar bill.

The hooker went out.

"This soap all right with you?" said the woman behind the bar. She smiled. Her false teeth had clots of dental fixative on them.

"Yah," said Madelaine.

Du Pré laughed.

They got some fives and they went to the video poker machines. The machines were shut off.

They went back to the bar and sat and a man in a workman's uniform came in and he carted the machines out the door.

The woman behind the bar never looked away from the television as the four machines went out the door.

Du Pré looked at Madelaine. He grinned. They both laughed.

An actress on the television was suffering from amnesia.

A commercial sold soap. Another, feminine hygiene.

Madelaine reached down and took Du Pré's hand and she squeezed his fingers.

They had another bottle of beer each.

The hooker in the nurse's uniform came in.

She handed Madelaine a slip of paper.

Madelaine glanced at it and she laughed and she handed over another hundred-dollar bill.

She gave the note to Du Pré.

"Ahhhhhhhhhhhhhh. Paint a great hit. Raster Creek," Du Pré read.

"We go home now," said Madelaine.

✤ CHAPTER 40 ✤

Du Pré was fiddling and Bassman and Père Godin were backing him up. Père Godin was famous for having been thrown out of a seminary in Quebec when three very pregnant young women accused him of fathering their impending children. He was in his late seventies now and he had fathered more than forty children. He played the accordion and he sang in a high falsetto, a tenor, a baritone, a bass. Double-voiced. Du Pré had never heard anyone else like him.

The Toussaint Bar was packed. There were local people and then many from Turtle Mountain and from Canada. The women wore bright dresses with beadings and bells, the men ribbon shirts.

Godin quavered to the end of the ballad and Bassman and Du Pré quickly finished. It was time for a break.

Du Pré was sweating in the heavy silk shirt that Madelaine had made for him.

He made his way over to her and he put an arm around her. She grinned and looked merrily up at him. Her face was a little flushed. She had been drinking her sweet pink wine.

"I never see so many Métis, one place, here," said Du Pré. There were about thirty in the room. One couple had come from Manitoba, a drive of nearly a thousand miles from their home.

"Why they here?" said Du Pré.

"Listen to my Du Pré fiddle," said Madelaine. "You are a very famous man, you know, them records you made, people listen to them."

Du Pré nodded.

Bullshit, he thought. They got plenty good fiddlers, Turtle Mountain, Manitoba, Alberta. Me, I am OK, not the best. Me, I do not want ever to be the best, anything I do. Does bad things to you, that best.

"That Père Godin, he have what, fifty children?" said Du Pré. "I hear he just had twins, latest wife."

"Ah, yes," said Madelaine. "He is very charming man I hear. One, my cousins, Canada, she have one of his."

Bassman was leaned up on one hand against the wall, talking to a pretty woman in a turquoise velvet dress, who was not his wife. His wife was home, swelling with child. Bassman and the woman went out.

Some of that grass, thought Du Pré, these musicians are some playboys. Good hearts, lots of damage, them good hearts.

Somebody handed Du Pré a glass of whiskey and water and ice. He drank thirstily. Playing made him burn. Tomorrow he would be exhausted.

Susan Klein bustled past. "What's the occasion?" she said. "I'm damn near out of some of my booze."

Du Pré put one palm up and he shrugged.

"Ver' charming man," said Madelaine. "Père Godin, he is some guy. There are some guys, Du Pré, that women just cannot get mad at. They are born, that. He is one of them."

Du Pré looked at the silver-haired old fart. He was fairly tall and rail-thin and he had big hands with very long tapered fingers.

"We go maybe outside," said Madelaine. "It is plenty hot in here."

They struggled to the door and went out into the cool night. There was no cloud or moon and the stars burned in the velvet black sky.

"Wheh!" said Madelaine. "This is some better!"

Du Pré felt the silk cold on his back where the little wind from the west was touching lightly. His neck itched. He took off the silk bandanna wound around it.

Ahh, he thought, I don't put it back on neither.

"I don't see Bart," said Du Pré.

"He come later," said Madelaine, "I talk to him, he will be along, probably a few minutes."

Du Pré nodded. Bart was so shy, really, that Du Pré couldn't remember him in any crowd.

Booger Tom was pissing in the shadow of a cottonwood in the little park across the road.

Du Pré looked down the street. One of Bart's Rovers was coming on, the big SUV pulled up and the rear window rolled down.

"Evenin'," said Rolly Challis. Bart got out and he went to the back of the rig and he opened it and he took down a wheelchair and he unfolded it and snapped the pressure rings together.

Bart wheeled the chair up to the door and it opened and Rolly swung his leg out and Du Pré went to help Bart lower him into the chair. Bart pushed the wheelchair over to the steps that led up to the front door of the bar and Du Pré got on one side and Bart the other and they lifted the chair up to the boardwalk and then Du Pré pushed Rolly on in while Bart went to park his rig.

Père Godin came and he cleared the way for Rolly's chair and Du Pré wheeled him up right next to the tiny stage. Susan Klein brought Rolly a big glass of whiskey. Rolly took tobacco and papers from his shirt pocket and he rolled a smoke expertly and he licked the paper and tucked it in his mouth.

Madelaine lit the cigarette for him.

Oh, Du Pré thought, now I am knowing why all of this.

Père Godin got up on the stage and he lifted the heavy accordion up and he shrugged into the harness and he checked it for tune. Bassman stepped up on the stage and he picked up his fretless electric bass and he put the strap on and he turned toward his amplifier and he ran a quick scale and then he bent and fiddled with the knobs.

Du Pré kissed Madelaine and he stepped up and he picked up his fiddle and he plucked the strings with his left forefinger and listened close to the harmonics. He twisted the peg for a string that had gone a little flat.

A Métis that Du Pré didn't know stepped up and he lifted a flat Celtic drum over his head and he began to beat on it with the stick, a fast rhythm with backbeats. Père Godin chuffed the accordion in time. Bassman did stops on his bass.

Du Pré nodded and he ripped off some icy little notes.

"Salteux!" screamed Père Godin.

One of the Métis war songs. The victory song.

Salteux, the Métis warriors, and this for the Salteur Du Pré and the Salteur Challis.

The Métis roared.

The ranch folk backed away and the Métis women went to the space in the center of the floor and they began to dance. They ululated, hands to mouths, while they bobbed, legs pumping. The floor shook. The many voices warbling the ululations blended, rose and fell.

Père Godin broke into riffs of reedy chords and notes not on the European scales.

Du Pré fiddled. He played notes from his blood. Smoke. Buffalo on the shortgrass prairie.

The Salteux had run the Sioux out of the Great Lakes country and the Cheyennes out of Wisconsin.

Du Pré fiddled between his two worlds of the blood.

He looked down at Madelaine.

Her eyes flashed crimson fire, so did her hair when the light struck just right.

Your babies are safe, Du Pré thought.